# BEHIND THE BONEHOUSE

**by**

**Sally Wright**

Print Edition ISBN: ·978-1533150295

Print layout by eBooks By Barb for booknook.biz

Because of Frank's grasp of chemical engineering,

and Caroline's eleventh-hour idea,

and Rod Morris's experienced editing

it became a better book.

# LIST OF CHARACTERS

Benoit, Camille – French woman; friend of Jack
   Freeman; painting restorer; member French
   Resistance in WWII

Buckout, Frank – Woodford County Kentucky Coroner

Cathcart, Terence – IRS investigator

D'Amato, Frankie – stable worker; enemy of Buddy
   Jones

Eriksen, Vincent – janitor at Equine Pharmaceuticals

Franklin, Booker – (Charles); founder, Blue Grass
   Horse Vans; Spencer, Richard and Martha Franklin's
   father

Franklin, Spencer – VP Manufacturing Blue Grass
   Horse Vans; Jo and Alan Grant's friend

Franklin, Richard – Spencer's brother; President Blue
   Grass Horse Vans

Franklin, Martha – Spencer's sister; VP Blue Grass
   Horse Vans

Franklin, Alice – Booker's dead wife; childrens'
   mother

Freeman, Jack – former OSS member; landscape
   designer; friend of Jo and Alan Grant

Freeman, David – Jack's father; escaped Russia 1918;
   physician

Freeman, Eloise – Jack's mother; injured in escape from Russia; former pianist

Grant, Tom – Jo Grant Munro's dead brother; former OSS member; Alan Munro's friend

Hardgrave, Kevin – lab technician, Equine Pharmaceuticals

Harrison, Bob – vet, pathologist; founder Equine Pharmaceuticals

Harrison, Brad – Bob's son; Accounting Manager, Equine Pharmaceuticals

Honeycutt, Garner – Bob Harrison and Alan Munro's attorney

Jones, Buddy – Breeding Manager at Mercer Tate's farm; friend of Jo and Alan Munro

Jones, Becky – Buddy's wife

Lawrence, Art – equine supply distributor in Canada

Lebel, Jean Claude – WWII French Resistance leader killed by a traitor in Tours during WWII

Miller, Annette – Equine Pharmaceuticals lab secretary

Miller, Mack – well known Thoroughbred trainer

Morgan, Butch – Production Manager, Equine Pharmaceuticals

Morgan, Frannie – Butch's wife; insurance company manager

Munro, Alan – VP Science and Technology Equine Pharmaceuticals; Jo Grant Munro's husband; OSS member during WWII

Munro, Jo – Jo Grant Munro; architect; co-owner broodmare care business with her uncle Toss Watkins; mother of Ross Munro; sister of Tom Grant

Munro, Ross – Jo and Alan's son

Nagy, Jean – lab technician, Equine Pharmaceuticals

Nevilleson, Elinor – neighbor of Carl Seeger

Peabody, Earl – Woodford County Sheriff (also called Stump)

Peabody, Cassie – Earl's wife

Phelps, Pete – Woodford County Deputy under Earl Peabody

Reynard, Henri – member French Resistance in Tours during WWII

Russell, Ridgeway – Booker Franklin's attorney

Seeger, Carl – Laboratory Director, Equine Pharmaceuticals

Seeger, Jane – Carl's wife; librarian at University of Kentucky

Shafer, Virgil – farmer who calls Alan to his farm

Smalls, Charlie – groom at Claiborne Farms; Esther Wilkes's twin brother

Smith, Doug – Equine Pharmaceuticals employee in packaging department

Tate, Mercer – owner of stud farm where Buddy Jones works

Thompson, Cecil – laboratory supply distributor

Trasker, Mertie Mae – finds Booker Franklin in Midway

Treeter, Mary – Booker Franklin's part time housekeeper

Watkins, Toss – Jo's uncle; partner in broodmare care farm

Wilkes, Esther – Carl and Jane Seeger's part time housekeeper

Zachman, Greg – Fisher Scientific salesman

# THE GATE

When I was lying in the hospital three months or so ago, after the boys and their children had gone home, Alan came back and kissed my forehead, and said, "It's time you wrote it down." He handed me a spiral notebook. Which I set on the bedside table without saying a word.

I didn't have to ask what he meant. Even after I'd finished writing *Breeding Ground*, when I wanted to tell a whole lot more of what we've watched here in horse country, this memory wasn't one I could touch. And what you won't look at festers, especially since I'd been putting off lancing it for a good many years with conscious intent.

Once I got home, and got stronger again, I got busy with every other part of my life. Till one night I dreamt about the river, and woke up sick and sweating, and it came to me, the way it always has, when I've made a decision in my subconscious mind, that the time had come to get it done.

It started thirty-two years ago, months before the wounding in the river, when the Woodford County Sheriff Alan and I saw as a friend stood right here on

3

the family farm saying words that tore our lives asunder without looking us in the eye.

It'd grown out of something we've all had happen —lies getting told about you by someone with implacable intent. Malicious intent, in this case, because it was no misunderstanding. It was someone setting out to twist the truth toward his own perverse purpose. It was his word and deeds against ours, which has always been part of living in this world, and will be till the last of us gets over being human.

I'd just turned thirty-four when it happened, and I didn't have the experience then to put it in perspective. I need to try now, while I still can, because the disease that's started eating into me makes delay a kind of denial.

I'll describe what happened like a novel, the way I did in *Breeding Ground*, slipping myself in like any other character, writing scenes I wasn't part of from interviews and supposition. I'll put in excerpts from my journal too, because they show what it was like from one minute to the next.

But if I can't convey what work means to both of us, the rest won't make much sense. How it's more a cause and a calling, for Alan and me—and Spencer, too, who's still our best friend today. But then those who actually love what they do have been given one of life's great gifts.

And yet work led directly to the death that bred the danger we faced. The stress that comes from outside and in. The expectations and ambition. The greed and pride that flesh is heir to compounded in one unsatisfied soul, in this case in an equine lab that brought out the best and the worst.

I'll have to talk about 1963, a year before the murder, and tell more about equine medicine than I ever imagined I would. I've got to explain what Jack and Spencer faced in their separate worlds (especially Spencer whose life had pinned him inside himself nearly as efficiently as ours). Because they both noticed what I couldn't, and helped make the way through.

But when worry had us on the run, when I was caring for our first son, without knowing hardly anything about how to do it well, there was still peace in quiet moments when my mind would finally wander away from it, even if my throat stayed tight and my heart seemed to rattle my bones. Sometimes it came when I worked on an architectural plan for one of my historic restoration projects. Sometimes it came when I tended the broodmares Uncle Toss and I boarded on the farm, feeding and brushing and filling their buckets. Mostly it settled in the center of my soul when I rode Sam, or laid my head on his shoulder, or kissed the side of his chestnut chin, or patted Emmy, our big boxer-mutt, and watched them both when they faced their own pain with patience and quiet good will.

That's the peace I understood. There was more, thank God, beyond human understanding I still can't begin to describe to someone who hasn't been taken up short by meeting it face-to-face.

Jo Grant Munro

December 10, 1996
Rolling Ridge Farm
McCowans Ferry Road
Versailles, Kentucky

# 1963

# CHAPTER ONE

*Wednesday, July 3rd, 1963*

It was five in the morning, and Alan Munro was alone, again, in the lab at Equine Pharmaceuticals. He'd just looked at the notes in the formulation notebook Carl Seeger, Equine's lab director, had entered the day before, and he tossed a red lab crayon on his desk with a look of deep disgust. He rubbed his eyes with both hands, and leaned back in his chair—then pushed himself up and limped, slightly, less the longer he walked, to the research corner in the back of the plant.

He'd converted a fifty-four gallon drum into a mixing tank they could use to develop the proper methods for converting a beaker-size experimental batch of his new horse de-wormer paste into an intermediate batch, before they moved to a commercial size tank.

This latest mixture was way too thin, and the solids hadn't properly dispersed in the methylcellulose, and as Alan read the batch sheet he muttered words he'd

almost never used since he'd come home from World
War II.


At 8:35 Alan walked into the main lab and asked Carl
Seeger if he could speak to him for a minute.

Carl was weighing white powder on a double pan
balance, and he didn't look up before he'd slid the
powder off one pan into a large glass beaker and
replaced the brass weights from the other in their
wooden rack. "I'm busy right now, Alan. I should be
free in an hour or so." He spoke calmly and quietly, his
thin mouth tucked under a wispy mustache, his pale
brown eyebrows pulled down in concentration, half-
hiding his small hazel eyes.

"It's important, Carl. We need to go out to the
plant. You need to see the problems we're having with
the de-wormer formulation."

"Alan, I'm the laboratory director. I'm not part of
the production team. My work is in the lab." He looked
up at Alan then, who was half a foot taller, and smiled
for a second, before reaching for a black-lidded bottle.

Alan Munro didn't answer right away. He saw the
lab secretary back by his office look up from her
typing, and the two lab techs at the bench on his right
pause and wait for him to speak. "I'd like you to join
me in my office."

Carl laid a thin metal mixing spatula on the black
stone bench top, then clipped a pen in the pocket of his
clean white lab coat before he followed Alan into
Alan's office at the front end of the lab and waited for
him to close the door. "I don't appreciate being talked

down to. I have a degree in chemistry, and I direct the lab, and I've been here longer than you."

"This is not a matter of who has what title, Carl, it's—"

"Then what is this about?"

"Our job, all of us together, is to produce excellent equine medications that benefit horses and their owners. That requires outstanding formulations, plus the ability to scale them up to consistent commercial size batches."

"And you've concluded that I disagree?"

"No. I didn't say that. The point is we have to have both. If we have a formula that sets us apart from all our competitors but we can't manufacture it consistently, it'll put us out of business. If we have the most sophisticated production methods in the world and no high-performing distinctive formulations, we'll go under just as quickly. We all have to work together, without barriers between departments, to make both possible."

"I'm responsible for the lab. Butch is responsible for the plant."

"And you both work for me. And right now we're going to go out in the plant and consult with Butch."

The three of them stood uneasily by the scale-up tank. Carl was the shortest, narrow shouldered and sedentary looking. Butch Morgan was an inch or two taller, stockier with a pockmarked face, but dark eyed and good looking. Alan—by far the tallest, broad shouldered and strong boned, and dark haired too, like Butch —was leaning over the three-foot-high metal barrel dipping a two-foot aluminum ladle past the twelve-inch stirrer into a thin colorless liquid clotted with irregular lumps.

Butch answered Alan's questions about the speed of the stirrer, and the order in which the raw materials had been added, and Carl spoke when spoken to. They discussed possible causes and adjustments that might be made—led through it step by step by Alan asking questions when he could, so he didn't look any more like a dictator than he could help.

Then he smiled and said, "I know scale-up is difficult. It's like telling someone who cooks for four to make stew for two hundred and fifty on a stove they've never seen."

"Butch and I *have* encountered the concept." Carl smiled condescendingly.

And Alan swallowed what he wanted to say. "Equine's never made a paste, and this one's demanding. The consistency has to be perfect so it can be sealed in a cardboard tube, and then get pushed out with a plunger into a horse's mouth. A de-wormer like this has never been done by anyone, and the—"

"So you've said before." Carl stared straight at Alan, his eyes cold and hard.

"It's important enough to repeat. You know how they treat worms in horses today?"

Carl didn't answer, and Butch shook his head.

"A vet shoves a ten-foot tube through a horse's nose and pumps the medication into his stomach with a hand pump. It can be fatal, even with a vet positioning the tube, and calling in a vet's expensive. Not only does the parasiticide in our product kill worms more effectively than anything else available today, if we can market this de-wormer as a paste a horse *owner* can safely administer, we'll revolutionize the horse world, and give Equine a market advantage."

Carl and Butch glanced at each other.

And Alan tried again. "We're going to have to buy an entirely different mixing system. A big S-shaped Sigma blade blender with a special tank that rotates so the paste can be dumped out. We'll have to design and build a completely new assembly line, which means Bob Harrison's investment's going to be huge, and we have to get this right. It'll be very interesting and important work, and you both can really contribute."

Neither one of them said anything. And Alan asked them to work on the tasks he'd already sketched out and report back at three.


They did. Reporting little progress. Shortly before a thunderstorm rolled in, and the power went off after a lightning strike that seemed to shake the earth.

That led Bob Harrison, the founder and president of Equine Pharmaceuticals, to visit each department and wish everyone a happy Fourth of July, and suggest they go home early.

Alan stepped out into the short side hall at his end of the lab, right after Bob had gone back to his office, to put mail in the outgoing box on the wall—and found Carl and Butch at the corner near reception with their heads together talking to Bob's son, Brad, who ran the accounting department (but gave Alan the impression that he saw himself as a masterful manager, waiting for a chance to show what he could do).

They stopped talking when they saw Alan. Then

Brad nodded, and walked off toward the front door, to the right beyond reception.

Vincent Eriksen, tall and thin and nearly crippled by shyness, who cleaned all of Equine every night, was standing in the doorway to his supply room across from the door to the lab, filling a cart with supplies. Alan stopped and talked with him a minute before he walked toward the others to wish them a good Fourth.

Before he got to them, Carl said, "Butch and I have been talking. Before you were hired, Bob worked with us directly managing the transition from the lab to production. If you don't feel able to do it on your own, why don't you bring Bob in to fix the scale-up?"

"It's a bigger issue than that. It's not just this one scale-up today that's important. It's that we *all* need to learn to do it now—to develop the ability to do this easily as a part of everyday business. It's not healthy for an organization to have one or two Mr. Fix-Its who solve every problem."

Carl smiled and said, "No? I thought speed was the issue."

"Not speed alone. And Bob shouldn't be bothered with it. There're too many things only he can do. The formulating and fermenting of the vaccines and antibiotics. Field testing them too, with the UK vets. Horse care products and simple medications aren't as interesting to him, and we need to master this ourselves. Chemical manufacturing processes are beginning to change more rapidly now, and this will help us keep up."

"My responsibility is the lab." Carl wasn't looking at Alan, but staring off toward reception.

But Butch looked at Carl, before he glanced at

Alan. "My responsibility is to take the formulas I get from the lab and manufacture the way I'm told."

"Precisely." Carl nodded and crossed his arms across his belt. "Again, as I said before, if you can't do it, and if speed in scale-up is—"

"Believe it or not, I have a great deal of experience with scale-up in pharmaceuticals, as well as formulation. But me being a dictator would end up being harmful. This is an opportunity for all of us to learn and develop." Alan stopped, and made himself smile, before he said, "Anyway, have a good Fourth. Hope you've got power at home."

Butch said, "You too."

Before Carl said, "Goodnight," and started toward the front door, with Butch following behind.

Alan sighed, then smiled at Vincent, and walked back into the lab.

*Friday, July 12th, 1963*

The following Friday night, Alan and his wife, Jo, went out to dinner in Lexington—Jo in a black linen suit with the skirt left half unzipped, and her tan silk blouse hanging loose to postpone the sewing of maternity clothes. Her pecan colored hair was wrapped on the back of her head so the curly ends swirled on one side, and Alan smoothed a stray end, before he sat down across from her.

They talked about all kinds of things the way they always did—her work as an architect helping to restore White Hall, the mansion that a hundred years before had belonged to Cassius Clay, the street-fighting

abolitionist who'd been Lincoln's ambassador to
Russia.

Jo talked about being pregnant for the first time too,
and how four months felt different than it had before,
and how she was trying to figure out what she should
stop doing now with the horses they boarded on the
farm.

But when Jo asked Alan how work was going, he
clammed up without warning.

"What about the antifungal shampoo you formulated? How's that selling?"

"Better than we expected. The fungicidal ointments
too. The exclusive contract with Bayer for the fungicide has given us a real advantage."

"How's the de-wormer going?"

"More or less the way I was afraid it would."

Jo leaned back in her chair, her straight black
eyebrows pulled close together over dark blue purpose-
ful eyes that were fixed right on Alan's.

She sat and watched him look away, the scar along
the left side of his jaw white against the five o'clock
shadow that had already taken control. Then she set her
elbows on the table and wove her fingers together.
"What?"

"What d'ya mean, what?"

"What's going on, Alan?" She watched him silently,
seeing more than he wanted her to, her eyebrows arched
analytically.

He told her then, for almost half an hour—about
Carl and Butch, and that during the last week, Bob
Harrison was either irritated with him, or avoiding him
altogether. Bob normally went out of this way to
consult Alan, and seemed to enjoy discussing the

vaccines he was working on, but he'd been keeping to himself, and hardly looking at Alan when Alan went to talk to him, and the chill rolling off him was getting hard to ignore.

"I don't want to worry you, with you being pregnant, but if there's a lack of trust, or some opposition from Bob, it doesn't bode well for my stay at Equine. I can put up with resistance from the rest, but I can't stay if Bob joins the others."

"Somebody's been gossiping behind your back. You know what I mean. Telling him something about you that's got him questioning what you're doing, and maybe what kind of person you are."

"That's nothing but speculation."

"Yeah, but I bet I'm right. Carl wouldn't hesitate, that's for sure. And yet why would Bob believe him? He oughtta know you better than that."

"Bob's very good with people in certain ways. He can talk about the principles that are important to him, and the medicine he's excited about, and where he sees the company going, and when he's done everybody who's heard him would crawl across cut glass for him.

"But there's something naïve about him too, and I've seen him get fooled. He's so straightforward himself he expects everybody else to be. So he doesn't catch the two faced, or the manipulative, and he can't see the boot kissing that goes on with some of the people there. 'Member how Spencer's mom helped Spencer's dad with all of that? That's what Bob needs. But his wife knows nothing about the business. All she seems to think about is getting their son promoted."

"That sounds ominous."

"It's definitely not a help."

"So how does Bob react when he sees somebody's dishonest, or trying to take advantage of him?"

"I think he tends to overreact. He's so surprised and appalled he can't see it as an everyday facet of human nature and try to be dispassionate."

"So if he thinks you've been undermining him, he won't respond well. Right? So what're you going to do?"

"You know how friendly he's been? How he's supported me, even when Brad's acted threatened by me?"

"Yeah."

"Well, yesterday, when I asked to talk to him about the Sigma blade options we need to research, he wouldn't even look in my direction."

"You're going to have to do something. You can't just let it go on."


They walked out into a blue-black night sprinkled with crystal stars, and stood by the curb in front of the steak-house and looked up and smiled.

A man's voice said, "Hey," off on their left, and they turned and saw Butch Morgan and his wife walking toward them from a barbecue place that was one of Lexington's favorites.

Alan said, "Hi, Butch. Hey, Frannie. How are your girls doing?"

"Enjoying their summer vacation." She answered before Butch, adjusting the belt of her dress, her heart-shaped sun-burned face looking slightly ill at ease.

Jo asked if she was still working at the insurance company, as she slipped her hand in Alan's.

"The branch in Louisville most days. I moved up

there this winter. Daddy comes in and helps three days a week here, but it's primarily up to me now. At the Louisville branch, and in Lexington."

Butch looked irritated before she'd finished, but then he slipped his arm around Frannie's waist, and looked directly at Alan. "Her dad's not much older than Bob Harrison, but he's real close to retired."

Alan said, "I can't imagine Bob retiring. He's only in his fifties, and work's the center of his life."

Butch was watching Alan now with a kind of wavering intent as though he might've had too much to drink. "You ever seen Bob lose his temper?"

"No. Not what I'd call losing it. Why?"

"I reckon he didn't like being told he's too old to do good work."

"Who told him that?"

"Carl told him what *you* said. 'Member? In the hall the other day? Manufacturing's changing so fast, you don't want him to help with scale-up. Like maybe his methods are outta date." Butch was smiling, rocking on the balls of his feet, taking in the shock on Alan's face.

"I didn't say that! Nothing even close to that."

"That's what *we* thought you said. But you know how it is," he was trying to take one of Frannie's hands in his, but she stepped farther away. "If ten folks see a bank holdup, you'll get ten versions of what happened. See ya Monday, Alan."

Frannie and Alan and Jo said goodnight, as Butch and Frannie walked past.

After they'd turned the corner, Jo said, "Well, now we know why Bob's irritated with you."

"Yeah, we certainly do. Crap."

"Did Butch and Frannie get divorced?"

"He hasn't said anything at work, but if she's moved, it—"

"She wasn't wearing a ring."

"How do women notice things like that?"

"Why do men not?"

They both smiled, and started toward their car, staring up at the stars again—before they started worrying about what Carl had told Bob.

*Monday, July 15th, 1963*

"I appreciate you meeting with me." Alan Munro set a glass of iced tea on the driftwood table under the old farmhouse's back arbor, between his chair and Bob Harrison's. "If the bugs get bad we can move inside."

"I was raised on a dairy farm. I worked as a large animal vet for eight years. I can put up with bugs. Jo here?" Bob's salt-and-pepper hair, with gray patches at the temples, ruffled in a gust of wind from the left end of the arbor.

"She's working on the restoration of a house south of Lexington."

A painful silence settled between them, while Bob Harrison, who looked like a coiled spring, tapped a finger on the arm of his chair as though that was all that was keeping him from leaping up in the air. "Look, I left work that I need to do, and I don't mean to be rude, but I'd appreciate it if you'd tell me why you asked me to meet you away from the office. I assume it's concerned with the business."

"It is. I'm trying to decide where to start." Alan Munro took a sip of iced tea before he turned toward

Bob. "I know Carl Seeger told you that I told him and Butch Morgan something that more or less means I think you're old and behind the times. That you can't help with the scale-up of new products, but that's not at all what—"

"How do *you* know that's what Carl said?" Harrison's eyes were gray and deep set behind black-framed glasses, and he stared hard at Alan, then looked away again fast.

"Butch. Jo and I ran into him and his wife outside a restaurant in Lexington Friday night. He might've had a bit too much to drink, and he looked like he was gloating when he said it. I've also noticed there's a distance now in the way you communicate with me."

Bob Harrison looked sideways at Alan for less than a second, then picked up his glass of tea.

Alan slid his director's chair counterclockwise till he faced Bob straight on, his green eyes determined, the small muscles under his cheekbones clenched as tight as his jaw. "What I said to Carl and Butch was 'Bob shouldn't be bothered with scale-up. That's our job. He has other things to do that only he can, like the antibiotic formulating and fermenting.' I said we need to master it ourselves. I've told them till I'm blue in the face that it's a good opportunity for us to learn, and work together as a team. Vincent Eriksen was in the hall when we were talking and he can corroborate what was said."

"Can he?" Bob was studying Alan now, his eyes cool and considering, his firm mouth skeptical. Then Bob looked away again, out across the lawn at the willow back by the pond, as he locked his hands behind his neck. "What's the root of the conflict?"

"I'm the VP of Science and Technology. I'm a chemical engineer trying hard to improve things, and they don't like my input impacting the way they've always worked."

"That's not unexpected. I would've thought you would've anticipated that reaction and gone out of your way to avoid it."

"I did, and I *have* gone out of my way. You brought me in to evaluate Equine Pharmaceuticals' existing product line, and help you determine what needs to be developed. To help the lab design reliable test methods too, for products and raw materials, and improve the way you test new products in the field. You've also wanted me to help your lab and production people take what's formulated in the lab and scale it up from a beaker-sized batch to full commercial volume."

"Correct." Bob said it as though Alan were stating the obvious and wasting valuable time.

"I don't know the veterinary science that enables you to develop vaccines and antibiotics and cutting-edge equine drugs. I can formulate other treatments, and help refine the health care formulas to optimize ingredients and improve production techniques. But I never could've started the business, or come up with the drugs you have."

"I do grasp the distinctions, Alan."

"Then why would I be stupid enough to minimize your contributions and imply that you're behind the times?"

Bob didn't say anything till he'd finished the last of his tea. "How would you evaluate Carl's and Butch's performance?"

"Carl has a degree in chemistry, and he's able to

perform lab-tech-type bench work under your and my direction, but he doesn't have the curiosity or the experience to do the more sophisticated thinking and development that I think a lab director should. It may be attitude, rather than aptitude, I can't say. I do know he's very determined not to get his hands dirty by helping with any of the scale-up work, and he resents my presence here, and the relationship you and I have had, because of our shared perspectives."

"And Butch?"

"He doesn't have the education and the training to be effective at the scale-up work, or develop new manufacturing techniques. I think he questions his own competence, and I think Carl has influenced him to be more negative and resistant to change than he might've otherwise been. He's capable of making the antibacterial shampoos and ointments, and the new fungicidal treatments, as well as the other equine health care products in the line, once we've developed the processes for him.

"But the new de-wormer paste, that's a whole new process, and I think it's got him panicked. But instead of being cooperative, and willing to say, 'I don't know how to do this, help me and let's work together,' he's fighting whatever is new and unknown and doing you a disservice."

Bob Harrison loosened his dark blue tie, before he glanced at Alan. "I've seen evidence of that myself, but I'd like to be able to salvage him, and Carl as well. Carl especially. He's was the first person I hired in the lab."

"Then that must make it hard."

"I did everything myself when I started the business. The microbiology, working with Elvis Doll at

UK's Vet School. The fermenting and the formulating, along with the manufacturing. I washed the floors and took out the garbage and did the packaging. When you're first starting up, you don't have the luxury of scouring the country for someone with the best degrees and the deepest experience, you hire the person you can afford and hope to be able to develop them. That's how I hired Carl, and I don't want to have to let him go."

"I'm not suggesting you let either of them go. But I would like you to look at the memos in this file. Annette did the day-by-day transcribing. You can corroborate their authenticity with her." He pulled a manila folder from the briefcase he'd set on the arbor's brick floor and handed it to Bob Harrison.

Bob read it, while Alan drank tea and patted Emmy, the boxer-and-something-else, who'd been lying by his chair since he'd first sat down.

"Your position's documented, I can see that. Carl's resisted too many reasonable requests, and seems to be more interested in standing on his own dignity than putting the health of the company first. Butch too. Though, as you suggest, his insecurities may play a larger part."

"I have *tried* to be collegial. I've invited them to dinner, separately and together, and tried to talk in encouraging terms, without being critical. I've described how chemistry and production methods are beginning to develop more rapidly, and how we could learn so much, and contribute so much, if we could work together. But it hasn't seemed to help."

"I see that in the lab and production reports."

"But I think there's more too. They both really respect you, and they feel as though I've come between you and them. That you and I work together more closely now, and some inside position they once had has been unfairly ripped away. I also have to be honest and say that Carl's attitude is such that I have real doubts that he can be turned around."

"It's an unfortunate situation."

"It is."

"I would like to speak with Vincent. It's not that I don't trust you—"

"I understand. And I've asked him if he'd be willing for us to stop by this afternoon. If that's something you have time to do."

"It'll be difficult for him. With his background." Bob was looking out toward the pond, shielding his eyes with one hand. "Look at the great blue heron."

He'd landed for a second, but then gathered himself and flown off again as Alan turned to look. "I don't know anything about Vincent, except that it's hard for him to talk to people, and he still uses a list to clean the offices every night, even though he's cleaned the building for years."

Bob Harrison smiled as he reached for the sport coat he'd hung on the back of his chair. "The fall before Pearl Harbor was bombed, Vincent was finishing his doctorate dissertation in mathematics at Harvard when a paper by a physicist at Oxford was published that anticipated his work. Vincent couldn't come up with a new dissertation topic, and he left Harvard on his own volition and came home to live with his parents, whom I've known for years.

"He tried to enlist, but his eyesight disqualified him. He took a job as a mail carrier for a while, but the personal contact with that many people was very difficult for him. In '55, when I was able to hire a person to clean the offices and the lab, I decided to try Vincent. It's suited him very well. He comes to work as everyone else is leaving and works till midnight, or so, then studies mathematics and astrophysics on his own during the day."

"I had no idea."

"Few people do. He finds it impossible to discuss."


Vincent Eriksen was waiting for them on the front porch of the small clapboard house he shared with his widowed sister. It was over ninety and humid, but he was sitting in an old rattan chair dressed in khaki work pants with a long-sleeved tan shirt buttoned at the collar and the cuffs.

He stood up as soon as he saw Bob's car draw up, very tall and slightly stooped, and so thin his black leather belt sat on a ridge of sharp edged bone. His eyes were anxious behind his horn-rims, even more than usual, pale blue and partly hidden under worried eyebrows.

Bob and Alan both said hello as they came up the walk, and Vincent nodded and motioned them toward the two rattan chairs perpendicular to his on the right end of the porch.

They tried small talk for a minute or two, but then Bob asked Vincent if he knew why they were there.

Vincent had been staring at the painted gray floor, rubbing his hands on his knees. "I do."

"So …"

"You want to know about the conversation I heard in the hall by the lab."

"Yes."

"The power failed on July 3rd at 3:52 p.m. The incinerator had been acting up, and I was worried that I was running late, and had consulted my watch a moment before." His voice trailed away as he stared at the street, his hands gripping his knees.

Bob had taken off his glasses and was rubbing the red places where they sat on his nose, when he said, "I know this isn't easy."

"I don't care to be a bearer of tales."

"Is that what you're going to do? Tell us a tale?"

"No. No. I detest disputes. I told Mr. Munro."

"But?"

"I agreed to speak, and I will." Vincent crossed one leg over the other and tucked his hands underneath his arms, hugging his ribs without saying anything for what seemed like more than a minute.

Bob said, "Take your time, Vincent. There's no rush. We don't want this to be stressful."

"I know you don't … I know, I …" He stared at the peeling floor, holding his breath, rocking forward and back, without seeming to notice.

Alan said, "So you were in the hall when Carl Seeger and Butch Morgan and I were talking."

"Yes."

He worked his way through it, with lurches and stops, and nervous twitches, but he told Bob Harrison what had been said with accuracy and order.

"Mr. Seeger was wearing his white lab coat, and adjusting the pens in his pocket. Even those two times when he said that Mr. Munro couldn't do the scale-up himself, Mr. Munro spoke politely." Vincent swallowed hard, as though his mouth and throat were dry, and his

Adam's apple shot up and down like a hockey puck sliding under skin.

Bob Harrison said, "Thank you, Vincent. You did the right thing to tell me."

"I don't want to get anyone in trouble."

"You haven't. You've helped me see how to do what's best for everyone at the company. We'll have to show Carl and Butch how much they can help if they work with me and Alan here to get our new products to market more quickly."

"I want to work on my own without interfering with anyone else."

"No one could do better work than you do. You're an excellent example of the dedication and loyalty we should all aspire to. Thank you."

"You're welcome." He was breathing too fast and the color had drained from his face, making him look parched and ill.

Alan said, "I really appreciate your help."

Vincent nodded, and then stood up and shoved his hands in his pants pockets as though he'd finished a distasteful task. A small ginger-and-white cat shot up the steps, and Vincent stooped and caught it, then patted it without looking up as Bob and Alan left.

# CHAPTER TWO

*Excerpt From Jo Grant Munro's Journal
Thursday, August 1st, 1963.*

*I'm five months pregnant and feeling totally unpre-
pared. I don't have nieces and nephews because
Tommy died before he could marry. And with Mom
dead, and Spencer's Mom too, I don't have an older
woman I can ask for advice.*

*I don't say much to Alan about it, because he's got
enough to put up with. Carl's tormenting Vincent now,
having figured out where Bob got corroboration for
Alan's side of the story, and that makes it even harder
for Alan to tolerate Carl.*

*I saw Spencer's dad at church last week, and I
wanted to talk to him about Equine, because Booker's
got years of experience with interoffice politics, first at
John Deere and now in his own horse van business. It
hasn't been much more than a year, though, since he
lost Alice, and you can see something's missing.
Booker's quieter, and way too thin. And when he
doesn't know you're watching, he settles into an*

*internalized sort of stare that makes me wonder if there's something someone ought to be doing to help him more than we are.*

*He's still riding Buster, and I hope that helps him the way riding Sam helped me after Tommy was killed. Being on a horse with great gaits who's the soul of equine comportment is the best way for me to loosen up my body and soften my view of the world. I've had to stop now, for obvious reasons, but brushing Sam, and talking to him, and watching him in the fields smooths away the interior wrinkles the world lays down every day.*

*And of course, horses being as delicate as they are despite their size, Sam developed a nasty abscess in his hoof a month ago, and he's put up with daily soakings and packings and occasional cuttings with character and kindness and the common sense of a gentleman, and he's made me evaluate my own reactions to the vicissitudes of life.*

*There's some progress restoring White Hall, but making practical* and *artistic decisions with a committee of volunteers with no professional experience is enough to make me shoot somebody.*

*Toss is doing most of the work with the broodmares and babies, and with the part-time guy he's hired, I don't have to do much on the farm, so Emmy and I do everything together with her boxerish dewlaps flapping. She is so coordinated it's amazing to watch her leap and jump and twist in midair.*

*I dreamt last night about England and Scotland. I still can't believe we got there on our honeymoon. Seeing the landscape, and the cottages, not to mention*

*the great houses and the castles, has influenced my*
*work a lot.*

## Saturday, August 3rd, 1963

Art Lawrence moved the wooden chairs closer to his
desk, then looked at his watch, and dropped into his
swivel chair. He opened his center drawer, and the top
right too, for at least the third time, then left them
partially open. He laid a ballpoint pen on the legal pad
he'd already set on his desk blotter, and adjusted his
red plaid tie. He sipped his coffee and stared at the
door, then consulted his watch again, and walked to the
window that overlooked the drive.

When he saw a turquoise-and-white Chevy sedan
with U.S. plates, he reached quickly into both drawers,
then turned a switch on the gray metal Dictaphone that
sat on top of his desk, and rushed out into the hall to
open the front door.

He stood straight and still as he waited, shorter than
average, and military looking, probably in his early
fifties, his shoulders back, his reddish blond hair
brushed till it gleamed, his shoes polished, his navy
blazer, well cut and pressed. He opened the door for the
two Americans and said, "Carl. Butch. Thank you for
driving all this way."

Carl Seeger smiled before he said, "Thanks for
meeting us on a Saturday."

Art asked how customs had been in Detroit, as he
led them down the hall, and Carl answered while Butch
looked uncomfortable and pulled at the sleeves of his

sport coat as though he'd been imprisoned in it and wanted to rip it off.

"Would you like coffee, or tea?"

Carl and Butch both said coffee, and Art filled two mugs from the percolator in the corner of his office.

Carl and Art compared and contrasted the large animal vet markets in the U.S. and Canada, while Art brought out sugar and creamer—both of them deliberately talking around what had brought them together, controlling the pacing, sizing up the other, each planning their final approaches, depending on how the conversation developed.

Art, because he was a born salesman with a gift for getting to know people and steering conversations to the kind of connections that helped him close deals. Carl, because he'd learned as a kid, working as a soda jerk, that customers who feel admired leave the biggest tips.

Butch, who looked twenty years younger than the other two, licked his lips and sipped his coffee as though he were having second thoughts about sitting there at all.

"So, Carl." Art took a sip of coffee and set his cup in its saucer. "Shall we discuss the subject you broached on the phone? I'm not saying I'm interested, but I am willing to listen."

Carl lit a Lucky with a dented Zippo, and reached for the ashtray on Art's desk. "Yeah, sure, as I said then, the new equine fungicidal shampoos and ointments Equine Pharmaceuticals has brought out this year are selling like hotcakes."

"I know they've sold tremendously well here. Canadian winters are so cold our horses' coats grow in terribly long and thick, and fungal-type skin infections can be extremely severe. Your products are the only ones that help control the problem."

"Nothing else on the market can touch Equine's line, and I did the formulations."

"I thought Alan introduced the active ingredient when he came to Equine, and did the development as well."

"He brought the active ingredient. He had a relationship with the manufacturer already, and he made an exclusive equine market agreement with them for Equine in the U.S. But I did the formulating."

Butch looked at Carl as though that had come as a surprise, but he wasn't going to disagree in public.

"I will say the anti-fungal products have made handling the Equine line even more attractive. I represent Pfizer too, of course, when they don't compete with Bob. His vaccine and antibiotic offering is narrower than theirs."

"Yeah, I'm sure it is."

"So …"

"So what we're proposing, Art—Butch and me—is that we take advantage of the opportunity we see to use the formulas I've developed, and the production methods Butch has perfected, and set up our own business here in Toronto. I know your brother has a blending operation, and we're proposing to pass on seventy percent of the gross sales here in Canada to you and your brother if you manufacture and sell in Canada. Butch would set up the manufacturing and packaging methods and provide ongoing technical support. I'd provide the formulas and application support, after I work out an exclusive with the fungicide manufacturer for the Canadian equine market. I'd try to get an exclusive for the equine industry in Europe too, because manufacturing here and shipping out the St. Lawrence Seaway offers another substantial market with no one in competition with anything like the performance we can provide."

"So this would include the formulas for the fungal preventative shampoo, the fungal treatment shampoo, and the topical ointments and powders that Equine Pharmaceuticals makes now?"

"Exactly." Carl stubbed his Lucky out in the metal ashtray and finished the last of his coffee, then blotted his mustache with a paper napkin, and watched Art with a satisfied smile on his soft pale face.

Art didn't say anything for a minute. He watched Carl watch him while he played with his ballpoint pen. "I take it you don't see any legal difficulties? I wouldn't want to open myself up to any sort of litigation."

"No, the attorney I've consulted sees no problem whatever. Both of our noncompete agreements with Bob Harrison apply exclusively to the United States. I developed those products, and I have a legitimate right to profit from my own work over and above the paycheck I get for directing the lab. Butch here, he figures out how to get these products made, and he ought to benefit too." Carl lit another Lucky and shrugged at his own common sense, his cool hazel eyes, under graying sandy hair, watching Art with a look that seemed to say, *I understand you. You're a man like me. The two of us can do business.*

"And you came to me as the logical person to partner with you in Canada?"

"You're a very successful independent veterinary supply and pharmaccutical distributor. You know the market extremely well. You represent large prestigious suppliers, and you and I have known each other since I joined Equine Pharmaceuticals. Your brother has a chemical blending business, and you're a sharp guy. I thought you'd be interested."

"I'll have to think about it. I've known Bob Harrison a long time, and he's always treated me well."

"He treats himself even better, trust me."

Art asked, "What about you, Butch? You haven't said anything."

Butch set his mug on Art's desk and slid a finger inside his shirt collar, before he looked at Art. "Well, I reckon we've got a right to benefit from the work we've done. I've always liked Bob, but things are different now. Alan Munro, he's changin' everything. The fun's goin' out of it, and I don't know how long I can hang on."

"So this would give you an income if you chose to leave?"

"That's the way I see it." Butch looked down at Art's desk with his hands set solidly on his knees.

"Well, you've given me a lot to think about. Percentages would have to be reconsidered, based on setup and production cost estimates. I'll have to discuss it with my brother, of course. Then I'll call you, Carl, at your home number."

Carl said, "Good. I look forward to us doing business together."


After Art had walked them to Carl's car, he sprinted

back to his office and pushed a switch on his Dictaphone, then pulled out two small six-by-eight battery
operated reel-to-reel tape recorders from the open
drawers in his desk. He pushed the off buttons, inserted
the power cords, plugged them into a wall outlet,
rewound both, and listened for several seconds. Then
he shut them off and placed a person-to-person call to
Bob Harrison in Kentucky.

"I got it, Bob. Two tape recorders and a Dictaphone! I'll make copies this afternoon and drive down
with them tomorrow. ... You don't need to thank me.
What you did for me when I was starting up makes this
an absolute pleasure. Those two deserve to be throttled!
... "I agree, yes, Carl's the motivating force. Butch
looks profoundly uneasy, but he's still willing to go
along with something he knows is wrong. ... Yes,
indeed. Tomorrow, late afternoon. ... Thank you. I *will*
spend the night, if you're sure I won't be imposing on
Rachel."

*Tuesday, August 6th, 1963*

Booker Franklin had left his office at Blue Grass Horse
Vans just before six, and ridden his horse, Buster, at his
son Spencer's farm. He'd hosed Buster off, and put
grain in his feed bucket, then turned him out in that
paddock, and started home with a very hard knot
lodged deep in his chest.

As he drove the winding, hazy, soft green hills, past
farm after farm of grazing horses, past corn and
tobacco and beef cattle too, on his way north from
south of Versailles toward his house up in Midway, he

thought back to a night when he was young, to the night of an Iowa blizzard, when his daughter Martha had been born.

She'd been so cute. So quick and determined and clever. And she'd been very good, right from the start, at batting her eyelashes and smiling at her daddy till he'd wanted to hug her and give in, even when he'd known better and forced himself to resist.

He hadn't loved her any more than the boys, but he'd tended by nature to be harder on them to help them grow up to be men. He'd found himself wanting to protect Martha from every ill in the outside world, when Alice, her mother, had known better, and had told him what he'd needed to hear when he'd needed to hear it.

Now he found himself in an unlooked for situation, in conflict with Martha that should've been avoided, and the time had come to take a stand before the rift got harder to repair.

He'd been very willing for Martha and her son and daughter to move in with him after her divorce from Hal, when they'd cut her job at the Gibbes Museum in Charleston. The cost of living in Lexington was much less, and moving back made economic sense.

He'd understood that the move home was temporary, but Martha had made no attempt to find a house, and she and the kids had been with him six weeks, and the turmoil was wearing him down. He was accustomed to living alone. Now. Since Alice had been killed. And he needed peace and quiet.

He had to have time to concentrate on what he was trying to accomplish at work, and how to do it without Alice. He still wasn't used to living without her, and it eased the loss and the sense of displacement when he could think about their years together quietly on his own. How they'd courted. And raised the children in Iowa. And what'd it'd been like to risk everything they'd hoped to have to move back to Lexington and start Blue Grass Horse Vans together.

He had to make plans for the future too, now, with what he was facing, without the quarreling and inter- ruptions from a nine year old and a seven year old, and all their comings and goings. He felt like a squatter in his own home. And he didn't have the energy to live like that much longer.

He'd taken his boots off on the back porch, and washed his hands in the kitchen sink, and he was walking barefoot across the heart pine floor when he heard Martha call him from the dining room next door.

Booker stood in the kitchen doorway and watched her measuring and making notes, as she talked about converting the dining room to a playroom when she rearranged the downstairs.

Booker made himself wait before he spoke in a carefully quiet voice. "I don't think that's a good idea, honey. And there're a couple of other matters too I reckon we need to discuss."

"What?" She was making a note on a notepad, bending over Alice's grandmother's long walnut table, and she didn't stop as she spoke.

"I was wonderin' if you've given any thought to getting a job at the art museum at the University of Kentucky. Being a curator's what you love, though the art department would suit you too, if you—"

"No, I can't say I have."

"I've also been meaning to tell you I've got a very good friend in real estate here, and he and I can help you look for a house to rent. There're lots of places in town, and out—in Lexington, or here in Woodford, County—that might suit you real well."

Martha looked surprised, and maybe half-amused, when she glanced at him over her shoulder as she said she thought she'd live with him, and was thinking of working at Blue Grass Horse Vans, once she and the kids got settled. "My furniture's coming next week, and I'll have to find a place to put it into storage temporarily, till I have a chance to rethink the house. After that I'll be ready to start. Maybe I could store it at Blue Grass, somewhere back in the plant?"

That was not what Booker had expected to hear, and he paused a second and swallowed. "You don't have any business experience. You don't. Not one minute anywhere. You have no interest in horses whatsoever. Why would you want to work for a horse van and trailer manufacturer?"

"I thought I could just work part-time, and set my own schedule around the children's school. You know I can't afford a nanny the way I could in Charleston before the divorce." Martha didn't look at Booker while she talked. She measured the outside wall in the dining room, then made a note on her scratchpad. She set one hand on a broad hip, her back turned to Booker, and considered the archway into the living room as though she didn't approve.

Booker said, "That's not the way it works, honey. The family has to set the example. We have to work harder than anyone else, and be the most professional.

You don't have any kind of background or experience, and it would not be viewed well by the people who've been there a long time and are really dedicated and good at what they do."

Martha turned around and looked at Booker for the first time, her blue eyes steely, her pointed chin set. "Mom didn't have any experience either, and she became the personnel director and did all the public relations."

"She started the business with me. She didn't do the engineering, and the trailer and van design I did, like Spencer does with me now, but she was the only other employee when we started out. She did all the accounting and the orders. She learned every bit of it from the ground up, just the way I had to. We worked with every lawyer and accountant together. We negotiated with the banks together. She developed and administered the office procedures much better than I do. And it's way bigger than that now, and much more complicated. When we had enough employees that there was such a thing as personnel, she took courses, and read a great deal, and worked with experts in the field to develop the way she needed to."

"I thought you'd *want* me in the company, taking Mom's place!"

"I'm sorry, Martha, but it's not a good idea." Booker's arms were crossed across what there was of his stomach as he leaned against the kitchen doorway, and smiled a sad gentle looking smile while he said what she didn't want to hear.

"What you mean is it's just because I'm a woman! You've got Richard and Spencer there, and—"

"That's not it at *all*. And having them both in the

business has not been without considerable conflict and difficulties, and I don't intend to make it worse. It's not because you're a woman. No. It's what I've already said. Your talents are in museum work. You could teach about being a curator as well as doing it, and that's what you love. There's the library at Kecneland Racccourse too, and their archives are exceptional, with paintings and drawings as well as the documents, and they're talking about building a new facility that will—"

"The UK museum is very small, and it wouldn't pay much even if they hired me, and at Keeneland—"

"You get dividends on the stock we've given you. I know they're not large, but it's something, and Hal's paying reasonable support. It's a lot cheaper to rent a house here than it would be in Charleston."

"I thought I could come home and get—"

"Taken care of? A place to live for free, and a job because you're my daughter, that you wouldn't have to work at very hard? I'm sorry to be so blunt, Martha, but that's not fair. I need to be alone here too. Mom and I raised three children. I don't have the energy to do it again, not when you're healthy and can care for them on your own. I love Jenny and Matt, but I have to have time alone. I'm still missin' your Mama, and I need to think and plan in quiet. I've also been having some trouble myself, though I haven't—"

"I never thought I'd be rejected by Hal and you too!" Martha burst into tears and ran out of the room, her thick curly bourbon-colored hair swinging around her shoulders the way it had when she was twelve, passing her son and daughter who'd come in quietly from the back hall in time to hear her yell.

*Wednesday, August 7th, 1963*

It was almost seven the following night when Booker came through the kitchen door saying, "Martha? Where are you, honey?" without getting an answer.

He threw his keys on the long maple table that'd come from his daddy's farm, and found two notes addressed to him waiting on the end near the sink.

Mary Treeter's note said she'd cleaned the upstairs and done the ironing and left him tuna-fish salad and green beans with bacon in covered dishes in the ice box, and that some fella named Ridgeway Peters wanted Booker to call him at home as soon as he got in.

The other note was from Martha. "I've taken your grandchildren out to dinner so we don't intrude on your solitude."

Booker sighed, and walked down the hall that was open on the left the whole length of the gallery, then turned right into the front hall and stepped into Alice's office. It was his now, but largely unchanged. And he sank down into Alice's black leather swivel chair and phoned the lawyer they'd both trusted enough to put on their board of directors.

Booker heard what he'd hoped to hear—the new will and supplemental document were ready to sign, and Ridge would bring them to Booker first thing in the morning before they both went to work.

Booker thanked him, and listened to Ridgeway talk about the summer sales at Keeneland, and the two year old he'd bought. Then he hung up, and showered, and dished up his dinner from the fridge.

He ate it on the terrace in back, outside the gallery where Alice had painted her landscapes the three or four weeks she took each year away from her everyday work. He looked at the boxwoods they'd planted together the year they'd moved in. And he watched the birds swirling around him, on the feeders, sometimes, that he kept out year round, and in and out of the redbud trees too, that he and Alice had loved, and the woods beyond that screened his view, that belonged to the farm behind him.

He hadn't eaten much, but he still felt full and uncomfortable. And he told himself it was time to tell Spencer what he knew he was facing. He'd talked to him about the will at least, and he thought that had gone fairly well. He'd said he truly believed he loved all of them equally, and he wanted them all to benefit identically. But his main obligation, in terms of the business, was to make sure his responsibilities to every-one who worked there were lived up to as best he could.

He'd told Spencer that he knew Richard and Martha would be irritated with Spencer for what he'd done himself. But if anyone could make them see the wisdom of the decisions he'd made, it would be Spencer. And at least Spencer'd be able to do what was best for everyone who worked for Blue Grass Horse Vans as time went on.

He'd seen that Spencer had felt uncomfortable, not wanting to talk about planning for Booker's death, though all he'd said was he knew it was something Booker had to prepare for, but that he had years left, that his whole family lived to see ninety.

A hummingbird settled on the sugar-water feeder five feet away, and Booker held his breath and watched the light flash on the green-and-turquoise feathers on a bird smaller than his thumb. Even so, he didn't watch as intently as usual. His mind was on his family and truths he couldn't change.

He told himself he shouldn't be surprised. *It's one of the mysteries of life, the way genes come out so differently. The shape of the head skippin' a generation. Or the arches in someone's feet goin' to one, but not another. Or seeing things the same way someone else does, so you can talk to your uncle, but not to your own daddy. Or to one of your kids, and nobody else, not in the whole family.*

*Maybe if I get up and walk for awhile, I'll start to feel some better.*


Booker stepped out his front door, heading straight east down his long drive toward Midway's main street. It was cooler after the shower that had come before he ate, and the lawn and the oaks lining the driveway, and the hydrangea bushes with their huge dark leaves tucked in the shade of the oak trees, looked less dusty and greener now than when he'd driven in.

He waved to old Miss Anna Eldrige, tending her azaleas across the street in her tiny front garden, and he told himself to sit on her porch and chat on his way home. He hadn't talked to Miss Anna since Martha'd moved in, and it was time he made the effort. There weren't too many left who knew her, and most of those couldn't get out on their own anymore, and had to wait for someone from church to drive them over for a visit.

Booker turned left toward the center of town, walking under the old trees on the west side of Main. They made him feel sheltered and calmer, though he couldn't have said why. Maybe the laciness, and the filtered evening light that dappled the cracked old stones in the sidewalk, and the soft green in the yards. It reminded him of walks with his grandmother, and with Alice too, through Midway, out past the horse farms on the south side, talking about their day at work, and how their horses were doing, and who was going to water the garden when they got home.

He was thinking he'd get him a pack of spearmint gum down in the center of town, as he walked past the Midway College president's house, all white-washed brick and pristine gardens as neat and tidy as Robert from the college had kept them for forty years.

Booker stayed on the west side of the next block too, and then crossed over to the east, where he stopped and stared in the window of Lehman's Antiques at an oval mahogany dining room table he knew nothing whatever about, except that it was a work of art that few could've made in his day.

He was feeling worse rather than better, even though he'd walked slowly and the evening had sunk into shade. Perspiration was running down his chest now, and nausea was sweeping through him. His left arm too had begun to ache, even before he reached inside the breast pocket of his shirt, and pulled out the small cardboard box that held his nitroglycerin. He'd taken two out, and was trying to get them under his tongue when a pain in his chest like a vise around his ribs knocked his knees out from under him, and threw him down onto the stone step in front of Lehman's door.

Mertie Mae Trasker was on the west side of Main, just across from Booker Franklin, coming up the hill from the railroad tracks, walking her collie after dinner, and she hollered out to poor Mr. Booker and hurried across the street.

He was dead when she got there, when she knelt down beside him. That's what she figured, but she chaffed his wrists anyway, repeating his name the whole time. The old tan-and-white collie was sniffing Booker's shoes when Mertie Mae tugged hard on her leash, and started trotting east toward home to call the county sheriff.

# CHAPTER THREE

*Excerpt From Jo Grant Munro's Journal*
*Thursday, August 8th, 1963*

*Poor Booker. Poor Spencer. No one had any idea Booker was ill, and I can see Spencer worrying that there was something he should have noticed, or should have done, and didn't. I've invited him for dinner tomorrow, and I hope he'll actually come.*

*We had our own excitement here tonight. Bob Harrison appeared at eight o'clock, without calling ahead, which wasn't like him at all, saying he needed to talk to Alan.*

*They went into our farm office/library, and I took Emmy out to visit Sam to give them time alone. When I got back, Bob was gone, and Alan managed to look stunned, furious, and gratified at the same time while he told me that Bob's distributor in Canada had recorded Carl and Butch asking him to take the formulas for Alan's fungicidal products and manufacture them in Canada.*

*Carl claimed he'd developed them, which is so far*

*from the truth it makes me crazy. But the larger issue,*
*obviously, is it's clearly criminal behavior.*

*Alan and Bob are both hopping mad, but Alan*
*thinks it's the treachery that's upset Bob most.*

*I'm not all that surprised with Carl, but I didn't*
*expect it of Butch.*


### Friday, August 9th, 1963

Carl Seeger laid the heavy black metal receiver back in
its oval cradle, telling himself again that Art Lawrence
had a large territory and traveled most of the week, so it
shouldn't be surprising that he hadn't returned his calls.

Carl stood behind the desk in his study, holding his
smoke-colored Siamese cat in the crook of his left arm,
stroking her back and listening to his wife put dishes
away in the kitchen. He set Cassandra down on the old
brown rug and lit a Lucky while he stared across the
street toward the honey-colored stone house where
Elinor Nevilleson was watering her roses and surveying
her neighbors' houses as though she were responsible
for decorum and civility, as well as all lawns and
gardens.

Carl was planning what to say to her the next time
she complained about Cassandra "defecating" in her
perennials—when Bob Harrison's long black Chrysler
turned into his drive.

Then he saw Harrison wasn't alone. His blond-
headed stork of an attorney had unfolded his reed-like
legs and was climbing out of the car, when Carl said,
"Damn!" and crushed his Lucky in the plastic ashtray
on his desk. *Garner Honeycutt. In a fine blue suit.*

*Stickpin in his tie. Honeycutt, Honeycutt and Whipple. Coddlers of the rich. Defenders of the predators who prey on people like me!*

*That explains why Art hasn't called. The little turd's talked to Bob! But it's still his word against mine and Butch's, so it's far from over yet.*


Bob Harrison had set a tape recorder on a side table in the living room, and was plugging it into the wall, when Jane Seeger walked in from the kitchen drying her hands on her apron.

"Hey, Bob. How are you? I didn't know you were coming over. Garner. My! I haven't seen you since you came into the UK library and made me drag out every volume of local history since 1826."

Garner smiled, and said, "You always did exaggerate, Janie. It's good to see you too." Then he looked at Carl Seeger, and Garner's long narrow face turned to chiseled stone.

Bob said, "I apologize for not calling ahead, Jane. But this is a business situation that Carl and I need to talk about away from the office."

Jane studied her husband, her intelligent eyes probing his, her wavy brown hair damp along her forehead where she smoothed it back with one hand, before she untied her apron. "I'd like to hear what you have to say, Bob, if it's all right with you."

Carl shook his head, before he said, "Bob wouldn't have come here if it wasn't a sensitive matter. Though I, for one, don't know what that could be."

Jane looked at Bob and Garner, her plain pleasant face still and concentrated, as she sat at one end of the sofa. "No, Carl, I have a good idea it does affect me, and if they have no objection, I'd very much like to hear what Bob and Garner have to say. Why've you brought a tape recorder?"

Bob watched Jane for half a minute before he finally spoke. "I think maybe you *ought* to hear both sides of the story." He took hold of one of the controls, then glanced over at Carl. "You may want to sit too. This will take several minutes."

Carl crossed the room and stood by the fireplace, then rested an elbow on the white painted mantelpiece, after he'd lit a Lucky.

The tape played, while Bob and Garner stared at Carl, Garner sitting in a chair on the other side of the hearth from Carl, Bob standing by the tape recorder, Jane looking shocked, and then repulsed, as though she'd touched something vile.

Ten minutes into it, Carl said, "I think we've heard enough. I believe I do have the right to pursue the use of my own formulations outside the U.S."

Jane said, "How could you steal Bob's formulas like that?"

"Don't comment on what you know nothing about!"

Garner handed Carl and Jane copies of Carl's employment contract, then settled himself in his chair. "Mr. Seeger, you are in violation of your noncompete, nondisclosure agreement as set forth in the employment document you signed when you went to work for Equine Pharmaceuticals.

"It clearly stipulates that you do not own any of the formulas you are asked to work upon, nor the trade secrets, nor any other information to which are given access while at Equine Pharmaceuticals.

"It further stipulates that you will not disclose any information or trade secrets you encounter there to anyone else, or use that information to benefit yourself or another. That you will not go to work for any business that competes with Equine Pharmaceuticals. That you will not yourself go into compctition with Equine Pharmaceuticals during your employment, and for a period of eight years after your employment has been terminated. It is only too clear from the testimony of Arthur Lawrence, and the recording we have all heard, that you are in violation of that agreement."

"I don't see it that way."

"Don't you?" Garner Honeycutt smiled stiffly, and adjusted the knot in his gray paisley tie. "On what do you base your position?"

Bob Harrison couldn't have smiled if there'd been a gun to his head, and he started toward Carl with his hands clenched, stopping himself three feet away. "How could you *do* it! Those are Alan's formulas! All you did was run the tests Alan and I asked for. For you to steal his work and try to—"

"Wait a minute! I—"

"Your education and experience didn't qualify you for the work we do at Equine. I went out of my way to mentor, and train, and encourage you, and I promoted you way beyond what you ever should've expected, when—"

Garner raised a hand toward Harrison, with mild blue eyes and raised eyebrows. And Bob Harrison turned around and sat down in the straight-backed chair beside the tape recorder at the end of the sofa near Jane.

"Besides." Carl was smiling now, smoothing his hair away from his forehead. "Tapes can be faked."

"But they weren't, were they? We have the originals and copies of two recordings and a Dictaphone belt as well, in addition to the testimony of Mr. Lawrence. Let us accept it as read, shall we? Now." Garner Honeycutt was still looking at Carl as he crossed one leg over the other, slowly tapping a file folder on the arm of his chair, his thin face calm but stern, his voice quiet and firm.

"There are three options open to Mr. Harrison. He can file a police report citing premeditated theft and ask the County Attorney to prosecute you on a criminal offense. If the County Attorney proceeds, with the evidence in our possession, a conviction would be assured. That could entail the possibility of jail time, court-ordered financial restitution for the damages to Mr. Harrison, as well as burdening you with a permanent criminal record. He can also—"

"The probability of the Woodford County Attorney taking that up is nil."

"Is it?" Garner Honeycutt smiled, a small, secret, predatory smile, and gazed briefly at the ceiling. "You're far more confident of that than I would be, were I to be in your position. It would be an easy case for him, and it would certainly show the voters here in Woodford County that he supports local business. Which I would think would be advantageous for a man with political ambitions."

"So what?" Carl's face was red now, but his eyes were cool, squinting under his sandy gray brows as he lit another Lucky.

"The second option open to Mr. Harrison is to file a civil suit and ask the court to *permanently* enjoin you from working for a competitor, as well as from competing against Equine Pharmaceuticals in any manner whatsoever. It would preclude you from disclosing trade secrets, and all other information acquired at Equine Pharmaceuticals.

"I draw your attention to the word *permanently*. If you were to appear in court, facing this evidence, you would have no choice but to *agree* to such an order. While that might reduce the chance of a criminal prosecution now, it would expose you to crushing defense costs, and ultimately the payment of all Mr. Harrison's financial damages arising out of the violation settlement for having willfully violated the contract you signed upon employment. The theft of a substantial trade secret, based on this evidence, will support punitive damages as well.

"At the end of the day, you would have a court order hanging over your head, and no employer, investor, or banker would ever touch you. If you were even to attempt to subsequently violate such a court order, you would be subject to contempt of court proceedings. The court has *very* broad powers in handling instances of contempt of court, and the violation of its own orders. You would risk having to pay additional damages, as well as Mr. Harrison's legal costs."

"And Mr. Harrison's other option?" Carl was sitting on the sofa now, leaning back, blowing smoke toward the ceiling, holding an ashtray in his lap.

"His third option is to draw up a document such as I have here. In it you acknowledge that your employment at Equine Pharmaceuticals is terminated as of today's date. You acknowledge that this agreement is binding and supersedes the employment contract you signed

when you were first employed. You agree to abide by
the following: For a period of ten years, in all of North
America, you will not work for a manufacturer of
equine pharmaceuticals and health care products, or
any other enterprise which competes with Equine
Pharmaceuticals, directly or indirectly. You will not
start such a company or go into competition with
Equine Pharmaceuticals in any manner whatsoever.
You will not use, or disclose, any formulas, trade
secrets or other information to which you were privy
while employed at Equine Pharmaceuticals. You will
acknowledge that if you violate this agreement, a court
will immediately issue an order to enforce the
restrictions and require you to pay the costs of such an
action."

"You expect me to sign that without seeing a
lawyer?"

"Mr. Harrison is a man with many demands upon
his time who wishes to reach a quick conclusion and
put this matter behind him as rapidly as possible. He is
consequently willing to extend the offer until six
o'clock tomorrow evening. After that, Mr. Harrison
will take the tapes he has in his possession and pursue
his other options. We took the liberty of determining
that Harold Rasmusson, whom you used when
negotiating your first employment agreement, is in
Versailles all day tomorrow, and has time available to
meet with you. We have played the tape, and discussed
the options with him, and shown him this contract. But
if you wish to consult another attorney, that's entirely
up to you. If you wish to sign now, no other attorney
need be subjected to hearing the tape Mr. Harrison has
in his possession."

"What about Butch?"

"That is not your concern."

"So you'll offer him the same deal?"

Garner didn't answer.

And Carl stared at the fireplace as he stubbed his cigarette out and set the ashtray on the coffee table. "I suppose I might as well read the agreement."

Garner Honeycutt handed a copy to Carl and another to Jane, then sat down again by the fireplace, where he thumbed through a *National Geographic* he'd picked up from a side table, while Bob Harrison put the cover on the tape recorder, and Carl and Jane read the contract.

Jane finished first. She was a university librarian who'd been reading since she was four, and she sat slumped against the blue flowered sofa, tears gathering in her eyes, her hands clenched on top of the contract in her lap.

When Carl looked up and lit another Lucky, Jane said, "You ought to sign it. It's the best resolution you can hope for, and nobody else would have to know what it is you've done."

"Don't expect me to give in to this, simply because you—"

"*I* was born and raised here! You weren't. I don't want one more person to know what you've done. How could you *do* it!" Her face was flushed, but her lips looked bloodless, as she glared at Carl, on the other end of the sofa with a grim but petulant smile on his face.

No one else said anything. And Carl read the three page contract again, taking his time, glancing at Garner Honeycutt twice, before he said he'd try to reach Rasmusson at home.

He walked out to the front hall, then turned toward the rear of the house, and was gone for fifteen minutes. The other three sat in silence, unable to contemplate small talk, tapping feet and staring into space.

Carl came back in, and sat on the sofa, and crossed his legs before he spoke. "If you make one addition I will agree to sign this now."

Bob said, "What is that?"

"That I will not be liable for legal costs, other than my own, pertaining to this document."

Garner said, "We would not be willing to entertain such a requirement concerning action brought about by your possible infringement of this second document."

"No, I mean at this time. Bob's legal fees relating to the work you've done and are doing now. Drawing this up, evaluating the first contract. I want it stated clearly that you can't come at me for costs."

"Bob?" Garner Honeycutt looked at Bob, his eyebrows raised inquisitively, making him look like a wild hare for a moment, nose quivering in the air.

"That's okay with me." Bob sat upright in his side chair, his spine a steel rod, his hands gripping the arms of his chair as though he needed to control them, his feet set squarely on the floor, ready to move fast.

"In that case, with Mr. Harrison's consent, I shall compose a draft of an addendum for consideration." Garner pulled a legal pad from his briefcase and wrote for a moment with a ballpoint pen.

No one said a word while Garner handed his draft to Bob first, and then Carl.

Both nodded, and Carl handed it back. Honeycutt asked if there were a typewriter in the house.

Jane said, "I'll show you," and led him across the hall to the study on the other side of the front door.

When Garner came back, he stapled addendums to the two originals and three copies, which Carl and Bob both signed. He had them both initial every page in every copy, and then Jane signed the bottom of the last page of the contract, and the addendum as well, as a witness. Garner handed an original to Carl and another to Bob, then put the others in a folder and slipped it into his briefcase.

Bob stood and picked up the tape recorder, and started toward the door—before he stopped and turned and looked Carl in the eye. "You fooled me. I'll give you that."

"That's the first time I've heard you admit a mistake!"

Bob stared at him and shook his head as though that didn't deserve a reply. Then he and Garner walked out the front door, closing it quickly behind them.

Jane was standing, clutching her apron, her eyes burning into Carl's. "I wish I could say I was as surprised as Bob."

"Shut up! You don't know what I've had to put up with, with Alan Munro, and the—"

"Oh, I knew there'd be an excuse!"

"Easy for you! *Your* father didn't—"

"Walk out. And my mother didn't clean houses like yours, or die when I was sixteen. *None* of that justifies what it is you've done!" Jane stalked out through the archway into the front hall, then turned left past the stairs and rushed on into the kitchen.

Carl heard the back door slam and gardening tools getting thrown in the wheelbarrow she'd left by the back door. He heard it thumping across the flagstones toward the garage—just as Cassandra sprinted into the living room from the front hall.

She rubbed against Carl's ankles, till he picked her up and stroked her throat as he stared across the street at Elinor Nevilleson, pretending to dead-head a rose bush while she watched Harrison's car turn toward the light at Main Street.

Carl said, "Bitch!" before he kissed Cassandra's forehead and carried her across the hall to the study.

He still held her while he dialed the phone and waited. "Terry, it's Carl. … Oh, not bad. Though I'm actually calling on a matter of conscience. … No, you heard me. I've decided to leave Equine Pharmaceuticals. I can't go into it in any detail, but there're practices being condoned there that I can't stomach. … I've also decided that it's my duty to tell you that you ought to investigate Equine's taxes. Bob Harrison's not doing business on the up-and-up. … I assume IRS auditors still get to keep a percentage of the unpaid taxes you uncover? … Good. So how soon can you start? … Well, even if you can't for a couple of months, it'll be worth your while when you do. … Okay. Sure. You wantta tee off at eight? … Good. Believe me, you won't regret looking at Harrison's books."

Carl smiled when he put down the receiver, as Cassandra jumped to the floor.


Butch Morgan was leaning back in a worn green velvet chair, his feet on the matching footstool, the sound off on the baseball game on the TV across the room, a beer cupped in his left hand, his wife on the phone in his right.

"Come on, Frannie. You know you don't want a divorce. You know you don't. You know how good we can be. 'Member before the babies were born when we'd go out to the river and take a … Okay, so you've filed, but you can stop it if you want. I can make you happy, honey, you know I can. … Yeah, I'm drinkin' a beer. One, that's all. I can quit whenever I want. … No! Why would I want to talk about Korea with some stooge in a white coat who's never fired a shot? I wantta forget Korea, okay? And bring you and the girls back home. …

"Anyway, I'm fixin' to pick 'em up tomorrow mornin' about nine. I thought we could go see the Clark Museum there in Louavull, and take a picnic lunch. 'Course, one day I'd like to take 'em to see Harrodsburg and show 'em where I grew up, but there won't be time tomorrow if we …

"What d'ya mean? Why don't they want me to pick 'em up? … I don't. Not every time. … Well, are you helpin' 'em to want to, or are you criticizing me behind my back, so that … Then I'll just come up there tomorrow mornin', and we can all spend the day and go out to supper. … I finished fixing up the kitchen. Tiling the floor, that's done, and I … I gotta go, Frannie. Somebody's at the door."


Garner Honeycutt and Bob Harrison had told Butch everything they'd told Carl, and he'd listened to them and the tape, sitting in the big green chair in the family room he'd added on at the back with a slider out to a side porch. He was holding a cup of coffee, staring at the slippery looking surface as though matters of consequence depended on how well he concentrated.

He asked questions about the options he was given, and eventually told them he'd sign the new agreement. And he did, the same one they'd offered Carl, all the copies and the addendums, once he'd called his next-door neighbor over to witness them too.

Then he sat, his square face sunken and crushed looking, his eyes tired and red rimmed, his dark hair thick and coarse, brushed straight back from his face, his heavy muscled shoulders straining against the back of the chair, while he stared at the turned off TV.

Bob Harrison watched him for a minute, then asked him in a neutral voice why he'd gone along with Carl.

"It wasn't you. I respect you a whole lot. You were real good to me right from the start. You didn't care that I dropped outta college, and it seemed like you trusted me to do things right."

"I did. Until this happened. But that doesn't mean that there wouldn't be new things that we'd all have to learn to keep the business growing. You can't stay the same in business. You either grow, or shrink, or go out of business altogether."

"It was Alan Munro changin' everything. You started talkin' to him and not me when we was trying to figure somethin' out. It's been him standin' in between us, actin' like he knows it all, and I got real tired of it. I figured I couldn't stick it out much longer, and if Carl and me had a business goin', there'd be some way for me to make a livin'."

"There'd be lots of ways for you to make a living if you hadn't done what you did. Then I could've given you a good recommendation. You're a hard worker, and you're very mechanical. What I don't understand is why you didn't just come and talk to me, if you were having trouble working with Alan."

"I wouldda looked like a cry baby. I was hopin' to be successful, and work on new products with Carl, and then you'd see I could do it without help from you or Alan."

"And you didn't see that taking the formulas was dishonest?"

"Carl said he'd checked with his lawyer. That he owned the formulas, for having done the work, and it wasn't wrong for us to benefit too."

Garner Honeycutt smiled and shook his head. "I very much doubt that he talked to his attorney. Harry Rasmusson wouldn't have said any such thing. Not if he'd consulted Mr. Seeger's signed employment agreement, which he had a hand in drafting."

Bob Harrison set his coffee cup on the table beside him and looked across it at Butch. "Carl did the experiments we asked him to do. Lab-bench-level experiments designed by Alan or me. That's not the same as designing the experiments, or doing the formulating, or creating a product. And even so, any work done at Equine legally belongs to me as sole owner and proprietor. That's absolutely standard. It's stated right in your contracts. What I did that most people don't was to give you and Carl bonuses when a new product did well. Even so, there's a difference between what's right and what's legal. Taking those formulas was wrong."

Butch set his coffee on the telephone table, just as

Garner Honeycutt thanked him for the coffee, and stood up and walked toward the door.

Butch stood too, and faced Bob Harrison, then dropped his eyes toward the floor. "I'm sorry, Mr. Harrison. I can see it better from your side now. And I wish I hadn't done it."

"I do too. I really do. I thought we could all work together."

Butch stood on the side porch after they'd gone, a bottle of twelve-year-old Jefferson bourbon open on the table by the hammock, a cocktail glass with an inch in the bottom hanging loose in his hand. He sipped at it again, then drank the rest down, and wiped his mouth on the rolled-up sleeve of his denim work shirt.

He stood and stared at the big old elms, tall and wide and half dead most of them, twisted gray arms sticking up toward the sky in the darkening dusk. He watched the old willow too, weeping across the ground, being torn by the wind on the far side of the creek just past the edge of his land.

A storm had come up, rolling in fast, whipping leaves across the lawn as the first flash of lightning lit the night somewhere off on the west. He counted seconds till he shuddered from the crash that must've been five miles away.

The next bolt exploded closer, and he jumped before he could stop himself. He closed his eyes and shouted at himself, saying what he needed to hear, hoping that this time it might even work. Knowing it wouldn't in the long run. Because by then he was crawling up a hill in Korea, icy rain pouring down his neck, mud sliding under his hands, slipping away from his knees, slithering under his cold soaked boots while artillery shrieked, splitting the sky, as it pounded the world all around him.

Butch pitched his glass at the porch step, watching it shatter, as another flash of lightning hit off to his left, still flying in from the west with a freight train screaming wind. He held his hands over his ears, and waited for the next crash that didn't come. Then he pushed his hair back with both hands and lifted his face to the rain, shouting "Damn Alan Munro! He's gettin' just what he wants!"

### Saturday, August 10th, 1963

Carl woke up on the sofa just before six, Cassandra curled on his chest, the ashtray overturned on the floor beside him. He sat up, as Cassandra jumped, and rubbed his eyes with both hands.

The house was silent, which was unexpected. Janie was always up by five, making coffee and fixing breakfast, or working in the study—and he called her name on his way to the bathroom, but didn't get a reply.

She could've been in the garden already, getting a start before it got hot, and he didn't give it much thought.

She wasn't in the bedroom, but her closet door was ajar, and when he opened it all the way, he saw most of her clothes were gone. Her suitcases weren't on the upper shelf, and her two favorite pillows were missing from the unmade bed.

Carl walked into the kitchen to see if her car was on the apron next to the unattached garage—but it wasn't. Which by that time was no surprise.

He splashed his face in the kitchen sink, looking out at the gardens she'd made, at the star-shaped leaves of the clematis vine getting tossed against the screen in a soft northerly breeze.

He grabbed a dish towel and patted his face, then went to the fridge for the can of Folgers, and noticed an envelope waiting on the counter addressed to him in her hand.

He turned it over, but laid it down again, then started the percolator, and made himself toast, and poured a glass of orange juice.

He ate the toast and drank the juice, glancing through the *Herald Leader* he hadn't read the day before, and finished his first cup of coffee too, and lit his second Lucky, before he poured another cup, and slit the back of the envelope.

*Carl,*

*I have left you not simply because of the revelations of last evening, but because it served as confirmation of the character traits I have observed in the course of our years together.*

*When we first met in Bloomington, I felt great compassion for you because of the deprivations you had faced as a child, and your determination to work two jobs to save funds for college.*

*What I came to see after we married was that you take whatever help you are given as your rightful due because of what you lived through. You were not grateful to the pharmacist who took you into his home and gave you a job in the Depression, any more than you were my brother-in-law for arranging a Chemistry scholarship at IU, and letting us live rent free.*

*Even so, I was proud of you for completing your degree, and being promoted to the lab at the dairy. Then, totally unexpectedly, in 1939, I was introduced to the pharmacist who had taken you in. I have never spoken of our conversation. I have tried to thrust it from my mind. He told me that when he had asked you the year before if you would help run the pharmacy for a week while his wife had surgery, you "preferred not to use vacation days coming to you at the dairy." You never returned his phone calls after that. And yet he spoke of you with sadness and confusion, rather than bitter resentment.*

*When war was declared after Pearl Harbor, I saw you rush to secure a job in a federal food lab that would keep you safely home. That disturbed me, though I chose not to let on. I married for life. And life is not easy. I kept my job at the IU library and wanted nothing more than a child.*

*After the war, when my mother was ill, and you were willing to move here so I could help care for her, I told myself that was an instance of unselfish concern. I later realized you were counting on my father to help you find a better job through his contacts at the bank. He did too. He introduced you to Bob Harrison when Harrison was getting started.*

*The hurt I have felt because you refused to adopt a child, I will not attempt to describe for it matters to you not at all. I have lived in emotional isolation, using the children I teach in Sunday school to help fill the very real void I have felt since we married—a work I do which you clearly scorn whenever the subject arises.*

*Yesterday, hearing what you have done out of premeditated greed and vindictiveness has forced me to make a decision I should have made long ago. I will file for divorce Monday. I no longer wish to communicate with you. I doubt you wish to speak with me. It will be the public embarrassment that troubles you most.*

*Jane*

Carl folded the letter and slid it in the envelope, then held a corner in the flame from his lighter. He watched it burn to ash in the sink, while he said, "What a bitch!" twice. *Leave it to Jane to run with her paycheck, right when I need it most.*

*I ought to dig out the mortgage. And probably copies of the wills. And find the insurance contract too.*

He threw down the last of his coffee, before he walked into the study—then coughed, and couldn't stop. He grabbed the corner of the desk and hacked for half a minute, facing the front window.

Elinor Nevilleson was raking her front lawn, surveying his house, and Terry's next door, her usual expression of curious contemplation fixed firmly in place, which seemed to make it harder for Carl to actually catch his breath.

# CHAPTER FOUR

*Excerpt from Jo Grant Munro's Journal:*
*Sunday, August 11th, 1963*

*...I don't know why, but last night I woke up about three, thinking about when Tommy was killed by the ninety-year-old farmer who couldn't see his motor-cycle. I started reliving what it was like bringing Sam and Maggie home from his place and having the horse trailer have a blow-out on a fog-bound mountain road.*

*I remembered being so filled with grief and frustration and anger that year, with having cared for Mom through the brain tumor, and then having Tommy die too—and it all came back right in the middle of the night with such power and detail it woke me up for good.*

*I went and got my first journal, the one I'd never intended to start, but did, right after Tommy's funeral —and reading that, while Alan slept on his side, breathing softly beside me, I realized even more than I had then how much Alan had helped me see how I'd been choosing to react.*

*Tommy had always been more than an older brother. He helped me grow up my whole life, especially after Dad died so young. Then worrying about him all through the war too, made him mean more to me than most brothers probably do. And Alan—having been in the OSS with Tommy, and spending time with him after the war—he helped me understand why Tom came back different. Why he'd taken engineering jobs all over the world before he'd moved to Virginia, and jumped out of planes for fun, at least every year on his birthday.*

*Alan had known how to talk to me the first day we met. He was older like Tom, and he'd been blown apart in France, and lost the woman who'd helped him heal. And yet he'd crawled out of the darkness, and it was his way of seeing, and his humor too, that helped me stop choosing to dwell on the worst and ignore what should've made me grateful. That, and the other workings of God. That I couldn't see then either.*

*It was Jack too, in a way. When I read again about him staggering onto my porch that night in a thunderstorm that rattled the world, dying and dirty and running from his torments, coming to Tommy for help—I could see clearly that it was having to help him, and having to help Uncle Toss too, after the stallion attacked him—it was doing something for somebody else, even though it seemed overwhelming, that helped me rejoin the world.*

*And now Spencer, after losing his mom in a truly horrible way, has lost Booker too. Alan and I need to figure out how to help him make his way through.*

*Monday, August 12th, 1963*

Ridgeway Russell thought it would feel more relaxed and collegial if he went to Booker's house to read the will instead of his own office.

When he climbed out of his car, he'd been telling himself character was more important, while hoping mightily that age would count for something. Richard and Spencer were forty-one and forty. Martha was thirty-eight. Age *might* indicate maturity. Though it still remained to be seen.

They settled in the dining room—Ridgeway, at one end of the oval table, his salt-and-pepper hair hanging long and thick, his face tanned and as creased as an old shoe after a lifetime of working farmland in whatever time he could find for it. His three-piece tan linen suit was clean but wrinkled wherever it could be, and his old white shirt and brown-and-black tie were frayed and soft and comfortable looking.

He set his tortoise-shell reading glasses on the very end of his long bony nose, and laid his dented gold pocket watch beside a thick battered cardboard file tied with a wide black ribbon.

He wiped his eyes with a crumpled handkerchief, while he talked about when he'd first met their mother and how much he'd thought of her, before he passed out copies of two wills, and studied the faces of the family. They opened the files, but didn't seem to read much as they looked uneasily from one to the other and waited for him to speak.

"Y'all know that I knew your father all my life. We both grew up on farms off the old back road to Paris. I heard all about it when he courted your mother, and he sent me pictures of y'all when you were small. We had good long talks when he and Alice were getting to the place that they were ready to move home here, from living in Iowa, and risk every cent they'd put aside to start a business of their own.

"Y'all were grown up by then, and I didn't get to know you that well, but you need to understand that I had nothing but respect for your folks. When they asked me to serve on Blue Grass Horse Vans' board of directors, I felt truly honored."

The family nodded, and mumbled a few words, though Martha glanced at the wills again, before she looked up.

Russell watched, and then cleared his throat. "We find ourselves in an unusual situation here, and it hasn't been easy for me to decide what tack to take, because just the day before your daddy died, he drew up a new will with a supplementary document, and asked me to rush getting 'em typed so he could sign 'em right quick. We got 'em finished the day he died. We talked on the phone an hour or so before he passed away, arrangin' that I'd bring 'em over here first thing the next morning so he could affix his signature before he went to work."

Richard, who'd been staring at the wall behind Spencer, leaned forward, his small eyes worried suddenly, as he looked over at Ridge. "He didn't tell me about any new will. How long did you say he made it before he died?"

"First thing the day before."

Martha had sat up straighter in her chair, and she turned to look at Spencer before she spoke to Ridge.

"It's not binding, whatever it says if he didn't sign it. Isn't that right, Mr. Russell?"

"Yep. That's right. But I figured you had a right to know what he intended. That way I'd be givin' you the opportunity to honor his wishes, if y'all were of a mind to.

"Now, as I figure you know, the previous will gives each of you equal shares of stock, voting and non-voting, and equal shares in his remaining property, which is limited to this house, two horses of no particular monetary value, a modest investment portfolio, and a savings account in the amount of twenty-two thousand dollars."

Martha said, "That's all?" while she watched Spencer with a speculative stare and fluffed out the sides of her hair.

"It is. Your folks took very little in the way of dividends after the business got out of the red and began to make some money. They bought this house, but other than that, they plowed the profits back in the business. And that takes us up to the new will here."

Spencer had watched Ridge till then, his face drawn and tight looking, his bright blue eyes partially closed, as though he felt the need to guard them against a punishing wind. But when Ridge mentioned the new will, Spencer stared down at the table, the two files tight in his long fingers.

Ridge said, "Old Booker set a high store by Blue Grass, but not as high as he placed on his family. It played out differently, but the family still came first. So in the new will y'all still get equal voting and nonvoting shares, which means equal dividends, should there be any. You get an equal interest in the house, and all other assets, the same way as before. The difference has to do with how business decisions get made.

"Booker chose to put the voting stock into a trust, with Spencer here being given the right to vote those shares. He would not profit in anyway more than the two of you, but he'd vote the shares as sole trustee, and chose his successor as well."

"I can't believe Dad would do that!" Richard was glaring at Spencer with what looked like anger and anguish, while Martha said, "It isn't fair!"

"Well now, Booker had every right to do exactly what he did. I reckon it was Spencer here havin' horses like he did, and understanding what they need in trailers and vans, and helping Booker the way he did with the design and engineering. He's been directing production right along, and helpin' too with marketin', and I reckon Booker felt like those aspects are the heart of the business, and Spencer knows what it needs.

"Now, I want y'all to believe me when I say that that in no way should be interpreted as though he favored him as a child. I know that for a fact. Booker made that clear as could be when he and I talked. It was just that the business would be best served, from the way Booker saw things, to put the decisions in one person's hands instead of split three ways."

"That's what it means, does it? That I, as the office manager, contribute less?" Richard threw the new will on the floor and shoved his chair from the table, his fleshy face turning splotchy.

"There was another document Booker wrote as well that established Spencer as president after Booker's passing."

That was met by a cold silence during which Spencer stared at Ridge, his big hands lying still on the table on either side of the files.

"Did you know about this?" Martha was asking Spencer, while Richard stared across the table as though he were having trouble keeping himself in his chair, his double chin, his small hands, his soft looking stomach almost quivering with agitation.

Spencer looked at both of them before he answered in a deep quiet voice and set his hands on the arms of his chair. "He talked to me about it when he came out to ride the night before he died. I never thought it was a final decision. I thought he'd live for years."

Ridge cleared his throat in the silence that followed, then turned his pocket watch in a slow careful circle. "If you folks decide you want to honor Booker's intentions, all you have to do is—"

"There's no question of that!" Richard pulled a pen from his shirt pocket and threw it on the table.

"All I can assume is Daddy wasn't in his right mind after Mother died." Martha crossed her arms across her stomach and tossed her hair back away from her face. "He treated me very differently than he would've before, ever since I moved back."

"Well." Ridge looked at each of them in turn, and untied the ribbon on the thick cardboard file. "There're a whole bunch of practical steps that have to be taken in addressing estate issues, so let's take a look at those. First of all, the house will have to be appraised, and its value included in the estate, so that we can establish how much will have to be paid in estate taxes."

Martha said, "Estate taxes?"

"Yes, ma'am, and with the Blue Grass stock that

won't be nothin' to sneeze at. The federal rate is upwards of sixty percent."

"What!" Richard spluttered.

And Martha looked incensed. "I plan to go on living here. We can't let putting the house in the estate interfere with that!"

"That'll be up to your brothers and you. The house is equally owned. If you want to live here, you'll have to work that out with them. Maybe you could pay rent to your brothers. But with all the money you'll owe in taxes, I wouldn't be surprised if y'all might have to put the house on the market, or sell stock back to the company, or sell Blue Grass outright to an outside buyer."

Martha said, "That's outrageous!"

Ridge considered her for half a minute, and then looked at the anger he saw in Richard, and said, "I reckon we can meet another time and discuss some of the other issues, if that suits y'all."

Martha and Richard nodded, both of them refusing to look at Spencer, as he and Ridge stood.


"Can I ask you something?" Spencer shoved his hands in the pockets of his khaki pants, while he squinted up at the flat-bottomed clouds being blown across to the east.

"Sure. I'm sorry about that debacle in there. I know how strongly Booker felt that you should take over the business, and I debated, and debated, whether to say anything about the new will, and now I wish I hadn't. I reckon I made the situation worse, when I'd hoped they'd honor his intentions."

"That's the last thing either of them wants."

"*That* came across real loud and clear."

They were standing by Ridge's car, heat rising off its gun-metal gray paint in quick shimmering waves, and Spencer took off his suit coat before he put on his sunglasses. "Did you know Booker had a heart condition?"

Ridge glanced at him, then looked away, gazing down the length of the driveway toward Midway's main street. "Well, I reckon I did, and I didn't. I figured when he made this new will, that he had some reason to rush it the way he did. I knew he wasn't feeling real well, but he didn't tell me straight out he had some concern with his health. Why?"

"That's what bothers me—that he didn't come out and tell me he had heart trouble. He and I talked. Better to each other than anybody else. We saw a lot of things the same way. We rode horses together. Went to church together too a lotta the time, on top of working the way we did. We didn't agree on everything, but neither of us thought we should."

"A blind man couldda seen that the two of you were real close."

"We're both kinda solitary. More than most anyway."

"Yep."

"But I thought we told each other everything important. I mean, he told me he felt more tired than usual, and he had heartburn some, but he said it was no big deal."

"He didn't give me that much. But he made me think it wasn't nothin' neither, the way he was in a rush."

"I keep asking myself if it was just that he was the

kind of man he was. You know what I mean, the kind that minimizes sickness and trouble as a fundamental principle of life. Or did he decide there was nothing that could be done about it, and he wanted to keep on living the way he always had. Riding Buster. Working hard the way he wanted, without me or anybody else makin' a big fuss."

"Maybe."

"It also could've been that he wanted to go, 'cause of Mom being gone, and didn't want anyone watching over him, keeping that from happening."

"Couldda been any one of those."

"He wouldn't have wanted to be an invalid, I know that."

"No, he surely wouldn't've. How do you think it'll go with the business, with Richard and Martha votin' their shares?"

"I'll be out-voted on everything, just the way Dad knew I would be."

"We're gonna have to fill seats on the board too, so you need to think about how to approach that. The way it looks right now, I reckon they might both wantta be on it, and you oughtta come on for sure, so that's gonna mean outside professionals'll have to step down. Sorry to rush, but I gotta go."

Spencer smiled and nodded, and waved to Ridge as he pulled out, then walked back into the house, wondering what he could possibly say that wouldn't make the situation worse than it already was.

## *September and October 1963*

Because Richard and Martha controlled two-thirds of the votes, they could determine who sat on the board. There were only seven seats, and the banker who'd taken Alice's seat and an extremely knowledgeable breeding farm owner both stepped down voluntarily so that all three members of the family could join the board.

The company's outside tax advisor, a training barn owner, a manager at Keeneland, and Ridgeway Russell stayed on, telling Spencer in private they hoped they could help him with Richard and Martha by teaching and by example.

When Richard and Martha asked the board to make Richard President, the outside board abstained. The family elected the board, and the professionals didn't want to give them an excuse to throw them off and pack the board with their own personal friends. Richard and Martha out-voted Spencer and made Richard President. They then elected Martha Vice President of Personnel and Public Relations (though as it turned out she never worked more than twenty hours a week).

She also thought there should be guaranteed dividends paid out every year, regardless of how profitable the company was. Spencer, along with the outside board, explained why profits vary. That the cost of materials and equipment changes. New personnel hires and capital investments are different from year to year, and all of that has to be subtracted from the income from sales. Sales fluctuate constantly too, especially luxury items like vans and trailers, which don't get bought in recessions. Other factors change as well—

taxes and maintenance and accountant and legal expenses—and dividends can't be set arbitrarily because of all those factors. Martha listened, but remained unmoved, while Richard dithered, thereby postponing a decision.

Spencer walked away from that meeting muttering one of Booker's favorite sayings, "Nobody gets it when there ain't any." *As they're about to find out.*

Richard had a very difficult time making the decisions that had to be made by a company president, and spent more and more time out of the office involving himself in his model train and historic train clubs.

But when a trailer design or production decision of Spencer's was involved, Richard, and Martha too, if she was there, began to question and pressure him to reverse whatever he'd chosen to do.

He generally kept his temper, and tried to explain what he was doing and why, but the second-guessing began to really get to him. He talked to the outside board members, and they talked to Richard and Martha, who claimed they understood the boundaries of responsibility and would abide by them and not interfere with Spencer's areas of expertise.

On October 11th, however, Spencer inspected the interior customizing job on a very expensive custom van, and discovered that the padding that the customer had ordered hadn't been put on the ceiling. It was intended to keep a horse from injuring itself if it reared, or threw its head up, or got loose loading or unloading. The heavy imitation leather was in place on the metal ceiling, but the three inches of extra padding hadn't been put in under it.

An experienced finisher had been doing the work, and when Spencer found him and asked why the padding wasn't in place, he looked embarrassed and said that the other Mr. Franklin had told him not to do it. That "it'd cut costs and increase profits if it wasn't put in."

Spencer found Richard in his office reading a train magazine, and asked if what he'd been told was an accurate representation of what he'd done. Richard looked cornered and fidgety, and admitted that, yes, he'd been going over the cost sheets for some of their production items, and that that particular padding material was more expensive than he'd realized, and should be eliminated whenever it could be.

Spencer didn't say anything for a minute. His heart was thundering in his ears and the same surge of adrenaline that got him across France and Germany was rushing through his veins, beating hard against his brain.

He waited, his face flaming and his fists clenched, the shrapnel scars on both his arms standing out white against his skin, as he made himself count to twenty, before he could trust himself to keep from reaching down and snapping Richard's neck. "Richard … what you did is unethical. It's a form of fraud. It's absolutely antithetical to everything Dad and Mom stood for! The customer ordered that padding for the safety of his horses, and yet you were perfectly willing to charge him the same amount for nothing but the eighth-inch backing attached to the plastic upholstery! Weren't you? Tell me that's not true!"

"Well—"

"He's a very successful trainer, and he would've seen he was being cheated immediately. So not only was it wrong, but just on a purely pragmatic level, our reputation would've been ruined with him and his friends forever. Not to mention the fact that that was *not your decision!* If you *ever* stick your nose in the plant again and try to rescind a directive I've given, you'll regret it. Do you understand me, Richard?" Spencer was towering over him, strong and fit and furious.

"I was just trying to be fiscally responsible when—"

"Gimme a break, Richard! Don't say another word!" Spencer stood there vibrating, his fists set on his hips. "No! I can't do it. I resign. You'll have my official resignation in the morning."

"Wait! You can't leave! Who else would run production?"

"Maybe you should've thought of that before you interfered with me time after time after time!"

Spencer walked into the plant, told the finisher to put the padding in, and walked out the plant door without stopping in his office.

Richard found Spencer's letter on his desk the following morning:

*Richard,*

*I have been dedicated to Blue Grass Horse Vans for many of the same reasons Mom and Dad were. I took great pleasure in making something that served a practical purpose: high quality vans and trailers that provided safe, comfortable transport for horses of all types and sizes. I was proud of the fact that Blue Grass maintained a strong commitment to producing excellent products at a fair price, while providing a pleasant, safe, environment for those who work here. I was dedicated to maintaining it as a company that: treated people fairly, customers and employees; expected honesty, competence, commitment and excellence, and attracted and rewarded people who valued that too, treating them with respect, and rewarding them well, in many more ways than only monetary.*

*In order for those principles and attributes to flourish, Mom and Dad clearly understood that they had to be embodied at the highest level by the family members who work at Blue Grass. This is no longer the case.*

*All that I have respected and admired about the design, production, business practices, and ethics promulgated in the company are now being undermined and I can no longer work at Blue Grass Horse Vans. I am, therefore, tendering my resignation.*

*Spencer Franklin*
*Vice President of Production*

The day after Spencer quit, he arranged for a friend to move into his house and take care of his mare and his parents' horses, while he trailered Tracker, his big dark bay Thoroughbred gelding, down to Tryon, North Carolina, just south of Asheville in the foothills of the Smokies, where he camped and rode for two weeks.

When he came back, he heard that the production foreman and the head welder had quit. And that Peggy James, Alice Franklin's secretary, who'd taken up the slack after Alice died, would be leaving the next week.

They all phoned and told him what had been driving them crazy and why they'd had to leave, and he tried to be neutral when he talked about Richard and Martha regardless of what the others said. It was right and professional, but it wasn't easy, and every time someone told him what was going on at Blue Grass, it made him more angry and outraged, and there were days he didn't even answer the phone. He had trouble sleeping, which hadn't happened since the war. He'd find himself staring into space too, during the day, not even knowing where he was.

He built a shed for his tractor. He worked at Jo and Alan's for ten days so her Uncle Toss could take a vacation. He rode Sam for Jo, who was too pregnant to ride.

But when he wasn't riding Sam or Tracker, or working hard on his farm, Spencer stared at his walls and watched images of disaster roll through his brain, trying to imagine what he could do. He had to start bringing in a salary, he knew that. And he had to find something to do that he loved. Though he couldn't imagine that actually happening anytime soon.

Then he heard that a friend of his from college had broken his hip in a car accident, and he went to see him in the hospital.

*November 1963*

On November 4th, Spencer started teaching a course on the American Revolution at Centre College, in Danville, Kentucky, for the friend who'd been hurt. They'd both been history majors (though Spencer'd minored in engineering too) who'd concentrated on Revolutionary America and the writing of the Constitution. Spencer hadn't taught in years, but he had his friend's course notes, and he drove himself relentlessly to teach the course as well as he would've wanted to be taught. He'd teach through January, which came to him as a godsend—something that would give him an income and keep his mind moving away from the breakdown at Blue Grass Horse Vans.

Carl Seeger wasn't coping with unemployment nearly that well. He'd taken to driving by Equine Pharmaceuticals two or three times a day, and he was seen several times parked across the street, giving rise to the rumor that he was hoping someone from the firm would walk across and talk. Then the week before Thanksgiving, which fell on the twenty-eighth, he visited two lab people at their homes without warning or explanation.

They were social calls, ostensibly. Though he gave them the impression he was fishing for information about how his leaving had been viewed at Equine, while he offered a sanitized version that blamed everyone but himself for his hasty departure.

He made both lab people uncomfortable. They thought he seemed unfair and unstable, and they hadn't known how to react. They told Alan together, since he was directing the lab (while doing everything else he'd been doing before Carl left), and he thanked them, and asked them to tell him if Carl showed up again. Then Alan talked to Jo, and pondered what to do.

The day after Thanksgiving, Alan was doing an errand two blocks from Carl's house, and he decided on the spur of the moment to drive over and talk to Carl. He sat in the driveway for a couple of minutes, but decided not to go in. Seeing him might set Carl off, and lead to something they'd both regret.

He'd wait and see what happened. If Carl pestered the lab folks again, he'd tell Bob and work out a plan. Bob did not need to be bothered before that. He was having fermentation troubles with his new Equine Viral Arteritis vaccine, while interviewing lab and plant people to replace Carl and Butch, and doing everything else too that presidents have to do. He was looking distracted and mildly on edge, and Carl's weirdness could wait.

# 1964

# CHAPTER FIVE

*Excerpt From Jo Grant Munro's Journal*
*Sunday, March 1st, 1964*

*...I haven't done much with the journal since Ross was born in December. He's sleeping better at night than he was, but I still haven't caught up. Alan goes to work at four so he can come home by six and help with Ross through dinner, but I have had moments of abject panic when Ross is screaming and I don't know why.*

*There was a baby in the nursery when he was born who had all his internal organs on the outside of his body. Watching his mom and dad staring at him through the nursery window made me feel terrible, and see even more clearly what a gift it is that Ross is whole and healthy. Sometimes we just stand by his crib and watch him breathe in wonder and amazement, and I suspect we aren't the only parents who've done exactly that.*

*We've been blinded, though, I think, in a way, in our quiet cocoon here. Because forces have been at work in the outside world that are far less than benign.*

*One being Carl Seeger who actually went so far as to get an IRS auditor to investigate Bob Harrison. This guy spent all of January and February at Equine Pharmaceuticals, and even took over Bob's office for a week so he could go through his personal files, and all he found, after all of that, is $2000.00 that Equine <u>may be</u> should've paid, depending on how you allocate some part of their inventory. Investigators get to keep a percentage of what they find, and Carl's friend Terry was pretty put out that he couldn't find more. Bob was beside himself watching this guy poke and prod, when he'd always been as honest as he knew how to be. Especially when he's so pushed at work he can hardly see straight.*

*Spencer's being tormented too by the ongoing muddle at Blue Grass. Folks who work there keep calling him asking him to do something to make it better, and all he can do is tell them there's no way he can help, and to do what's best for them.*

*During their January board meeting, the outside directors asked him to come back and take over, with Richard and Martha actually agreeing to let him be president, since the company's losing customers, and lots of folks have quit. Spencer said he can't come back if R. and M. can still outvote him, and that they'd have to agree to the rest of the stipulations in his dad's will. Richard and Martha refused, of course. And how they'll pay their inheritance taxes, nobody seems to know. I think part of Richard's animosity comes from the fact that his social climbing wife left him two years ago because he wasn't being promoted as fast as she thought he should be, and they both blamed Spencer for standing in his way.*

*One good thing was that Spencer was approached by a group of venture capital people, not too long after the teaching job ended, who asked him to evaluate a pre-cut custom pole barn manufacturer that's just east of Lexington. The owner's ill and has to sell, and they wanted Spencer's opinion as to whether the quality of design and production is enough above the industry norm to make it a business worth buying.*

*He dodged around it for a while, because he wasn't sure he'd know enough about that business to help, but he ended up doing it, and he's found it interesting. It looks like they're going to buy it and ask him to run it for them.*

*Maybe even more importantly, Spencer met a woman there, a widow who's the office manager, who's intelligent and educated <u>and</u> a long-time horse lover, languishing without a horse, who seems like a very reasonable person, and they've started going out. After what he went through two years ago, he deserves to be with someone who's actually worth his time.*

*We haven't heard anything from Carl for quite a while. He's stopped showing up at people's houses, but I know he had lunch at least once with Jean Nagy (the lab tech I secretly think of as Eeyore), since I ran into them at the Wagon Wheel. Carl being quiet makes me vaguely nervous.*

*Butch, on the other hand, calls Alan at two in the morning every two or three weeks in a drunken stupor, to pour vitriol in his ear. Sad. But hard on Alan.*

*I'm designing the renovation of an old farmhouse toward Harrodsburg that's in bad shape, but has great bones, and I not only think about it when I'm doing the dishes, I dream about it at night. I love doing what I do, and I'm grateful I get to.*

*Riding Sam again too is making me feel like myself. Being a mother changes things. You stop just being who you've always been—much less what it is you do. You're responsible for a helpless child twenty-four hours a day, and you will be till he leaves home. I also suspect you never stop worrying even when they're grown. Ross can tear my heart out in ways no one but a child ever will.*

*Which means cantering through the fields on Sam makes me forget about being a mother and blows cobwebs out of my brain.*

*Emmy comes with us, of course, with her ears flopping around her. I looked at her today and thought about the night she showed up two years ago just as a thunderstorm blew toward us—a tiny tan puppy shivering in the wind—and I can't believe what a great dog she's been.*

*Monday, March 2nd, 1963*

It was late afternoon, and Toss had put grain in all the feed tubs and was throwing flakes of hay in the stalls while Emmy sat and watched him as though she were grading his performance.

Jo had left Ross with a babysitter at the house, and she had Sam in the crossties at the back end of the aisleway, and had just unsaddled him, after having taken him cross country. It'd been so warm, after the cold of February, and Sam's winter coat was so thick and long that steam was rising off his back, and his coppery chestnut hair was wet and curling and dark with sweat.

Jo was pulling a shedding blade through his coat, scraping out handfuls of hair and shaking it out in clumps on the floor. He was itchy everywhere, and he liked the scratching and the scraping, and he threw his big head straight up in the air and curled his upper lip above his teeth, then shook himself all over.

"Feels good, doesn't it? I'm going to give you a bath too, and use Alan's new shampoo. Look at the piles of hair on the floor! It looks like you oughtta be bald."

Toss came out of the last stall and pushed the wheelbarrow into the tack room, then told Jo he'd pulled up the handle on the pump in there so the hose was ready to go.

He walked past Jo and Sam to the back door, and gazed across the small paddock at a dark bay mare and her new foal nuzzling at her side. Toss squinted as he took off his battered straw cowboy hat and wiped his forehead with his sleeve. "You looked at the new foal? The colt by Tap Dancer out of Virginia Dare?"

"First thing this morning. Why?"

"Virgee had kinda a hard time. I don't reckon he lacked for oxygen. We got him breathin' right quick, but he seems kinda weak."

"I didn't notice anything, but then—"

"I called Mr. Breckenridge, and he'll be along first thing tomorrow. He's real partial to old Virgee, and he's done real well with her foals."

"He has."

"I'm gonna go ahead and call Doc Dutton. The little

guy might need a supplement or somethin'. He don't seem to be nursin' real good."

"Has her milk come in the way it should?"

"Seems okay, but I'd like to get 'em both checked to make sure we ain't missin' nothin'.'"

Jo kissed the side of Sam's snoot, and patted him on the shoulder as she walked past him to stand by Toss, who was scraping mud off a flat-heeled boot on the edge of the concrete floor.

Jo watched the tiny bay colt walking behind his mother, a collection of bones in a tight skin bag, as Virgee led him away. "He is wobblier than some, but there's a whole lotta variation when they're this young."

"I know. I know. And his confirmation looks real fine, but … You hear somebody walkin' on the drive?"

Emmy was flying toward the front of the barn, and they both turned to look after her, and saw a short plump man with tiny hands and feet silhouetted against the sun at the other end of the aisleway. He was wiping his forehead with a handkerchief, holding a briefcase in his other hand, while Emmy sniffed both his shoes and he looked uneasy. "A woman at the house said I should try here. I'm looking for Jo Grant Munro."

"I'm Jo. Emmy, come."

She came, and sat next to Jo, close to Sam's head.

"I'm from the Internal Revenue Service. I'll be auditing your farm business, your LLC architectural firm, and yours and your husband's personal tax returns."

"Why? We've never—"

"I'd like to establish an office here today so I can get straight to work first thing tomorrow."

"So you're Carl Seeger's neighbor, Terry."

"Carl Seeger has nothing to do with it."

"Right." Jo looked at him as though he'd offered her the Brooklyn Bridge, while he pulled a card from his suit coat pocket and held it in her direction.

"If you wouldn't mind stepping out here …" He was watching Sam and Emmy with a wary, disapproving look on his smooth round face.

"You can come in the barn. Sam and Emmy won't hurt you."

Toss hooked his thumbs inside his belt, then smiled serenely at the man by the door. "You oughtn't to pressure him, Jo. You can see the little fella don't want to risk it."

"I beg your pardon! I don't want to get my shoes dirty." He was looking at the piles of hair around Sam.

Jo raised an eyebrow at Toss, then walked over to the IRS man and took the card from his hand. "You'll have to wait for me to finish grooming my horse. You could walk back to the house and sit on the porch if you'd like, and I'll be there in fifteen minutes."

He considered it, and turned around, and started off down the north-south drive that ran along the high ridge from the barns back to Jo's house.

"Damn!" Toss's fists were on his hips, and blood was flooding across his face, as he kicked the barn cat's water bowl out the back door.

Sam's head jerked toward the ceiling, and his whole body levitated like a tennis player leaping for a serve that doesn't clear the net. He kept himself from jumping into Jo, and then stood right where he'd been and shook all over.

"Sorry, Jo. I wasn't thinkin."

"Sam's okay." She laid her arm across his withers

and told him he was just fine, and then went back to currying him. "You know it's because of Carl. This guy spent eight whole weeks at Equine. Here he's got two separate businesses, plus Alan and me. He could be here for months!"

Toss went out and picked up the cat's bowl, and set it back on the floor, then took his hat off and ruffled a hand through his thick graying hair. "You fight in their wars for 'em. You hard-scrabble every day trying to make a livin', and maybe, if you're lucky, you put somethin' by for your old age so you won't be a burden to your family. Every year ya live they tax your every dollar, and then they do it again when you die—when you already paid taxes on every cent you ever made! What gives them the right?"

"You're preachin' to the choir here, Toss."

"You and me, we never even thought about cheatin'. We've cared for horses as good as we can, and treated their owners fair, and paid our dues to federal, state and local. And what do we get for it? A fireant like Carl Seeger tellin' his buddy to make our lives a livin' hell! This here, Jo, this is real persecution! What's to keep 'em from turning you inside out 'cause they don't like the way ya vote?"

"You know that'll happen. What am I saying? I bet it already has."


*Thursday, March 12th, 1964*

Spencer wasn't completely asleep when he got the call. Tracker had had a mild case of colic, and he'd walked him around from eleven o'clock on. He hadn't been in so much pain that Spencer'd thought he had to oil him, and when Tracker had finally pooped on his own just before two-thirty, Spencer'd come in to get some sleep, before he checked on him again at four.

He was just dozing off, finally, when the phone rang at three. He rubbed his eyes, as he said hello, and felt his chest pound the way it does from a call in the middle of the night. A voice he didn't recognize said, "Mr. Franklin?"

"Yes."

"This is Chief Anderson from the Fayette County Fire Department. Blue Grass Horse Van's on fire. We're doin' our best to save it, but I reckon it's touch and go."

"What!"

"Blue Grass Horse—"

"Sorry, I heard you. Was anybody hurt?"

"No, sir."

"Good. Thank God for that. I'll be there as fast as I can."

*Saturday, April 4th, 1964*

They were racing at Keeneland, and although Alan and Jo hardly ever went to the races, a three-year-old she and Toss had foaled and raised the first nine months of his life was running in his fifth race, so she and Alan and Toss got dressed up the way everybody did—Jo in a dress, Toss and Alan in sport coats—and went off to the races.

They talked about Blue Grass burning, wondering what caused it, and what it would mean to Spencer, all the way to Keeneland, where they drove in the west gate, and parked on the backside next to the track kitchen. Then they walked up the road to where the runners were stabled on both sides of the drive in long rows of shed roofed stalls—facing each other, most of them, across pea gravel paths, with ovals of grass in the center.

They talked to Wilder Son's owner, and the trainer Toss had known since they were kids, while the groom finished the final brushing and wrapped the big colt's legs. They walked with them to the paddock, where there were two rows of trees planted in the center of small circular walks numbered according to post position.

They led Wilder to circle number six, where Toss talked to him, and stroked his shoulder, while the groom held his lead shank and the trainer discussed the race with his jockey as he smoothed the purple and turquoise cloth across Wilder's broad chestnut back.

He threw on his lightweight racing saddle and half tightened the girth, as Jo and Alan talked to the owner again, a quiet woman with wavy gray hair whose mares Toss had cared for for six or seven years. They stood to one side then and watched Wilder and his people walk round and around the number six tree. They studied the other runners Wilder seemed to be eying too, comparing conformation and discussing who was riding whom, till a gate was opened and the horses were led into the walking ring outside the jockeys' room.

The trainers and jockeys conferred, while the horses were led around the oval, completely surrounded outside the fence by race goers watching their every move. When the "jockeys up" call came, the trainers tightened girths and gave their riders a leg up, then walked their horses around the ring one more time in postposition order before leading them across to the tunnel that led out to the track.

Jo and Alan and Toss walked through the north entrance under the grandstand, and out toward the track, having decided to stand by the rail and watch the horses warm up with their lead ponies, before they were called to the gate.

When Jo and Alan were halfway across the sloping concrete apron, heading toward the rail, Carl Seeger stepped in front of Alan, staring directly at him with a lopsided smirk.

"I hear you're in trouble with the IRS." He was grinning under his narrow mustache, squinting up at Alan, sunglasses perched on top of his head.

Alan stopped and stared at him, letting go of Jo's hand, his eyes furious, his jaw a ridge of knotted muscles, his wide soft gentle-looking mouth clamped in a fierce line. He stepped straight toward Carl with his arms clamped at his sides.

"Get away from me!" Carl stepped back as he said it, bumping into an elderly woman who was reading the race program behind him. "Don't come any closer!"

"Why? You're not afraid, are you Carl? You haven't done something to me that's making you nervous?"

"No, of course not! I haven't done anything to you!"

"Stealing my formulas? How 'bout that? Siccing the IRS on Bob, *and* me, *and* my wife, *and* her uncle? You think that might tick somebody off?"

Carl looked around him with a half-amused,

condescending expression at the bystanders who were listening now, even when they pretended they weren't. "*You* are a liar, and this attack's unprovoked."

"*I'm* a liar! *That's* interesting! If you'd fought in the war with the rest of us you wouldn't have gotten away with the kind of crap you pull. Maybe it's time somebody taught you how to act like a man!"

"Is that a threat?" Carl stepped off to the side this time, and the watchers cleared him a space.

"You and your IRS buddy don't have a principle between you."

"Alan?" Alan didn't look at Jo, but she still said, "Why don't we go watch Wilder? The race is about to start."

Toss was staring at Carl, his hands on his hips, his old tan sport jacket tucked behind them, his face hard, his mouth pinched under his Sunday Stetson, when he said, "Your mama'd be ashamed. 'Least mine wouldda been, if I'd carried on like you."

"You! Who do you think you are?"

They turned away from the rail, Alan walking fast enough Jo had to trot to keep up. Toss walked backwards for a minute, straightening his tie as he stared at Carl, then he turned and followed Jo and Alan on their way to the grandstand stairs.

Toss got waylaid by Virgee's owner, and the trainer who worked for him.

But Jo and Alan climbed the stairs together, her hand tucked under Alan's elbow. She could feel the anger in the iron in his arm as he took the stairs fast. "Alan?"

"Yeah?"

"I haven't seen Carl since November, but I think he looks different. Did you? Thinner, maybe, or—"

"I was trying to keep myself from picking him up by the neck and crushing his windpipe with my thumbs."

"I think you did rather well."

"No. I should've ignored him. He wanted to get me going, and he did. I stood there and insulted him in public when I should've walked away."

"Still—"

"What do you think of Wilder's chances?" Alan was telling her he was done talking about Carl.

And Jo squeezed his elbow, as she said "Hey," to a farmer who lived up the road. "He's alert without being nervous, which is good. He's fit, and he's fast. But I never have an opinion. There're too many other factors. Heart. Guts. Getting out of the gate without getting mugged. Luck, as much as anything."

As it turned out, Wilder Son came in second. Though neither Jo nor Alan could've told you if you'd asked them two weeks later. Their world cracked in two in between. An avalanche swept in from the outside and drove everything before it.

### Monday, April 6th, 1964

Alan woke up at two. His left leg ached the way it always did, the scarred tendons and sliced muscles more usually than the bone grafts. He stretched it and kept it moving for a minute—and used it to remind himself that he was alive when too many others weren't.

Tens of thousands of vets were in much worse shape still. He'd seen them from his hospital bed after he got back from France. He'd watched, and worried for them, and tried to help whatever way he could for more than a year in the hospital, and what he'd seen still woke him up in the darkest part of the night and made him pray for the faces that floated across his brain.

He turned over on his right side away from Jo, trying not to wake her, and listened to Emmy dreaming on her bed on the floor next to Jo. He knew he wouldn't be able to sleep, so he slid out of bed in his boxer shorts, and grabbed a T-shirt from the chair by the door.

He walked through the living room, then passed the front stairs and went on into the dining room, where he turned right, along the length of the table, and limped down two ten-foot-wide steps into the farm office/studio/study, and on through to the kitchen. He drank a glass of water, staring out into the silvery dark, then opened the back door and walked out under the arbor toward the big oval pond.

He heard the screen door slap behind him and looked around, disgusted with himself for having waked Jo, and saw Emmy trotting toward him across the wet grass, a shadow moving in dappled moonlight under the lace of the locust.

He'd sat down in an old Adirondack chair just past the willow by the pond, and she came and lay down beside him, and he stroked her smooth head and rubbed her warm ears, telling himself that he'd been wrong, even though he'd been justifying himself ever since it'd happened.

*Why did I do what Carl wanted? He set out to goad me, and I fell for it like a fool.*

*It's not that I don't have good reason to be outraged, but yelling at him in public played right into his hands. It was nothing but anger and pride on my side. And I ended up looking like a petulant child.*

*The fact that that bothers me more than what he said is pride too. Which is not the way I want to live.*

*There's nothing I can say that'll change Carl. It's spittin' in the wind, as Dad would say, which doesn't end well.*

*So what am I supposed to do?*

*Go on.*

*Make yourself say it.*

*Forgive him for what he's done. And whatever he does next.*

*Yeah? How? God's gonna have to make a move here, 'cause that's the last thing I want to do.*

*I s'pose I could apologize. Sometime. Just for yelling at him in public. And tell him we need to get over this and learn to act like adults.*

*'Course I'd rather eat a worm sandwich and wash it down with lye.*

"Right, Emmy? You don't ever have to apologize. You can just wag your tail and look ashamed and everyone tells you how cute you are."


Alan pulled into Carl's drive at six-twenty that night. Carl's Chevy was there, parked in front of the unattached garage. And Alan sat with his hands on the wheel, talking himself out of shoving the gearshift into reverse and heading home fast.

He climbed out, finally, and walked to the front door, where he rang the doorbell, after another conversation with himself.

He waited. But no one answered.

And he went back to the car and took his legal pad out of his briefcase and wrote Carl a note of apology, then clamped it into the edge of the screen door right at eye level.

He backed out, and drove off, nodding to the elderly woman who was watching him, as she watered her gardenias, across the street from Carl's.


*Wednesday, April 15th, 1964*


Jo pulled into Jack Freeman's driveway on Pisgah Pike at a little before two, and drove through the deep ruts, climbing the long hill, then left past the creosoted tobacco barns and the smaller barn full of tractors that belonged to the man who rented the land. She parked under the cluster of hardwoods up the hill from Jack's house, then stood for a minute and watched the wind fluttering paths through the leaves.

It was the house Alan had rented before they'd married, the stone and clapboard Cotswold cottage halfway down the slope from a fenced in cattle pasture that ran west across the top of the hill.

Jo started down toward the back of the house, but Jack came out before she'd gotten fifty feet, carrying his army pack and a small canvas suitcase.

He was grinning, the way he never had when she'd first met him, and though he was probably forty now, or maybe forty-two, he looked ten years younger than he had two years before.

Jo waited for Jack to lock the kitchen door and walk up to her, watching the tall grass swirl in the breeze that came sweeping down toward Pisgah Pike, looking at the gardens too that Jack had planted—the vegetable patch beyond the rope hammock by the screened-in porch, the new boxwoods flanking the stone path Jack had laid to the tiny flagstone entry outside the kitchen door, the peony bushes where there'd only been raw red clay.

Jo said, "You're the kind of tenant *I* want."

Which made Jack laugh, as he set his bags in the truck. "It's fun for me. Experimenting on my own gardens makes me relax. How long will it take to get to the Cincinnati airport?"

"We've got to count on three hours, though it probably won't take that long. What time does your plane leave?"

"Seven-forty-five."

"Good. We've got time to spare for construction."

"Thanks for driving me up."

"It'll be good to talk. I've got Ross over with Buddy's wife, and I feel like a free woman."


They talked about Jo's newest client, and the work they were both doing at White Hall (her renovation and his landscaping), and the difficulties he was having making his landscaping business profitable. They discussed Alan's job, and the troubles with Carl, and moved on to her Uncle Toss and their broodmare business.

They'd driven about forty-five minutes when Jack got quiet.

His thin face seemed pulled in on itself, the hazel eyes searching the distance, the sharp nose and the chiseled cheekbones, tanned now, when they had been pasty, making him seem strong and reliable in ways Jo couldn't have explained.

"What're you thinking about? Not that it's any of my business." Jo laughed as she glanced at him.

And he looked back and crossed his arms across his sport coat, then sighed before he spoke. "I've been brooding about this trip since 1945."

"I would've, I know that."

"And yet actually going and doing it isn't without risk."

"If someone had set me up to look like a traitor, I'd feel downright nervous, going back to find out who."

"That would be an understatement." Jack rubbed his hands on his thighs, and turned toward Jo. "Being made to look like I'd turned the Resistance into the Gestapo? It made me insane for years. You saw that yourself."

"Well—"

"It's not that I don't want to go track down who-ever it was. I want it more than anything else I've ever wanted. But I know it's a nearly impossible task, the way it always has been. That's what used to paralyze me. I absolutely have to try. But that doesn't keep it from being daunting, especially with limited time."

"How will you go about it?"

"My number one suspect is Henri Reynard. He was a Resistance member who worked as a photographer for the Tours paper and the Vichy police. He photographed crime scenes, and any dead that turned up, so he knew what the police and Gestapo were up to from one day to the next. That information helped the Resistance, but gave him a network on their side too. I have no concrete evidence. And there's research I need to do first, but I think my best bet is to find his ex-wife."

"She was a painter?"

"Who taught during the war in what we call a high school. She'd been trained as an art restorer, and that was her real love."

Jack was silent then for quite awhile before he smiled at Jo. "Actually, and I've never said this to anyone else, I admired her a great deal. I could talk to her about all sorts of topics. Literature. Art. Legal practices in our disparate cultures. She made me smile at the oddest times, and I found her quite attractive."

"Good for you! I hope you find her. Did she know you were an attorney before the war?"

"No. Agents in the OSS did *not* discuss their backgrounds. She's probably remarried, and she may well not want to help me, but I've got to at least try."

"Yes, you do."

"Did Alan ever tell you about the talk he had with me that first year I came here? I'd stopped drinking, so he was letting me stay in his spare room, and he—"

"He didn't mention a particular—"

"He was telling me I had to put it behind me— being set up and thought of as a traitor—so I could make myself a new life."

"I know he talked to you in general terms, but—"

"He told me that holding a grudge, even when it was justified, was like taking cyanide and expecting the other guy to die. That may not have originated with him, but he was right. It made me absolutely livid at the time, but it helped in the long run."

"I'm glad. He would be too. Especially since he's having to struggle with something similar now."

"Funny how that happens."

"Yeah."

They talked about other things then. Styles of landscaping in Europe and the US. The integration crises in Louisville. The easier time they'd had in Woodford County, speculating too on why that might be.

Then Jack fell asleep, much to his embarrassment when he woke up. "I'm sorry to leave you to drive alone. Where are we?"

"Pulling in to the airport."

"There was something else I meant to tell you. What was it?" He was putting his sunglasses in his army pack, checking his pockets of his corduroy jacket for his passport and his ticket, tightening the knot in his dark green tie. "I know what it was. This morning. Maybe quarter after five. I was driving to Equine Pharmaceuticals to mow the lawn and show the guy who's working for me how I want it done while I'm gone. I was on my way to the back lot, and when I passed the front driveway Alan's car was the only one there, but a man was standing in the lot, and it looked like Carl Seeger. He was—"

A car honked behind them. And Jack waved at the driver. "It's no big deal, but remind me to tell you later. I better run. Thanks, Jo."

"I hope you accomplish what you want to accomplish, and that your friend isn't married."

Jack actually blushed, then nodded and thanked her

again, and waved as he walked into the airport to try to make sense of his past.

# CHAPTER SIX

Alan had just gotten home and put on a pair of cutoffs and a T-shirt, and had poured himself an ice tea from the fridge, and was telling Emmy that they'd trot up and down the front drive a few times, then feed Sam and Maggie an apple—when the phone rang in the study.

The man identified himself as Virgil Shafer, a farmer Bob Harrison had known for years, who'd asked to try their experimental equine viral arteritis vaccine on his daughter's quarter horse mare. She was about to take her to a series of shows where she could get exposed to the virus, so Bob had inoculated her that morning, and Virgil was calling to tell Alan what he didn't want to hear. "The mare's having a real bad reaction. I couldn't get Bob, and I've called out another vet, but I figure you oughtta come out right quick."

Alan put on Levis and paddock boots in less than half a minute and drove to the north side of Versailles, while Emmy watched the world whip by through the back right window. Alan turned left onto Elm Street (which changed its name to McCracken Pike half a mile on), and drove five miles past Carl Seeger's house to the Shafers' farm, turning left into their driveway, climbing the hill through the woods in second, pushing the Dodge hard.

When they pulled up into the circle at the front of the old brick farmhouse, Virgil's pickup wasn't there. It wasn't in the back drive either, though Georgia's station wagon was. And when Alan knocked on every door, and looked in all the windows, there wasn't anyone home—not Virgil, or his wife, or his daughter.

Alan checked the barns and the paddocks, and found Susie, the mare who'd been inoculated that morning, cropping grass in the west field with two gray geldings.

Alan examined her as carefully as he could—not with the knowledge a vet would've had, but with two years' experience helping Bob Harrison with horses in field tests.

She wasn't sweating. There were no hives. She was breathing normally. He pried her jaws apart and looked at her throat, which didn't seem to him to be swollen. Her legs weren't swollen anywhere either—and she communicated clearly but politely, sniffing his hands and then backing away, that if he didn't have an apple or carrot secreted about his person, she'd appreciate it if he'd leave her alone to eat dinner in peace.


As he drove back toward Versailles on the winding one-lane road that followed a shallow creek, he gazed at horses and glanced at dry stone walls, but he couldn't pry his mind off the call. Because why would anyone drag him out on that kind of wild goose chase?

*Whoever it was knew about the vaccine, and that Virgil's horse got injected this morning.*

*And maybe the point was to get me away from home. To hurt a horse. Or steal one. Or take something from the house.*

*Anyone who knows Toss would know we don't leave the horses alone for long. That he goes to his place before dinnertime during foaling, and comes back at nine or ten to oversee the mares at night.*

*So if whoever it is knows Jo and Toss were both gone, I'd be the one to get rid of.*

*Butch? He's not doing much that makes sense at the moment. Maybe he'd think it was funny.*

*Carl might do it just to inconvenience me.*

*And they both have contacts at Equine who could tell them about the vaccine and who was getting it when.*

*It could be something more sinister too. Though what that could be I don't know.*

When he got home, he took Emmy with him and checked all the barns. Nothing was missing that he could see, and the horses were all accounted for, there, and in the paddocks. He went through every room in the house, where everything seemed normal. And though that was a relief, it made the call more inexplicable. Which made him more uneasy.

He scrambled some eggs, and sliced a tomato, and made a sandwich on whole wheat toast. He sat under the arbor in back, his plate on his lap, his iced tea on the side table, and read *The Agony And The Ecstasy* till he found himself staring into space, his ribs tight and his breath shallow, his eyes beginning to ache.

*Who knew Jo would be gone?*

*Bob Harrison. And probably Brad. I think he was there when I told his dad.*

*I might've mentioned it in the lab too, though I don't remember that I did.*

*Jo could've told all kinds of people.*

*And me sitting here speculating won't do any good.*


*Thursday, April 16th 1964*


Esther Wilkes climbed out of her husband's rusty red Ford pickup, pulling herself up with her right hand clutching the top of the doorframe.

She was a large woman. What some might've called stout. But she was firm looking, and she stood up straight, and her small-striped tan-and-blue dress fitted well and was perfectly pressed. She'd made the dress so it fell halfway between her knees and her ankles, and she'd sewn a belt of the same fabric, though neither of them looked homemade. She was wearing stockings, in spite of the heat, with lace-up black oxford shoes with sturdy squared-off heels. She carried a large brown pocketbook in one hand and a hand-kerchief she'd embroidered in the other, and she waved it once at her husband, before she blotted her forehead, as he backed out of the driveway and headed to work in Midway.

She stood for a moment on the sidewalk, thinking about her brother, Charlie, on his way up to the Belmont track with one of the Claiborne four-year-olds who'd be running there that summer. She hadn't talked to Charlie since he'd gone back to work, and she was worried he wasn't over his bronchitis. He'd had a weak chest since he was the tiniest child, and it'd sounded real croupy when he'd coughed in church on Sunday.

'Course, Charlie Smalls was no kinda fool. He was a Negro man respected by white folks *and* by colored, by rich folks *and* by poor, as a man of honor and good common sense. And if she knew he neglected himself, being his twin and having seen it all her life, all she could do was pray that his loyalty to Mr. Bull Hancock and the horses he put in his care didn't make Charlie ignore his own health a good deal more than he should.

She had her own troubles too, to get through now, and she needed to collect herself and prepare for what was coming. She patted the chignon on the back of her head, while her broad big-boned ebony face composed itself against the dread that fluttered deep in her chest. She adjusted her belt then, and let out a sigh, and started down Carl Seeger's drive toward the turquoise-and-white Chevy sedan in front of the unattached garage.

She followed the flagstone path that started at the drive just behind the house, and curved off to the left, that Mrs. Seeger had laid with her own hands clear to the kitchen door.

Esther knocked on it twice—the white painted door with small paned glass filling the whole top half—and didn't get an answer. That hadn't ever happened. Not since Mr. Seeger had lost his job and been home all day long. She tried the handle, but it was locked like she expected, and she walked into the garage and got the key from the coffee can where Miz Seeger had hid it for her years before, that he didn't know was there.

She knocked on the door again, to be on the safe side, but when Mr. Seeger didn't appear, she unlocked the door, and opened it an inch or two, and called Mr. Seeger's name. She didn't want to vex him mightily by barging in unannounced—not on the day she was fixing to quit and ask for what he owed her.

Things were real different since Miz Seeger had left, and you couldn't count on how he'd react. She s'pposed he mightta gone out for a walk, or forgot she was coming. But she knew he wouldn't have trusted her with a key, and she put it back in the garage, telling herself that hard as it was, she'd have to tell him she'd had it all along, once she'd let herself in.

She opened the door, and stepped inside, the reek of cigarettes making her cough—and almost tripped over Cassandra, stretched out on her side, four feet past the door, lying dead right there on the floor.

Esther said, "Poor little thing!" *Lord knows what couldda happened*, as she closed the door real quiet like, and stepped around the thin grey body to set her purse on the counter. She looked back at the stiff matted fur, and shook her head, before she smoothed her dress and stepped on out into the hall that led to the front door.

She was listening hard for Mr. Seeger. For water in the shower, or the toilet getting flushed, or the typewriter clickin' in the study. She didn't hear nothin' but the grandfather clock ticking under the hall stairway, and she called his name softly again, then louder by the front door.

He wasn't in the study, and he wasn't in the living

room. And the bathroom was empty too between the study and his bedroom at the back, just off to the side and a little in front of the kitchen.

The door to the bedroom was standing ajar, and she knocked real quiet like, and called his name, then pushed the door wider.

There was a big window on the wall facing her, and another off on her left. The curtains were open, but the wooden louvers were half-closed, yet enough pale early morning light slipped through the slats for Esther to see Carl Seeger on the far side of the double bed against the wall on her right.

The bedclothes were twisted and crumpled around him, and as Esther walked toward the foot of the bed she could see his right foot dangling off the mattress, his right arm hanging off it too, his mouth stretched wide, under staring eyes that were fixed right on her.

Esther Wilkes had been looking at death since the day she was born. Chickens and calves and hogs on her papa's farm. Too many kinfolk and friends to count. And she knew what she'd seen from the door. It was the look on his face that made her clasp her hand to her mouth and whisper, "Oh, my dear sweet Jesus." *There ain't no peace in this death, no, sir. There ain't no hope at all.*

His photographer had finished in Carl's bedroom, and Earl Peabody, the Woodford County sheriff, stood on the left side of Carl's bed and stared down at his body, which was mostly covered in pajama bottoms and a dingy white T-shirt stained with all the bodily fluids Earl expected with death.

There was one of the new plastic type hypodermics on the floor beside the bed not far from the outstretched arm, and a small glass vial with a black plastic lid overturned on the bedside table. Earl rocked back on the heels of his boots, his hands in his back pockets, and made a noise low in his throat that sounded like sadness at the waste before him, and what was coming next.

Frank Buckout was standing on Earl's right, his strained face turned away from Carl as though he couldn't look at him, as he said exactly what Earl expected, which caused Earl to keep his face on straight and try to look like it made good sense for him to wait on instructions.

"As Coroner of Woodford County in the Commonwealth of Kentucky, I pronounce Carl Winslow Seeger dead. I add furthermore that I consider it to be an unexplained death. That means you got this one, Earl. You and your boys proceed."

"Right."

Frank turned toward Earl then, and set a hand on his shoulder before he started toward the door, stating the obvious one more time to make sure Earl hadn't missed it. "The investigation's been placed in your hands from this minute on."

"Yes, sir, I understand. We'll get the body to the medical examiner in Louavull soon as we can. My guess is he died last night. That's what the M.E. figured at first sight, but we'll know a good deal more after he's done the ortopsy."

"Fine. Give my best to the wife."

He was gone then. And Earl thought for the hundredth time what an odd situation it was—that everyday ordinary folk with no medical or forensic training got elected county coroner. All they got was a two-week, on-the-job course after their election, and yet they were the ones to declare the death and assume responsibility for the whole investigation. They had no idea how to begin one, much less carry it through, and they'd hand it on to the Sheriff in a second, so what was the blasted point?

Not that it mattered a whit.

Not when Carl Seeger was lying dead with a puncture wound in his left arm. A syringe under him on the floor. A vial of something turned over on the table next to an ashtray half full of butts and a piece of typing paper, with type in the middle, it behooved him to read again.

> *I have no reason to go on. All I care about has been lost to me: job, wife, reputation. Now that Cassandra is dead too, I have nothing left to look forward to, tomorrow, nor any day after.*

Earl slid the note in a plastic bag, then picked up the syringe and smelled it, before he slipped it in another and laid it on a chair. He looked under the bedside table, then picked up the dust ruffle and looked under the bed—and there he found a black enamel pen, just past the edge of the fabric, with a gold band at the base of its top engraved with an inscription:

> *With Love from J. to A.—12/8/62*

Earl said, "J. to A.? Jane Seeger to … who?"
*I'll have to ask Miz Seeger, and Esther Wilkes too.*

He pulled the top off and saw it was a fountain pen, then dropped it in another bag—just before the gurney rolled through the bedroom door.

His deputy, Pete Phelps, sidled in behind it, saying, "We checked every door and window like ya asked, Stump, and everyone of 'em's locked, so we can eliminate a break-in right off the bat."

"Good. Ask Burt to shoot photos of every room, and outside the kitchen door too. Stones and all, up by the door. There looked like dirt was kinda dug up and scattered. Have him shoot the front door, and around the garage. With the concrete drive and all, we won't get tire tracks, though there might could be mud prints from tires, with the shower last night and all. Ask him to look for that. Have you dusted the typewriter in the study?"

"Yep."

"Good. And would ya tell Miz Wilkes I'll be with her in a minute, soon as I finish here?"

"Got it, Stump." Pete, who was six-feet-five and thin as a stick, adjusted his flat-brimmed WWI style campaign hat on his bald head, and disappeared toward the back.

When the mortuary men had lifted Carl onto the gurney and wheeled him out the door, Earl was still staring at the bed. It looked to him like it was an old mattress, thin and sunken where Earl and his wife had lain for years. But it seemed like one part of the bottom edge looked bumped up higher than the rest.

He pulled the mattress up right about there and slid his hand in between it and the springs, and pulled out a brown leather book.

It was a diary, or some kinda journal, two inches

BEHIND THE BONEHOUSE          121

thick, or close to. Written in Carl's handwriting, based on what he'd seen on his desk. He leafed through it, and found the last entry, dated the night before.

*April 15, 5:45 P.M.*

*I've had as much as I can take. Alan Munro's persecution has lost me my livelihood and my reputation. Even Jane has turned against me because of Alan's actions at Equine Pharmaceutical and his vendetta against me. His visit here in November was solely to deliver a private threat, and was just the next in an escalating series that's continued ever since.*

*The verbal abuse he heaped on me at Keeneland during the racing was an indefensible humiliation. And <u>then</u> he came here to harass me two days later! I know he killed Cassandra. He's threatened to repeatedly. For as soon as I came home and found her, and saw sticky smears beside her on the linoleum, the smell left no doubt that the substance was Dylox and had come from the Equine lab. It constituted the next step in Alan Munro's plan that ends with my own demise.*

*He could've gotten a key from Esther. Her brother is a friend of Buddy Jones, who's very close to Alan and his wife. Esther could have taken an impression of my key, or Jane's in the garage (which Esther doesn't know I know about, being nearly as oblivious as my former-wife). Esther could have given it to Buddy so he could give it to Alan. If Alan wanted a key, he'd have found a way to get one, of that I have no doubt.*

*I can no longer tolerate his attacks. His killing of Cassandra, who'd never done him any harm, shows the vicious bent of his insanity. Munro was a trained assassin during World War II, and I know it's only a matter of time until he makes a concerted attempt to murder me too.*

*All I can do is leave tomorrow as quickly as I can pack. I could return to Bloomington, or maybe try Nashville. Destination doesn't matter. I have to escape Munro's persecution and preserve this journal too, in case the worst happens.*

Earl Peabody shook his head, and stared out the window that faced the foot of the bed, the journal held carefully by one leather corner in his huge tanned hand. "Carl musta gone off the deep end, 'cause Alan Munro wouldn't a killed him."

*I know Alan. The way he dealt with that killer two years ago, without takin' revenge. No, he and Jo are real fine folks, and Seeger's way off base.*

*Gotta run it down anyway, and get to the bottom of it quick as I can.*

*'Course, the inscription on the pen, that's* something. *"J to A." From Jo to Alan? They got married about then, from what I remember. Not that Alan killin' Carl makes any sense at all.*

Earl took the suicide note into the study and turned on the turquoise electric typewriter that sat in the center of the desk. It was one of the new IBM models, like the one they'd just gotten at the Sheriff's Department after months of wrangling over funding, the model that had a revolving ball, with the type stuck on all around it, that could be replaced to change the font.

He pulled a piece of typing paper out of a bottom drawer and held it up next to the note by Carl's bed so that the light coming through the front window was right behind them both.

There was a watermark on the one from the bedroom, and one on the paper from the desk too, but they weren't the same marks the way he'd expected.

He typed the same message that'd been left by Carl, and saw right away that the type was the same, but the "o" was chipped on the one from the bedroom, and wasn't on Earl's typewriter.

*So it ain't just what you'd come to expect. Not right outta the chute. Not some everyday suicide. Not with different type.*

*'Course it's not like suicide's an everyday occurrence with folks here in the county. I don't reckon there've been twenty all together, not in the past eighteen years.*

Earl sat and swiveled, and hummed to himself for a minute, then looked through the papers in the top center drawer, and pulled out a handwritten list in the same handwriting that was in the journal, and slipped it in a file inside his satchel.

Then he walked into the kitchen and asked Esther Wilkes if he could have a word.


"Thank you, ma'am, for waitin' on me. And I'm real glad you went outta your way not to touch nothin' you didn't have to and all. Did my deputy get your finger-prints?"

"Yes, sir, he did."

They were sitting in the study—Earl in Carl's desk

chair, Esther sitting with her pocketbook in her lap, her lace-up oxfords planted right together, her back straight in her overstuffed chair.

"We did that to eliminate your prints, as we try to see what we got here."

Esther didn't say anything. She looked at Sheriff Peabody as though she were waiting for him to do his job in whatever way he would.

"So did you notice anything missing, or rearranged in the house when you got here?"

"No, sir, I didn't. I thought about that too. I kinda walked around and inspected, while I waited for y'all to get here."

"Can you identify this handwriting?" Earl handed her the list he'd taken out of the desk."

"That's Mr. Seeger's writin'. No doubt at all."

"You've known him a good long while?"

"I worked for Miz Seeger a good many years."

"So how would you describe Mr. Seeger? Has he seemed depressed, or upset at all?"

"I only come in one day a week. Thursday, like today. And a 'course till last fall he'd be goin' to work, and I wouldn't see him hardly at all before he left the house. He'd just walk through on his way out the door, and that'd be all I seen. Miz Seeger, she works in the libery over to the university, and her hours change some, but she'd be here when I come, and usually for some little while so I know her a whole lot better. I like to come early, in the cool of the day, and we'd talk some while I got to work, and I think she's a real fine woman." Esther, set her purse on the floor and clasped her hands in her lap.

"Did Mr. Seeger seem different after she left in the fall?"

Esther hesitated, and it looked to Earl like she was asking herself how blunt she could be with a white county sheriff she didn't know from Adam. "I hope you'll say just what ya think, Miz Wilkes. That's the way you can help."

"Well. *I'd* say he got a whole lot more fractious and short tempered. Kinda rude, if ya want the whole truth. He'd be here every week to let me in, and he made it real plain that he didn't want me to have a key, or be here on my own. Some folks I work for give me a key a my own. But he'd sit in the living room, in his chair with the footstool, and read till I'd finished my work, comin' in though, wherever I was, more times than you'd expect. It was like he was watching my every move. Like he figured I'd try to steal from him if he weren't makin' sure."

"And that's stayed pretty much the same since the fall?"

"I wouldn't say that altogether."

"No?"

"I b'lieve I saw a change. Seemed like he got real quiet. More than normal. I'd look over and there'd be this stoney-like scowl on his face, and he'd be workin' away at something in his mind. 'Course, what, or why, I have no idee."

"When was this?"

"I cain't say for sure. Mightta been January. Might-ta been early February. Then sometime around then, I'm not sure just when, he got busier than he'd been since he'd stopped going to work. He spent more time in his study with the door closed. 'Course, I only seen him one day a week, so I cain't say for sure. It's just the impression I got."

"Did you usually come in the back door, or the front?"

"Back door. Yes, sir."

"Was it unlocked today?" Earl was leaning back in his chair, a notebook in his left hand, his right holding his pen.

"No, sir, it was never unlocked, not once. Not since Miz Seeger left. She used to leave it unlocked, but not him, no sir."

"So how'd you get in on your own?"

Esther stared silently at her feet, then smoothed her dress toward her knees, before she looked Earl right in the eye. "Miz Seeger put an extry key in a coffee can in the garage for me, in case I ever needed it. Once in a while, she'd have me come an extry afternoon, when she was gone, to do somethin' special. Ironin' and what not. And she trusted me to come in on my own. He wouldda been real put out if he'd had any idee."

"Did ya ever show anybody else the key?"

"No sir, I did not!"

Earl nodded, and pushed his glasses up his nose, then asked if there was anything else she figured he ought to know.

Esther thought for a minute, gazing past Earl toward the row of encyclopedias on the bookshelf behind him. "I was fixin' to quit today, and ask for my back pay. I been workin' for Miz Seeger at her new place, and I'm fixin' to start for her sister. I was dreadin' it. Tellin' Mr. Seeger. I knew he'd throw a fit and make it real unpleasant. He owed me for three whole weeks."

"That don't sound like he was treatin' ya right." Earl took a small plastic bag out of his canvas carryall with the fountain pen inside it and handed it across to Esther Wilkes. "Do you recognize this?"

"No, sir. I never seen it before."

"Can you think of anyone Miz Jane could've given a pen to with that inscription?"

"No, sir, I cain't." Esther looked slightly perturbed, as though the question had been in questionable taste, or an affront to Miz Seeger's good name.

"Alright then. Thank you. I appreciate your help."

Esther said, "You're welcome," and pushed herself out of the chair.

"One other thing. I'd like you to give my deputy a sample of your handwriting. I'll get one from Miz Seeger, too. We'll need them for comparison as time goes on."

"Can I ask you somethin', Sheriff?"

"Sure."

"You figuring this was murder? 'Stead of him committing suicide?"

"Well, I'll tell ya, Miz Wilkes, the whole truth is I don't begin to know, but we gotta look at it all."

"Yes, sir. D'you see the sticky stuff on the floor by Cassandra?"

"I did."

"Smells like nothin' I ever smelled."

"Yep, I know what ya mean. If you think of anything else, I hope you'll give me a call."

"Yes, sir, I surely will."


Earl went through the rest of the desk, and the tall file

cabinet next to the door, and found nothing that seemed to help him put the death in better perspective.

He walked down the hall to the bathroom, and looked through the medicine cabinet, then took the top off the toilet tank, and looked behind it too, more out of thoroughness than with any expectation of making a discovery.

But when he picked up the toilet seat, there was a fragment of cream-colored vinyl that looked like a piece of the new type disposable gloves they'd started using in hospitals, stuck right there on the rim of the toilet bowl, like a glove had been cut up and flushed maybe, and one piece got stuck.

He pulled it off with tweezers, and slipped it in a plastic bag, thinking that, with any luck at all, they'd get him a latent print up at the state police lab.

He walked through the kitchen, opening and closing drawers and cupboards, before he looked in the ice box. He opened the back door and considered the dirt scattered across the flagstones. There was some plant, low and creeping, growing between most of the stones, that might've been planted, he couldn't tell—but between the two closest to the door, it looked like it'd been dug up accidental, getting shoved by a shoe, or a hoe. He yelled for Pete, who was upstairs in the guest room, and asked him to take samples of the dirt and the plant material too, when he was done upstairs. "Anything interestin' up there?"

"Nope. Don't look like it gets used. There's a small bedroom, and a storage room like a little attic where there're suitcases and old chairs, and a bathroom with rust in the sink, but that's about all."

"I'll be up in a minute."

Earl went into Carl's bedroom again, and stared at the carpet on Carl's side of the bed, then took a utility knife out of his satchel and cut a patch eight inches square and put it in a bag of its own.

"Pete?"

"Yeah?"

"I'd like you to vacuum the carpet in here. Could be we'll get some fibers to compare to somebody's shoes."

"Got it."

"You always have to say 'Got it,' do ya?"

"Guess not."

"You dusted the phones down here?"

"Yep."

"Good. I gotta make me a call."

# CHAPTER SEVEN

*Excerpt from Jo Grant Munro's Journal:*

*...Buddy Jones drove his wife over to watch Ross this morning, and we talked for a minute. He's done so well at Mercer Tate's he feels like he's ready to help Mercer train a new stallion manager and try to find himself a job with one of the local trainers, like he's always wanted. He's put out a couple of feelers, and then—out of the blue—he got a vicious letter from Frankie D'Amato threatening to tell lies about Buddy to whatever trainers he approaches.*

*Frankie! The ne'er-do-well groom who offered to secretly breed one of Mercer's studs to Buddy's mare a couple of years ago so he could pocket the fee himself, which would've been grounds for lynching a hundred years ago. So when Buddy told Mercer (who only fired Frankie when he could've prosecuted him) Frankie took it out on Buddy's mare.*

*What is it in human nature that makes a person hate enough that years later he'd still be looking for ways to inflict pain?*

*Short word. Three letters. Starts with the letter "s".*

Earl Peabody stood on Carl Seeger's front porch, his huge hands settling his dark brown wide-brimmed WWI style sheriff's hat on his head, as he gazed across the street at the elderly woman in a big straw hat deadheading some sort of plant, while looking across at him.

He was just about to cross the road, when the door opened on the house on his left, and a short pear-shaped man with small hands and feet hurried across his lawn toward Earl.

"Excuse me. I'm a friend of Mr. Seeger's. Has something happened to Carl?" He was tying his tie, a suit coat thrown across one shoulder, his shirt tail not quite tucked into the front of his pants.

"May I ask your name, sir?" Earl was staring at the man's thin brown hair, wondering uneasily if it'd been sprayed into place.

"Terrence Cathcart."

"Well, Mr. Cathcart, I'm real sorry to have to tell you Mr. Seeger's passed away."

"How? Of what?"

"We're not rightly sure yet, but we're gonna be lookin' into it real close."

"If he was murdered I know who did it!" Cathcart's plump face was red now and prickly, and his eyes looked incensed.

"I beg your pardon?"

"Carl told me Alan Munro's been persecuting him for months. He called me last night and told me he'd found his cat dead, and he was sure Alan had killed her."

"What time was that?"

"I can't say to the minute. Maybe six-fifteen, or so. Something like that."

"Do you know Mr. Munro?"

"Not to say 'know.' I work for the IRS, and I'm in the process of auditing his and his wife's finances."

"Today?"

"Yes. I'm on my way there."

"What led you to undertake the investigation?" Earl was looking down at Terry, his broad shoulders stooped, his upper body bent slightly forward as though he might be having trouble hearing the high pitched voice.

Cathcart hesitated, and pushed his arms into his jacket, while he glanced off to his left toward town. "We often receive reports of malfeasance. I'm responding to such a report."

"And who gave you that report? If you don't mind my askin'."

Terry Cathcart adjusted his tie, and patted his stiff shiny hair. "I'm not at liberty to say."

"This is an unexplained death investigation, Mr. Cathcart. There'll be a formal enquiry. You'll have no choice but to answer that question, and pro'bly a whole lot more, all of 'em under oath."

Cathcart stared at his shoes, before he glanced at Earl. "Carl told me there was very good reason to investigate Munro. He had pertinent information, having worked with him at Equine Pharmaceuticals."

"Was there bad blood between them, would you say?"

"On Alan's part, yes. He caused Carl to lose his job. He threatened the cat. Cassandra. He came over a week or so ago and threatened Carl's life. And that was just a couple of days after he'd accosted him at Keeneland in front of the whole crowd."

"You heard him yourself, did you?"

"Well," Terry brushed a speck of lint from his coat, then glanced across the street. "Not directly. Carl told me about it."

"Can you describe Mr. Munro's car?"

"It's a dark-blue Dodge sedan, several years old."

"When was the last time you saw it?"

"Last week. In Carl's drive. I haven't seen Munro when I've been working at his house. He leaves before I get there, and comes home after I've left."

"Well, sir, I thank you for your help. Someone from my office will ask you to make a statement. Today, or maybe tomorrow."

"Fine. I'll be more than happy to tell what I know about Alan Munro."

"I'm sure you will." Earl nodded and started across the street, leaving Terry standing in Carl's driveway tucking his shirttail in his pants.


Elinor Nevilleson had pulled off her gardening gloves and laid them on top of the clippings in the wicker basket that hung from her left arm. She straightened herself to her full heighth and held out her right hand. "Sheriff Peabody. Elinor Nevilleson. I hoped you'd be interviewing Mr. Seeger's neighbors. May I offer you a cup of tea?"

"Thank you, ma'am. I'd like that."

The thick walls of her old stone house sheltered it from the heat, and her parlor was cool and dark. The cream-colored crewel-work drapes, half-pulled across the tall windows, softened the early sun. The mahogany framed Regency sofa and Georgian tables and chairs, fighting for space on the blue oriental that covered most of the heart pine floor, the gilded mirrors and Victorian portraits, filled the parlor with history and style, but made Earl feel cramped right off, like he was too big for the room.

"Sugar, Sheriff?"

He sat at one end of the brocade-covered sofa, wiping his hat on his sleeve before setting it down on the pale yellow silk, lying shiny and smooth on his left. "No, thank ya, ma'am, but I will take a piece a lemon since ya got it right there."

She passed him the plate, then slipped a slice in her own tea, before she looked at Earl. "Having seen the mortuary van depart, and having seen Miz Wilkes drive away with her husband, I can only presume Mr. Seeger has passed away." She sipped her English Breakfast tea from a blue-and-white Chinese porcelain cup, then set it carefully in its saucer, as she studied Earl over gold-framed glasses with sharp brown eyes.

"Yes, ma'am, he has. Did you know Mr. Seeger well?"

"I did not, no. We had what I can only describe as an adversarial relationship. He was a rude and vindic-tive person whom I chose to have little to do with."

"What makes ya say he was vindictive?"

"Ah." She smiled then, and swept a curl of thick white hair off the side of her forehead. "His cat has an unfortunate fondness for my gardens. She comes here to do her business, apparently preferring my double dug beds to the soil she finds at home.

"When I asked him, most politely, to discourage her behavior, he spoke to me in the crudest possible manner. Not long thereafter, he deposited a piece of decomposed fish under my camellias at four o'clock one morning, leading her behind him, of course, to forage here on her own."

"Not what you'd call neighborly."

"No, sir, it wasn't. I don't sleep particularly well, and I watched his entire performance from my bedroom window. I took him to task later that day, in what *I* considered a restrained tone, but the response I received was vituperative, and will not be repeated by me."

"Sounds kinda mean-spirited."

"The irony, of course, is that rotted fish is wonderful for the soil, though I doubt that he was aware of that fact." Elinor Nevilleson smiled, a slow wry smile as she said, "Singularly peculiar, though, wouldn't you say?" before she set her cup and saucer on the mahogany tea table that must've been worth a small fortune.

"Did he have many visitors? Folks you might've noticed when you're workin' in your front yard?"

"No, sir, he didn't. His wife, who is a lovely woman, had several friends who stopped by frequently, but other than the Internal Revenue minion whom you've already encountered, I'm unaware of anyone else who chose to visit Mr. Seeger with any regularity." She handed Earl a plate of tiny homemade orange cookies, and after he'd taken three, she set the plate on the table.

"There *was* one recent visitor, though whether his visit is of particular significance I, of course, can't say.

A tall man, quite good looking. I noticed a tendency to limp a bit, when he walked to Mr. Seeger's door."

"Did you see him well enough to describe him?"

"I did, yes. He had dark hair, and distinctively shaped eyebrows, and he made me think of … you may find this amusing, Sheriff. The sentimental fancy of an elderly spinster. He reminded me of Gregory Peck."

"I'm real glad to hear that. Gives me a good clear picture. When did he visit Mr. Seeger?"

"Let me think … Yes. Today's the sixteenth. They finished running at Keeneland on the fourth, if I'm not mistaken. So I b'lieve it must've been Monday the sixth. I normally water my roses first thing in the morning on a Monday, and spray them as well when it's still cool, but I had an appointment with my physician that morning, and didn't tend to the roses until six o'clock that evening. I never water, *or* spray, during the heat of the day, and rarely water in the evening."

"That's what the wife says too."

"She's a plantswoman, is she?"

"She is. An outdoors woman, and real practical. Broke horses on her daddy's farm when she was just a little child."

"She wasn't a Montgomery, was she? One of Clarence Montgomery's daughters?"

"No, ma'am. But I know just who you mean."

"Well. In any event. I was spraying my roses with nicotine, when a blue sedan drove into Mr. Seeger's drive. The tall man I described earlier sat in his car for a bit, as though he were trying to reach a decision. Or steeling himself, perhaps, for a rather unpleasant task. He eventually got out, and rang the bell.

"It elicited no response, however, and he returned to his car and sat behind the wheel for several minutes more. I found it rather odd, you see, for Mr. Seeger was very much at home. His car was parked in the drive. He chose not to answer the door."

"That's interestin', ain't it?"

"Still, the young man walked to the door once again carrying a paper in his hand. He knocked on the doorframe, and when there was no response, he opened the screen and tucked the paper into the frame, closing the screen to secure it. He then drove off the way he'd come, heading east toward Main."

"You make a real fine witness, ma'am. Your eye for detail is exceptional, it really and truly is."

"Thank you. I'd hoped to become a novelist, and deliberately honed what observational faculties I possessed. As fortune would have it, that ambition went unfulfilled. That, as well as others." She smiled softly, to herself more than Earl, and sipped again at her tea. "I taught English in a secondary school for forty-eight years, and found it thoroughly rewarding."

"You said he was a young man. How old would you say he was?"

"In his late thirties, or perhaps his early forties. Both seem very young to me, Sheriff. I shall celebrate my eighty-third birthday on the twenty-ninth of this coming month."

"Was that the only time you saw this man at Carl's home?"

"No. No, there was another visit in the fall. That was a bit unusual as well. It was the day after Thanksgiving. I remember because I was removing the Indian corn from my front door. I always remove it the day after Thanksgiving, as my mother did before me, in preparation for Christmas."

"So what was odd about the visit?"

"That same blue Dodge … did I mention that it was a Dodge? My younger brother has one very much like it. In any event, it pulled into the drive in the afternoon, and the driver, who was clearly a dark-haired male, but whom I was unable to see particularly clearly, sat in the car without getting out. He turned off the ignition when he first arrived, and yet, suddenly, and very unexpectedly, he started the engine again and drove off toward the center of Versailles without once approaching the house."

"Does seem kinda odd, don't it?"

"I'm sure there's a perfectly reasonable explanation."

"Yes, ma'am. I 'spect there is."

"If I'm not being too inquisitive, Sheriff, how did Mr. Seeger die? He was my neighbor after all, and I would regard the revelation of anything which might affect my safety here as a single woman a courtesy on your part. Or was it perhaps suicide? He did seem to have become even more irascible after his wife departed."

"We don't know how he died for sure. And we have to look into every possibility, as I reckon you'd expect."

"Of course. Yes. I do see that. Of course." She was looking at him contemplatively, intelligence in her cool brown eyes, a slight smile on her dry looking lips, her head cocked slightly away from him. "I knew your oldest sister, you know. Carrie was three years behind me at Centre College, both of us on scholarships."

"I commend you and Carrie, I surely do. It was a hard row to hoe for a woman, getting an education, when you two was young."

"The path was strewn with obstacles, yes, if I may so express it. Still, the benefits of confronting adversity are not to be undervalued. You may think that the inherited furnishings in this room suggest a privileged background, but that would be an erroneous conclusion. My family suffered severe deprivation in years past, as did so many others of my acquaintance, before and during the Depression. And you? Were you able to attend college, Sheriff?"

"No, ma'am. I went into the military before I took up law enforcement."

"I've always maintained that formal education can be overemphasized. Wide-ranging curiosity. A dedication to excellence. Respect for the unvarnished truth. Those are what matter most in the final analysis. Though whether one can maintain the last, and continue to be elected by the populace we have today remains to be seen."

"It ain't easy, that's for sure. I feel called to law enforcement, but I don't take to politics. Never have. And I cain't say I'm lookin' forward to fightin' this comin' election."

"The electorate *can* be terribly fickle. And the news sources we have today seem very much taken with sensationalism."

"True. 'Course, I reckon they always was subject to pressure, and pro'bly prejudice too. But thank you for your help. I'll send a deputy to take your statement later on today."

"One other thing, Sheriff, not that it may mean

anything. I did see what I took to be that same Dodge last night as it passed my house on its way into town."

"Was it coming from Carl's?"

"I didn't see it in the driveway. It was closer to the center of town when I looked up. I can't say for certain that it was the same car, but it looked to be the same model, and the driver was definitely male."

"Thank you, ma'am. You've been a big help. You didn't happen to get the license number? You've noticed a whole lot I wouldn't't've expected."

"I do remember that the number plate of the car in the drive on those earlier occasions contained my mother's initials, the letters E and A, together in that order. As to the rest I couldn't say."


Earl Peabody parked his big Ford Sedan in the circle in front of Jo and Alan's house, just behind Alan's Dodge. He studied the license plate, and made a note on the pad in his shirt pocket, then picked up his satchel and opened the car door. Emmy was there, wagging her whole body, and he stopped to rub behind her ears before he climbed out of his car in his perfectly creased tan uniform.

It'd turned out to be a gorgeous day, cooler than normal, somewhere in the middle-eighties, the sky a shining porcelain blue, the clouds high and huge and blinding-white, blowing soft out of the west. He stood there, and stared at the sky, and the green rolling land spread out around him on that high ridge the old house rode, edged by hardwoods and horse fencing.

He slammed the white door with the Sheriff's shield decal stuck in the center of it, and sighed as he glanced at the round blue light sticking to the roof with a magnet. He'd tried to get an official car into the departmental budget, so he didn't have to use his own car every day of his life, but with everything else they'd needed—one new deputy, two new typewriters, one of the new Xerox machines, plus a brand spanking new teletype—he'd lost the car in the shuffle.

He turned then and started toward the house, and saw Jo on the porch steps. "Hey, Jo. I didn't see ya there. How's the baby doin'?"

She'd opened the white front double doors and been standing there, tall and thin, waiting for Earl to stop staring into space. She smiled at him, and kept herself from laughing, as she propped Ross against her left shoulder. Her dark hair was pulled back in a ponytail, and her indigo eyes were smiling too, when she said, "Ross is doing fine. I have a question for you, though."

"Shoot."

"How come Toss, and folks who've known you a long time, call you Stump?"

He laughed and smoothed his windblown hair, then pushed his glasses up his large bony nose. "Shucks, Jo, it started-up in high school. Goes back to when this teacher nobody cared for much, 'cause he was kinda sharp and critical, he asked me a question one day when I wasn't payin' attention. He said, 'Come on, Earl, don't sit there like a stump. Try to answer the question.' Everybody thought that was real funny, and since I was near a foot taller than him, and he looked like a stump in comparison, it made it funnier too. So is Alan home, is he?"

"Yep. Come on in. He's getting you both some iced tea. I can make you a sandwich if you'd like."

"That's mighty kind, but I already had my lunch. We can talk while Alan eats his."

They'd sat down under the back arbor, and Alan said, "So what's up with you?", then took a bite of his chicken salad sandwich with his eyes on Earl's big broad face with its carefully neutral expression. "Why'd you ask me to meet you here on my lunch hour?"

"I figured it'd be easier than talking at Equine. I got called over to Carl Seeger's this morning by Esther Wilkes, the maid who worked for him one day a week. She found him dead in his bed first thing this mornin'."

"What?" Alan set the sandwich on his plate and stared hard at Earl. "What did he die of?"

"Don't rightly know."

"He was definitely a chain smoker. That couldn't have done him much good."

"There was a half-empty vial of somethin' on the table beside his bed, and a puncture wound in his left arm, and a syringe there, lyin' on the floor. One of them new plastic types you can throw away. You know if he was right handed?"

Alan stared out across the lawn, as though he were picturing Carl, before he said, "I think so. But I can't say for sure."

"Looks like he died early evening of yesterday, though I don't know that for certain. Wasn't earlier than that, and I don't think a whole lot later, based on what the medical examiner said after seein' him at the house."

"I don't know what to say. It somehow doesn't seem possible."

"Yep."

"What was in the vial?"

"Don't rightly know."

"I can't really picture him committing suicide."

"No?"

"He was too enamored with himself. But then I didn't know him that well."

"His cat was dead too. And there was drops of the fluid from the vial by Carl's bed there on the floor beside her body, like she'd been injected too maybe. The M.E. will check her out, to see if he can find an injection site."

"What kind of person would do that? Deliberately kill a cat?"

"Don't know. But you could be a big help if you'd take a look at a couple things."

"Sure."

"Carl left what looks like a suicide note, but he hid a journal too, and it's real contradictory to what got said in the note."

"How?"

"Well, first, you got any idea what that fluid might be? Thought maybe it might be somethin' Carl got from Equine." Earl pulled two plastic bags out of his satchel and handed them to Alan—one containing the glass vial with the black plastic lid, the other a wet looking Q-tip. "We've already photographed and printed the vial, and taken samples of the fluid, so you can take the lid off and give it a sniff. We took prints ourselves, but we'll send everything along to the state police lab in Frankfort too. The other bag's got the swab we used to take a sample of the fluid on the floor by the cat. Seems like the same thing to us."

Alan unscrewed the lid, using the plastic bag to keep from leaving prints, and held the bottle three or four inches below his nose, then waved his other hand toward his face across the open top so he could get a whiff without inhaling much, in case the substance was toxic.

Alan screwed the lid back on, then smelled the Q-tip, and said, "It's the same substance in both. It's made by Bayer in Germany. It's called Bayer L 13/59. It's generally known as Dylox here in the States. It's an organophosphate we've tested at Equine, but decided not to work with."

"What's an organophosphate?"

"An insecticide. Bob wanted us to investigate treatments for fleas and lice and ringworm. But we both agreed this was too toxic, and he's decided it's not a product line he wants to get into. Not as an application for using on horses, and not with a product like that. Nor does he want to expand now into products for dogs and cats. We stopped the experiments last summer, having done a handful of tests in the lab."

"So Carl would've known about it?"

"Sure. He did some of the bench work."

"Could it kill somebody?"

"Oh, yeah. But an analytical lab would have a heck of a time identifying it in human tissue. At least with the instruments most of them have now. It works by inhibiting acetyl-cholinesterase. So basically, without going into all the chemistry, in addition to everything else it does, it would paralyze the respiratory center, and you'd stop breathing fast. If you ate it, you'd be sick as a dog before you died. But if you injected it, you'd die within seconds, and pretty much painlessly. Even if you just injected it in a muscle death would be that quick. You wouldn't have to shoot it directly into a vein."

"It'd kill a cat too?"

"Oh, sure. Bob could tell you a lot more about it. I'm a chemical engineer. He's a pathologist, as well as a vet."

"That's a brand new way to kill somebody that not too many would know about." Earl was leaning back in his director's chair, the chair's front legs off the ground, his thumbs hooked inside his belt, his big legs straight in front of him, his eyes fixed on Alan.

"But Carl would've known all about it."

"I'd like ya to take a look at this." Earl pulled the plastic bag out of his satchel and handed it to Alan. "I found that syringe by Carl's bed."

Alan held the bag up and studied it without taking the syringe out. "It's one of the disposable types labs and doctors are starting to use."

Neither of them said anything else for a while. Alan ate the rest of his sandwich, and drank some of his iced tea. Earl sipped, then hummed for a minute, something that sounded almost like a hymn, but could've been an old time mountain song. "I told you about the note."

"Yeah."

"I got me a Xerox here." He handed it to Alan, who read it fast, then shook his head in disbelief. "That makes it sound like he couldn't go on because of losing his job, and his wife, and then having the cat die on him. Right?"

"Yep. That make sense to you?"

Alan stared at the pond for a second, before he turned to Earl. "Not really. But like I said, I didn't know him that well."

"Did you like what you did know?"

"No. I didn't. He took a formula Bob and I developed up to a guy in Canada and tried to get him to manufacture it up there, which was stealing, first of all, and a violation of his contract too. He did it in cahoots with Butch Morgan, who was production manager then. But Carl was definitely the instigator. When Bob brought in the lawyers, and fired Carl, and made that all go away, when he could've gotten Carl sent to jail, was Carl grateful that he didn't? No. Carl sicced his neighbor, who's an IRS auditor, onto Equine Pharmaceuticals. He spent two months hounding Bob and only found two thousand bucks in inventory allocation that could even be considered iffy, and then only depending on how one accountant or another decides to interpret it. So basically he found nothing."

"Bein' investigated musta burned Bob."

"It did. But I'm the one Carl hated. He thought every attempt I made to improve processes in the lab, which is what I was hired to do, was nothing but a personal attack."

"So that's gone on awhile."

"Almost two years. Pretty much since the day I arrived. And then I found out two weeks ago—when the auditor showed up here unannounced—that Carl had also gotten him to investigate Jo and me, *and* her part-time architectural business, *and* the broodmare-care business Toss runs with her. Carl was a vindictive person, Earl. And he'd started a vendetta against me."

"Anybody corroborate that?"

"Sure. Bob Harrison. His lawyer. Jo. Does it need corroboration?"

"Would you say Bob holds a grudge?"

"No. I mean he's disgusted by Carl, like you'd expect. But nothing out of the ordinary. He's reacted like an honest man faced with someone who's dishonest who's done him deliberate harm. You have to learn to see it for what it is, and then go on about your business. Bob's worked for a big pharmaceutical company. He's had his own equine vet practice. He's taught in vet schools. He's got all kinds of experience with business politics and career ambition, and he knows how to walk away."

Earl didn't say anything else for a minute. He just gazed out at the pond, tapping his index fingers on the arms of his chair. "Carl said it was you who'd been threatenin' and tormentin' him. Said he feared for his life at your hands. Not those words exactly, but that's the gist of it."

"What! Where'd he say that?"

"In a journal he hid for safe keepin'."

"Crap." Alan stared at Earl for a minute, his heart picking up speed, a wave of heat rolling up his chest, cresting against his face. "May I see the journal?"

Earl hesitated and crossed his arms before he said, "Don't figure it'd be proper for me to let ya see it."

Jo walked out of the kitchen, and stood behind them, right at the back of the arbor. "Earl, your deputy's here. Pete somebody."

"Phelps. Thanks. Would you mind tellin' him to wait in his truck? I'll be there in a second."

Jo nodded and went back in the house, before Alan said, "What's going on Earl?"

"You ever seen this?" He handed Alan the plastic bag holding the black enamel pen with the engraved gold rim.

Alan looked at it without taking it out, and said, "Jo gave it to me as a wedding present. It's been missing a couple of weeks. I had it in my desk in the lab, and then it just disappeared. I came to work and it was gone. I lock my desk when I leave at night, and my office too, so having it go missing didn't make sense. I asked people in the lab if they'd seen it, thinking maybe I left it someplace, or it fell out of my pocket. So they'll pro'bly know how long ago that was. Where did you find it?"

"Under Carl's bed. Right under his body."

"No!" Alan swung his chair around to face Earl, his face red and his green eyes on fire, his hands crushing the arms of his chair. "I didn't put it there! I've never even been in his house. I can't believe you're telling me this!"

"I gotta ask ya, ya know I do. Where was you last night?"

"Do you really think I'd murder Carl and kill his cat? Earl! Come on! You know me. I'd never do something like that."

"I wouldn't think so. I wouldn't. But I gotta do my job."

"I know. Damn. I know you do." Alan sat frozen for a minute. He even ignored Emmy when she came up and laid her head on his knee. "I got home from work a little before six. I changed my clothes, and was going out for a walk with Emmy when the phone rang, and a man's voice said it was Virgil Shafer calling, and that a horse Bob had injected with an experimental vaccine that morning was having a bad reaction, and he couldn't get Bob on the phone. He said he'd called another vet to come out, but I should come too.

"I jumped in the car, and drove out McCracken Pike as fast as I could." Alan stopped and stared at Earl. "Nobody was there. Nobody. The horse was fine too. So I figured it was a crank call. Or something more sinister that didn't make any sense. Anyway, I got Virgil on the phone about ten last night, and he said he never called. He and his family had gone to a potluck supper and Wednesday night service at their church. That the horse had had no reaction at all, and somebody was pulling my leg."

"That make any sense?"

"No, it doesn't. I can't think of anybody who would've done it as a joke."

"What about the other guy ya mentioned. Butch."

"I s'ppose he could've done it, but it doesn't sound much like him. He's drinking a lot and kind of having trouble organizing anything. At least from what I can tell."

"How was he with Carl?"

"As far as I know they were commiserating with each other for having been treated unfairly. Strange, don't you think? When they were the ones who stole the formulas and were trying to go into business to compete with Bob?"

"Was Jo here when you got the call?"

"She was driving Jack Freeman up to Cincinnati to catch a plane to France."

"Toss?"

"Nope. He brings the pregnant mares in about five during foaling season, then goes on home for dinner. He comes back around nine or so, to keep an eye on them during the night."

"So somebody who knew you folks, and the farm here and all, could know that?"

"Yeah. They wouldn't have known Jo was going to be gone, necessarily. Even if she's working away from home, she's usually home by six. And whoever it was would have to have known that the horse was inoculated yesterday."

"Got any ideas?"

"No. Right now I'm in a state of shock."

"Somebody did see your car last night on McCracken Pike, there where it gets to be Elm Street, so you explainin' why you was there's a real good thing."

"I can't believe this is happening. I can't." Alan was breathing fast, his eyes boring into Earl, both feet tapping the old brick floor.

"Is it true that you accosted Carl at Keeneland during the races?"

"Geeze, Earl. It sounds like you're actually seeing me as a serious suspect!"

"I have to, Alan. I do. Not that I believe it. But I gotta follow through."

"I know. I know." Alan set both hands on his head and held them there while he spoke. "Yes. I did confront him at Keeneland. It was right after the IRS guy showed up here and started the 'investigation,' and

Carl walked up to me and said, with an intentionally insulting smirk on his face, how he heard I was in trouble with the IRS. He'd set the whole investigation up! And him saying that was a deliberate slap in the face. Rubbing salt in the wound might be a better way to put it. So I did yell at him. And I regretted it afterwards. And I went to his house a couple days later to apologize. He was there. His car was in the drive. But he wouldn't come to the door. So I wrote him a note of apology and stuck it in the front door."

"But you don't have a copy?"

"No. I just grabbed a legal pad out of my briefcase and wrote him a quick note."

"You ever been in Carl's house?"

"No. Never. I told you that a minute ago."

"Right. I gotta have Pete get your fingerprints. And get a sample of your handwriting too. I'm just doing that with everybody. Miz Seeger too, 'cause you never know what you'll find, and I'm just trying to anticipate every eventuality."

"Fine."

"Then I'd like to get your permission to examine your house and your car. You don't have to let me do that. You could make me get a warrant. But if you've never been in Carl's house, we can use what we find to clear your name. If there're no fragments of carpet in your shoes, or dirt from his grounds in your car, and that kinda thing, it'll help you prove your innocence."

"Fine with me. Whatever you have to do."

"You folks use Selectric typewriters at Equine?"

"We have a couple. Maybe three or four."

"Ya got one here?"

"No. Why would you ask that?"

Earl didn't say anything for a minute. He seemed to be considering how best to answer as he finished his tea and stared at the pond, then leaned forward with his elbows on his thighs, clasping his hands between his knees. "I think it'd be better if I didn't explain. It'd make it better for you in the long run."

"Really!"

"Down the road, if it comes to it, would you be willin' to take a polygraph test?"

"Of course I would. I'm telling you the truth."

"Good. I reckon you folks use some kinda gloves in the lab for doin' experiments?"

"Yeah. We use B&D plastic disposable syringes too, just like the one you showed me."

"That saved me a question. Thanks. And I figure it's to your credit for bein' real straightforward.

"I didn't kill him, Earl. I've got nothing to hide."

"I hear what you're sayin'. And I thank you for all the help. I better get movin', though. You willing to show me your clothes and your shoes? I'll set Pete to looking through your car. I'd like to see your desk too, along with the rest of the house."

"Wherever you want to start."

"Oh, yeah. One other thing. Were you an assassin during World War II?"

"It's not what I did, no."

"Can ya tell me more than that?"

"You ever hear of Wild Bill Donovan?"

"He the guy who started some behind-the-scenes outfit that turned into the CIA? An intelligence group, kinda like the Brits had?"

"Yeah. I worked for him in Europe. Jo's brother did

too. There were demolition groups in uniform. And intelligence agents who weren't."

"Must still be pretty hush-hush. I never hear nothin' about it."

"It is. I can't legally talk about it. But I didn't assassinate anyone."


Earl left with the paddock boots Alan had worn the night before, and the black lace shoes he'd worn to work that morning. Pete Phelps took a sample of dirt from the driver-side floormat, and searched through every other part of the car, and might've taken something else—from what Jo could tell, as she watched from the porch, without any idea what was happening.

Alan came out, and was standing beside her, when Earl and Pete drove off—Earl in his sedan, Pete in his pickup, decals starting to curl on both Pete's doors.

"What's going on, Alan?" Jo had begun to feel sick, even before she stared at the hard closed-up worry that had taken control of his face. She'd never seen him at a loss before. But that's where he was now.

"Pray, Jo."

"I will. For what?"

"Help. I don't know exactly. But I'm beginning to think Carl figured out a way to make it look like I murdered him."

"What!"

"We need to give some thought to who we'd use as a lawyer if I need one. Somebody who does criminal work, not just civil."

"Alan!"

"I know. I know. I'm sorry, Jo. We'll talk about it tonight. I've got to get back to work and tell Bob what's going on too."

# CHAPTER EIGHT

Earl Peabody had called Jane Seeger at home shortly after he left Carl's house that morning. It turned out to be her day off, so he arranged to meet her at her house at two that afternoon.

She'd been a few years behind him in school, but he'd known her since they were kids, and he figured talking to her would be pretty straightforward. She'd started out as a down-to-earth sort of practical person, naïve in a way when she was young, but less so now, from what he could tell, since she'd moved back from Indiana. But then Earl figured you either learned the lessons of living longer, or got run over in the road.

'Course, he also figured if you stayed a cop long enough, you'd see so much crazy meanness you could start to thinking there weren't many decent folk left on top of the earth. It caused him to worry some, and question his wife too when he did or said something that scared him into thinking he was losing hold of his heart.

But when he was driving to the office from Alan's, he got to thinking about his dad. How he'd lost the farm and had to move to town because of the Depression with hardly a word of complaint. And then he started wondering how many young folks in 1964 knew how good they'd got it. Or would've been able to face hard facts the way folks before them had, too many days to count.

He knew he couldn't answer it. And he told himself to concentrate on organizing the evidence to get it driven up to Frankfort to the state police lab before the end of the day. He'd gather materials at Equine that afternoon too, and get them up there the next day, hopefully before noon.


Talking to Janie an hour later gave him more to go on, at least in terms of picturing Carl as a flesh-and-blood person. It surprised him in some ways too, because her divorce had just come through, and he'd expected a lot of emotion from Jane, and bitterness most likely too.

She seemed cooler than he'd figured. Analytical almost. Like she'd been figuring Seeger out over time, and had long ago lost the love and the illusions she said she'd had at the start. She told Earl she'd gotten to the point a long time before that she didn't expect hardly anything from Carl, and had stayed to honor her vows.

The respect had been the first to go, because she'd seen for herself, a couple years in, that he was kind of a vortex of a person. Which made no sense to Earl, and he'd asked her what that meant.

"He took a tendency that's a part of all of us, and shrunk himself down so it was all there was. He saw the whole of life—every person, every object, every opportunity, or kindness, or slight, only as it applied to him. Nobody was seen for who they were on their own, but only in terms of how they affected him—beneficial or harmful, one thing or the other.

"When Carl met me back in Bloomington, he saw that if he married me, my sister's husband could help him get a scholarship to IU, and provide a place for us to live rent free. So he went ahead and married me, with no more thought than he'd give to buying a pair of shoes."

Jane said she'd also seen years before that he'd lie when it suited him. When something he wanted would come of it, or something unpleasant would be avoided. "And when I asked him to do the one thing for me that would've meant the most to me, the answer was no, the instant I asked, and hasn't wavered since."

Janie didn't tell Earl what she'd asked for, but he could see it was still an open wound. And he asked if she'd been surprised when Carl stole the formula, partly just to change the subject.

"That was simply the last straw. That, and his total lack of guilt, much less a sense of thankfulness to Bob Harrison for choosing not to prosecute. But even so, I don't hate or despise Carl. I feel nothing much but weariness when I think of him, and regret that I stayed so long."

She said she hadn't talked to him for more than a month, and she was glad Esther Wilkes had decided to quit. Carl spoke to Esther with such condescension and impatience, it was time Esther was actually appreciated for the fine work she did.

When Earl asked if she knew Alan Munro, she said she'd met him only once, but she knew Jo slightly, and liked the little she'd seen. "Bob Harrison I do know, and he certainly behaved with professionalism and consideration. He was determined to put the situation behind him as quickly as possible without excessive legal entanglement, and I can understand that. But it might've done Carl an unintended disservice. It protected him once again from the painful results of his own behavior.

"He's been running from those his whole life long, and going to court might've helped him. Losing his job was something, but he rationalized it, and explained it away to his own satisfaction so he didn't have to take any blame."

Earl asked what she knew about his death. And if Carl brought chemicals home from the lab. And if Alan Munro had seemed hostile, or threatened Carl in anyway.

Jane stirred her coffee before she answered, and then stared down at her hands. "Suicide would be a surprise. Other than that I can't say. I never knew Carl to bring substances home from the lab, and as far as I know Alan Munro never treated Carl in any way that was anything but professional. Carl fought against Alan from the day Alan arrived at Equine. Primarily because, from what I could tell, Carl was secretly afraid Alan knew more than he did, and he wouldn't be able to keep up."

When Earl asked how the divorce had gone through as fast as it had, she said, "Because I asked for nothing. Not the house, not the furniture, no money whatsoever. I took two rose bushes and three camellias and an antique stone dog from the garden beds in back, and left the rest of my past behind."

Jane gave Earl a sample of her handwriting, and let

herself be fingerprinted, and agreed to come to the office on Friday to give him a formal statement.

Then Earl finally asked where she'd been the night before.

"I was working on the research desk in the history library at UK from one p.m. until nine."

She'd said it quietly, before sipping her coffee, a furry brown puppy asleep by her feet, and she'd looked to Earl like a woman who'd settled into her own life exactly the way she wanted. Like she'd thought a lot about what mattered, and found some sort of peace that didn't depend on anyone else, but facts she'd faced herself.

That's what Earl told his wife on the phone that afternoon, when he'd called to say he'd be late coming home. That when he'd asked Janie how she felt about Carl's death, she'd looked at the wall behind him for a minute, then opened a drawer in the table by her chair and pulled out a spiral notebook.

"I feel nothing about his death for me. I'm not sad, or glad, or relieved. The tragedy was his. He wasted what he was given. He never saw that anything *was* a gift. Or there was any better way to live."

She'd said, "This may sound strange to you, Earl. And I surprised myself when I did it. But after I left Carl I copied out every reference to forgiveness in the Bible in this notebook. And when I was done, I was done with it. With the hurt, and the anger, and the wanting him to suffer I'd felt before."

It'd made Earl feel real uncomfortable. Like it was something extreme, and too personal to hear about. But his wife had said, "That musta been hard for her, and

I'm real glad it did her good. I'd like to have her over for supper, when you're done workin' on this case."

Earl had said, "Sure. I guess." And hung up the phone, hoping Jane wouldn't bring it up, if she did come over to eat.

Bob Harrison's secretary ushered Earl into Bob's office at four thirty-five, and said he'd be there as soon as the lab meeting finished.

Earl walked around from wall to wall reading the captions to a collection of black-framed black-and-white photos—some big, some small, the early ones faded and grainy.

The first showed Bob in 1930, the year he graduated from Ohio State's vet school, hunkered down by a cow's udder. The next showed him in 1934, working in a vet practice, standing beside a draft horse whose ribs were sticking out and whose head was hanging low. That was followed by a shot two months later when the Percheron looked fat and happy and Harrison was beaming.

The next photo showed him in 1939 sitting at a desk in Rahway, New Jersey, in Merck's Institute for Therapeutic Research, a masters diploma in pathology hanging above the desk.

The one after that showed him in a big plant during WWII with rows of covered metal tanks, where a whole group of pharmaceutical companies were working together to develop something called "submerged fermentation" to produce penicillin for America's troops.

Earl was looking at the photo of Bob in 1950,

staring down the throat of Hill Prince, that year's Horse of the Year, with someone named Dr. Elvis Doll from the UK vet school—when Bob walked through the door.

They shook hands, as Bob said, "Well, at least we have one thing in common. Your glasses are exactly like mine. Your wife pick yours too?"

They both laughed as they sat down in the two chairs in front of Bob's neatly organized black metal desk.

Earl reached in his shirt pocket and pulled out his notebook, as he said, "Looks like you've had a real interesting life."

"I've been very fortunate. If businessmen in Plain City, Ohio hadn't gotten together and helped me go to college, my life would've been entirely different."

"Bet that don't happen too often."

"Those men assisted several. Eight members of the Chamber of Commerce, they got together and helped pay my way. And because of the start they gave me I was able to learn from some really outstanding scientists, before and after the war."

"How you'd end up startin' Equine?"

"I got frustrated being a large animal vet in the thirties. We could diagnose fairly well, but there wasn't much we could treat. I wanted to help develop drugs and treatments. And ended up wanting to have my own business so I could control my own work. Took me a good long while to get it up and running, though. Antibiotics and the new vaccines? They've revolutionized the world."

"They have. They surely have. Penicillin alone."

"So anyway, Alan came to me after lunch and told

me about Carl's death. It was a big surprise to both of us, Alan as much as me. Especially since the Dylox must've come from here. The UK vet lab might have some, but with Carl having worked here, I presume this is where he got it."

Earl said, "You're figuring it was suicide then?"

"I don't have enough data to have an opinion. But I can't imagine anyone else from Equine, including Alan, murdering Carl."

Earl laid his huge hands on his knees and leaned toward Bob Harrison. "Do I have your permission to examine your laboratory for materials that might be pertinent?"

Harrison folded his arms across his rib cage—his gray eyes studying Earl behind the thick lens. "You do have my permission, but I wonder if you could give me some idea what it is you're searching for."

"Surgical gloves. Typing paper. Glass vials and plastic syringes to compare to those at the scene. I can come back with a search warrant, but—"

"No, we'll cooperate in any way we can."

"Thank you. I decided I oughtta come late in the day 'cause I figured it might be easier for y'all if I went through the lab after the lab folks left. It'd be less disruptive, if ya see what I mean. Not get everybody talkin'. 'Course I'll most likely have to come back another time to interview a couple a people, once I see my way clear."

"You do realize that Carl would've had access here to all those materials?"

"I wouldda figured that once you'd fired somebody who'd up and stole a formula you wouldda taken the first opportunity to change all the locks."

"We did. The same night I fired him."

"When was that exactly?"

"Friday evening, August ninth."

Earl made a note in his notebook before he looked up at Bob. "So, if I understand you right, you're sayin' Carl would've gathered the materials I mentioned that were found at the scene before you let him go?"

"No. I imagine he'd have come up with some way to get in after he was fired. Carl wasn't an honest person, Sheriff. He was also very adept at persuading other people to do his bidding without them recognizing the purpose he had in mind."

"So you're sayin' he wouldda found a way to get a key and get in?"

"I think so. *If* he committed suicide. Which does strike me—and this is pure speculation—as fundamentally out of character."

"That's what Alan said too." Earl slipped his notebook in his shirt pocket and buttoned the flap before he spoke. "So would it be too much to say, that with him trying to steal your formulas, and bringing the IRS here and all, you bear him some kinda grudge?"

"Yes, it would be too much to say. I never would've trusted him again, and I wouldn't have given him a reference, but I didn't even choose to prosecute him when I certainly could have. I have better things to do with my time, *and* my mind, Sheriff, than to let myself dwell on a man like Carl. I dealt with the situation, and I'm getting on with my work, which I find much more compelling."

"I can see that. 'Specially with what you do. Would this be a good time for you to show me the lab? That's if you figure your folks'll all be gone."

"Everyone but Alan. He'll still be working."


Bob took Earl into the supply room off the lab and watched him take samples of gloves, syringes and plastic-lidded vials from the boxes on the shelves. Earl wrote down the manufacturers, and the lot numbers, and any other information he could find.

Bob then pulled out their bottle of Dylox, and used a bulb pipette to put a sample in a sterilized vial for Earl to take as well.

Alan showed Earl where there were opened boxes of gloves, syringes and vials in the cabinets under the lab benches, and Earl took samples, and notes on the manufacturers' lot numbers from those too. Then he took samples of the second sheets of the letterhead, and the everyday typing paper, from the lab secretary's desk.

He typed something on the proportional space IBM Bob's secretary used, the accounting department Selectric, and the Selectric in the sales department. He typed another sample on the Selectric in the lab. And after having looked through all the boxes of Selectric type balls in those offices, he put a Courier font ball from the lab secretary's desk drawer into a plastic bag —while Alan stood by and watched.

"I know she ordered a new ball of one of the fonts and it came from IBM fairly recently. Which typeface I'm not sure, but she said one of the letters was chipped on the typeface that she thinks is easiest to read."

"I need to take this one with me. I've written a receipt for the items I'm taking, and I'll give it to Bob before I leave."

"Why are you taking the Selectric ball?"

"It could be connected to the investigation. Can you think of anyway Carl could've gotten back in the lab when no one was around after the locks were changed?"

"Someone could've met him and let him in I guess. Though I can't think who that would be. It'd have to be someone with keys to the front, *or* the plant door, and keys to the lab too. And in order to take my pen, he'd have to have gotten keys to my office and my desk."

"Was there anyone here he was particularly close to?"

"Not that I know of. He didn't seem to make friends very easily. He did stop by the houses of two people from the lab after he was fired. Stopped by more than once, I think."

"Could you give me their names?"

"Sure." Earl wrote them down before Alan said, "He made them both uncomfortable. They came and talked to me about it, hoping I'd try to persuade him to stop."

"Did you?"

"No. I thought about it. But I decided that me getting in touch with him might make it even worse. I was doing an errand near his house the day after Thanksgiving, and I drove over, but then changed my mind and left without getting out. He stopped on his own right about then. At least no one's mentioned it if he kept it up. I can't think how Butch could've gotten keys either. He's been pretty belligerent with folks when he happens to run into them."

"What's he doing for a living?"

"He was working as an auto mechanic last I heard. Whether he still is I don't know."

"Where, do you know?"

"I don't. No. But I guess one thing you ought to know is that since he was fired, I've gotten calls from Butch in the middle of the night every couple of weeks. Two, three o'clock, something like that, when he's really loaded and feeling the need to tell me how much he loathes me. I don't think he's violent, or anything, and I see no reason whatever why'd he'd want to kill Carl. But he'd be more than happy if the death could be pinned on me."

"Then I better have a talk with Butch."

"Bob's secretary oversees personnel, so Bob should be able to find his address in her files."

"Thanks. If ya think of anything else that seems related, let me know. Unfortunately, we're spread kinda thin right now. We had a farm break-in and robbery two weeks ago, and—"

"I read about that. Wasn't it one of the big farms near Midway?"

"Yeah, and another one last night. So there's plenty of folks screaming for my blood, and round-the-clock protection."

"I'll bet. Anything valuable stolen?"

"Jewelry worth a whole lot last night, and a silver tea set, and trophies too, and some kinda fur coat. Some of the items had plenty a sentimental value, and the family's got a name around here, and with this bein' an election year, you can see how that could go. I was lookin' into Carl's death this mornin' when the theft was discovered, and I had to send a deputy out, and that didn't go over real big."

"No."

"Anyway, I think I'll get a deputy over here tomorrow to ask your lab folks and all if they've got any information, or have been in touch with Carl."

"I'll let them know one of your men'll be in."

"Thanks. Give my best to Jo." Earl looked almost embarrassed when he nodded at Alan, like he'd rather be doing anything else—that his personal feelings were fighting each other and he didn't like it one bit.


Butch was on his side porch when Earl drove up. He stayed where he was, and hollered at him to walk back around the side, and he offered Earl a beer when he took off his hat and stepped up on the porch.

"Thanks, but I won't right now. Okay if I sit?"

Butch waved a hand toward the other split-wood chair on his side of the family room slider.

Earl sat, and threw his hat on the white rope hammock hanging at the end of the porch, then pulled out his notebook. "I need to ask you a couple questions, 'cause with what's—"

"What kinda questions?"

"'Bout your relationship with Carl Seeger."

"Why? What's that gotta do with you?"

"Carl died last night in unexplained circumstances."

"Carl!"

"Yep."

"Like what? Circumstances like what?"

"Well, he might couldda killed himself, but it could be somethin' else."

"You sayin' he was murdered?" Butch was holding the bottle of Bud so it dangled loosely from his left hand, hanging over the arm of his chair. He was slouching against the back, his legs stretched out wide across the porch.

"Don't know. I gotta look at it all. When was the last time you talked to him?"

"Me? Three or four weeks maybe. I don't keep in touch much."

"Why's that? I thought you two were good friends?"

"No, sir. We worked together was all."

"Weren't you plannin' to get into business together too?"

"Who told ya that? Alan Munro! Bob Harrison? They can go to hell!"

"Sounds like you're bearin' 'em some kinda grudge."

"Munro ruined my life! He come to Equine and took over everything. He lied to Bob Harrison about me, and everythin' fell apart!"

"How'd he lie?"

"Made it sound like I don't know nothin'.'"

"So you didn't try to steal their formulas?"

Butch didn't say anything then. He finished his beer and set the bottle carefully on the table between them as though he were afraid he couldn't if he didn't concentrate.

"Well? Did you and Carl do that or not?"

"It was Carl's idea. I wish I hadn't gone along. I wish I'd never listened."

"Would Carl have had any way of getting new keys to Equine after the locks was changed?"

"I don't know. I don't know nothin' about it. But if Carl wanted keys, I reckon he'd find a way."

"He didn't say anything to you about tryin' to get keys or nothin'?"

"Nope." Butch's dark hair was hanging down on the collar of his work shirt. His jeans looked dirty, and there was grease under his fingernails. He hadn't shaved in days and the strong, square, good-looking face, in spite of the pock mocks he'd always hated, was starting to look soft around the jaw. "How'd he die? You can tell me that. You know it'll be in the papers."

"Looks like he died from some kinda poison."

Butch looked right at Earl, his eyes suddenly focusing. "What kinda poison?"

"We're not releasing that to the public."

"Lots a poisons at Equine to choose from. You better look into it real close. Even if Mr. Robert Harrison contributes to your campaign fund."

"He doesn't. Neither does Mr. Munro."

"'Mr. Munro?' You know Alan, don't ya? From that killing years ago."

"I've interviewed him, as you'd expect."

"You knew him before?"

"That's not your business. You need to be concerned with your own—"

"*He*'s why you're here! Munro sent you to investigate me!"

"No, Mr. Morgan. He didn't. Here's my card. If you think of anything that might be connected to Carl's death, you need to give me a call."

"If you're lookin' for a murderer, Alan Munro's where ya look."

"Why? What evidence do you have?"

"Motive. He hated Carl's guts, just like he does mine. You tell him for me, I ain't gonna forget he sent ya here to me!"

*Friday, April 17th, 1964*

First thing the next morning, Earl had to deal with the wealthy family that'd just been robbed, and he sent Pete Phelps, his most experienced deputy, to Equine. Pete asked the lab folks if any supplies had been missed from the lab benches or the supply room, and got a "not that we noticed." He asked if Carl had approached anyone with a request to copy their keys, and the people in the lab, the plant, and every other department gave him a negative response.

He made a plea to everyone to contact the Sheriff if they had any knowledge concerning Carl's death, or had been in touch with him any time that spring. He took the two men Carl had visited in the fall off on their own and asked what they could tell him, which amounted to next to nothing.

He asked the receptionist if she'd seen Carl approaching, or coming into the building since his employment ended the previous August. And when she said no, Pete Phelps left.

When Earl had done what he could to mollify the big Midway farm owners, he drove out and questioned Jo about what she knew—which didn't turn out to be much. Everything was secondhand, or supposition on her part. She'd been appalled by Carl's attempt to steal the formulas, and his deliberate attempts to persecute Bob Harrison and her family with the IRS investigation, which should be about fairness and justice, not imposing the government's power to carry out targeted vendettas. She told Earl she'd met Carl, but never known him, and she'd been driving Jack Freeman to the Cincinnati airport the afternoon of the fifteenth, then driven home alone, getting back about eight.

Earl talked to Toss for ten or fifteen minutes, the preponderance of which was spent discussing Carl's vindictiveness and the hubris of the IRS investigator he'd foisted upon them.

Earl told Jo not to worry, and drove away in the rain.


Jo and Alan hadn't been out to dinner without Ross for five or six weeks, but that night they got a sitter and went to a small quiet restaurant on the Lexington Road a mile or so east of downtown Versailles.

They spent the whole time going over the evidence that looked like it'd been planted in Carl's house—the pen, the syringe, the vial, the Dylox, and maybe a glove (or a fragment thereof), because why else would Earl be so interested in Equine's gloves? They then came to the tentative conclusion that the suicide note must not have been typed on Carl's own typewriter, and maybe not on the paper found in the house. Because why else would Earl have taken the IBM typeface ball, and the paper samples too?

That meant Jo picked at her food. And Alan turned silent, after asking more than once how Earl could think that he'd make mistakes that were that stupid.

They walked out into a hot humid Kentucky night —the sun down, the bugs buzzing, the streetlights already on—with worry walking inside them.

Alan was pulling his keys out of his pants pocket,

when Jo laid a hand on his arm, and said, "Look over at the car."

Butch Morgan was leaning against the passenger fender ten feet away, his arms crossed, his clothes clean, his eyes looking glazed and unfocused.

"Hey! Alan! Saw your car. Thought I'd wait and say hello."

"Butch." Alan slipped the keys in his coat pocket as he stepped halfway in front of Jo, then stood with his arms hanging loose at his sides.

"Looks like you're in big trouble this time. R-e-a-l big trouble. Murder! I told the Sheriff where he oughtta look and he took it right ta heart. Wantta come in the Oaken Bucket and talk about it awhile?" He was yelling, and people were looking at him, and at Alan and Jo, then turning away and hurrying on.

"We have to go rescue the babysitter, and we need you to move away from the car."

"Why would I make it easy for ya? Ya never helped me! Ya lied to Bob Harrison and made me lose my job! And now, you mother, you sicced the Sheriff onto me!" He was standing a foot away from the car, unsteady on his feet, glaring across at Alan.

"No, I didn't."

"You liar!"

"I've got no quarrel with you, Butch. Just step away from the car so Jo and I can get in."

"Make me!"

"I don't want to make you. We don't need to do this. Go on in the bar and get something to eat, and we can talk another time."

"So smooth, aren't ya? So smart! So in control! You make me wantta puke!" Butch took a few steps toward Alan, then tripped suddenly, and fell, and Alan reached down to help him up, which seemed to make Butch even madder. He screamed, "Get away from me you son of a bitch! You're gonna regret this, ya hear me! I ain't gonna let this lie!" He grabbed hold of a parking meter and pulled himself up while folks on both sides of the street watched, then glanced away.

Butch straightened up and started down the sidewalk toward the Oaken Bucket, as Alan put his arm around Jo.

They stepped off the curb, and crossed the road, and climbed into their car, not saying a word—Jo feeling sick to her stomach, Alan keeping his eyes fastened right on Butch.

### Sunday, April 19th, 1964

Sunday afternoon, having called Saturday and made arrangements, Earl drove over to Esther Wilkes' house in Frog Town to talk to her and her twin brother, Charlie Napoleon Smalls. Earl had had to time the visit between their morning church service, and the evening one they went to, and he got there right at three.

The house was perched on the top of a low hill, and he climbed up the steep front yard and knocked on the screen door of the small white clapboard house, and saw Esther walking toward him across the front room. She pushed the screen open as he said, "Afternoon, ma'am. I appreciate ya makin' time."

"No trouble at all, Sheriff. There's a cool breeze on the porch there, if you'd like to make yourself ta home. I'll bring us somethin' to drink."

Earl waited there by the door till she'd come back
carrying a tray of lemonade and cookies, then held it
open and moved a geranium off a barn siding table so
she could set the tray between the chairs.

"Charlie hasn't been to the house in a month or so,
and he's out back lookin' at the vegetable patch, but
he'll be here directly."

He walked through from the house right then, not
wearing the Clairborne Farm uniform that always
looked to be part of him, but his Sunday suit with a
starched white shirt, though he took the jacket off and
laid it on a chair at the other end of the porch.

Earl and Charlie had met before when a hot walker
had stolen a whole lot of Claiborne's tack, and they
nodded to each other, and smiled kind of neutrally, as
they both sat down on rush-seated chairs and took the
glasses of lemonade Esther handed round.

"Thank you, ma'am."

Esther said, "You're welcome, Sheriff," as she sat
and smoothed her dress. "I surely do want to cooperate,
in every way I can, but I don't understand why ya'd
want to see me again, or Charlie either one. I told you
everythin' I know about Mr. Seeger just the other
mornin'."

"It's 'cause of somethin' I found that he wrote.
According to that, he knew about the key in the garage,
and he—"

"And he let it go and never said nothin' to me?
That's real hard to believe!"

"He was sayin' he figured Mr. Alan Munro had him
a key 'cause he had a way of knowin' about the one in
the coffee can Miz Seeger left for you."

Esther was wearing a black linen dress with a wide

white lace collar, and she folded her arms across the hand-sewn tucks decorating the bodice, her eyes looking mildly put out, before she glanced away. "Sheriff, I don't know Mr. Munro, and I never told nobody 'bout that key."

"No?"

"No."

"Not even your brother Charlie here?"

"You did, Essie." Charlie was thin and strong looking, and no taller than Esther, his wide black face unlined, though there were strands of silver in his short cropped hair.

"When!" Esther stared, and shifted in her chair, before she picked up her glass.

"'Member?" Charlie was nodding at Esther, a sugar cookie in one strong hand, a tall glass filled with lemonade and crushed mint in the other.

"No, I don't."

"It was the day before Thanksgivin'. You and me we went and got the turkey from that ol' gentleman down by Harrodsburg, and we brought it here and was pluckin' it together, here in the backyard, and we got to talkin' about when we was kids, and that old German fella who owned the peach trees down the road. How he was always accusin' every little child of stealin' his peaches, and how him being so hard and mean and suspicious and all, made us all *want* to snitch some, even though we didn't 'cause Mama wouldda skinned us."

"I remember him, sure." Esther was sweeping sugar cookie crumbs off her bust, looking down the road toward a dun-colored Chevy pickup stirring up a trail of dust like a plume of smoke behind him.

"Well, ya told me he made you think of Mr. Seeger. The way he acted suspicious all the time, and like he spied on your every move, and that if he knew 'bout the key Miz Seeger left you in the garage he wouldda had a fit."

Earl asked Esther if that brought it to mind, and she said, "Maybe. Kinda vague and all. If I was gonna say it, I'd say it to Charlie, and if he remembers it that way, I reckon it's the way it was. He's always had a real good memory. He recollects all the family stories and passes 'em along."

Charlie said, "Is this real important, Sheriff?"

"Could be. I don't rightly know. But I gotta follow every lead as far as it can go."

"So you want to know right now did I tell anyone else about Esther's key?"

"I do. That's it in a nutshell."

"I'm 'fraid I did. And I ask ya to forgive me, Essie."

"How could you! You never in your life blurted out something private, even as a little child! Even when Burt held your wrist in the candle."

Earl finished the last of his lemonade, and moved the ice in his mouth to one side so he could talk around it, and asked Charlie who he'd told.

"You know Mr. Mercer Tate?"

"I do. Mostly by reputation."

"Well, the young man who's his stallion manager I've known for a good long while, and when I took one of the Claiborne mares over to him to get bred, we done the job, and got the mare in the van with a net full a real nice hay, and then we got us a Coke."

"And?" Earl picked up another cookie, his eyes fixed on Charlie.

"We talked about this and that for awhile, and how he's good friends with Jo Grant, who married Mr. Munro. I don't recall just how it come up, but he said his wife heard Jo and Alan talkin' one night, and Buddy said Carl Seeger tried to steal a formula for somethin' that Mr. Munro had come up with, and that's why he got fired." Charlie looked at Esther and waited for a minute, his hands on his knees, his feet planted straight and solid right underneath them.

Esther said, "Go on. I gotta hear it all. I don't know what got into you."

"I reckon it was knowin' all these years how cold he treated you, and Miz Seeger too, and then hearing about him being a thief, it kinda got my goat. Him not wantin' you to have a key, was like him sayin' he figured you'd steal, when you'd rather cut your hand off. And to find out *he* was a thief, I reckon I just—"

"Well? What'd you go and say?" Esther's eyes were hot, and her mouth looked like she'd bit some-thing sour.

"I said it made me feel some better to know that if Mr. Seeger had any idee Miz Seeger'd put a key in his garage for you, he'd be fit to be tied, him being so suspicious and all."

Earl looked up from his notepad and stared hard at Charlie. "Did you mention the coffee can?"

"Don't think so. Can't swear to it. This was back in the fall. Buddy and I, we laughed some. And I took my mare on home."

"Miz Wilkes? You got anythin' to add?"

"I do not. 'Cept I cain't believe Mr. Seeger knew about the key and never took me to task. That don't make no sense. And I cain't believe my own brother, who's generally real quiet, and sensible, and never gets to meddlin', would say that to Buddy Jones!"

Charlie nodded solemnly, and then picked up a sugar cookie, as Earl said, "We may need a formal statement later from y'all, but my notes is fine for now. I appreciate the cookies and lemonade. You're a fine baker, Miz Wilkes, and I thank you very kindly."

# CHAPTER NINE

*Monday, April 20th, 1964*

Buddy could've had one of the grooms who worked for him lead Arctic Ghost out of the breeding barn, the sixteen-and-a-half-hand twelve-year-old gray stallion, who bred better than he'd run. But Buddy liked him specially, and he was leading good the way he always did for Buddy, swinging his head some, but stepping careful, and Buddy brought him into the stallion barn and took the lead rope off him in his stall, and had just checked his water buckets, once he'd locked his door— when the phone rang in the tack room.

It was Becky, his wife, telling him the Sheriff had called, and wanted to see him at home on his lunch hour, and she'd told him he'd likely be home at one. Buddy asked her what he wanted, and she said she didn't know. "I didn't like to ask, with him bein' the Sheriff and all."

Buddy spent the next four hours shuffling that question around in his head, while he oversaw the scheduled breedings—handling his grooms, and the client's people, making the three owners who wanted to watch their mares get bred feel like he was being hospitable, while he made sure everything was done for their safety, for the mares' and the stallions', and the folks handling both.

It was Frankie D'Amato flickering through his mind that made Buddy feel halfway sick. Making him wonder if Frankie'd been messing around behind his back again, trashing his good name and shedding blame on him for something he couldn't imagine.

Word had it Frankie'd gone and broke a good stud's leg deliberate with a sledge hammer or something like it, to get a cut of the insurance money from the owner, who was naturally thought to be in it too. It hadn't been proved, but it was being looked into. And him knowing the lengths Frankie'd gone to before was enough to make Buddy feel real uneasy. And waiting made it worse.

At five to one, Buddy was in his truck, past Mr. Mercer's big-pillared house, turning left out the long shady drive onto Route 1685. He turned left again onto the Old Frankfort Road, driving beside moss-covered stone walls, then right between two tall stone pillars into a dark-dappled open-work woods.

He passed the old stone pioneer house that had been in Mercer Tate's family since the Revolution (that he rented now to distant cousins), curving his way to the left beyond it, then out of the woods and across the pasture where the breeding sheep grazed—black faced, and easy to startle, skinned looking too, having just gotten sheared.

The sheriff's car was in front of Buddy's house, the small stone-and-cedar farmhouse that came with his job for Mr. Tate. It was the sweetest little house he'd ever hoped to live in—a story-and-a-half peaked-roof cottage with a one-story room built off both sides. If he got him a job with a trainer the way he wanted, leaving that house would be real hard. Not half so hard as leaving Mr. Tate. That gnawed at his insides right then, soon as it come to mind.

But then Buddy slammed the door to his truck and took the front steps in one leap, his flat-heeled boots sounding hard on the flagstone stoop. He pulled off his wide straw hat as he walked through the door into the center hall, and saw Earl Peabody at the dining-room table through the living room on his left. Earl was facing Becky, with a twin on either side, sitting in their high chairs in yellow dresses, cookies clutched in greasy-looking hands.

Earl said, "You got you a fine family here, Buddy. They're eatin' real good for not being two."

Buddy nodded and said, "Thanks, Sheriff," as Becky got up and fetched him his plate from the kitchen.

"There's cold chicken and coleslaw, and I got more cornbread too, if ya want. The sheriff ate before he come. I'm puttin' the girls down for their nap, so y'all can talk in here. Would you like some more iced tea, Sheriff?"

"Thank you, but I'm doin' fine."

Becky pulled the twins out of their chairs and herded them toward the stairway, with a detour or two from both of them before their hard-soled baby shoes could be heard hitting the stairs with pauses between each one.

Buddy said, "What can I do for you, Sheriff?"

feeling his heart pounding in his ears, and his throat closing up on his chicken.

"You heard Carl Seeger died?"

"Read about it in the paper."

"I can't go into a lotta detail, but I talked to Charlie Smalls, and he told me he mentioned to you when you was shootin' the breeze in the fall that his sister had her a key to Carl's house put away in his garage. Miz Seeger'd put it there for Esther, and left it alone when she moved."

"I can't say I recall." All six–foot-three of Buddy looked hunched and squeezed into the metal dinette chair that he'd kept pushed a foot or so out from the table. He leaned over his plate, holding a fried chicken breast in his hands, pulling meat off with his teeth, his eyes looking sideways at Earl.

"Charlie said it was when you two was talkin' about how Seeger had got himself fired for stealin' a formula from Equine."

"I 'member tellin' him that."

"Charlie said something like, 'Then there was justice in Esther havin' a key when Carl wouldda been real upset. He treated her like she'd be one to steal, when he was a thief himself.'"

"Okay. Yeah, I guess that's about right." Buddy could feel the heat in his skin starting to die down, and he took a big breath and let it out, because Frankie D'Amato hadn't entered in.

"Did you tell anybody about that key? Anybody at all?"

"Why would I?"

"I don't know, but did ya?"

"I don't recall." Buddy had finished his chicken

breast and was holding his hot buttered cornbread in one hand, staring at the kitchen wall. "I didn't give it much thought, and I can't see why I'd tell anybody. Gossipin' when you're in the horse business can not only get ya fired, it can hurt a lotta folks."

"Did ya tell Becky?"

Buddy raised his voice and said, "Honey, could you come here a minute?" He wiped crumbs off his mouth with a paper napkin and swallowed half his iced tea.

They could hear Becky skipping down the stairs, and then she was in the living room, standing in the middle of the floor, six feet from the dining room doorway, a rag doll in her hand. "Buddy?"

"Did I tell you about a key bein' in that guy Carl Seeger's garage?"

"Yeah. You did. Last fall, I think."

Earl asked Becky if she'd told anybody else.

"No, I never did."

"Buddy?" Earl asked again, holding his glass in both hands.

"Nope."

Becky said, "I thought I heard you say somethin' to Jo."

"Me? When?"

"Few weeks ago. She was telling you 'bout Carl getting the IRS guy to come pester them after he finished with Mr. Harrison." Becky was short and thin, her blond hair pulled back in a ponytail, a blue-and-white checked shirt tucked into her denim skirt, her blue eyes looking nervous. "I thought you said somethin' like 'If ya ever want to leave a dead rat in his kitchen, there's a key in his garage.' You were just kiddin'. I mean you were just—"

"Me?" Buddy's hand had frozen with a forkful of coleslaw halfway to his mouth.

"You were pickin' me up at Jo's after I'd watched Ross, when Mama had the twins, and you'd been helpin' Toss out at the barn. Sometime this spring. March maybe. Or early April?"

"Okay. Maybe. Somethin' like that."

"You both sure of that?" Earl was holding his notebook, his ballpoint pen poised above the paper, his black-framed glasses sliding down his large nose, his eyes studying theirs.

Becky said, "That's the way I remember it."

"I guess, yeah. You're making it sound important, Sheriff." Buddy was beginning to look worried, like a minefield might be opening up right underneath his feet.

"Don't know that it is, but it could be. Ya mention it to anyone else?"

Buddy said, "Not that I can think of. I wouldn't a said a word about a key to some folk's house unless I thought whoever I was talkin' to could be trusted not to break in. Jo and Alan? They'd never do somethin' like that. Never in a million years."

"Did ya know Seeger, did ya?"

"Nope. Never met him."

"You know anything else about him, maybe something from Esther, or the Munros?"

"Just that he was real hard on Esther, and what he did with the formula at Equine made me think of him as a no account. The IRS business too."

"Well. If ya think of anything else connected to Seeger, give me a call at the office."

"I will."

"I'll arrange to get a deputy to take a statement later."

"Sure." Buddy got up and walked him out the door, then sat down on the stone stoop and lit himself a Marlboro with a kitchen match as he watched Earl drive away, thinking, *How am I gonna tell Jo and Alan?*

*Excerpt from Jo Grant Munro's Journal*
*Tuesday, April 28th, 1964*

*It looks as though Blue Grass's burning must've been something electrical. The insurance folks have been investigating forever, and though the final report isn't in, they've said it doesn't look like arson. Which Spencer hadn't expected, of course, but the insurance money will be critical, and I'm sure it's been hard waiting to hear what they think.*

*We haven't heard anything more from Earl, but Buddy called a week or so ago, and told us that Earl had asked him if he'd told anyone about the key in Carl's garage.*

*I've always thought you just tell the truth and even if somebody else isn't, it'll work out fine in the long run, so I never would've wanted him to hedge around it. But finding out Earl knows we knew about the key made my stomach turn over right then. Alan's too, probably, even if we didn't talk about it much.*

*There're been anxious silences every day when we've worried alone so as not to upset the other—interspersed too with feverish discussions of the circumstantial evidence Earl's got. That's when we*

*weren't talking about Ross' diarrhea, and us not*
*knowing how to make it stop.*

*But not hearing from Earl has eased us back into*
*more of a routine—of Ross, and our work, and helping*
*Toss some, of taking walks with Emmy, and me riding*
*Sam and Alan riding Maggie (who seems to have*
*gotten attached to Alan, which pleases him no end).*

*I've been praying every day that Earl's eliminated*
*Alan as a suspect, and this is not just the lull before the*
*proverbial maelstrom.*


*Thursday, April 30th, 1964*


Ross was sleeping in his buggy late that afternoon, in
the shade of a huge old maple, next to the sand riding
area just past the south barn.

Jo was sitting on Sam at the south end watching
Alan canter Maggie. She'd been asking Alan to pick up
the canter from the walk, *and* the trot, then bring
Maggie down to one gait, and then the other, to help
him work on his position in transitions, and get quick
responses from Maggie too, instead of letting her
shuffle a couple of strides before she responded to his
aids.

Jo said, "I'm glad you came home at five for once.
It's too beautiful not to ride."

"That's why I came home."

"You've really learned a lot in two years."

That made Alan laugh, before he smoothed a hand
along Maggie's neck as she rushed a couple of strides,
then settled into the canter. "Oh, yeah? Then why is
this so hard?"

"You're both learning. Good transitions take a lot of hindquarter strength too, and Maggie's just getting back in shape after having that last baby."

"Her canter's getting smoother."

Jo nodded, and had just said, "And you're beginning to get more precise in the way you apply your aids"—when she heard a car coming toward them on the long drive from the house.

It was a white sedan, and when it'd gotten close enough for her to see the insignias on the front doors, her heart lurched against her ribs, and blood rushed to her face. "Alan!" There was worry and warning and misery in her voice.

And Alan brought Maggie down to a walk, and looked across his left shoulder to see what Jo had seen.

The car stopped just north of the barn, and Earl opened the driver door and squeezed himself through. Pete Phelps climbed out the passenger door and stood looking like an embarrassed egret, as he stared into the small paddock of mares and newborn foals.

Earl nodded at Jo, and squinted at Alan as he said, "I need to talk to you a minute."

"Sure. Let me just get Maggie unsaddled and turn her out in her paddock."

"Ya reckon Jo could do that for ya?"

Alan had climbed down and was leading Maggie toward Jo, who'd already dismounted and was walking Sam toward the back of the barn. Alan met her at the open door to the aisleway and handed her his reins, before he started toward Earl, who was pulling a paper out of his shirt pocket, without taking his eyes off Alan.

"I got no choice, Alan. I feel real bad, but I gotta ask ya to come with me. I got a warrant here for your arrest for the murder of Carl Seeger. I hate doin' it, but I'm gonna hafta handcuff ya too and take ya into the department. I can cuff yer hands in front. It don't have to be in back. But that's the procedure I gotta follow."

"Earl!" Jo was white-faced and rigid, Sam and Maggie standing close together just behind her, her voice sharp, her hands gripped tight on both sets of reins, just as Ross started screaming. "He didn't kill Carl! You know better than that!"

"Can't ignore the evidence, Jo. County Attorney give me no choice. I gotta take Alan in and book him, but you go ahead and get you a lawyer, and work on makin' bond as soon as it gets set."

"Do I get to change my clothes? I'm dirty, and sweating, and I need to get cleaned up." Alan was glaring at Earl, as he peeled off his riding gloves and unbuckled his helmet.

"Sorry."

"I'm going to take my chaps off, and wash up with the hose. You can come with me and watch if you feel the need." Alan was unbuckling his rawhide chaps without looking at Earl, his face hard and angry, his green eyes, when he took off his sunglasses and wiped his forehead with the back of his hand, hot and pinched and focused on the tack room door as though nothing in this world could have made him turn aside.

Earl watched him pull the handle up on the pump in the tack room and drag the hose out behind the barn, and wash his face and hands. Jo and Earl were staring at Alan's back when Alan said, "Jo, get Bob Harrison's lawyer. Then call Bob at home and tell him what's happened."

While they took his mug shot and fingerprinted him again in the Woodford County jail in Versailles, Alan told himself to calm down and watch his mouth.

*This is nothing compared to France.*

*Demolition before D-Day.*

*Setting up local army governments.*

*You dealt with nothing but deceit.*

*Use what you learned then.*

*Listen. Read between the lines. Don't aggravate Earl.*


Earl walked him into the Sheriff's Department next door to the jail, past the old scarred counter in the front room, where a plump deputy looked up with ill-disguised hostility as they passed into Earl's office.

The brown linoleum was old and cracked, the desks —Earl's facing the door, Pete's against the wall on the left—were banged-up metal under chipped tan paint. There were gray metal chairs with red plastic seats sitting in front of Earl's desk, and Earl sat in one, and waved Alan to the other. Pete swiveled his desk chair toward them, and folded his arms across his bony-looking middle, while he stared across at Alan.

Earl pulled a stick of Juicy Fruit from his shirt pocket and peeled off the silver paper, folding it into his mouth, before he held the pack out to Alan—who shook his head and leaned back in his chair, his hands spread on the arms.

Earl sat and watched Alan for a minute with his thumbs hooked in his belt. "As you know, we got circumstantial evidence against you, and we gotta go through it again."

"You think I'm stupid enough to do it the way it was done?"

"Meaning what?"

"Use a toxin that could only come from my own lab. Leave my pen at the scene. Leave a syringe and a surgical glove. I figure there must've been a glove, or a piece of one, of the type we use in our lab there too, since you took samples from the lab. And with you taking the Selectric ball, and samples of Equine paper, there's a good chance that the note Carl left didn't match his typewriter, or his typing paper either. How dumb would I have to be to make mistakes like that?"

"Can't ignore it though, can I?"

"No, I know that, but—"

"What other explanation can you offer for the evidence? No alibi neither. Your car seen just past his house close to the time he died."

"And if I were going to go to his house, would I do it so my car would be seen? No! I'd plan it a whole lot better!"

"You gotta admit you got motive."

"What motive? That he tried to steal my formula, and he got the IRS to hassle Jo and me? I would not *murder* somebody over an IRS audit! And he didn't get *away* with stealing my formulas. He got fired. He got stopped. It means I think he was a dishonest son-of-a-pup, but it doesn't mean I'd kill him."

"There's more evidence besides what I've mentioned before."

"What? Anything new from the autopsy?"

"I'm not obligated to reveal our evidence, not at this stage of the proceedings."

"Earl, it's me. Alan Munro. Remember the murderer

I helped you arrest, when I could've killed her with my bare hands for what she did to Jo! You know in your gut I didn't do this."

"I wouldn't a thought it, but the County Attorney he don't know you from spit, and he's the one weighing the evidence and asking the judge for a warrant so he can take you to District Court."

"Do you have any evidence placing me inside Carl's house?"

"I can't answer that."

"You don't. You can't. I've never set foot in his house! You don't have my prints on the vial, or the syringe, or anything else. You can't!"

"Well, you cain't tell me you wouldn't a worn gloves."

"Right. And I wouldn't have been dumb enough to make all the other stupid mistakes!"

"The question I cain't answer, and I don't figure you can either, is why would Carl kill himself just to set you up? Unless you got some other suspect."

"I don't know. I admit that that's a serious question. And I don't have another suspect. But I'm not giving up on finding one."

"Fine."

"Do you have Carl's appointment calendar?"

"Why do you ask?"

"Well, it seems like maybe what he'd been doing, and who he was meeting, might give us some kind of clue."

"Actually, we didn't find one. And consider that a concession on my part to pass on that information."

"I do. Thank you."

Earl pulled a legal pad off his desk and handed it to

Alan. "You write down your side of things. Your history with Carl Seeger, when you went to his house like ya told me before, and all-and-everything, and what you was doin' the day and night of the fifteenth. Then Pete and me, we'll sign it after you as witnesses that it's your words."

"Crap, Earl!"

"You can wait for your lawyer if you want. If you—"

"No. I'll write it now. I don't have anything to hide."

"One thing I will tell ya, that I don't have to, is that the final ortopsy report got real delayed. The M.E. from up in Franklin who did the preliminary examination, after I talked to him that morning, he was in a real bad car accident on his lunch hour. They doubt he'll be out of the hospital for another week or ten days. They don't have nobody else to fill in. So it ain't been finished."

"That seems fairly outrageous. That they'd only have one doc."

"The other one they used some turned out to be a drunk, and they fired him not too long before all this happened, and he up and moved outta town."

"Still seems unprofessional."

"Well, we're kinda small potatoes around here. We don't get hardly any unexplained deaths, and there's never been a big need. The doc had no doubt Carl's death was caused by the injection, and his blood was on the needle and all, and the cat'd been injected too. He found that before he got hurt, but we'll have to wait for the rest."

"But you know they're going to set bond for me?"

"I reckon they will, yeah. You're not much of a flight risk, with your family and job and all. 'Course, this bein' late in the day, I reckon you'll have to spend the night, but tomorrow your lawyer can go to work, and the bond'll get set, and then Jo can talk to the bank and all, and get ya out after that."

"Not tonight?"

"I'd be surprised. And you better prepare yourself for this bein' all over the papers. This is real big for Woodford County. Lexington and Louavull, they'll be on it too. We ain't had a murder case like this in Versailles, premeditated and all, pro'bly since 1949. This ain't no knifin' outside some bar late some Saturday night."

"Except for the one two years ago."

"Right."

"When can I take the lie detector test?"

"Takes awhile to schedule it. Earliest next week."

"Jo does *not* need to go through this, Earl. She knows everybody in a fifty-mile radius, and it's bound to be horrific for her."

"I reckon that's true, but it cain't be helped."

"Still—"

"You may be kinda a newcomer 'round here, but everybody's gonna know you now, that's for darn sure."


It was past two when Alan woke up and threw the blanket off his face. He sat up shivering, sweat pouring through his shirt, his jeans sticking to his thighs, trying to see where he was.

He'd been back in France, running from a train they'd booby trapped with plastic explosives, and it was night, and there was machinegun fire behind him, and Gary Prescott had just been blown apart fifteen feet to his right.

It'd changed then the way it always did, to him running across a stone square in a tiny village up near Amiens, where he saw a guy from the French Resistance lob a grenade at a woman who'd been posing as a collaborator, but had worked with Alan and the OSS before American troops moved in.

He could see the grenade flying toward her—the perfect arc, the effortless throw—Marie not seeing it as she walked away from him. And then Alan was running faster and faster, screaming at her back. And then he felt himself stumble on a chunk of rubble and hit his face on the edge of a curb—where he watched her get ripped apart against a café window that shattered on her as she fell.

That's when he woke up, shivering and sweating, and told himself to open his eyes.

He wasn't in France.

There wasn't a grenade.

The woman he'd been trying to save had been.

He'd been ten feet away. And he hadn't stumbled.

And the war was over and done with.

He was in Versailles, Kentucky.

In jail for murdering Carl.

That made Alan laugh—and not be able to stop for longer than he could explain—before he pulled his threadbare blanket up around his shoulders, and told himself to calm down and take a deep breath.

There was light in his cell, from a streetlamp, falling on the concrete floor through the bars on the one high window in the wall on his right where he sat on his metal cot. There was light from a bulb too, in a wire cage, in the hall ceiling beyond the two-foot square of bars in the door on his left.

He heard another door open at the end of the hall, and the clap of hard-soled shoes hitting concrete, heading toward his cell.

The footsteps stopped outside his door, and he looked up and saw a small guy with yellowish skin, holding a mug of coffee in his hand, staring at him through the bars. "You okay in there?"

"Sure. I'm fine. Nothing to worry about here."

The deputy didn't answer. He blew on his coffee and took a sip, then walked back to the end of the hall and closed the door behind him.

# CHAPTER TEN

*Excerpt from Jo Grant Munro's Journal*
*Friday, May 1st, 1964*

*We debated taking out a second mortgage on the farm to make bond, which they set as half the value, which means we had to pay ten percent of that. Neither one of us wanted to put the farm in jeopardy, and put more pressure on Toss with the horse business, so we pretty much emptied the savings account, hoping we've got enough left to pay all the legal fees. Whatever they may end up being.*

*Alan's been unnervingly quiet. He never talks just to hear himself. If he has something to say, it's something worth listening to—but this quiet is different.*

*He spent a long time in the shower when he got out of jail, then shut himself away to write up what he knows about the whole situation to give to Garner Honeycutt, who's agreed to represent him.*

*We did talk at dinner, which came as a relief. I don't do well with uncomfortable silences. But we're both so much in the dark, the only good it does is to get it out in front of us.*

*We met with Garner at the jail today, when he asked Alan to write that report, and he's filed some sort of paper, telling the County Attorney (which is the same thing as a prosecutor), and I assume the District Court Judge, that he's representing Alan, and that Alan pleads not guilty. This will eliminate a preliminary hearing. Whatever that is.*

*The first hearing in District Court (which is different than what got waived) will be Monday, since they only meet on Monday in Woodford County, and Garner doesn't want to delay. This will be an open court with Alan there, when the County Attorney presents his initial case. If the judge thinks there's a "preponderance of evidence that shows probable cause," he'll "kick the case up to the grand jury."*

*The press will be there, and Garner wants to keep it short so Alan doesn't get run into the ground by the prosecution and let them prejudice the community any more than it probably is now. The news coverage has been awful. We've got reporters and TV folks camped out at the gate. And the queasy feeling around the boulder in my chest makes it hard to swallow.*

*Saturday, May 2nd, 1964*

*We took Ross with us, and spent the morning with Garner going over what we did the day Carl died, and what we know about Earl's evidence, and the questioning he's been doing. We won't get all the evidence the prosecutor has for some time to come apparently. Even the results of the autopsy, if the report's finally in.*

*I've never known much of anything about the procedures leading up to a criminal trial, and having to learn still seems surreal. But I've got to come to grips with it, and figure out how to help. Standing by and doing nothing, I've always been bad at that.*

*Alan went off on his Triumph about one this afternoon and was gone for five hours. He normally rides for an hour or so, and it scared me.*

*Tommy was killed on a bike because of somebody else's mistake, and whenever Alan goes off, I worry. Not cripplingly. I get over it. But when I see him drive in there's a definite sense of relief. He always wears a helmet (though Tommy did too, and it didn't help), which is how Alan got me wearing one when I ride horses. He calls it our anti-suicide pact.*

*It's also true that a Triumph Bonneville is notorious for losing its electrics. It's a great bike in general. Steve McQueen rode one in* The Great Escape. *But just a couple of weeks ago, Alan had to push it home when the electrical system went out.*

*And yet, now, with the murder charges, when he was gone for five hours, a small part of my overly wrought brain said, "What if he's run away?" Even though I know he wouldn't. And "What if he cracks the bike up on purpose?" When I'd pretty much stake my life on Alan never considering that.*

*That's what happens to the brain—or the heart—in traumatic situations. You call everything you know about someone into question because you're floundering in the unknown, tripping in the dark.*

*He was easier with himself when he came home.*

*Less tense. More talkative. Though still not his usual
self. And why would he be, with what he's facing? How
could he not be changed?*

*I'm writing more in my journal. Getting it down on
paper makes it easier to deal with, though why I don't
know.*


*Monday, May 4th, 1964*


"Dad! How can you be so blind! Alan Munro is an
embarrassment to Equine Pharmaceuticals. He's been
arrested for murder, and you still defend him." Brad
Harrison was standing in his father's office, his hands
on his hips, glaring at Bob across Bob's desk.

"We need to cultivate the same approach we use in
our scientific work. We can't jump to a hasty conclusion any more than we would when testing a new
drug."

"The District Court Judge just today took the evidence seriously enough that he's sent it on to the grand
jury! What more do you want?"

Bob was sliding that day's correspondence into
hanging files in a lateral file drawer with his back
turned to Brad. "You're the one who studied law.
Aren't we innocent until proven guilty?"

"I've never trusted Alan. I've told you that before."

"No, you trusted Carl. Perhaps because you shared
his animosity to Alan."

"Now wait—"

"Carl's the one who stole Alan's formulas, and
tried to start a business to compete with us! Doesn't
that mean anything to you?"

"They were your formulas."

"No. They were Alan's conceptions and formulas, based on a fungicide he brought to us. All I did was help with the very last raw material adjustments in two of the formulations."

"But—"

"And what about Carl getting the IRS to hound us for months when there was no objective reason for us to be examined?"

"I'm not defending Carl. It's Alan's ability to harm Equine I'm concerned about."

Bob swiveled his chair around to face Brad, and folded his hands on his desk. "You want my opinion on the overarching situation?"

"Yes." Brad didn't look as though he did. His nearly chinless face with its small tight-lipped mouth looked startled, and maybe even marginally frightened, as he glanced down at his dad, then turned toward the wall of photos.

"I'm going to be more blunt than I ever have been with you, because I believe the time has come. You have always felt threatened by Alan because he understands the science *and* the business at Equine in ways you don't."

"No, now when you say—"

"You've had your mother, who loves you very much, but doesn't comprehend the complexities of the business, telling you that you have a right to succeed me, and that you need to push me for faster promotion. Then you see Alan, standing in your way, and it makes you less than objective."

That was followed by a stunned silence in which the ticking of Bob's father's old brass desk clock measured off the distance between them. "I'm sorry, Brad. But that's the way it looks to me. I have real respect for Alan Munro. I don't believe he's guilty of murdering Carl, and I'm not going to throw him to the wolves when he's in trouble. How would you feel if you'd been wrongly accused of a crime? He needs to be given a fair chance."

"I'm being wrongly accused right now!"

"How so? You don't think you have a right to succeed me? Or you don't feel threatened by Alan?"

"If I'd taken the bar exam, you'd feel differently."

"Only in the sense that then you would've followed through with your original career plan. Having passed the bar would not qualify anyone to direct a company like Equine. I think you do a very good job of managing the accounting department, and I give you credit for going back and taking the accounting courses you did. But that's not the heart of the business. It's the science that created and sustains it, and it always will be. Or if not, it will have evolved into a totally different company, based on a different market. *Assuming* it can survive at all. And that's a big if, with the well-established, very large pharmaceutical competitors we struggle against for survival."

"And when Alan Munro gets convicted? What will you do then?"

"*If* he is, I'll find another chemical engineer with his kind of depth and breadth of background who can help develop the products, and the processes in the lab and manufacturing."

Brad turned, and walked out the door.

Bob sat and watched him go.

### *Tuesday, May 5th 1964*

They were all there in the plant—all of Equine's nineteen employees, standing around in a circle (except for the receptionist, who was still answering the phone at her desk, and Vincent, the custodian, who'd gone to Williamsburg on vacation with his parents, and the lab secretary too, whose husband had had a heart attack).

Bob Harrison raised his hands, and the muffled noises of an ill-at-ease crowd wound down before he spoke. "I know you've heard about Alan Munro's arrest for the murder of Carl Seeger. It's been in the papers, and there're been plenty of folks speculating around the coffee pot, just like you'd expect. I want to ask you to not speak to the press, or the TV folks, or the radio news people, or anyone else anywhere for the good of the company. I know that's a lot to ask, but I believe it's extremely important.

"I also want you to get a chance to hear Alan speak for himself. I have absolute confidence in Alan's innocence, and I hope none of you will jump to any hasty conclusions, but will cooperate and work with him the way you always do. He has much to contribute to our enterprise, as I'm sure you know."

Alan walked across the concrete floor to stand next to Bob, looking thinner than usual, and tired too, as he faced the faces around him—awkward looking, most of them, as though they'd rather be somewhere else—though some seemed to be trying to hide curiosity and excitement. One looked noticeably skeptical, and maybe even satisfied—Brad, leaning toward the woman who worked for him in accounts receivable, whispering something in her ear.

"Well ... first of all ... I never thought I'd be standing in front of anyone saying anything even vaguely like this, but I didn't murder Carl Seeger. I didn't. I had nothing whatever to do with his death, and yet circumstantial evidence has come to light that appears to the police to implicate me. It's my belief it was deliberately planted, and we're working to try to make sense of it.

"The legal process is going to take weeks— possibly even months to unfold—and I ask you *please*, to give me the benefit of the doubt, and work with me the way you always have for the good of Equine Pharmaceuticals.

"But if ... *if* ... any of you knows *anything* at all that might shed light on Carl's last months—and especially on whatever events could've led up to his death—please talk to the Woodford County Sheriff. And if you think, that in all good conscience, you could talk to me about it too, it might help me to defend myself to know whatever you know. Thank you."

Brad said, "What if what we know is even more incriminating? You want us to talk to Sheriff Peabody then?" He was smiling, as he watched Alan, in the second before Alan responded.

"If you, or anyone else knows anything pertinent, they should talk to the police. Do you know something, Brad, that'll incriminate me, or were you speaking hypothetically?"

Brad looked surprised, as he said, "Hypothetically."

Then Bob stepped up and said, "Thank you, folks." And the crowd began to break apart.

A few people came up to Alan and shook his hand and wished him well. Most walked away without saying anything, to him or anyone else.

## *Wednesday, May 6th, 1964*

"So …" Garner Honeycutt was leaning back, his long legs crossed at the knee, on an old wooden bench in the Woodford County courthouse, shoe-horned in between Jo and Allan so he could speak extremely quietly and make sure both of them heard. "As I told you the other day, this grand jury hearing is closed to you and the public. The foreman, on behalf of the jury, *could* ask for you to testify, Alan, but there's no reason to expect he will. Even so, you must remain here throughout the hearing, in case they decide to call you."

Alan nodded, then rubbed the scar on his jaw.

"The sheriff will testify, and a forensic expert may as well, probably from the state police lab where the evidence was last examined. If all twelve of the jurors, and I emphasize that unanimity, agree that the prosecution makes a compelling case, they will indict you, and send the case to Circuit Court."

Alan said, "I understand," leaning forward, elbows on his knees, refusing to look at the *Lexington Herald Leader* reporter who was smoking one cigarette after another with his eyes pinned on Alan from thirty feet down the hall. "And if they do indict me, then you'll be able to get all the evidence they've got?"

"I'll be able to go to the County Attorney's office and look through the file, yes. I've already filed a 'chain of custody of evidence' request, which will tell us who's had custody of the items, when, and in what order, in case any sort of tampering might have taken place. Not that I expect there to have been any deliberate tampering, but carelessness can't be ruled out. Asking for the order is simply a wise approach."

"Good." Jo was clutching her purse in her lap as though something important depended on it—her face drawn, her eyebrows crushed together—looking stoical but worried.

"I'll talk to the County Attorney, if the indictment's handed down here, and make the necessary arrangements to see the file tomorrow. I can copy whatever we need in its entirety using their new Xerox machine, but they'll charge at least two dollars a page, and I'll try to take as many notes as I can in order not to squander your money."

"Do what you need to do. What about copies of the photographs taken at the scene, and that sort of thing?"

"I'll arrange for those as well, though they won't come through quickly."

Jo said, "It all seems to take forever," as she dropped her purse on the floor.

"Actually, in comparison to how many cases are treated, the County Attorney seems to be hurrying this case along. But most importantly, as we begin to prepare our own case, if our contention so far is that Carl Seeger killed himself with the intent of incriminating you, formulating a reasonable motive for his suicide is where we need to focus. If you folks can think of anyone else who would've wished him dead, that'd be important, to say the least. Either way, if you can come up with other people we should interview who had dealings with him over the years, it'd be well worth the effort."

Garner Honeycutt looked across at the Sheriff's deputy—who'd opened the courtroom door, and stood, holding it open, while he nodded at Garner. Garner said, "I'll join you here shortly," as he rose to his feet, buttoning his charcoal suit coat over its matching vest. The suit fitted perfectly, and had been very good quality originally, but was worn looking and threadbare at the cuffs. His shoes were old and plain. His tie was somber. His face was composed and restrained. It didn't behoove a defense attorney to look too slick and prosperous, not with a jury in Woodford County, Commonwealth of Kentucky, in 1964.

Alan opened his briefcase and pulled out a file of lab reports and another of product field evaluations, and began reading and making occasional notes on a yellow pad. Then he put his pen down and looked at the wall across from him. "I have no idea why Carl would've killed himself. And I don't know what to do next."

"Maybe Jane Seeger would have some idea of who else we should talk to. Maybe I should go see her." Alan didn't answer. And Jo opened her case and pulled out a mechanical pencil, an architect's rule, a pad of drawing paper, and a roll of ochre tracing paper the same width as the pad.

She was working on a renovation and redesign of a small, simple farmhouse south of Versailles over-looking the Kentucky River that was about to be saved from ignominious ruin by a retired army couple who'd vacationed in the bluegrass many times in the past.

She drew the existing floor plan on the drawing pad first, then added a kitchen wing off the back on a piece of tracing paper she'd torn off the roll and smoothed across the plan. She drew, and erased, and drew again. Then balled up the tracing paper, and the sheet on the pad, and shoved them into her briefcase. "I can't get anything right. It's like the architectural part of my brain died when you got arrested!"

Alan was staring at the courtroom door, his files lying still in his lap.

"But it does pass the time." Jo drew another plan, and smoothed another sheet of tracing paper on top of it. Then drew small exterior elevations to see what would happen to the roof lines.

Alan picked up the files again, while he looked at his watch. The newspaperman had gone off, but it was too much to hope that he wouldn't come back.

Two hours later, he was walking up and down the hall, smoking one cigarette after another again, crushing them out on the floor.

He'd tried to talk to Alan and Jo when he'd first appeared, but Alan and Garner had both told him to back off, and he had so far, biding his time, till there was something new to report.

Half an hour later, a photographer arrived, and the two of them started talking baseball loud enough to irritate Jo. She looked away, as she slipped her hand inside Alan's elbow, and kissed the side of his face.

He laid his hand on her thigh, and squeezed gently in an encouraging sort of way, as he leaned over and kissed her mouth, then put the files in his case.

She whispered, "It seems to be taking an awfully long time," for what might've been the tenth time, as she slid her materials back in her briefcase.

It was right then that the door opened, and three or four people they didn't recognize came out of the courtroom, followed fast by Garner, who walked over, as Alan and Jo stood up, his face giving nothing away.

"They indicted," he said, quietly, close up between them.

And Jo said, "Crap," feeling her face turning red while her heart battered her ribs.

"The County Attorney is trying to schedule the first hearing with the Circuit Court on Wednesday, the twentieth. Otherwise we'll have to wait another month, and he doesn't want to. Which doesn't surprise me. This is an election year, and he wants to push forward so he looks like a go-getter. But that shouldn't be a problem for us. We'll have progress meetings with the judge in between to make sure we're on track with that timetable. I'll get on to the evidence tomorrow. This isn't a surprise. You shouldn't feel disheartened. Now we can get to work. Let's go out through the courtroom and take the stairs from the judge's chambers to try to avoid the press. There's quite a crowd outside."


Jack Freeman knew nothing about what Alan and Jo were going through. If he had, he would have phoned, at the very least, and might have even flown home.

He'd spent three weeks in France in total isolation trying to track down Henri Reynard and his ex-wife, Camille Benoit. He'd spent countless hours in Paris at the Musée de l'Armée, as well as newspaper archives, the American Embassy, various French government offices, and three different libraries trying to trace both. He'd found references to Henri's postwar attempts at establishing a political career that apparently went nowhere, but after that the trail disappeared. He found nothing whatever in the sources in Paris about Camille Benoit, the painter and restorer.

He stayed with his mother's Russian relations, who'd left Russia and settled in Paris months before the Revolution, and had taken his parents in after they'd escaped in 1918. His aunt and uncle had died, but their son (and his wife) had an extra room, and his sister helped Jack with his research. He'd been born in Paris, and he enjoyed speaking French again, while getting to know his cousins.

Even so, he'd left Paris on April 24th, hoping that in Tours, where he'd known Henri and Camille, where he'd worked with the Resistance and been wrongly accused of turning them in to the Gestapo, there would be some trace of a trail.

He did what he'd done in Paris. He went to government offices, libraries and newspapers—but all records that had to do with the Vichy government and the war years in Tours were closed there, as they were all across France. The telephone records offered no one named Benoit who was related to Camille. Henri Reynard wasn't listed either, and he decided not to randomly phone the other Reynards and risk alerting Henri of his presence in France.

And of course he spent too much time standing and staring at the new concrete apartment building where the café had stood in '44; the café where the Tours Resistance had been ambushed by the Gestapo and the Tours police. Its leader had been butchered there. Too many of its members had been seized, to be later tortured and killed. While he'd been taken and released in such a way that it looked as though he'd been the traitor.

Finally, when Jack was beginning to feel desperate —as though all the time and money he'd spent, and the hopes he'd had of coming to France and finding who the real traitor had been, slipped away as he lay in bed, staring up at the ceiling—he decided to visit the art museum on the slim chance that someone who worked there would know what had happened to Camille Benoit.

It felt to him like a last chance. And yet he found himself postponing the moment—walking the cobbles behind the cathedral, past the Lycée where Camille had taught in 1944; sitting in the cold, dark, much embellished church, studying the interior—before he walked to the Musée Des Beaux Arts that almost grew against the southern side of the old cathedral.

The stone walls around the museum were ten- or twelve-feet high, and it wasn't until he'd walked under the tall, pillared, carved stone arch that he could see the museum and its garden.

Then Jack hurried, running up the stone steps, rushing through the huge front door to the imposing antique reception desk, where he asked if anyone knew Camille Benoit and how he might get in touch.

It took six more days of wandering in the dark while the woman curator made undisclosed calls to unnamed contacts before he received a message from Camille. She was working at Château de la Flocellière, five hours or more southwest of Tours, restoring a painting. If he wished to meet her at the château there in the village of Flocellière, she would be willing to speak with him.

It was May 6th when he saw her face for the first time since 1944—the thick curly amber hair escaping in wisps around her face, the rest wrapped loosely, fastened with a tortoise-shell comb on the back of her elegant head. The strong bones and wide mouth. The dark eyebrows. The gray-green eyes that seemed to pierce his soul.

*Excerpt From Jo Grant Munro's Journal*
*Thursday, May 7th, 1964*

*Alan and I made love last night after he was indicted like we might never get a chance again. Like nothing else existed in the world but us trying to climb inside each other's skin. And while we loved each other, for all that time, we were free of the horror of his life being laid on a razor-thin line.*

*I woke up an hour later, half pinned under Alan, with Ross crying across the hall, on the other side of the dining room.*

*I'd breast fed him for three months, but I'd never had nearly enough milk, so I held him that night just as close and gave him a bottle of formula, and told myself I was doing what I could. Which was when I thought about the medical study I read a year or so ago in which it was claimed that the smaller one's breasts, the higher one's IQ. It may not be true, of course (medical studies being what they are), but it made me smile, when I needed to, before I kissed the side of his head.*

*I was almost dozing again myself while I rocked him, when I found myself unexpectedly remembering something Alan had told me sometime in the fall. That there'd been a lab supply distributor that Carl had bought a lot of stuff from, who lost Equine's business after Carl left when they found they could buy more cheaply from other suppliers. Someone had said he was upset with Carl, though I don't think I ever knew why.*

*When I got back to bed, Alan was awake, and I asked him what he knew about the guy, and he said he'd look into it.*

*Alan took his lie detector test this afternoon. He seemed to be very calm about it, because he said every answer he gave was true, and if the test was reliable at all, they'd figure that out. It can't be introduced as evidence, but it may help Earl begin to rethink his assumption of Alan's guilt. I just hope the test results end up being accurate.*

*Friday, May 8th, 1964*

Spencer trailered Tracker over about five thirty, and he and Alan rode cross country for over an hour while Jo watched Ross and cooked dinner. She'd always cooked more elaborate dinners on Friday night than normal, making it into a minor celebration when they sat and talked longer than usual, and even drank a glass of wine, while they looked back on the week, and discussed what they were reading, and planned the rest of the weekend.

They ate in the dining room (where they always ate when they weren't out under the arbor), and they used good china and silver from Alan's mother's family. That night it was chicken in mustard sauce, with brown rice and mushrooms, and crisp cooked kale from Toss' garden.

Alan opened a bottle of wine from the Rhone Valley that his mother's family had sent him from France. And they talked of what had befallen them all since they'd last had dinner.

"I was all set to manage the barn manufacturer, but Blue Grass burning down made me reconsider. Rebuilding would cost an arm and a leg, even with the insurance money, and there's not much left of the business. If we tried to start up again, I'd still be left with Richard and Martha outvoting me. So …" Spencer had been twirling his wine in his glass, watching the deep red swirl, before he thoughtfully inhaled the fruit and spices, and took another sip. "I decided to talk to Everett Adams."

Jo said, "I know Everett. He was pretty much my parents' age, and he used to manufacture some kind of small equipment for the war effort. He got into horse vans afterwards. Right? I haven't seen him in three or four years."

"Yeah, that's exactly right. So to make a very long story short"—Spencer held his glass out toward Alan, who poured him another inch in the big balloon glass —"he and I have come to an agreement. I'll buy him out over time, giving him a steady income without a huge one-lump-sum to have to pay taxes on, while I try to combine our businesses."

"What about Richard and Martha?" Alan set his elbows on the table as he looked across at Spencer.

"Their advisors told them there's not enough left of Blue Grass's client base to make it worthwhile to try to rebuild. So they'll take two-thirds of the insurance money, and I'll take my third, assuming, of course, that we actually get it, and use it toward buying Everett's.

We'll sell the Blue Grass land, and what's left of the buildings. The small warehouse is still intact, and it's a good commercial location. We may have to pay for the demolition, but someone will end up buying."

Alan said, "Buying out Adams sounds like a real commitment."

"It is. I've been evaluating Everett's operation, which has plusses and minuses like you'd expect. And I'm hoping I can bring back the folks who worked at Blue Grass I really relied on, and attract our old customer base too, adding it to his. It's risky. I'll sell the farm if I have to, but it's what I want to do. Maybe you guys can help me come up with a new name that's similar to the old one, but different enough too."

Jo said, "Didn't Everett have a son in the business?"

"A mechanical engineer. That's what made Everett willing to sell. His son got an offer to work for someone up in Pennsylvania he went to college with who makes medical prosthetics, and he finds that more interesting. Which I can understand too."

"Yeah. More rice?" Alan passed the bowl to Spencer and asked how Richard and Martha were taking it.

"They think they're being unfairly treated. As though I haven't taken care of them the way I should. But I have to make a life, and do what I know how to do, and work with people I trust."

Jo said, "Good for you."

"We're going to have to sell Mom and Dad's house too, which bothers me, because they loved it so much, but taxes have to be paid. Martha's going to have to get a real job, and so is Richard. And I think that's what they both need."

"What about the woman you were dating from the barn building company?"

"Elizabeth. We're still going out, but I can't rush into anything, that's for sure. And if she's as serious a person as I think she is, she won't run from the risk, and will find the horse business interesting."

Jo said, "Good. I hope so. I like her."

Alan was pouring coffee into his cup and Jo's, and refilling Spencer's. "Have you ever had Buffalo Trace bourbon? I almost never drink any kind of liquor, but a guy I work with gave me a bottle for Christmas, and I've never even opened it. You want to try a taste?"

Spencer raised his eyebrows, and smiled across at Alan. "Sure. I guess. I don't drink much whisky either. Maybe one on New Years. But sure, I'll take a small one. I do want to talk about the evidence in your case, though. There's got to be something we can do to help figure this out."

"The County Attorney and the cops aren't getting to it. They think they've got their case made."


Jo gave Ross his bath and played with him for awhile, then fed him a bottle and put him to bed, and finished the dishes while Spencer and Alan talked on in the dining room.

When she came back in to clear the coffee cups, they were both talking loudly, and waving their hands more than normal, and laughing way more than seemed reasonable, and she realized, like a knife in the chest, that they were both close to being all out drunk.

She stood there with her back to the archway into the farm office/study, trying to think of something to say. She'd never seen Alan even marginally loaded, or Spencer either one, and it made her feel panicked, as well as irritated, laid on top of everything else that had gone wrong in their lives.

They'd been drinking the bourbon neat, half an inch in a cocktail glass, but there must've been plenty of refills, since the bottle was less than half full. She picked up the last of the coffee cups and saucers, and reached for the bottle of bourbon, but Alan put his hand on it and said, "Hey, Josie. We might want one more. I'll put it away in a minute."

She wanted to say "You've both had more than enough." But she didn't. It wasn't her job to tell Alan what to do. And she didn't want to embarrass him in front of Spencer.

Then Spencer stood up and laughed, and said, "I don't know, Alan. I'm more loaded than I thought." His face was pink under his tan, and his blond-brown hair was sticking straight up as though he'd been rubbing his scalp.

"You think so?" Alan was staring up at him as though focusing took concentration.

Jo looked from one to the other, and said, "Spence, I'll make up the guest bed for you. You can't trailer Tracker home. You wouldn't want to take that chance."

Alan said, "Do I detect a note of censoriousness?" He was smiling, but there was a warning somewhere inside it.

Jo stood and stared at him, without knowing how to react.

Spencer watched her for a minute. Then nodded and said, "Hell. I haven't been loaded in years. Not since France, at the end of the war. And one thing I do know, I'm not gonna like it in the morning. You either, brother. What were we thinking?"

He and Alan both more or less giggled, which made Jo feel even worse.

She went into Ross's room off the south side of the dining room—her parents' bedroom, the one they'd built at the south end with a bathroom behind it. She took Ross out of his crib there, and settled him in his bassinette, watching him turn on his stomach without waking—his head to one side, his behind in the air—before she rolled him through the dining room, across the hall, and into the living room, where she settled him close to their bedroom door.

Alan and Spencer stayed at the table, standing and talking and weaving around some, while she put clean sheets on the guest bed in Ross's room, and more towels in the bathroom, with her mind in an uproar as the men laughed on.

The two of them finally went to bed about one, when she was feeding Ross again, but Jo couldn't bear to go to bed, and she put Ross down, and sat on the front porch in an old wicker chair, feeling as though her life had turned dangerous in ways she'd never expected.

She'd drunk half a glass of water, and was blowing her nose, and trying not to cry, watching the stars getting hidden behind clouds—when she heard boot heels on gravel coming up from the barns on the south.

Someone was walking toward her, wading across the grass, and she waited and listened, hoping it was Toss, and not Scooter, the barn hand, who helped at the heighth of the foaling.

"Josie?" Toss appeared, outlined against the darkness, his soft low musical voice reminding her of her mother's.

"Hey."

"What are you doin' out here?"

"Just sitting."

There was light sliding out onto the porch, soft light from the hall and the dining room, and Toss must've seen her face when she looked to her right toward him.

"Mind if I sit too?"

"Nope."

"I'll use the facilities I come for, and be right back out."

While he was gone, she tried to swallow the stone in her throat, and worked at not wanting to cry, but the more she tried the harder it got, and when Toss came back and sat down next to her, there were tears washing down her face, and the noises she made made her furious. Embarrassed, and humiliated, and disgusted with herself for crying like a little kid.

"Good thing we put a gate up at the road last year. There were folks from the TV and the papers there till right before Spencer pulled in."

"Yeah."

"What's the matter, honey?"

"You haven't called me honey since I was ten years old."

"I haven't found you crying alone in the dark since then when your daddy died, even when you had reason. What's happened?"

He handed her a large folded handkerchief, and she blew her nose and swallowed. "Alan and Spencer got drunk after dinner. I hate seeing people drunk. We have a glass of wine on Friday and Saturday. Maybe two, at most, one of those nights. But I've never seen Alan drink like that. What if he turns into a drunk? I couldn't stand it, Toss! I couldn't. I've got to respect Alan. If that goes, I don't know what I'd do."

"I understand what ya mean. I do. But—"

"If I can't rely on Alan to be strong and sensible and trustworthy, I can't face what we're going through. I can't! He'd be just like Jack used to be. And Butch, falling in the street. I couldn't stand it!"

"He won't turn into a drunk. He won't, honey. He's a real responsible man. Like your daddy. Like Tommy too. You married a man, Josie. He ain't about to let you down."

"Why would he get drunk? It only makes things worse!"

"Look at the pressure he's under. Accused of murdering somebody he didn't? Facing jail time? Losin' you and Ross forever? Don't you reckon that weighs on his mind?"

"Of course! But why would he go and get loaded?"

"He didn't plan to."

"That makes it scarier in a way. That if it happened once, he could slide into it again, just the same way without meaning to."

"Why's it scare you so much?"

"Drunk people act like fools. I saw it in college all the time. The guys from the war as bad as anybody. You start out a reasonable person, and a few drinks later, you're either a raging bully, or a pathetic looking idiot, who's lost every shred of dignity and basic common sense."

"You ever get drunk?"

"Twice. The first time totally by accident because I

didn't know how much I could drink, and I with people who were drinking a lot. The other time, when I was … when I realized the guy I was engaged to up at the U of M was sleeping with anybody wearing a skirt. I went out pretty deliberately and got myself soused."

"How'd you like it?"

"I hated it. I got sick as a dog. I made a complete fool of myself and couldn't even remember half of it. And it made getting over Nate a whole lot worse."

"Right. That's what Alan's gonna think in the morning. It mustta been a desperate kinda thing he did tonight, but I'm tellin' you, it ain't in him to make a practice of it. I've seen drunks all my life, and I've overindulged myself from time to time, when I was a youngster, before you was born. I grew up and got over it."

"He's old enough to know better." Jo started crying again, and struggled to stop, then drank the rest of her water. She gulped and sighed, and shook her head. "It's kinda like the straw that broke the camel's back."

Toss didn't say anything for a minute. He lit a cigarette, and clicked the lid on his Zippo back and forth, while Jo pulled herself together.

"You know, I was born in nineteen hundred. I turned eighteen the last year of World War I, and I went right out and enlisted. I never went overseas. I spent most of my time in Kansas, carin' for a bunch a cavalry horses on a post in the middle a nowhere." Toss stopped then and smoked for half a minute. Then turned and looked right at Jo. "Your mother ever tell you 'bout me bein' engaged?"

"No! Are you kidding? I never heard a word."

"Well. I was. I knew Margaret from the time I was

two or three. Church socials. Going to a one-room schoolhouse. She was older than me, three years, and she was way smarter. I used to listen to her recite, and answer questions real good, and work problems out on her slate, and I marveled at how quick she was, and how pretty, and good, and sensible, and all. I won't say she didn't have a temper." Toss snorted quietly, and clicked his Zippo, and sat for most of a minute.

"She had a brother, who was younger like me, who had a real ugly harelip, and kids, being the nasty little brutes they are, they'd tease him, and make fun of the way he talked. He never seemed to pay it much mind himself. But Margaret couldn't stand it, and she bloodied more than one nose, and I helped too, a time or two, when some cuss had it comin'." Toss chuckled and stubbed out his cigarette, and rocked his chair back on its back legs, swaying it forward and back.

"I don't know what it was she saw in me, but she saw somethin'. She went off and got trained as a nurse, and come back just when I was fixin' to enlist. I asked her to become my wife, and Margaret … Margaret agreed." Toss was quiet again. Staring at the sky.

Jo held her breath as she watched him, in a haze of light from the house. He'd never said much of anything about his past—not in her whole life—and she knew it meant more than she could understand, and she had to meet it just right.

"I reckon you know there was a big Spanish flu epidemic, hit right that year, brought back by our boys from France. Folks was dyin' like flies. Just like flies. A *quarter of a million* right here in the States. Millions of folks died around the world. Think about that for a minute. Two hundred and fifty thousand folks—right in the blink of an eye. The schools got closed for a whole year. Families got wiped out. Two, three, four generations. And my Margaret, she died nursin' the sick, with me out there in Kansas."

"Oh, Toss. I'm sorry. I had no idea."

He nodded, she could see it in the light from the hall. But he didn't say another word till he'd lit another smoke. "I was real upset. Real upset. I'd loved her as long as I could remember. I did. But the worst of it was … and I'm gonna tell you this 'cause you need to hear it. But I've never told nobody else, and I ask you not to repeat it."

"I won't. I promise."

"The worst of it was, there was this secret, hiding, cowardly piece in me that was actually kinda relieved." He stopped. And Jo held her breath. Before he started again. "Lord help me, Josie, but I was real afraid of the responsibility. Of having a wife and kids. Of providin', and makin' a home. I felt like I might not make good, or do it right, or live up to the way I wanted to be, and that Margaret'd look at me one day, and wish she'd chosen another."

"Toss—"

He held up his hand, with the Lucky in it, and Jo shut her mouth. "Not trying was safer than failin'. And I've lived that way ever since. I've squired one lady or another, from time to time. I've had me someone for companionship for awhile. Someone to flirt with, and go out dancin'. But I made damn sure I was never responsible for another human being. And I done that outa fear and cowardice, that's shamed me all my life."

"Toss, you take such responsibility for the horses, and the folks who own them, and the help—"

"That ain't the same thing. It ain't. Alan ain't like me, Jo. He takes on folks and cares for 'em, and puts himself on the line. I reckon he worries about you and Ross, and what this'll do to you, way more than he thinks about himself. He don't moan and whine. He takes it in hand."

"I know. I agree. That's why it felt so awful seeing him get drunk."

"Give him some leeway here, honey. It'll be fine, I'm tellin' ya." He took another drag, then crushed the butt on the porch floor with an old scuffed boot. "'Nother thing I never told ya. Last time I talked to Tommy on the phone. Prob'ly a month 'fore he was killed, he told me 'bout Alan. 'Bout how he reckoned the two of you would fit real good together. Told me how Alan had thrown himself on some woman in France and took the blow from a grenade himself. That he was a man who'd stand up, and do his Josie proud."

There were tears on Jo's face again, and she wiped at them, and blew her nose, before she said, "Thank you. I appreciate you talking to me."

"Least I can do."

"Uncle Toss?"

"Yeah?"

"I love you."

The silence went on for almost a minute, and then he said, "I love you too. You're all I got in the world, girl. All I got in the world." He stood up and leaned back like his back hurt, before he said, "I don't reckon Abby's gonna foal tonight, but I better get back and check." He coughed then, long and hard, as he started down the stairs, before he said, "I'll look in on Tracker too and get him fed and watered."

Then he was gone. Boots swishing through the unmown grass. Crunching away across gravel.

# CHAPTER ELEVEN

*Saturday, May 9th, 1964*

When Jack and Camille had met at Flocelliere, when they'd settled in the sun, down the hill a little behind the ruins of the oldest part of the turreted stone chateau; when they'd sat self-consciously, catching glimpses of each other, and looking away as though too much might be said by half-familiar faces expecting to see the past; when they'd leaned back in old wicker chairs by clipped box parterres where sorrel and strawberries and tarragon grew, where they wouldn't be seen by the Vicomte or Vicomtesse, or any of those who worked for them; when they talked about the white puppy first, who'd followed them down the hill—there was wonder, and worry, and interest between them that Jack had let himself hope for, but hadn't begun to expect.

First they talked about the early eighteenth century painting she was restoring—the woman in a sweeping dress of deep teal silk, that might've been an unattributed Fragonard, which Camille would finish varnishing by noon the next day. Then they touched on their lives since the war, quickly, lightly, without detail or emotion. Finally they turned to Tours in '44, and the treachery that destroyed the Touraine Resistance.

They worked their way slowly and carefully, as the sun sank beside them, to Jack's suspicion that Henri Reynard had been the traitor. He told her eventually, as the air grew chilly and her eyes disappeared in the night, that being suspected had tortured him for years. That he'd drunk himself nearly to death, living in a shack in a North American forest, that he'd only stopped two years before and begun to reclaim his life.

Camille listened, and nodded, and told him what she had witnessed during and after the war—the lives warped and lost and perverted, the souls saved and restored, the joy and gratitude that abounded in some, in spite of hatred and horror.

But it wasn't until the next afternoon, as Jack drove them northeast on winding roads as narrow as farm tracks, that Camille told him she knew for a fact that her former husband, Henri Reynard, had told the Gestapo and the Tours police where the Resistance would be meeting. He'd deliberately made Jack the scapegoat and laughed when he'd told her how he'd arranged his alibi.

She'd left Henri long before that conversation, but he'd still chosen to appear from time to time, and it'd been in the middle of a terrible fight, early in 1945, that she'd accused him of having engineered the Gestapo raid and the death of Jean Claude Lebel.

Henri had admitted it, three-quarters drunk and bragging, telling her how clever he'd been—claiming it'd been a political necessity, and a fine example of the political will that revolutionary history demands. The kind of will and vision she would never have.

He'd said his goal, and that of countless others, was a people's postwar France, and that leaders like Jean Claude Lebel who opposed the Communist wing of the Resistance had to be eliminated for the ultimate good of the people.

He'd said too that he'd ensured her release, so what more could she have asked?

Camille had long before filed for divorce, and it came three months later. Yet, he'd pounded on her door late one night a month after it was final, and shouted his way in. He said he knew she'd never reveal that he'd helped the Gestapo. He "knew" full well she still cared for him, no matter what she claimed. And more importantly still, she had no proof of his guilt. It never would be more than her word against his, and his political supporters would systematically destroy her if she spoke out against him.

Camille stared out the window for a minute, as she brushed a shred of lint off her sleeve and smoothed her dark green linen skirt down below her knees. She told Jack then that Henri had tried to establish a political career—first locally, then nationally—but had never achieved any sort of success. Not even in the Touraine, in the whole of the Loire Valley, where his leadership after Lebel's death had alienated rather than unified.

Camille had sat quietly again, while Jack drove. She'd sighed and blown her nose, and folded her hands in her lap, before she went on to tell Jack that Henri had moved to Paris in 1948, and married a wealthy leftist dilettante, and had lived with her on Isle Saint

Louis in a grand apartment two blocks north of Notre Dame.

He'd done fashion photography, using her family connections with the haute couture community, which couldn't have been easy to explain to his leftwing friends. But the day came when his wife threw him out. And where he went from there Camille had never heard. She'd tried hard not to know, deliberately choosing to distance herself from their mutual friends.

Jack asked if she thought she could find out where he was now.

And she'd said she could try, once she got home to Esvres sur Indre where she'd rented an old grist mill, twenty-five kilometers southwest of Tours, outside the tiny village. "Could I perhaps persuade you to converse in English? I would like an opportunity to improve my grammar."

"Isn't that where Henri said he'd been—at Esvres sur Indre? And that he couldn't have gotten back to Tours in time to have told the Gestapo where the Resistance was meeting?"

"Yes. The one who swore Henri was there was nothing but a petty crook who lied in exchange for black market goods. It-tis only a … how do you say? … only a coincidence that I now live in Esvres sur Indre. A childhood friend purchased the mill, and refurbished it after the war. He allows me to rent three floors in a building that … is it sets or sits? Off on one side?"

"Sits."

"Thank you. There I have a studio, and a comfortable home. From there I travel to fulfill commissions, or restore those sent to my studio."

Camille turned and looked at Jack, and her eyes were hard, and uneasy. "Why is it you wish to locate Henri? I cannot see that there will be a legal means for him to be punished. We have no … how would you say? … no evidence of his guilt? The governments of France too, ever since the war, they have hidden all actions then, to protect our collaborators no matter their crimes."

"I want to look him in the eye and tell him what I think of him, and maybe even knock him down, if he reacts the way I think he will."

"And how is that?"

"With arrogance and contempt."

Camille nodded, and looked out the window. And there was silence again as Jack turned onto a one-lane road running through rolling farmland. Several moments elapsed uneasily before she placed her handkerchief in her purse, and reapplied her lipstick. Then she told him he was welcome to stay in her apartment at the mill while she telephoned those she knew who might help her find Henri. "There are two bed chambers. You must not feel an imposition."

"I'd like to. Thank you. Thank you for helping me. I was afraid you wouldn't, him having been your—"

"It is nothing. You deserve to accuse him to his eyes."


"So much for bourbon." Alan was sitting at the dining-room table, toast and strawberries in front of him, a mug of coffee in his hand, staring painfully across the old walnut table at Spencer Franklin. "My stomach's not doing well."

Spencer laughed, uncharacteristically softly, and said, "Mine too. And I left Toss to take care of Tracker. How could I do that? We're old enough to know better." He smiled, as though his eyes hurt, and drank all of a tall glass of water.

Jo walked in, carrying Ross, and her own second cup of coffee, and said, "Don't expect any sympathy from me." She'd laughed when she'd said it, and tried not to look as though she were gloating.

Spencer said, "By the way, do you know if the police checked the phone records to find out if Carl called you that night? To get you out to that farm so you wouldn't have an alibi?"

"I don't know what they've got. We won't until we talk to Garner after he's seen the prosecutions' files. Why?"

"Just curious. You'd think that might help. Anyway. I've got to load Tracker and get home. I've got so much work to do to pull off this buyout, I can't take off more time today."

"I need to get to the office too. I've been so distracted, I'm way behind at work."

Jo said, "I'm going to take Ross and go down to Shaker Village and see if they've started the renovations. I think I need to get away and do something fun."

"Good." Alan was standing beside her, and he leaned down and kissed her. "I've been thinking about what you said the other night. About the lab supply distributor, and what he was up to with Carl. Let's talk when we get home."

"What did Garner say when he called this morning? When does he think he'll be done with the file?"

"He thought Monday. But it'll probably take him all day to finish his notes and do the copying."

## *Monday, May 11th, 1964*

Alan asked Kevin Hardgrave, who worked on the lab bench, and did some pharmaceutical manufacturing in the fermentation room under Bob's direction, to come in and talk to him after his lunch hour.

When he did, he looked more or less like normal, calm and steady and hard to rattle, with humor hovering at the corners of his mouth. He was average size, and somewhere in his forties, and he sat down and looked at Alan, holding a notepad and a pen.

They talked for half an hour, about short- and long-term projects, and what they needed to accomplish that week, and what milestones ought to be met by Wednesday.

Then Alan asked him about the lab supply distributor they'd bought a lot from the year before.

"Cecil Thompson?"

"Yeah."

"He's a strange bird. One of the old-style salesmen who think nothing matters but relationships. You know what I mean. Handing out tickets to a Wildcat game. Not price, or value, or the quality of a product."

"But Carl did a lot of business with him?"

"Yep. He bought more and more from him last year as time went on, and less and less from other suppliers. Cecil would come in and Carl would take him into the supply room, and they'd stay in there for a considerable time, and then go out to lunch."

"Did Carl spend as much time with other distributors?"

"Not that I saw."

"So from Cecil Thompson Supply we were buying basic reagents, some proprietary raw materials, glassware, gloves, syringes, and maybe a balance, or a microscope?"

"Yep. A lot of our glassware. Pipettes, stirrers, paper filters too, lab crayons, that kind of thing. His chemical line was limited. He wanted to expand in that direction, but I don't think he had the scientific background. I know Carl would let him look in our cabinets, so he could've known the products we used and who else we bought from."

"What I recall, is that after Carl left in August of last year, you and I, when meeting with Fisher Scientific and others, found out we could save a significant amount of money by switching suppliers. We'd always used more than one supplier. We'd be fools not to. But it was after Carl left that we diverted most of our orders to two of Cecil's competitors. Do I have the timeline right? I was busy with a lot of other things."

Kevin said, "That's what I remember. And Cecil went kind of crazy when I told him. I didn't just phone him, because he was a small outfit, and I knew we were a fairly sizeable customer for him, so I didn't want to drop the bomb over the phone. I took him out to lunch and explained the situation, and told him we'd still buy from him occasionally, but that we had to find the best prices for ourselves."

"What did he say?"

"He tried to talk me out of it, and then said he'd

bought an unusually large inventory because of conversations he'd had with Carl, and it wasn't fair for him to bear the brunt of Carl having overpromised.

"I told him I didn't know anything about that. That the orders I'd seen placed by Carl were for similar amounts to what we'd been ordering. That he had increased them in the summer some—last year, in '63 —but that we'd have to work through our inventory before we purchased more, and then it would be with suppliers who offered the best deals."

"How'd he take it?"

"He drank two martinis and ate hardly any lunch, and got more and more upset. By the end, he was almost begging me to give him another order. I was actually afraid he'd burst into tears."

"When was this?"

"I can check my calendar from last year, but I'd say last September. He still called on us after that, at least once a month like usual, till … well, I guess it was probably late March. I haven't seen him since. I heard from the Fisher Scientific salesman in April that Cecil's gone out of business."

"Greg Zachman, right?"

"Yeah. He works out of his house on Morgan Street in Versailles. His territory's big, though. Cincinnati, Louisville. Indianapolis. Probably down to Knoxville. If he's not working his territory here, he's gone for at least a week."

"Thanks. You've been a big help."

Kevin started toward the door, then looked back at Alan. "It's none of my business, but are you doing okay? I don't believe for a second that you killed Carl."

"Thanks. I appreciate that. I do."

Jo wouldn't be home until seven, when she would've picked Ross up from Becky and Buddy's, and when Alan got home at six, having talked to Greg Zachman at his house on his way home, he decided to squeeze in a ride on Maggie.

They worked in the sand riding area for fifteen minutes, warming up and working on transitions, Emmy watching from the sidelines, hoping they'd go cross country.

When they started off, heading north till they could angle west to the path in the woods, they were walking along the paddock fence where Toss had put all the mares without foals who had been, or were about to be, bred again.

Alan had Maggie on a long rein, letting her stretch her neck after working with more collection, and he was humming something quietly to himself, more relaxed than he'd been in days—when a horse thundered close up behind him, running right at him on the other side of the fence. He was just starting to look over his right shoulder, when Maggie spooked, shying straight left in a fraction of second, unloading him on a fence post, as she bolted toward the woods.

The same mare squealed and snorted a foot away from him as he landed on his right side on rock hard ground. He was stunned for a second, lying crumpled on his side—when Maude, the mare who'd charged the fence, galloped away down the fenceline with the rest of the herd behind her.

Alan lay there, thinking about Maggie, loose somewhere in the woods, stirrups slapping her sides, where she could stumble, or fall on the reins, or tangle herself in branches and underbrush, or break a leg on a tree root.

All his body parts moved, when he tested them, inside the generalized pain. And he grabbed a fence rail and pulled himself up, rubbing his right hip and the length of his thigh, trying to get his knee to bend more than it would on its own, while Emmy licked his arm.

A boot could've gotten caught in a stirrup, dragging him off to his death. His head could've hit the post a lot harder than it had, and bones could've been broken— and he told himself to stretch and get moving, because Maggie was running on a narrow trail through a maze of bare roots.

Alan hobbled a few yards, and then trotted, more or less, limping now on both legs, something wet running down his arm, his helmet lying where he'd landed, Emmy running in front of him.

When he got to the break in the trees where the trail started, he could see Maggie standing sideways a hundred yards ahead. Her head was hanging, but she was watching him, quivering enough he could see it. And then she started walking, limping on her left fore, the loop of reins around her right, as she picked her way up the trail toward him, instead of running the other way, thank God, the way a lot of horses would've.

"Hey, sweet girl. What'd you do to your leg?"

She stopped and waited for him, slick sweat staining her bay coat black, foamy sweat white between her legs and circling the edge of her saddle.

Alan picked up her right fore, and untangled the reins, then ran a hand down her left leg without seeing a cut or a lump.

He stroked her neck and patted her shoulder, and

started leading her out toward the field, limping beside her left shoulder, saying, "Why were you so silly? You know Maude, and what a jerk she is, doing that on purpose. She took me by surprise too, so it's my fault as much as yours." Alan knew Maggie didn't understand, but it calmed her down to hear a reasonable voice, and it gave him something to do besides wonder how badly she was hurt, while his own pain rolled in in waves.

Jo and Toss both worked with Maggie, looking for heat in the tendons, looking for swellings to suddenly appear, putting her leg in a bucket of ice water, hoping to head it off.

They gave her a dose of bute, and walked her around for quite awhile, then put her in her stall and figured out a schedule for checking her during the night.

Alan got a shower, then doctored the cut on his forearm while watching Ross, and getting dinner on the table—cheese omelets, and boiled potatoes, with a spinach-and-bacon salad—before Jo came in from the barn.

"I think she'll be okay. If we're lucky it's just a bruised hoof. Sole, or frog, either one, from a tree root, or maybe a stone. How 'bout you? Your head's okay? No blurry vision or anything?"

"No. I'm okay. I'll be sorer tomorrow, but nothing to worry about."

"So did you talk to anyone about the supplier?"

Alan told her what Kevin had said about Cecil Thompson, as he dished himself up more salad. "I called the Fisher Scientific rep, Greg Zachman, too. I actually got him at his house while he was doing paperwork, so I stopped and saw him on the way home. He lives across from Mack Miller, the trainer Toss thinks so much of."

"What did Zachman say?"

"A lot, actually. He worked at another supplier with Cecil twelve or fifteen years ago. Cecil left and started his business, just about the time Zachman went to Fisher. He got along okay with Cecil, but he didn't respect him. He knows for a fact that he gave a kickback to a purchasing agent at one of his customers when they worked together. And from what he's heard, and it's only hearsay, Cecil did the same in his own company, and Carl was said to be one of his recipients."

"How does he know that?"

"He doesn't know it for a fact. But someone he knows, who worked for Cecil part time, says that's what happened. He says that last fall Carl gave Cecil to understand he was going to need a broad range of products, and hinted that he would be going out on his own and would make it worth Cecil's while. So Cecil bought a lot of inventory when prices were high. 'Member when raw materials went up in August, because of the teamsters threatening to strike? Petroleum products were really up too. And then Cecil got stuck with a whole stockpile of stuff when Carl got fired."

"Carl could've asked for a cut. That wouldn't surprise me."

"Right. And *if* Cecil was giving a kickback to Carl, that would explain why we could find his products cheaper from other sources. He was selling top dollar to cover the kickback, and bringing in larger inventories to get a quantity price break for himself."

"So then when Carl leaves, and his Canadian business falls through, Cecil's in a hole."

"Exactly. And then, when the raw materials costs went down in January, things got even worse for him. He'd bought high, and was going to have to sell low to compete."

"So he could have a grudge against Carl."

"Especially once his business folded with a lot of debt. He drinks a lot too, which may not help him be rational about who's to blame for what."

"When did the business fold?"

"Probably in March. And he obviously had all the same syringes and gloves and vials we have at Equine. He sold a lot of them to us."

"What about the Dylox?"

"He never represented Bayer, but he was in our lab, and in our storeroom. I expect he could've figured out how to get himself a sample. Take the pint of Dylox to the restroom and fill a small bottle. I don't know exactly how he'd do it, but it wouldn't be beyond the possible if he'd wanted to kill Carl.

"No. It wouldn't."

"Even if that's a long shot."

Ross started crying in the red canvas seat of his windup swing, and Jo got up and wound it again so they could talk in peace. "So what can we do to investigate him? I could talk to Jane Seeger, and see if she knows anything about Cecil. Did he go to their house? Did Carl say they were fighting? Did she know if there was a kickback?"

"Sure. You'd do it better than I would. I think I oughtta go take some aspirin." He was carrying their plates down the two steps to the study, limping slowly, looking as though his pelvis was twisted off to the left.

Jo watched him pass through the kitchen doorway before she said, "Maybe you oughtta get your back adjusted. The DO Toss went to, after he broke his legs."

"I'll see how I feel in the morning."

"I'll go look at Maggie again, if you'll change Ross's pants."

### Tuesday, May 12th, 1964

Jo tried to get Jane Seeger at home early that morning, and then called the University of Kentucky library and was told Jane was away at a conference and would be in the library on Friday. Jo made an appointment to see her at work Friday morning. Then threw the dishcloth into the sink from halfway across the room. "I can't keep doing nothing! There's gotta be something I can do to help!"

When Alan was getting himself a cup of coffee at Equine that afternoon, Doug Smith from packaging walked up to him at the coffeemaker and asked if he could speak to him. Maybe they could step out back while Doug had a smoke?

They stood under a big gnarled redbud, and once Doug had lit his Camel, and pushed his glasses up his nose, and wiped his forehead with a red bandana, he shoved it back in his uniform pants pocket, and slowly cleared his throat. "This ain't easy to talk about. It ain't about the business."

"Oh. Well, if it's not, I—"

"I don't wantta get nobody in trouble, and I don't know if it means much, or it's just me bein' stupid."

"You say what you think you should."

Doug watched Alan for half a minute, then said, "It happened in the winter. February most likely. See, I got me a big dog, some kinda hound mix, maybe blue tick, or bloodhound in him, and it was a Saturday, and it was warmer than it'd been. The day before'd been warmer too. And I just felt kinda itchy, like I had ta do something different, so I drove down to Cumberland Falls State Park."

"How far's that?"

"Eighty-five, ninety miles, somethin' like that. I figured to take my son, and Merle the dog, and hike for a couple hours. Have a picnic and all in the car, then come on home. We left about six, and Joey was real excited, leavin' in the dark, 'fore his sisters was up. And when we got there, and pulled into the parking lot, Carl Seeger was there too. Standing outside his car talkin' to this other fella."

"Did he recognize you?"

"Nope. Never looked my way. I drove right past, and parked a ways away, and he never paid no attention. Other fella didn't neither, that I could see. And he's the one that's got me worried."

"Why?"

Doug Smith crushed his cigarette out with a work boot, then shoved his hands in his pockets. "It was Brad Harrison, and they was talkin' real concentrated like. Noddin' their heads, and lookin' like whatever it was was real serious and important. Like a couple a agents in a spy movie."

"You couldn't hear anything?"

"Nope. No way. But it seemed real strange to me, that they'd go so far away to meet up. Know what I mean?"

"Yeah, I think I do."

"So now what? I mean, I don't want no trouble with Brad or Mr. Harrison. But I felt like I oughtta tell ya."

"You did the right thing. Thank you."

"That mean I should call the Sheriff?"

Alan looked up at the redbud, and picked off a sliver of bark. "I don't know. I wouldn't want to do any damage, if Brad doesn't have anything to do with Carl's death. Or get Brad put out with you either. Would you let me think about it for awhile, and then let you know how it seems to me?"

Doug looked at Alan for a second, and Alan could see he was thinking, *What if I'm wrong? What if Munro killed Seeger?* But then Doug nodded, and said it was time he got back to work.


After he'd left, Alan thought about going right to Bob, and asking him to help decide what to do—to talk to Brad himself, or approach it some other way.

*But Brad could've gotten the Dylox, and everything else. Easier than Cecil Thompson, or Carl Seeger. And blood's thicker than water. An old cliché that's usually true. It makes more sense to consult Garner before I talk to Bob.*

*Wednesday, May 13th, 1964*

It took Camille till May 11th to track Henri Reynard to Lyons. She and Jack left the next morning, passing through Tours, and on east through Orleans, then south down through Burgundy—past mile after mile of stony tan ground striped brown with rows of grape vines just beginning to sprout new leaves—stopping finally in a B&B that had been a farm workers' cottage just down a hill from the Chateau de Messey, a small country mansion outside of Oszenay, three hours north of Lyons.

They left early in the morning, and drove south to Lyons, parking on a side street not too far from the Centré d'Histoire de la Résistance in the university district.

The streets were littered and dirty, even where the buildings were old and beautiful. The shops were dingy and pedestrian looking, the traffic heavy and noisy, the smell of exhaust making Camille cough, as they threaded their way through streets thick with students —walking, and talking, and smoking at crowded tables crammed in outdoor cafes—while Camille and Jack studied street numbers.

Henri's apartment was on the second floor above a rundown corner tobacconist's, his door facing the side street. The outside of the building was smeared with graffiti and tattered posters, with advertising handbills and radical propaganda, even two red guerrilla slogans written in Italian.

When Jack shoved the street door open, they were assaulted by the smell of cat urine, and garbage cans, and what might've been dried vomit. The overhead

bulb had burned out, and they had to work their up
around litter on worn wooden stairs, before they stood
by a peeling gray door and looked at each other for
most of a minute, before Jack knocked.

They heard voices, and shuffling feet, and locks and
chains clicking and rattling, before a young woman,
who might've been a college student, opened the door
wide. She was barefoot and tiny, not more than five
feet tall, wearing a man's pale blue shirt tied in a knot
at her waist above short white shorts. Her legs were
sturdy, and her face was pale and round, her dark eyes
outlined in thick black liner, her lips pouting under
white lipstick, her blond bangs hanging in tendrils, the
back twisted on top of her head in a Bridget Bardot
tousle.

She gazed at them, one hand on her hip, before she
said, "Qui est vous?" as she looked Camille up and
down.

The end of a greasy brown sofa was visible just
beyond her, and there Henri sat in dirty chinos and a
half-buttoned shirt holding a pack of Gauloise in one
hand, while he lit the one in his mouth with a large
embossed silver lighter. There was a glass of red wine
on the coffee table in front of him next to an open
newspaper, and though it was almost eleven, there were
dirty dishes and clothes and magazines strewn all over
the room—on the mattress on the floor too, and
wherever else there wasn't a piece of camera equipment. Pamphlets were stacked in a lopsided pile under
the window that faced the front, its glass so filmed with
grime and smoke, the buildings on the opposite side
were a smudged yellow blur.

Henri's face had frozen—a stunned wariness in his

narrowed eyes, his mouth falling open—the instant he'd recognized Camille and Jack. He shot off the sofa and barricaded himself behind the far end, his back to the front windows, before he asked why they were there. Which was when the girl moved across to him, watching them the way he was, as she asked who they were.

Henri looked nothing like he had in 1944. His stomach strained against his shirt like a watermelon hanging above his belt, and the black hair—once wild and wavy, helping to make him look dashing and romantic—was reduced to a patchy fringe. His face was puffy, and his eyes were red-rimmed and strained above pale pouches, but there was the same old seduction in his smile when he told the girl to leave. This was business. He'd call her later to arrange when they'd meet.

She said no, why should she leave? She was his fiancée. She kept no secrets from him. And he pulled her against him, and whispered in her ear, then slid a hand across her rear end, telling her to go on and go, that they'd talk before they met for dinner.

She slipped on her sandals, and walked out, but she didn't look mollified when she snatched a green canvas satchel from the floor, and slammed the door behind her.

Jack stepped toward Henri, stopping just beyond the end of the sofa by the door, his hands clenched at his sides, before he said, "I know what you did to the Resistance in Tours," in a sharp clipped voice.

"Do you?"

"You wanted Lebel killed. You turned us into the

Gestapo and the Vichy police, and if the rest got tortured to death, too bad. Because you—"

"Camille was released. That was not an easy accomplishment when—"

"And you set me up to take the blame."

"What do you have to complain of? You were released! You, the interfering American, the—"

"And it's time the families of the people you murdered finally hear the truth."

"Is it? And who would believe you? You have no proof! I have a following who read and support my work. My testimony is in the archives of the Musée de la Résistance giving a very different explanation. The Centre d'Histoire de la Résistance et de la Déportation here in Lyons as well, they record the events *very* differently, I can well assure you. No, monsieur, no one will believe you, *or* my dear Camille, for she herself is suspect, as the only member of the Resistance released by the Gestapo. Aside from you, of course. The lone American."

Henri was smiling now, shaking a cigarette from the blue pack, a chuckle bubbling from his throat. "You, who were thrown from a Gestapo automobile to land indelicately in the gutter! No, there are many still in the Lourraine who have long suspected dear Camille's complicity. Yours, *and* hers as well. Without proof?" Henri shrugged, then leaned against the greasy coffee-colored wall and lit his Gauloise. "Your claims will fall upon closed ears."

Jack walked behind the sofa, the entire stained length of it to the end by the window, his whole body clenched and sweating, as he stared at Henri Reynard.

Jack stood absolutely still then, arms straining, rigid

at his sides, fighting back revulsion, as he watched Henri Reynard's fleshy lips sipping blood red wine. "I've lived with what you did to Lebel—and me, and all the rest—since 1944. I will not stand by any longer and let you—"

"Oh, mon coeur, it bleeds, yes! Quelle une tragédie! The poor simple American!" Henri had tossed off the rest of his wine and was pouring another glass.

Jack watched him in silence for half a minute, knowing too well what it was like to *not* be able to *not* drink another glass, or open another quart of vodka, or keep from crapping yourself in the night and puking on the floor. He took a deep breath and exhaled slowly, his eyes still on Henri. "Of course seeing what you've become makes me think that—"

"Oh? And what would that be, monsieur?"

"That justice has been done."

"And you mean by that what?"

"You were handsome and quick and charming. Now you're a middle-aged hanger-on. One of those we've all seen. Even when we'd rather—"

"Oh?" Henri had saluted Camille with his wine glass, even before he asked, "And what sort is that?"

"The artsy poseurs. The leftwing cranks. The ones who cling to the fringe of every college campus trying to impress immature kids who don't know enough to see what you've become, while—"

"And you! Who are you, and what do you know of the—"

"While you're hoping you don't look too out of shape to seduce someone susceptible."

"This is so much fantasy! And you! The American who could not even comport himself during the war as—"

"I wasn't a traitor who murdered his own people!"

"Oh, and you appear and lecture me? The coddled American, who came to manipulate *us*! *We* who had waged war through all the dark years! *You*, with your little gadgets, and your parcels of money. And childish Camille, so easy to lie to, so willing to believe when—"

Jack grabbed Henri by the throat and pinned him against the wall. He held him there, glaring at his red-rimmed eyes, before he let him drop and crumple on the floor.

Henri screamed, "You bastard! You think I shall let you walk out—"

Jack had pulled a thin silver rectangle from his pocket and was holding it at shoulder level, smiling at Henri.

"What is that?" Henri was pushing himself off the floor, tugging his trousers in place.

"One of those American gadgets. A tape recorder the size of a lighter that recorded everything you said."

"Wait!"

Jack had already stepped into the hall, when Camille said, "The families of the dead? It is time they learned how their loved ones were killed!" She closed the door, and ran down the stairs, hearing the door fly open, and Henri hollering behind them.

"Is it really a tape recorder? One so small without a cord?" Camille was watching Jack's face intently, as they made their way through a milling crowd, heading toward their car.

Jack laughed, and said, "No, though I wish it were. It's a Minox camera. Used during the war by American army intelligence. Did you see his face?"

"I did. It made the drive worthwhile. And you? Was it enough for you?"

"What else could we do? We don't have any proof. So, all things considered, it's the best I could've hoped for. Thank you. I couldn't have found him without you."

"And you are satisfied? You did not wish to kill him? Or make him suffer pitifully?"

Jack didn't answer until they'd gotten to their car. "Two years ago it would've been different. But, no. He admitted what he'd done, and I got to clamp my hands around his throat and drop him on his rear end. I couldn't have asked for more." Jack smiled.

And Camille smiled back at him and slipped her arm inside his.


Garner Honeycutt's office was in an old brick feed store in downtown Versailles on the west corner of Rose Hill and Main, two blocks south of the court-house.

The faded black door stuck at the bottom and creaked when Alan shoved it, and the scarred pine floor squeaked as he and Jo walked across it to stand in front of the receptionist's desk—broad and deep, and piled with files—with no one sitting behind it.

They stood there. Waiting. Feeling conspicuous—till they heard a door open on their right halfway down the hall that ran to the back of the building.

A tall stooped elderly man, with swirling white hair above an ancient black suit, carrying a sheaf of papers, shuffled away toward the end of the hall, muttering something and waving his free hand, till he turned right and disappeared up a flight of stairs.

Jo and Alan looked at each other, eyebrows raised in surprise, as Jo whispered "Now *that's* a character out of *Bleak House*"—before another door opened on the left side of the hall and a gray haired woman in a brown shirtwaist dress strode straight toward them.

"Mr. and Mrs. Munro? Sorry to have kept you waiting. If you'd care to take a seat, Mr. Honeycutt will be with you shortly."

They sat and watched her turn sideways away from them, as she fitted the ends of a gray plastic headset inside her ears, then switched on the Dictaphone next to a large gray IBM.

She used a pedal to start and stop the Dictaphone belt, and they could just barely hear snatches of dictation in the short pauses when she wasn't typing at what seemed like blinding speed. She answered the phone and transferred calls with equal precision.

And Jo had just told Alan, whose fingers and toes were tapping as though he'd drunk too much coffee, that she wished she'd brought a book—when they heard a door open, followed by rapid footsteps approaching from down the hall.

"Alan. Jo. Sorry to have kept you. I've set out the evidence in the conference room." Garner opened the door just beyond the receptionist desk, and led them into a front corner room, with windows facing Main and Rose Hill, their louvered shutters half-open spilling filtered light across the carpet while holding back some of the heat.

"Now." They were all seated at the conference table, Jo and Alan next to each other, Garner at one end. "I'll begin with a summary of the autopsy. They ultimately sent the tissue samples to the FBI Lab in Virginia, because the State Police Lab in Frankfort had a tough time figuring out what caused Seeger's death. One pathologist at the FBI eventually isolated organo-phosphate residue in the cat's tissue, as well as Carl's, but he had difficulty managing the analysis."

"He would." Alan finished looking at a photograph of Carl's kitchen and handed it over to Jo. "If he hadn't been given a sample of the Dylox, he would've had even more difficulty."

"But how did Carl really die? Was it what Alan said before? That he more or less just stopped breathing?" Jo was watching Garner as Alan laid a photograph in front of her of the suicide note on Carl's bedside table.

"Yes, respiratory function ceased. Though I'm not clear, based on this report, how the Dylox caused it."

Alan had poured Jo a glass of water from the pitcher in front of them, and was starting to pour another. "Garner?" Garner shook his head, and Alan took a glass for himself. "Dylox is a cholinesterase inhibitor. It keeps the neurotransmitter enzyme that enables nerves to communicate with each other from sending or receiving any impulses. If it was injected intravenously, or in a muscle, either one, the respiratory center would've been paralyzed. And he would've stopped breathing very quickly."

Garner seemed to consider Alan for a minute, before he said, "I see."

"The inhibition of cholinesterase would've inter-fered with all the other functions nerves control too, but breathing would've been first." Alan was sliding a ballpoint from one hand to the other and back again, without seeming to notice. "Which wouldn't have been a bad way to die, actually. Swift and pretty much painless, and Carl would've known that."

"The most significant finding, in my opinion, in the whole autopsy report, which was certainly new information to me, was that Carl was suffering from lung cancer."

"Really?" Alan's head had snapped up, and he stared hard at Garner.

"The pathologist thinks he wouldn't have had more than three or four months to live."

"Then that's a motive for suicide!" Jo was sitting forward now in her chair, elbows on the table. "If he knew he was dying, and it was going to be painful, he might have wanted to put an end to the pain, and make Alan suffer too."

"I believe a case could be made for that. But there is more evidence to consider, which doesn't look as favorable. They've matched the soil and screenings from outside Carl's kitchen door to your paddock boots, Alan, *and* your dress shoes, *and* the driver's side floormat in your car."

"They couldn't have! I've never set foot by his back door!"

"It'd be possible if it'd been planted, wouldn't it? What if Carl put that dirt on the floor mat of your car?" Jo looked from Alan to Garner, then back at Alan.

He shrugged as he said, "That would account for it, though we haven't got—"

"When I drove Jack Freeman up to the airport in Cincinnati the afternoon Carl died, just as he was getting out of the car, he told me that early that morning, a little after five, when your car was parked in

Equine's front lot, he was driving past, intending to park in the back lot and start mowing there, he saw a man in the front lot that he thought was Carl."

Alan stared at Jo as he said, "Why didn't you mention that earlier?"

"I don't know. It didn't seem connected till I heard about the dirt. Jack didn't have time to tell me anything more about it either, because somebody honked behind me, wanting to pull in by the curb, and Jack grabbed his bags and rushed away, but I had the feeling there was more he'd intended to tell me."

"We need to interview Jack Freeman as soon as we can." Garner's pen was poised above his legal pad and he was looking straight at Jo.

"He's in France. I thought he was coming home this week, but he hasn't yet."

"Can you reach him by phone, or telex?"

"I don't know how now, but I'll figure it out." Jo said it as though it was a covenant of some kind.

And Garner Honeycutt laughed. "Do. Please, also, you should know that the telephone company traced all calls from Carl Seeger's house, and none was placed to your number."

Alan was twirling his pen on his legal pad when he said, "There wouldn't be. Carl wasn't stupid."

"No, I don't think he was."

"What about fingerprints?"

"Yours were found nowhere in the house, or on the vial, the syringe, the suicide note, the fragment of vinyl glove, or his typewriter. His fingerprints were on the syringe and vial, but positioned and smeared in such a way that his fingers could have been deliberately positioned by someone else."

"Couldn't Carl have done that himself? Deliberately smear his own prints, so they looked like someone else did it?"

"One could certainly posit such a theory. The smears on the glove fragment were such that no print could be lifted. The only prints on your pen were yours. But the pen could have been handled by someone else so that no other prints were left."

"That has to be what happened." Jo's eyes were fierce, and her whole body seemed so concentrated and intense, she looked as though she could've hovered up above her chair. "I saw in the pictures of Carl's bedroom that there was carpet on the floor. Did Earl take samples from the carpet? Did they vacuum or anything?"

"They did. And Earl cut a sample of carpet to test and compare to Alan's shoes and car. I meant to mention that earlier. No carpet or other fabric fibers were found on Alan's shoes or floormat."

Alan said, "Well, that's something at least. How do they explain that?"

"I suspect they're trying to overlook it. Or suggest that you removed your shoes before you entered the house. If asked they also might take the position that their techniques aren't advanced enough to draw final conclusions."

Alan said, "Typical. Their minds are already made up."

"It's an election year. The County Attorney, and the Sheriff too, are not above hoping to create the impression that they've swiftly solved a difficult case as men of action and ability."

Alan nodded before he said, "I would've thought

Earl would be above that, but he's human. What about the lie detector test?"

"The results do indicate that you've told the truth, but it's inadmissible in court."

"At least that's something. Earl has to think about that when he considers my case."

"Largely, however, it's out of his hands."

"We've stumbled upon some information too that you need to hear." Alan started with what they'd learned about Cecil Thompson, the lab supply distributor and his dealings with Carl, and how his business had folded in March, and Garner agreed that that was worth pursuing.

Jo said, "I've made an appointment to talk to Jane Seeger at the UK Library on Friday, and I'm going to ask her what she knows about Cecil Thompson, because if he really did blame his bankruptcy on Carl, that could be a substantial motive. And with him having access to all the lab supplies they have at Equine, it's got to be worth looking into."

Garner said, "Yes, indeed," and made a note on his yellow pad.

"There's more too." Alan told him then about Brad and Carl meeting in February at Cumberland Falls. "Brad could've helped Carl set me up. Supplying him with everything from Equine. Though I have to say I find that hard to believe. He's too careful, and too self-protective. I can see him taking verbal pot shots at me behind my back, and being suspicious of my relationship with his dad, because of how it might affect his own ambitions. But him actually taking an active role in incriminating me, or helping with Carl's suicide?

Even if his morality's that warped, and I don't have any reason to think it is, I don't think he'd take the risk."

"Have you spoken to his father, or done anything else with this information?"

"No. We waited to talk to you."

"Let me think about it till tomorrow. I may wish to speak to Brad myself."

"Fine. By the way, how professional do you think the Sheriff's Department's investigation of Carl's house was? Were they good at not contaminating the evidence, and being as exhaustive as they should've been?"

"I wouldn't say it was particularly professional. Not the way law enforcement's developing these days from what the national legal journals are beginning to describe as routine. As an example, the investigating officers didn't wear protective gloves at the scene."

"What! So they could've left their prints on anything?"

"They could have, though I haven't seen evidence to suggest they did. I'm sure they handled the items as carefully as they knew how. You have to understand that in most small towns today the investigating officers wouldn't have done anything differently. Crime scene investigation is changing very rapidly, and here in Woodford County we have limited experience, and resources as well. We hardly ever encounter a case remotely like this. Bar brawls, breaking and entering, alcohol-related automobile fatalities, those are fairly routine. But sophisticated suspicious deaths with this many factors involved? Not in living memory."

Alan said, "Nuts." And shook his head.

"The lack of professionalism can work in our favor, as well as against us, and it's too soon to see its significance. Yet, we do need to pursue the Cecil Thompson and Brad Harrison angles. I'm sorry to say the private investigator I normally employ is out of town on another case and doesn't expect to be back in Lexington until sometime next week."

Jo said, "I can ask Jane Seeger about Brad, and see if she knows anything. And what about Carl's doctor? Should I ask her about him?"

"Yes, because so far we don't know who his doctor was. There was nothing in Carl's papers to indicate the physician he consulted. There was no appointment calendar, or personal address book found in Carl's personal affects."

"That's odd." Jo made herself a note to ask Jane about Carl's doctor, even though she knew very well she wasn't about to forget. "You'd think his doctor would know something that might help. When he told Carl about the cancer, and how he reacted."

"Whatever you can learn will be a help. So." Garner looked at them both, and then folded his hands on the table. "Our primary working hypothesis remains that, unless new evidence leads to a different conclusion, Carl Seeger amassed the materials from Equine and deliberately implicated Alan, while in fact committing suicide."

Jo said, "And *that* means we need to establish a straightforward method by which Carl could have entered the Equine building, once the locks were changed. Not only would he have entered the building, he would have made his way into the laboratory as well, *and* into Alan's office, requiring three separate keys. Correct?"

"I know! I know." Alan was leaning back in his

chair now, staring at the ceiling. "Four, actually. Counting the key to my desk."

"The Selectric font from the lab *was* in fact the font used in the suicide note, as was Equine's typing paper."

Alan said, "The lab secretary's been out for weeks, ever since her husband had a heart attack. She says she'll be back tomorrow, and I'll talk to her then and see if she knows anything that will help."

"Good. It's an interesting case."

Alan and Jo stared at him.

And Garner Honeycutt smiled. "I'm sorry. My criminal work is normally confined to the pettiest of criminal behavior, so from my perspective, this case offers a welcome change."

"I'm glad I'm providing a distraction." Alan almost smiled as he dropped his pen on the table and crossed his arms across his stomach. "So what do you think of our chances?"

"It's much too early to say. Their case is based on circumstantial evidence. If we can present conflicting evidence which effectively challenges their inter-pretation of the facts, one that suggests a very different explanation, we could prevail. But we're a very long way from being able to present any such array of evidence." Garner looked at his watch.

And Jo said, "May I ask you one more question?"

"Certainly."

"We saw a very elderly, white-haired gentleman walking away down the hall, and I wondered who he was."

"Ah." Garner Honeycutt chuckled. "Uncle Emmett. He's ninety-eight, but we still consult him on the intricacies of deeds and wills, for his grasp of the land disputes in Woodford County, ancient and modern, is nothing less than encyclopedic. His son took away his car keys this morning, and we've all been awaiting the eruption when Emmett discovers what he's done."

# CHAPTER TWELVE

*Excerpt From Jo Grant Munro's Journal*
*Friday, May 15th, 1964*

*Yesterday Alan talked to the lab secretary, Annette Miller. Her husband had a heart attack before Carl died, and yesterday was her first day back.*

*What she said about the Selectric font shows it was tampered with, though not, of course, who tampered with it.*

*She'd come to work on March 19th (she remembers the date because it's her son's birthday) and found a different font on her Selectric than she'd been using.*

*She normally uses Courier for the interoffice memos and reports because it's easy to read. If she's typing a letter for Alan on letterhead that goes out of the office, she uses something fancier. The font she found on her typewriter on the 19th was a Courier, but it wasn't hers. She asked every typist who has a Selectric if they'd switched their font for hers, but no one admitted it. It wasn't that it mattered, it was that it was so odd. The "o" was chipped on hers, but it wasn't on the new one. She said she'd already ordered a replacement for the Courier the week before from IBM, but the new one hadn't arrived.*

*The next day, March 20th, her old chipped Courier ball was back on her machine when she got to work.*

*So the question is who took it the night of March 18th and replaced it the night of the 19th so it'd be there on the 20th?*

*Alan got her to write down her account of what happened, and it's one of the pieces of evidence we're both praying will help.*

*Even so, I'm hardly sleeping, and I'm edgier with everyone, even when I try not to be, poor Ross included. Sometimes when he's crying it's almost more than I can stand.*

*It hurts to see Alan protecting himself in public too. The way he looks to see if people on the street are going to stare at him with loathing, and whisper when he walks by.*

*His lower back's been miserable too since he got thrown off Maggie, but I'm hoping the DO got it back in place with the second adjustment this week.*

*We try not to talk about reporters much. The junk they keep printing to whip up excitement and sell more papers, and get more viewers for the local news, shows only too clearly that they've condemned Alan already and don't care about the truth.*

*Sometimes when I walk up behind Alan when he's thinking about something else (and when isn't he thinking about something besides me, with everything else going on?)—when I slide my arms around him, just to stand there and hold him and settle my cheek against his back, I feel him startle and stiffen as though he's preparing for a blow, before he realizes who it is and I feel him begin to relax.*

*I know he's so busy at work there's pressure from that too, doing his job,* and *Carl's, and training a new production manager. Though I think it's probably a very good thing. Keeping his mind on work, where he knows he can accomplish something, has to be better than brooding.*

*It has helped me to finally have something to do that might actually be useful—aside from praying, which has taken on a whole new intensity. Why is it we say, "All I can do is pray," as though it's nothing but a last resort, when it may actually be the most important thing? And yet, getting to talk to Jane Seeger, and working on tracking Jack down is almost a physical relief. I'm a hothead by nature. Waiting around with nothing to do makes me want to scream.*

*I've never been comfortable with our new minister, who doesn't seem to believe much of anything except we all should be "nice" to each other, and I called Reverend Will yesterday in Louisville where he went when he left here. I wanted to hear his voice again, and get his perspective on our situation, and get him praying too. His wife answered, and hesitated a minute before she told me he had a heart attack six months ago and died the next night. They were incredibly close for a whole lot of years, and I wish I could've thought of something useful to say.*

*Emmy punctured her foot on something early last week and it's isn't healing the way it should. She still lets me squeeze it, and drain the wound twice a day, and she'll keep her foot in a pan of Epsom salt water with the kind of patience I should have and don't.*

Jane Seeger led Jo through a double wooden door from the History Reading Room in the UK library into a warren of back corridors to a low-ceilinged fluorescent lit room, packed with row after row of metal book-shelves crammed with cardboard boxes, to an old desk in a corner.

Jane sat behind it, unbuttoning the jacket of her navy blue suit, as she gestured Jo to the other chair, and said, "I'm not sure how I can help."

"I'm not sure either, but there're questions I think I ought to ask. First of all, has anyone told you about Carl's autopsy."

"No. I haven't heard a word."

"They discovered that Carl had lung cancer."

"Ah." Jane didn't say anything else for a minute, as she folded her hands on the desk. "I suppose that's not surprising, after all the years he smoked."

"The odd thing is, there was no mention anywhere in Carl's papers of who his doctor was. Our lawyer would like to consult him, but we—"

"Dr. Frazier. Augustus Frazier in Midway. Right on Midway Road."

"Thank you. That helps a lot. There was no appointment calendar in Carl's things either. Do you know if he had one?"

"Yes. Definitely. He kept it in the top right drawer in his desk. It should've been right there." Jane smooth-ed her pale brown hair from her forehead and looked at Jo with mildly puzzled eyes.

"They also couldn't find an address book."

"That doesn't make any sense. He kept it in that same drawer. Imitation red leather with phone numbers and addresses."

"Something else completely unrelated. Do you know anything about Carl's dealings with a lab supply distributor named Cecil Thompson?"

"Not from Carl, but I got a call from Mr. Thompson here at the library."

"When was that?" Jo was holding a pad and pen, staring straight at Jane.

"I think it must've been sometime in March. Though how he knew where to find me I don't know. He said he'd been trying to reach Carl at home, and was there anywhere else he could try to contact him. He'd gone to the house and left a note, but Carl didn't come to the door, or get in touch later."

"That's interesting."

"Yes. I told him to try Rotary. Carl went to the Rotary meeting every Tuesday at 11:30 at the Italian restaurant in Versailles. Georgiano's. On Lexington east of Maple. Whether Mr. Thompson went there to find him I don't know. I suppose you could ask the insurance salesman from Midway. He's in that large old firm that's … Burroughs and Burroughs and some-thing. I can't think of his name. Martin something. Baumgartner. I think that's right. He's one of the Rotary officers, and attends every meeting."

"Thank you. I'll give him a call today."

"Anything else?" Jane looked at her watch, then pulled down the cuffs of her pale blue blouse.

"Brad Harrison. Bob's son. What was his relation-ship with Carl?"

"They talked on the phone from time to time. What I heard of Carl's side of the conversation seemed to largely consist of Carl criticizing your husband. But, of course, whether anything changed after I left Carl, I don't know."

"Did Brad ever come to the house?"

"Not that I know of."

"Anyway, thank you for talking with me. I'd better let you get back to work."

"I don't know your husband, but I can see you're thoroughly convinced he's innocent."

Jo actually felt tears gather behind her eyes, and she took a deep breath before she spoke. "Not just because he's my husband either. Because of the kind of person he is."

"Then I hope what I've told you helps."


When Jo got to Dr. Frazier's office in Midway, the waiting room was packed, and there were three people waiting at the receptionist's desk. Jo stood behind them and watched the receptionist, who was probably in her late twenties, handle the brusque, the meek, and the confused with quiet, patient, practical concern.

When it was her turn, she asked if she could speak to Dr. Frazier for a minute or two, once he was done with his patients, on a matter concerning Carl Seeger's death.

"Dr. Frazier retired."

"When?"

"March 15th. He sold his practice to Dr. Patterson."

"So Dr. Patterson would have taken over Dr. Frazier's patients and have their files?"

"He would if the patient stayed on with him. Quite a few didn't."

"Do you know where I could reach Dr. Frazier?"

"He said he intended to travel, but where I don't know."

"Does he have family I could speak with?"

"He has a son in Louisville. His first name is Winston, and I expect you could find him in the phone book there."

"Thank you."

"I *can* tell you that Dr. Patterson doesn't have Mr. Seeger's file."

"Why is that?"

"The last time Mr. Seeger was here to see Dr. Frazier, he took his file with him when he left."

"Did he?" Jo was staring at the receptionist without seeing much of anything, wondering what to do next.

"He did." She considered Jo with obvious intelligence, and curiosity too.

"When was this, do you know?"

"If I had to guess I'd say January. Though it could've been early February. I can check the appointment book if you'd like me to."

"I would. Thank you."

The receptionist opened the large brown leather book that lay at one end of her desk and rifled back through the pages, in between phone calls, and newly arrived patients.

Jo stood off to one side and waited, watching the lame, the frail, and the very sick who were filling the doctor's day, beginning to think that there were worse things in life than being accused of murder.

"Yep. Here it is. January twenty-third. It was the third appointment in two weeks. And when he left, he took his file."

"Thank you so much. You've been a great help."

"I know you, you know. I'm Missy Rhodes. Your mama taught my Sunday school class when I was in junior high. She was the only interesting teacher I had, and I was sorry to hear when she died."

"Thank you." Jo's throat had suddenly closed up, and she swallowed carefully before she said, "She had a brain tumor, and wasn't herself for quite a while, and hearing you say that means a lot."

"I hope it all comes out okay." Missy Rhodes looked uncomfortable when she said it, as though she were picking her words, not wanting to come out and say, "I hope your husband isn't sent away for life, or executed, either one."

Jo thanked her, and waved as she walked away, while Missy answered the phone.


Jo called Martin Baumgartner from home, and found out that late in March, or possibly early April, a man had come to a Rotary meeting looking for Carl Seeger. Martin hadn't talked to him himself, but he did hear Carl say his name, and it could've been Cecil. He remembered that the meeting had just broken up when he got there, and that he heard him ask Carl to go next door to the Woodford Café. Whether Carl did, he couldn't say.

Jo had picked Ross up at Becky's before she called Baumgartner, but she didn't want to wait to find out more, and she took Ross with her, and drove back to Versailles to question whoever might know something at the Woodford Café.

One of the two waitresses who were working that afternoon, was a middle-aged woman named Louise

Beck, who said she remembered Carl Seeger coming in with a guy that she didn't know, and that they'd sat in a booth along the far wall, and had argued a good bit. She wouldn't have remembered it herself, but now that Jo said the name, she thought Carl did call him Cecil. They got real hot under the collar, and the other guy ended up storming out.

He'd stood by the door and turned around and yelled, "You ruined me! And you won't get away with it!" Something real close to that, if not word for word.

Seeger'd laughed at him, and everybody in the place had looked real uncomfortable. But Seeger'd sat there, waiting a good long while before he left. He refused to pay for the other fella's coffee too, but the Woodford's owner was working that shift, and he'd insisted Carl pay. So he paid up and left, saying that was the last time he'd darken their door if he lived to be a hundred.

Jo wrote down everything Louise said and asked her to read it and sign it. And she did, even though she dithered a while, after Jo explained she was trying to help her husband who'd been wrongly accused of murder.

The library in Versailles had copies of telephone books in other cities, and Jo stopped there, before she went home, and got the number for Winston Frazier, Carl's doctor's son, in Louisville. She then copied out every listing for a Freeman residence in Detroit, Michigan. Jack had told her he'd be calling his folks every Sunday, because once he'd gotten back in touch with them, he'd seen how frail and overworked his father was, and wanted to talk with him every week at least.

Jo tried to remember what his dad's first name was while she drove home, but didn't come up with it. She fed Ross, and put a load of diapers in the washer, then called Winston Frazier in Louisville, without getting an answer.

*Excerpt From Jo Grant Munro's Journal*
*Saturday, May 16th, 1964*

*It's 2:15, and I can't sleep. I went in to check on Ross too, and discovered he was sopping wet, so I changed him, and watched him sleep for awhile, wondering what he'll be like when he grows up. Who he'll marry. What kind of trouble he'll have to go through. What he'll end up doing. Hoping he won't be "the murderer's son," but a responsible kid from a regular family trying to make his way.*

*It was Alan who woke me up. Alan, the way he is today. He was repairing the water heater tonight, just before dinner, replacing a metal rod of some kind, and he was struggling with the mechanics of it, the screws or the bolts or something, and he started swearing, which he almost never does, and he threw a screwdriver and wrench across the pantry, then slammed the pantry door. He grabbed his helmet, and the key to his Triumph, and rode off without saying a word.*

*He didn't come home till after 8:00, and he apologized then, and said he didn't know what had come over him. And he fixed the water heater, and ate his dinner, and lifted weights before he went to bed.*

*But when we were lying there about 11:00, Emmy snoring on her bed, my head on Alan's shoulder, he said, "You know what bothers me, Jo? It's that even if I end up being acquitted—and I've got no reason now to think that's going to happen—there'll always be people who think I'm guilty and got off because of somebody I know, or some kind of technicality. Think what that would be like. For you, and for Ross too. I don't see how we'll ever be done with it."*

*I talked to him about it for a good long while, with me telling him we've got to turn it loose, and not worry about what we can't fix now or in the future. (Advice I ought to take myself and almost never do.) I don't know that I said anything that helped. Except that Bob Harrison believes he's innocent. He hasn't vacillated at all. And he's talked to practically everyone he knows telling them too. Alan said, "Yeah, that helps." And wrapped his other arm around me before he finally got to sleep.*

*At least I talked to Jack's father. Finally. And Alan will watch Ross so I can leave in the morning. I figure I'll make it to Toledo tonight, and leave for Detroit really early tomorrow. Jack will be six hours ahead, and he usually calls by 1:00, from what his father said.*

*Emmy's paw isn't healing, and I can see the vet's getting worried.*

*Sunday, May 17th, 1964*

It was late morning when Jo finally found herself in a very nasty part of Detroit not too far from the bridge to Canada. She'd passed through block after block of urban horror—crumbling unpainted buildings, trash blown into every doorway, sad, grim, hopeless looking people shuffling past bars and pawn shops, where once there'd been well kept-houses and small family-owned businesses.

The things of man run amok. They made Jo wince and feel sad and sick, since neither she, nor anyone else, had figured out what to do.

When she turned into Jack Freeman's parents' side street, there were a few more livable houses and fewer commercial wrecks. And then, unexpectedly, two blocks ahead, she saw what looked like a tangled jungle —a green oasis in a concrete desert that turned out to be theirs.

It got stranger as she got closer—a huge lot, there in the city, completely hidden by high trees and overgrown shrubs woven through a rusted chain-link fence that looked like it bound the whole property.

An even taller iron gate had been left unlocked for her, and she shut it again behind her, then drove across an acre of weeds in scrubby grass on a cracked meandering concrete drive that ended in front of a huge Victorian shingle-sided house that had once been painted gray.

Slates had fallen from the roof. Moss grew on the siding. Paint hung in strips from the window frames and the moldings around the front door.

Decay on such a scale depressed her, and Jo told herself, as she stood and stretched beside her pick-up, not to let herself look too appalled in case someone inside was watching.

The rain she'd been driving through since the Michigan line gusted around her, under overgrown trees half-blocking the sky, as she picked her way across weeds in the walk to the heavy mahogany door, and knocked twice, waiting uneasily, before it was opened by an elderly woman who was nearly six feet tall.

She looked almost skeletal, which may have made her seem older than she was. The heavy caked makeup too, seeping into cracks and wrinkles, the nonexistent eyebrows painted into place, the turquoise eyelids, the magenta lips—turned her into a caricature of what she once must've been.

She wore a sleeveless, flowered, diaphanous silk dress with a yellow silk scarf that hung to her knees. And she stared at Jo silently for entirely too long once Jo had introduced herself, before she said, "You may enter," in a husky Russian accent. "Dr. Freeman is at the hospital finishing morning rounds. I shall show you my collections until he returns."

"You're Mrs. Freeman?"

She nodded as though Jo were feebleminded, before she turned, limping on her right leg, and crossed the front hall.


It was a surrealistic experience, watching Eloise Freeman—listening too, to her ongoing monologue, as she led Jo from room to room—from library to morning room, from ballroom to withdrawing room, from guest rooms to nursery—showing her a priceless collection of antique musical instruments from every peak, and jungle, and back alley of the world.

"The keyboard collection is the centerpiece of my life's work. This pianoforte we know with certainty to have belonged to Amadeus Mozart from 1774 to 1777 when he was a child in Salzburg. The piano on your left was Frederic Chopin's when he lived in France with the adventuress Amantine Dupin, known to the world as George Sand. Another equally important piano acquisition will be brought to fruition shortly. Early harpsichords we will see displayed in the next room.

"The sackbut on the far wall, the serpent there, and the lizard, are early medieval horn instruments with substantial historical significance."

There were many Medieval and Renaissance stringed instruments Jo knew nothing about—the dulcian, the gamba, the rebec among them. There were violins owned by famous makers and performers, and ceremonial temple sitars from India and Nepal, along with seemingly unlimited varieties of drums from places Jo had never heard of.

The breadth and depth of the collection was astonishing. But also distinctly disturbing. The house could collapse, the grounds become jungle, the neighborhood a war zone, while Eloise Freeman wandered alone from one room to the next, hiding her injured hand in her scarf, caressing her obsessions.

Jo said, "That's amazing," and "That's really beautiful," till she thought she sounded like a much-impaired parrot, while she studied Mrs. Freeman's painted face for perceptible signs of Jack.

Then—when the guided tour had gotten to what had started as a sun-room—Jack's father walked through the door from the garage, carrying a worn black medical bag, smelling faintly of rubbing alcohol, mixed with glycol and soap.

He looked slightly older than his wife, probably in

his mid-to-late eighties—a small man with a serious face that examined Jo's carefully, as his heels clacked across cold terrazzo, hurrying toward her.

His hair and beard were gray and neat. His eyeglasses were rimless. A gold watch-chain hung across the vest of his three piece black suit. And though his eyes had faded to a soft gray-blue, Jo saw what looked to her like world-weathered astuteness there that brought any hint of easy softness into dispute.

He asked if she'd been offered refreshment, and when Jo said no, he suggested they go through to his study where he'd make her a glass of Russian tea.

Mrs. Freeman walked away, back toward the room that was filled with pianos, while her husband took Jo's hand and held it for a second, before he led her through the opposite door.

"I am so pleased to meet you, after all you have done for Jack. You know, the first Christmas after the war, when Jack had returned from Europe, one could see he had suffered emotional trauma. And yet, he spoke of your brother with such respect I was happy to have Jack leave us and visit him in Kentucky."

"I remember that visit. Tom really liked Jack."

"I had hoped Jack would agree to consult a colleague of mine at that time, who worked exclusively with returning soldiers, but, alas, it was not to be. Readiness and timing can be of great importance."

"He's doing really well now."

Dr. Freeman nodded, and almost bowed in Jo's direction, before he began making tea on a hot plate on a library table under one of the north windows. She wandered the perimeter of the room reading titles in the bookcases that covered the walls, unable to think of something useful to say. She finally asked if she remembered correctly that Mrs. Freeman had been a pianist.

"A very fine pianist indeed. The injuries she suffered robbed her of that artistic outlet, as well as her career. Would you care for milk or sugar?"

Jo shook her head, and he motioned her to a leather chair on the right side of the fireplace.

He sat and sipped across from her, then set his glass, with its ornate silver handle, on the slate-topped table between them. "One would have hoped that Jack could have spoken to us, but he rarely did, of his inner life, even as a child." Dr. Freeman raised his hands above his shoulders in one of the "what-can-you-do?" gestures understood around the world. "It can be terribly difficult to confide in one's family in the best of circumstances. Though since Eloise and I did endure many dangers and difficulties in our escape after the Bolshevik Revolution, we would not have been crushed by hearing of the hardships Jack overcame as well. I have sometimes feared he chose not to speak to spare our feelings, rather than his."

"Jack was born in Paris?"

"Where we first emigrated, yes. It was here I legally changed my name to David Freeman. Here I have been truly free for the first time in my life."

He sipped his tea, and stared at the empty hearth before he spoke again. "I cannot tell you how relieved I was, how joyous, for that I believe is the only suitable word, when Jack phoned two years ago, after you and your husband had been so kind to him."

"We didn't do anything that—"

"I sobbed, I assure you, like a very small child. For

to hear his voice! To see him again, after seventeen years of not knowing whether he was alive or dead—I ask for nothing more as long as I shall live." There were tears in his eyes, and he brushed them away with a folded white handkerchief he'd pulled from a vest pocket. "To have an opportunity to assist you now, is a very great pleasure indeed."

"We didn't do anything anybody else wouldn't have done for Jack. I think it was more a matter of timing, and him being ready to change."

"He would disagree. He has told me that without your—"

The phone rang then, and Dr. Freeman rose stiffly from his chair, and stepped across to the desk. "Yes, operator. This is David Freeman speaking. ... Yes, I shall wait. ... Jack my son! Good. ... You *did*! Thank God! ... Yes, yes, I agree. Still, there is someone here who wishes to speak to you with the greatest urgency. I shall hand the phone to Mrs. Munro."

Jo was standing by him by that time, and she grabbed the old-fashioned metal receiver and told Jack as fast as she could what had happened to Alan. "Can you tell me more about Carl that morning, when you saw him standing in the parking lot? How near was he to Alan's car, and was there anything else you noticed?"

Jack told her, making blood rush hot to her face, making her grip the receiver even harder before she spoke again. "If I give you two telex numbers—one for the Sheriff's Department and one for Equine—could you write out everything you saw and Telex it to Sheriff Peabody, and to Alan too? I know it'll be expensive, but I'll pay you back when you get home ..." She gave him the numbers, and then asked when he'd be back.

"Wednesday. Good. I can pick you up. You wouldn't believe what Alan's been through. ... Thank you. Yes, I know you do. ... I can go find your mother while you talk to your father, if you want to ... Then I'll give him the phone. I'll see you Wednesday afternoon."

*Excerpt From Jo Grant Munro's Journal*
*Saturday, May 23rd, 1964*

*I haven't written in the journal in days. This last week has felt like we're living in a pressure cooker. One minute we'd be picking our way across a minefield, the next we'd be thinking there was some chance we could prove Alan's innocence—right before the rug would start moving, making us scramble to stand.*

*Garner talked to Brad Harrison on Monday the 18th on Brad's lunch hour, and asked what the heck he was doing in February down at Cumberland Falls State Park talking to Carl Seeger. I guess Brad looked totally shocked and flustered, which always makes Brad bluster, and then he backpedaled and refused to answer, accusing Garner of undue pressure and putting him under duress. Garner's good, though. He got him calmed down and kept him from feeling threatened, without ever telling him who'd seen him, so that Brad eventually told him that Carl had called him earlier that week and asked if he could see him somewhere discreet that Saturday where they wouldn't be observed.*

*Brad was driving down to Williamsburg, Kentucky*

*that Friday to be in a friend's wedding, and if he wanted to meet on Saturday it would have to be there, or somewhere close by, in the morning. They chose the parking lot at the park. And he said Carl asked a lot of questions about how Equine was doing. What new products, if any, there were. How people in the lab were putting up with Alan. How the new production manager was getting along. Mostly, he wanted to complain about Alan and compare the "era under his rule" with the way it once had been.*

*Garner had led him to whether Carl had asked for keys, or materials from the lab, and Brad denied it hotly. Garner ended up believing it was as accurate a report as he was likely to get, and none of us could see how it helped our case.*

*Garner went to meet with the Circuit Court Judge on Wednesday and laid motions before asking him to have the case dismissed (and got the motion dismissed instead, pretty much the way he figured), then asked for a court date postponement till the court meets the third Wednesday in June, which the judge granted.*

*I picked Jack up in Cincinnati that same Wednesday evening, and we started out talking about him seeing Carl by Alan's car. I told him Alan's doors had been unlocked like always, and Jack said Carl had been standing by the car, and had then bent down beside the driver's door. It could've been to keep from being seen. But it certainly made it possible that he'd dumped dirt on the floormat.*

*I talked for a long time about what it'd been like going through the arrest and the rest of it, and Jack listened, and asked questions, and I felt better when we finished.*

*Then we talked about what he'd done in France, and it was good to get lost in something else. To hear how he'd found Camille, and how well they'd talked, and how glad he'd been to be with her, and how he'd confronted the jerk who'd set him up, who actually stood right there in front of them and justified what he'd done. It was so good to see Jack happy, and then watch while he blushed bright red telling me Camille had said she'd come visit this fall.*

*I said, "You know one thing you can count on, she's bound to like your house. I mean who wouldn't like a Cotswold Cottage on a piece of land like that?"*

*Jack looked kind of panicked then, and said, "I need to clean better than I've been. And I might paint the upstairs too. I also ought to get the lease renewed early. I don't want to have to move."*

*He looked mightily embarrassed, and I laughed, and it felt really good. Normal. The way life used to. Before I'd started imagining Alan behind bars.*

*Jack had a long talk with Earl Peabody on Thursday morning. And amazingly enough, Earl called that night. I answered the phone, and he sounded mighty awkward, but he told me he really did wish Alan well, and could he have a word with him. He told Alan he was glad to get Jack's statement about seeing Carl by Alan's car.*

*Alan asked Earl what locksmiths and hardware stores they'd taken Carl's picture to to find out if he'd gotten duplicate keys made, and Earl was willing to tell him. So that was kind of encouraging. That there was some sign that Earl was after the truth, and not completely set against us.*

*That same day, of course, another escape route*

*collapsed around us. The lab supplier who'd blamed Carl for him losing his business and had looked like a possible suspect, Garner tracked him down in Louisville, and there's no doubt whatsoever that he was in the hospital when Carl died, having just had a hernia operation that kept him there for a week.*

*Then yesterday, Friday, the 22nd, I finally got Carl's doctor's son, Winston, on the phone. It seems that after his dad retired and sold the practice, he bought a pickup truck and had it modified as a camper. His wife died last summer, and he had no intention of hanging around home. He'd read Steinbeck's* Travels With Charlie, *and he'd decided to do what Steinbeck had done—travel the country in a compact camper, with only his dog for company, wherever he felt like going with nothing planned ahead.*

*The son had just spent two weeks with him in the mountains of western Virginia, but he didn't know where he'd gone from there. He's on his way to Maine, but how far he'd gotten, Winston didn't know. His dad did phone him from time to time, and when he called next, Winston said he'd tell his dad about us, and find out where we could meet him, or phone at the very least.*

*So all we can do is wait to hear how Carl took the news of his cancer, and if anything he said seemed consistent with planning to kill himself, and blame Alan for his death.*

*Emmy's foot isn't getting better and we're changing antibiotics.*

# CHAPTER THIRTEEN

*Sunday, May 24th, 1964*

When they got home from church, Jo rode Maggie for the first time, having lunged her for two weeks and watched for any sign of lameness. She decided she was sound, but needed to be brought back slowly and carefully, even though finding the time to ride her wasn't going to be easy.

Jo and Alan spent the rest of the afternoon working away at the ultimate obstacle to proving Carl had set Alan up: How had Carl gotten the keys, and spent time in the lab unseen?

It was Jo thinking about how sometime early in the fall she'd seen Carl having lunch with Jean Nagy, that got them headed in the first direction that seemed to have potential.

Jean was a lab tech at Equine who'd worked for Carl, and who by then had a new key to the lab. Alan didn't think Jean would've deliberately given it to Carl to copy, and she only had a key to the lab anyway, not the front door, or Alan's office, which Carl would've needed to steal his pen.

But what if she'd gone to the restroom, or spoken to someone else at the Wagon Wheel, and left her purse on the table? Carl could've pulled out her keys and made an impression that would've allowed him to get a copy made at any locksmith's anywhere.

And if he had just that one key? How could he manage the rest?

Alan and Jo picked at it for an hour more, and the eventual scenario they worked out began to make some sense.

Carl would've known the receptionist's schedule, and he could've stood in the trees at the end of the front parking lot during the afternoon and used binoculars to see when she left her desk to go to the restroom, or stepped away on her coffee break.

The way the building was laid out, if he'd come in the front door, between 3:15 and 3:30 or so, and he'd gotten past the receptionist's desk when she was away, he could've taken a quick left down the short side hall where the lab's side wall was on the right, and the janitor's supply room was opposite the lab door on the left. There was an office storage room next door to the janitor's, and Carl could have hidden in that storage room (where they kept brochures and labels and paper supplies) till he was sure the plant people were gone. They got off at 3:00, so if he'd gotten there sometime around 3:30, if he was very careful, between then and 4:00 (when Vincent, the janitor, came in), he could've gotten out to the plant and climbed up the metal stairs to the open mezzanine storage area where no one went for weeks on end. He could've hidden behind the old files and furniture and stayed there until after midnight, when Vincent would've gone home.

He could've gotten into the lab with his copy of Jean's key and taken everything he needed—the syringes, the font ball, the paper, the Dylox, the vinyl gloves too—except for Alan's pen. Then, if he'd gone back to the storage room, across from the door to the lab, he would've heard Alan come in at 5:00 or a few minutes after, and been able to stay there and listen till he heard Alan go out to the plant between 6:30 and 7:00 to discuss the day's batches with the new production manager.

The plant people couldn't have seen him leave the storage room, and at that hour of the morning, no one would've been in the lab, or in the reception area. Bob Harrison came in early most days, but his office was down the long hall from reception at the far end of the building. The week the Selectric ball was switched, he'd been out of town too, which Carl could've learned from Jean the lab tech, or from Brad Harrison.

So if he'd waited in the storage room till Alan went out to the plant, he could've snuck in the lab and into Alan's unlocked office, and taken impressions of the keys to his office, his desk and the front door, which Alan would have left in the pocket of his sport jacket hanging on the back of his door. While Alan was in the plant, Carl could've snuck out the fire door, halfway up the long hall toward Bob's office from the receptionist's desk, which was always unlocked from the inside. The plant people, who started at 7:00, came in the plant door, and no one would've unlocked the front door until shortly before 8:00, when the receptionist went to her desk.

That same night, using the keys he would've had made that day, Carl could've come back after midnight, when Vincent had finished cleaning, and put the ball back on the Selectric, and taken Alan's pen.

Of course, he could've sat down and typed something there in the lab the first night instead of stealing the ball and having to bring it back. But maybe he hadn't wanted to risk more time in the lab than he could help. Because what if Vincent forgot something and came back? Or Alan came in even earlier? And he did sometimes, by 3:00 or 4:00.

Alan and Jo thrashed it out, with "what ifs?" and "that wouldn't work," till they wrote this version down, thinking that if anyone could've seen Carl, it would've been the receptionist—seeing him, in the trees in front, watching her desk. Or Vincent, making his rounds, maybe even hearing someone in the storage room next to his supply room.

Vincent had just spent three weeks with his parents in Virginia, and his first day back would be Tuesday, the 26th. Alan told Jo he'd talk to Vincent as soon as he came in and see what he could find out. Hearing about Carl's death would've been traumatic for Vincent, before he went on vacation. And then learning that Alan had been charged, once he got back, must've upset him too. So figuring out how to talk to Vincent would be even harder than normal.

Jo said she'd tackle Jean Nagy after work on Monday, since she'd been the one who'd seen her at the Wagon Wheel with Carl in the fall. If Alan talked to her she might feel pressured and decide to take offense. Jean was touchy. A chronic complainer in sensible shoes who seemed to resent most of what she faced in life, and criticized whoever wasn't standing in front of her.

<br>

*Excerpt From Jo Grant Munro's Journal*
*Friday, May 29th, 1964*

<br>

*It's been another week of living on nerves and caffeine. It's 1:00 in the morning now, and Alan hasn't come home from the office. He came home for dinner, and played with Ross for awhile, but then said he had to go back and get some more work done.*

*Monday I talked to Jean Nagy. It wasn't easy to get her talking, but she did admit that she'd had lunch with Carl more than once, the last time probably in January, or maybe early February. She was incensed at what she took as an implication that she might've given her key to Carl to make a duplicate, but she did acknowledge that she'd left her purse on the table in the booth on more than one occasion when she went up to the counter to chat with the waitress she's known since high school. Whether he did make an imprint of her key she had no way of knowing.*

*Alan tried to talk to Vincent Tuesday night, but he was working in a blind panic after having been gone, and he said he couldn't concentrate on his work and talk to Alan too. Alan could see he wouldn't get anything out of him that night, and he also felt even more sorry for him than normal because he seemed so flustered, partly because of the poor job done by the cleaning service while he was gone. Consequently, Alan decided to give Vincent a couple more days before he tried again.*

*Spencer called Wednesday night. He's been working so hard trying to get the buyout of Everett Adams's van business organized we haven't seen him hardly at all.*

*But he called to say he's had an idea he thinks might help. He didn't tell us what it was, because he "doesn't want to get our hopes up," but he is "pursuing a line of inquiry" (which he said in an English accent as though he were Sherlock Holmes).*

*I was telling him about trying to track down Carl's doctor, waiting for his son to hear from him and tell us where he's gone, and Spencer said, "When you do, I'll drive wherever he is and get a written document."*

*I was speechless—before I thanked him. I'd been worrying about what we'd do, because Alan can't leave the county. And it'd be hard for me to travel very far with Ross.*

*On Thursday, Alan and Bob Harrison went to Vincent Eriksen's house to see if they could talk to him. Vincent was there, but he didn't come out. His sister said he was having "emotional difficulties"—perhaps from being away from work, and feeling unsure of accomplishing the work as well as normal, though she said she thought there was more to it than that, but what she didn't know.*

*Bob explained that it was very important that he or Alan speak to Vincent soon to see if he knows anything that might help Alan. She said she'd talk to him, and see what she could do. But that timing was very important with Vincent. If you waited till he was ready, the outcome was always better.*

*So. We wait. It makes sense, but it makes me crazy. I've been praying for patience most of my adult life, because I was born wanting to move at a hundred miles an hour and when I can't I fume. Life inside this bonehouse can feel like an endless obstacle course to someone as restless as me.*

*Mom used to say that the way a prayer for patience gets answered is that you're put through a string of situations that make you really impatient, and then you're made to wait. I see why that works. I just wish there were another way.*

*Emmy's paw isn't getting any worse, but not much better either, so we're doctoring three times a day. Sam sliced his flank on a split fence board in his paddock too (which we found with some difficulty and replaced), and when the vet stitched him up, Sam turned his head and looked him in the eye in a considering sort of way, but stood stock still till he was done.*

*Monday, June 1st, 1964*

Friday night the phone rang, and a thin wavery male voice asked to speak to Alan. When Alan got to the phone, the other person hung up. Which made Alan and Jo begin to worry. Though whoever it was sounded so unsettled it didn't seem like a threat.

Unlike the calls Alan was getting from Butch once or twice a week. They'd gotten more and more vindictive, and he'd begun to sound unhinged.

Then Saturday morning at eight Jo got a call from Dr. Frazier's son, Winston. His dad had called from Williamsburg, Virginia, and the son explained what had happened to Alan, and got his dad to agree to stay there, and visit the Williamsburg Inn for messages until someone appeared.

Jo called Spence, and he said he'd get a neighbor to take care of his horses and he'd leave within the hour. He called at ten that night after having talked to Dr. Frazier, who'd said Carl had looked shocked when he'd heard about the cancer, more or less like anyone. But that then he'd said, with an oddly unpleasant expression on his face, "So I don't have anything to lose." The doctor said Carl had laughed then in a way that had made Dr. Frazier uncomfortable, before he'd reached over and grabbed his file off the doctor's desk and left without another word.

Spencer asked Dr. Frazier to write down everything he remembered, which he did right away, and Spencer would bring it to them the next day. The Doc said he'd call Winston more often too, in case Garner or the Sheriff wanted to talk to him directly so a time could be arranged.

The next day, Sunday, Jo got a call from Buddy. He and Becky and the twins had come over on Saturday, to see how Jo and Alan were doing (and so Buddy could look at the yearlings too, with an eye to the July sales).

Alan had told him their theory about how Carl could've gotten into the lab, and how they needed to talk to Vincent to see if he'd seen anything, since the receptionist hadn't.

Buddy went to the same church as Vincent, and he said he'd try to talk to him. He called Sunday afternoon and told Jo he'd talked to Vincent that morning, and he'd ended up agreeing that if Alan and Jo came to his house Monday morning he'd be willing to talk.

It was torturous for Vincent, trying to describe what he'd seen. And though there were stops and starts and much staring off into space in the telling, the long and the short of it was that in March, at two in the morning on the 20th (he'd written the date in his monthly calendar, while he tried to decide what to do), Vincent had realized after he'd left work at midnight, and gotten home and gone to bed, that he hadn't emptied the trash cans from the lab, which were by far the most critical because of the chemicals, the drugs, the hypodermics, and the glassware disposal, that all had to be handled differently with very precise controls.

"I got dressed right away. And I drove to work. I went in the back way at 2:40 a.m., through the plant, the way I always do, and along the hall under the mezzanine. It's a narrow hall, and there's a door at the end that opens into the long back hall. That's the hall that goes to the left the length of the lab by the plant."

Vincent stopped.

And Alan nodded. And then said, "I remember."

"There's a window there into the lab that faces the plant wall. And another window in your office, where it sits at the corner by the side hall. And as soon as I started to open the plant door opposite the lab, I saw ... I saw movement inside your office."

Jo and Alan waited, watching Vincent stare at the street, till Jo finally asked him in a very quiet voice what had happened next.

"Only the desk lamp was on. I know that for a fact. And I stood there, holding the door only slightly ajar, and I ... I saw Mr. Seeger standing by your desk. ... I know it was Mr. Seeger. I watched him for quite awhile. Opening drawers and picking something up, though what it was I couldn't tell.

"It upset me. Seeing Mr. Seeger. I knew he shouldn't have been in the building, and certainly not in your office. But I didn't know how to respond. I thought that perhaps I … I finally chose to leave the building without taking care of the laboratory trash. I knew I shouldn't have done that. But there was nothing else I could think to do."

Vincent said he'd eventually decided that he should talk to Mr. Harrison, but the longer he postponed, the harder it got to make a move. Nothing bad seemed to have come of it. Weeks went by, and then Carl died, so what difference would it make? He went on his first vacation away from home, and then heard from his sister that Mr. Munro had been arrested, and the horror of it paralyzed him. Was he responsible for Carl Seeger's death by not telling Mr. Harrison? Did Mr. Munro really kill Mr. Seeger? Vincent didn't think he would, but how could he be sure? And what would happen if Mr. Munro found out he knew something and hadn't been able to make himself talk? Did he harm Mr. Munro if he didn't speak up? He didn't know that what he'd seen mattered, and thinking about it was making him ill.

But that Monday morning, as hard as it was for him, when Jo and Alan talked with him, Vincent told them everything he knew, and then wrote it down, slowly and carefully, and even told Alan he'd talk to the Sheriff if they thought he should, but he didn't want to go to his office.

It made Jo feel awful, watching Vincent torture himself. He looked so sad, and so apologetic. And then he'd asked Jo if she could forgive him. That maybe if he'd told what he knew, Alan wouldn't have been arrested.

Jo thought about that for half a second, because that might indeed have been perfectly true, but watching Vincent suffer in ways she couldn't fathom, made her say, "You're a very good man. You did the best you could. There's nothing that needs to be forgiven."

He'd jumped up then and said, "I have to go now." And rushed into his house, his hands shaking as he picked up his cat and closed the door behind him.

Jo was worrying about what talking to them might've done to Vincent by the time they walked toward their car, which was when Alan said, "He works so hard, and he's so reliable, and I don't think we'll ever know how much that costs him."

"Or how much work comforts him too. Don't you think it gives him a sense of purpose? A way to contribute that makes him feel worthwhile?"

"I do. I think it helps keep him going. I also think his one piece of information could change the whole case."

"I hope."

"I'm going to take tomorrow off and drive up to Georgetown. Earl's men got to the locksmiths in Lexington, and the smiths and hardware stores in Versailles and Midway, but no farther than that. I'll take a picture of Carl and go up to Georgetown, and Frankfort if I have to, and Louisville after that, till I find the locksmith who made keys for Carl."

*Tuesday, June 2nd, 1964*

Before Alan got back the next day, Spencer drove over right before supper. He slammed the truck door, and ran up to the house, and Jo saw him from the long drive when she was walking back from the barns. She had Ross with her in his stroller, and Emmy was limping back and forth beside them—though she took off toward the house, faster than Jo wanted her to, as soon as she saw Spence.

He rubbed her chest and talked to her till Ross and Jo got there, and when Jo saw Spencer's face, she knew he had good news. But all she said was, "You look hot and sticky. Want an iced tea or a lemonade?"

"You aren't going to offer me a bourbon?" He was laughing, looking down at her, a paper rolled up in his hand.

"No, I'm not! Let's go sit in back."

"Emmy's foot must be better."

"It is. Thank God. It was touch and go for weeks. The vet even talked about having to amputate, before it turned around."

Jo put a comforter on the floor of the arbor, and plopped Ross down on that with pillows arranged in a circle around him. He'd just started sitting up, and she didn't want him to crash over and hit his head on the bricks. "So what is it? You're grinning from ear to ear."

"You 'member last week I said I'd had an idea, but I wasn't going to tell you what? It'd finally occurred to me that the public phones in Versailles and Midway are privately owned. The owners put up the phone boxes, and collect the coins, and have all the records of what calls were placed."

"I'd forgotten, if I ever knew."

"Well, I know the guy who owns them in Versailles. And there's one phone box almost at the corner of Main Street, maybe one block east of Carl's house, and half a block south."

"And?"

"My friend looked through the records, and at 5:59 p.m. on April 15th, a call was placed from that phone box to your home number." Spencer's blue eyes were crinkling at the corners, and he looked like a teenage boy who'd just bought his first car. "So though we can't prove that Carl placed the call, we can prove that such a call was placed from close by Carl's house, so that's some corroboration for Alan's side of the story."

"Thanks, Spence." Jo's throat was fighting against her and she swallowed before she could say anything else. "You've done so much for us. Driving to Williamsburg, when your own work's so overwhelming. I don't know how we can—"

"'Member helping me two years ago? 'Member how you saved me from the worst mistake I couldda made? That would've—"

"Still."

"You would've done the same for me."


Alan came home after Spencer left, having found a locksmith in Georgetown who recognized Carl from his picture. He'd brought putty impressions of three keys sometime in March, and he'd told him these were to his mother's house—to an outside door, as well as her bedroom, and her desk. That she'd gotten horribly demented, and she'd lock herself in all the time, and then fall, and he couldn't get in to help. Carl had said she couldn't recognize him anymore, and she didn't want him to have her keys. So he had to get them copied to care for her the way he should.

Alan had found another locksmith in Franklin who'd made a copy of one key for Carl in late February or early March. And he had written documents from both of them with Carl's photo attached.

Jo was stunned, standing stock-still and staring. And Alan wrapped his arms around her and held her head against his chest.

*Friday, June 5th, 1964*

Garner and Alan presented their case to Sheriff Peabody at Garner's office. Jo stayed home to take care of Ross, who was sick as a dog with stomach flu.

It was tense—polite and respectful on both sides—but tense. Earl considered the materials they presented and listened to the extract of the case from Garner:

—Carl Seeger had terminal lung cancer, which
    gave him a motive for killing himself to avoid
    suffering. He destroyed the records that
    revealed his illness and the identity of his
    doctor, including his engagement calendar and
    his address book, so no motive for suicide
    would be obvious.

—He obtained access to Equine Pharmaceuticals, using impressions of four keys to obtain duplicates (details and documentation attached), where all materials left in his house to incriminate Alan had been procured.

—He was seen by an eyewitness (document attached) in Alan's office, taking something out of Alan's desk early in the morning of March 20th, when the Selectric font ball was also replaced on the lab secretary's typewriter (document attached).

—He was seen the morning of his death beside Alan's unlocked driver's door (document attached), where he could have deposited the samples of dirt from outside his kitchen door that were found on Alan's shoes and floormat.

—A call placed from a public phone box less than two blocks from Carl Seeger's house (private phone company records attached) to Alan at 5:59 that same evening caused Alan to drive down Carl Seeger's road, thereby being seen by a witness, leaving him without an alibi for the time of Mr. Seeger's death.

—Carl Seeger's hatred of Alan is well documented (see attached).

—No evidence exists that places Alan in Carl Seeger's house.

Earl took his copies of the materials and rose to leave Garner's conference room, when Alan asked if he could speak to him alone for a minute.

Garner left. And Alan and Earl looked at each other from opposite sides of the table, Earl holding the file in one enormous hand, his big brown sheriff's hat in the other. His face was flushed, and he was sweating, and he seemed to be avoiding Alan's eyes.

"Earl, I've always had real respect for you, and I think of you as a friend. I don't hold this against you. I don't. You had limited resources, and it's been a complicated case. If Jo and I and Garner hadn't had help from several other people, we wouldn't have gotten the new evidence.

"But this could still drag on. It may not be easy to get the County and the Commonwealth Attorneys to be willing to drop the case. I don't want Jo to have to go through anymore of this if we can help it."

"You're not askin' me to do nothin' outside the normal legal procedures and all?" Earl looked mildly indignant for half a minute, as though he were hoping for something to hold on to that would put Alan in the wrong.

"No! Not at all. I just know that if you go to bat for us, the case will get dismissed a great deal faster than if you stay on the sidelines."

"The case ain't open and shut. There're still factors to be considered, that—"

"Like our County Attorney being an ambitious man who'd like to look like an aggressive prosecutor in the middle of an election, and isn't going to want to admit he's brought a case against an innocent man?"

Earl's big broad face seemed to freeze, even in the

heat, and he didn't blink behind his black-framed glasses for what seemed like more than a minute. Then he put on his hat, and walked out the door, telling Alan he'd talk to him later.

*Excerpt From Jo Grant Munro's Journal*
*Sunday, June 7th, 1964*

*The waiting's getting harder. It's been two days since Alan talked to Earl, and we keep thinking every time the phone rings it'll be him saying he'll talk to the County Attorney and try to get the case dropped.*

*It's never Earl, though. It's Butch on the phone more than I can bear. Gloating. Still. Telling us what'll happen to Alan when he gets to prison. He makes me want to say something mean that'll give me some kind of satisfaction besides just hanging up.*

*I don't, because I shouldn't. But it's getting harder over time.*

"Earl?" Cassie Peabody had been watching her husband dry the same plate over and over while he stared out the kitchen window.

"Yep?"

"You thinking about Alan?"

"Some."

"Well?"

"What?"

"What're you gonna do?"

"It ain't all that easy."

"You think he's guilty?"

Earl laid the last plate in the cupboard and hung the dishtowel across the towel bar, then grabbed a clean glass and poured himself iced tea. "You want another glass, Cassie?"

"I do. Thank you. Well?" Her warm brown eyes were smiling at him, teasing him in a way he knew well.

"I reckon ya wantta hear about it."

"Yes, sir, I do."

"It ain't clear cut."

"We got time. I'll make us some popcorn and bring it out to the screened-in porch."


Earl told her all of it. The history of what he'd seen, and heard, and what he'd found at Carl's and at Equine, of all the folks he'd talked to, and the circumstantial evidence that'd piled up as he went, and what the labs said later.

He told her what had just come to light, what Garner and Alan had given him that week. And then he sat and stared at the pasture beyond their small backyard where their grown kids' old gray pony tossed his head and swished at flies as the sun burned up the strip of west woods on the far side of his paddock.

Cassie didn't say anything when he'd finished. She let the silence stretch out between them as she picked up the bowl Earl had all but licked, and set hers inside it, then put both on the wicker table at her end of their wooden swing.

She looked so small sitting next him, her toes just touching the concrete floor, as she hummed a tune from one of the big bands she'd loved when she was young.

His legs were stretched out, keeping the swing

swaying, while two male hummingbirds did aerial combat around the feeder outside the screen beside Cassie. "Well?" Earl didn't look at her when he said it. "You're fixin' to say somethin'. You might as well go on."

"I got a good notion what you'rc gonna do."

"Even when I don't?"

"I do. Just like when you fussed and fidgeted buying the pickup last year. You read every car magazine, and you traipsed all over creation, looking at this one and looking at that, and I knew you'd get you a Ford just like the time before."

Earl didn't say anything more. He set the swing to swinging again and drank off half his tea.

"I know what kind of man I married."

"A de-mobbed kid who had to drive a gravel truck, and couldn't get elected dog catcher."

"Didn't keep me from marryin' you."

"Nope." He squeezed her right hand and held it on his knee. "But whether you or me likes it or not, this here's an election year, and I gotta deal with the County Attorney, who ain't an easy man."

"Guess it comes down to why you'd want to be sheriff."

"You know why I do it."

"Yep, and that's why I know what you're gonna do."

Earl didn't say anything.

And Cassie asked what he would've done different.

"Interviewed every damn employee at Equine Pharmaceuticals. Gone to every locksmith and hardware store in a sixty mile radius. Checked the private payphone owner here and in Midway. Don't know why I didn't think of that. Just worked with Bell Telephone, and let the rest ride."

"I know, but with the robberies, and all, with all the rich folks in the whole county up in arms, it didn't look like you had time. And didn't you just tell me two of 'em at Equine who knew somethin' important were outta town for weeks?"

"The janitor and the secretary with the typewriter thingy that got took."

"Well, then."

Earl didn't say anything. He leaned back and knitted his hands together on the back of his head.

Cassie watched him and sighed before she spoke. "The County and the Commonwealth Attorneys were looking for a case that would be real high interest, and they didn't just climb on the bandwagon they pushed it fast as it could go. I 'member when you first talked to Lou here in Woodford, you weren't ready to arrest Alan, and he jumped ahead."

Earl drank the last of his tea and set the glass on the floor.

"Could you use this as an example of why the Sheriff's Department needs more funding?"

Earl didn't answer.

And Cassie kissed the work shirt between her and his shoulder. "Never mind. You are who you are, and you'll do what you'll do." She looked up at Earl with the smile on her face she'd had when she was three, when he'd lived down the street from her and their folks played cards every Friday.

He patted her thigh with his huge left hand, then covered her hand with his.

Cassie squeezed it back, then went to answer the

phone, hoping it wasn't one more call that'd take Earl out into the night.

# CHAPTER FOURTEEN

*Tuesday, June 9th, 1964*

It was 7:30 when Earl parked his wife's pickup in the circle by Jo and Alan's front porch and climbed out as though his back were killing him. He bent over anyway, even though it looked like it made it worse, so he could talk to Emmy and rub behind her ears. He hauled himself up, one hand on his driver's door, and stared at the old brick farmhouse, at the black shutters and white-framed windows, at the old handmade glass, wavy and bubbled in the small narrow panes.

He told himself to stop putting it off, to go and get a move on. And he straightened his shoulders, and tucked the back of his work shirt farther in his jeans, as he climbed the steps with Emmy beside him, trying to lick his hand. He knocked on the door, and rocked back and forth on his boot heels, his thumbs stuck inside his belt, till Jo opened the door.

"Earl." Jo looked as though her heart had hit her ribs as soon as she saw who it was, and how hard it was for Earl to look her in the eye.

"Evening, Jo. Wonder if I could talk to you and Alan."

She stood where she was, holding on to the door, before she could wave Earl in.


Alan was sitting at the far end of the dining-room table, and Earl sat down on his right, on the long side opposite Jo. He eased himself into the chair, then sat straight up, not touching the chair back, his hands gripping his knees.

Jo said, "You look like your back hurts."

"Threw it out Sunday stackin' wood for the winter. Anyway, the reason I come, I want to tell you folks right to your face that I come to believe the evidence you dug up provides real good reasonable doubt that you're guilty of Carl's death."

Jo said, "Thank God!" while Alan watched Earl without saying a word.

"I b'lieve you had nothin' to do with Carl Seeger's death. Nothin'. That he went out of his way to set you up real deliberate."

Jo was sitting so tensed in her chair, holding her breath as she held on to Ross, that when she made a small strangled sort of sound she didn't even notice.

Alan said, "I appreciate you coming out to tell us." He said it almost formally, with a quiet sort of private restraint, as Jo put Ross in his high chair.

"I'm real sorry for the part I played in your troubles. I will say that Lou Wainwright, the County Attorney, he moved faster than I thought we oughtta, in arresting you and all. But I played my part too, and I sure do regret it. And if I had it to do over, I wouldda interviewed all the folks at Equine with a whole lot more attention."

"I don't blame you. I don't. I blame Carl." Alan folded his napkin and laid it by his plate.

"I'm fixin' to talk to Lou tomorrow. I got a meetin' set up with him and the Commonwealth Attorney, and I'm askin' Garner to meet with us too, and then my intention is to meet with the Circuit Court Judge as soon as can be, and put all this behind us."

Alan stared at Earl, then looked over at Jo, before he took a very deep breath and let it out fast.

"The thing workin' in our favor, is that neither one of them attorneys is gonna want go to court and *lose*. No sir, 'specially not durin' a campaign. All you gotta prove is reasonable doubt, and you done that, good and proper. If that don't make 'em go along, I'll be real surprised. We gotta do what's right, there ain't no doubt about that. And it won't take 'em long to figure out how to make hay out of this for their own campaigns."

"Human nature being as self-serving as it is." Jo handed Ross a bottle, and helped him prop it up.

"I figure we need to make a real big public point of how we're releasin' an innocent man, talkin' to the TV and all, and givin' interviews to the papers. If Garner will go along, and do the interview with us, it'll look real good for everybody."

"Except Alan. There'll be folks around here all his life who still think he's guilty."

"Jo." Alan looked at her as though he thought it would've been better if she hadn't said that.

But Jo didn't look like she agreed.

"She's got a point, Alan. If I could turn back the

clock, I would. I feel real bad for what you've gone through." He was watching Jo when he said it.

And she let him watch in silence.

"Jo?" Alan was staring at her.

After a long awkward silence, she sighed and nodded her head. "I know. I believe you, Earl. I know you didn't want to hurt us. It's just been really hard to bear." She could feel herself getting ready to cry, and she gritted her teeth and took control.

*Excerpt from Jo Grant Munro's Journal*
*Saturday, June 13th, 1964*

*It's almost midnight. After a day of peace. Of looking forward to the future too, for the first time in awhile. Yesterday at nine in the morning Earl Peabody, the County Attorney, the Commonwealth Attorney, and Garner Honeycutt held a press conference and told the world that Alan was absolutely innocent of Carl Seeger's death.*

*They said the Circuit Court Judge presiding over his case had officially dismissed it. That recent evidence absolved Alan and indicated that Carl had intentionally killed himself after having constructed a string of evidence to deliberately incriminate Alan.*

*Bob Harrison called the Versailles paper and asked to be interviewed, which they did that afternoon. The TV people came out to the farm yesterday too, and I actually got to tell them how their assumption that Alan was guilty made the whole experience harder than it had to be. Much to my amazement, some of it got on TV.*

*Alan's interview was aired last night, some at six o'clock, and then again at eleven, and they did it reasonably neutrally.*

*Toss enjoyed talking to them about how Carl had gotten an IRS investigator who was a personal friend to come and torment us, as well as Equine, which—and I have to give him credit—he did without mentioning Terry by name.*

*Interesting too, that the only thing old Terry has found that we should be doing differently is that when I drive the truck for my architecture business, I should keep mileage records, with separate ones too when I use the truck for the broodmare business. That, of course, amounts to nothing, since I never deducted my mileage as a business expense, having never given it a thought.*

*Anyway, that was yesterday. Today we invited Spencer and his girlfriend, Becky and Buddy and their twins, Jack and the Harrisons, and Jane Seeger, Vincent Eriksen too (who naturally didn't come), Garner and his wife, and Earl and his (who had other plans), plus Esther Wilkes and Charlie Smalls (who didn't come but sounded glad that we'd asked them) to come for dinner to celebrate here on the farm.*

*I got a lot done ahead, and then Becky came over to watch Ross in the afternoon, and Alan and I rode Sam and Maggie. I worked Sam on the flat for half an hour, and then we went cross country, giving Maggie a chance to build her endurance without asking too much.*

*We rehashed all of it, this time with a kind of overwhelming relief I can't begin to describe. To have*

*Alan here with me, with his good name restored—I think we're both so grateful it feels like a sacred thing.*

*It's a gift from God, the way we see it. A reconciliation with justice and mercy we'd almost come not to expect, and couldn't truly appreciate till we'd gone through something this extreme.*

*There're so many things that could've kept Alan from being cleared. If Vincent hadn't forgotten to empty the lab trash for the first time in his life, he wouldn't have seen Carl in Alan's office. If Vincent hadn't agreed to talk—and I think I know how close he came to not being able to. If Jack hadn't been driving past the parking lot right at the very moment when Carl was by Alan's car. If the lab secretary hadn't been able to say exactly when the typeface disappeared. If, when Alan went to all the hardware stores and locksmiths, the person who'd waited on Carl hadn't been there the day Alan came in (if he'd taken the day off, or moved to another job, or hadn't been observant enough to recognize Carl and remember what he'd said), where would we be now? If Spencer hadn't known the guy who owned the public phones, and <u>he</u> hadn't been willing to go out of his way to search through the records. If Buddy hadn't known Vincent well enough to persuade him to talk—so much might not have come to light that would've left Alan condemned for life.*

*I know this is a cliché, but I really do get chills when I think of it, and the hair stands up on my arms.*

*Then ... having dinner with all these folks who went out of their way for us, was overwhelming. I had to go out to Sam's paddock about nine and kiss him on the nose and feed him a carrot and pat him for awhile, and let myself reorganize quietly in private.*

*The food turned out as well as I could've hoped. We did my grandmother's potato salad, with charcoal grilled ribeyes, and green beans and bacon, followed by homemade rhubarb pies, with fresh strawberries on top of good vanilla ice cream. Summer on a plate. Horses watching over fences. Emmy chasing sticks. Iced tea and root beer floats and cold beer and good champagne and Châteauneuf du Pape from Alan's mother's family.*

*We all walked around and looked at horses. We sat by the pond, near the bonfire Alan'd built that we lit just before dark. We told stories of our families from long ago, when they came to Kentucky from the east and the south, and why we feel the way we do about the land we live on.*

*Alan never talks much at a party. We can talk to each other for hours on end, but we both like conversations with one person, or two or three, not big groups at once (small talk having been repellent to both us from infanthood on).*

*But tonight was different. These people saved us. And Alan talked to everyone for a long time, singly and in groups, laughing and grilling and handing out food, as though the reprieve he'd been given had opened a floodgate of wanting to show how much he appreciated the ones who'd had enough faith in him to stand against public opinion in the towns we love where it counts.*

*Anyway, it was humbling. It was an honoring of the hope they'd given us when we'd thought we'd live lives as outcasts, condemned to the fringes, gossiped about* and mistrusted, forced to build impenetrable shells to protect us from human hatred.

As I sit here and write this down, not being able not to, with Alan snoring quietly on his side of the bed ten feet across the room, I feel as though nothing else that will ever happen could be as painful as what we've gone through.

I know that's not true. And it's frightening to even think it. Like it's tempting fate in a dangerous way. But I have such a sense of relief, I want to sit here and wallow in it while I still can.

Of course, the phone rang a second after I wrote that, and I answered before it woke Alan.

Butch, naturally. Telling us this time that he won't let Alan get away with it. He'll make us pay for what Alan did in ways we can't imagine.

How pathetic is that? Losing his wife and his children, wasn't that enough? I mean why can't he put his life back together? I don't wish him ill. Not like I did Carl through all this (which probably did me more harm than it clearly could've done him). No, I really wish Butch could stop drinking and do something useful. He fell prey to _Carl_. And whatever Korea did to him, which Alan thinks must've been significant from what he could tell when he worked with him.

The call was unsettling, though. It's not that I can see him doing anything dangerous, but it was a different kind of call. A threat this time. Unspecified. When before it was mostly gloating.

## *Monday, June 22nd, 1964*

Butch Morgan woke up in the chair in the family room when the phone rang. He didn't make any move to answer it, but he pulled himself up, and leaned forward, elbows on his knees, and laid his head in his hands. His mouth was dry and his eyes burned and his hand shook when he reached to turn off the lamp.

When he'd gone to the bathroom and made coffee and put on his work boots, he walked into the backyard where he'd built a mound of dirt the year before so he could shoot in the backyard. There was a sawhorse in front of it, where he'd set beer cans and bottles, and an old tree trunk post beside it where he sometimes nailed paper targets.

He'd nailed one up the day before, two days after he'd gotten fired from the gas station in Lexington, when he'd seen the picture in the paper.

Alan Munro was grinning at his wife, his arm around her shoulders, wearing a suit and looking smug, like he'd gotten away with murder.

Butch smiled as he walked toward the photo. He'd put thirty rounds in it the night before, and he stood and considered his handiwork while he finished his mug of coffee.

He thought about adding a belt of bourbon to the next cup, but he told himself to wait till later. There was work to be done that only he could do. Work that would right a collection of wrongs. And he'd have to wait to celebrate until the deed was done.

Jo spent that morning at the farmhouse she was

redesigning south toward Shaker Town on a bluff above the Kentucky River.

The floor plan had been accepted by the owners, and she met with the general contractor who'd be doing the carpentry and bringing in the subs.

They talked about the moldings that had to be copied inside and out, and the best way to hide the heating ducts and electrical outlets, and who they should use to mill the lumber.

It was at a stage she really enjoyed, and she was whistling to herself when she got home. She chatted with Becky, who'd come to watch Ross, and then gave her rhubarb from Toss's garden, and a bag of lettuces too.

She worked in her office between the dining room and the kitchen while Ross took his afternoon nap and she finished the laundry.

It'd started raining by four thirty, and was pelting down hard, blowing in from the west by a quarter to five—which was when the phone rang for the first time all day.

She was changing Ross' pants, but she got to it by the sixth or seventh ring, and heard a faint breathless labored sort of voice that identified itself as Stoker Randolph, her neighbor from down the road.

Stoker was ninety-three, and he owned close to two thousand acres there on McCowans Ferry. His fine old farmhouse was three houses north of hers, but he owned the back strip of woods and fields behind the houses between them where he'd always let her ride.

He still farmed, driving his ancient tractor. Mending fence, usually without help, though he was stooped now and almost skeletal, and he moved so slowly and tentatively Jo often marveled that she'd never seen him fall. He was tall and sinewy and had the sun-toughened tan of a hardworking farmer. He was notoriously tough in every kind of transaction, and a determined lifelong bachelor. An introvert who liked being solitary. Who spoke gently and quietly. A man who'd shown her mother great kindness, and Jo as well, once her mother and brother had died.

Jo took him pies sometimes, and bread, when she baked it. And they talked horses, and breeding, and the price of hay. And when Jo heard how weak he sounded, her blood started pounding in her ears.

"I'm real sick, Jo. Pneumonia. Fell a good long while ago … just now crawled to the phone."

"I'll be right there. Stay right where you are!"


She was in her truck in less than a minute, with Ross sleeping in a basket carrier beside her on the bench seat. The rain was so heavy she could hardly see the road, but she'd still parked by Stoker's front door within a couple of minutes.

It was locked. And she didn't want to knock and make him try to get to her. So she ran around through pounding rain to the porch door in back.

She rushed through into the kitchen—and saw a very surprised Stoker Randolph eating vegetable soup at a round pine table in the center of an old brick floor.

"Josie!" Stoker looked astonished. His wrinkled mouth had dropped open, and he was staring at her with his spoon in midair, his sunken old cheeks peppered with stubble, his faded blue eyes on hers.

"You didn't call me?"

"No, ma'am. Not that I'm not pleased to see y'all." He looked a little embarrassed then, and ate the soup off his spoon.

She told him about the call. And they both pondered who could've done it and why. They chatted then for a minute about Alan's release, and the way Stoker's wheat was shaping up.

Jo left, pulling the hood of her raincoat over her head, an unsettling flash of fear twisting her insides as she slammed the truck door behind her.

She couldn't stop thinking about the call Carl had placed to Alan to get him out where he wanted him, and then she thought about Butch, as she started the pickup and pulled back out onto McCowan's Ferry Road.

The rain was blinding and her windshield wipers weren't keeping up, and yet she could see that head-lights had come up close behind her once she was on the road.

Too close. Way too close on her tail. And she began to wonder what that could mean, as she put on her turn signal and slowed to turn right into her own drive.

Then the car was there beside her, pulling straight in front of her, forcing her off the road on the right.

She kept from hitting the big stone pillar at the opening of the drive, but she scraped the right fender of the other car as it pulled in front of her, and she hit her head against something hard.

Ross's basket had slid across the seat into the passenger door, and Ross was screaming, and she was trying to scoot over and pick Ross up—when her door was wrenched open.

Butch Morgan was filling the doorway, holding a gun at her head.

"Out. Get the kid."

"Butch—"

"OUT! NOW!"

Jo grabbed the basket and the diaper bag, and Butch backed away from the driver's door enough for her to climb out.

"Put the kid in the backseat of my car."

"He's scared, and he's gonna cry if—"

"NOW!"

Jo did, trying to think. Too stunned to see what else she could do.

"You're gonna drive. If you don't do EXACTLY as I tell you, I'll kill you and the kid. The kid first. So you can watch."

"Butch—"

"Shutup!" Butch was on the passenger's side of the bench seat in his old sedan. And he smelled of cold sweat and old booze and he looked half out of his mind.

Jo put it in gear, feet on the clutch and the brake, blood trickling down her forehead from a cut up close to her hairline, as he told her to drive north to Versailles, then take 33 south.

Ross cried all the way into town. Butch told her to shut him up, and she tried just by talking, and though he quieted down for a minute or two, he started crying again. When they got to Rose Hill and turned south onto Main, right where Main became Rt. 33, Ross sobbed even louder and pushed himself up in his bassinette. It fell on the floor against the front seat and he screamed till he sounded like he'd choke, and Butch told her to pull off. He grabbed the bassinette and got it back on the seat, and shook Ross by the shoulders, the pistol still in his hand.

Jo said, "That'll make him cry more. Let me calm him down!"

"Shutup and do what I tell you, *if* you want him to live."


The rain was still torrential, and Jo could hardly see the twists in the old pot-holed road, though Ross eventually began to calm down, and seemed finally to doze as they climbed one low hill after another, and rolled through the valleys in between.

Fifteen minutes turned to thirty, and they still weren't where they were going. And then, when 33 dead-ended into 68, Butch told her to turn right, still heading south on the road that led to Shaker Town.

Jo could hear Butch breathing, in the quiet times when he wasn't blaming Alan for what was wrong with his life. Jo learned the hard way not to argue with him. To listen, and drive, and try to figure out how Butch saw what had happened.

She struggled to see through the fogged-up windshield, with blowing rain beyond, and tried not to do or say anything at all that would set Butch off, praying she'd have some idea sometime of how to cope with whatever it was Butch was planning to do.

His silence carried as much weight as the hate. And driving took real concentration. Jo didn't even recognize the house she was restoring as they passed below it, with the quiet then, and her own fear, stretching on ahead.

By the time they'd been on 68 for twenty minutes,

they crossed the Kentucky River on an old stone bridge, where the river was bound on both sides by high rock cliffs. A jagged wall of rock rose straight in front of them as soon as they'd crossed, turning Rt. 68 to the left.

The rain was beginning to slacken, and Butch told her to slow down and look for an abandoned roadhouse down the incline on their left where the ground fell to the river.

Jo saw what looked like an abandoned boat house, covered with vines, the roof line sagging, then nothing else for a quarter of a mile.

The remains of an old painted sign, dangling lopsidedly between two posts up close to the road, was suddenly caught in their headlights, maybe fifty feet up ahead. Then she saw the outline of a building behind it down the slope, a long collapsing rectangle, the dark rotting wooden frame listing off to the left.

"Stop!" Butch had his window open and he was peering out ahead, when he took a bottle out of his pocket and shoved a pill in his mouth. "Couple a feet more, and you angle down a drive just past the road-house. It's real steep and muddy, and there's a pull off to the right. Pull in there and turn around and park behind the building."

It was hard to see what she was doing, but Jo eased the car past the crumbling roadhouse and parked in what had been a gravel patch behind its right end.

Butch grabbed the key out of the ignition, and walked around the car heading toward Jo, who was trying to reach over the seat and get Ross and his bassinette.

"Out." Butch had pulled the driver's door open and was holding the revolver up against her head.

"I'm getting out as fast as I can." Jo eased out from behind the wheel, then opened the back door with her back to Butch.

Ross had fallen asleep from exhaustion, but when Jo pulled the bassinette toward her, he woke up and cried. It was misting by then, not pouring, and Jo picked Ross up and held him under her raincoat, then put the diaper bag in the soft sided bassinette, and turned and faced Butch.

"Up the hill. Toward the road. Into the trees with your back to the bridge. Get movin' now!" He was standing behind her, off to one side, with the gun aimed at her back, motioning toward a tangle of underbrush and close-grown trees.

"I don't see any path."

"There. Between the bushes." He shoved her into a thicket of shrubs.

And she asked him where they were going.

"If you want the kid to get there, keep your mouth shut!"

It was hard going, carrying Ross and the basket, shoving her way through the brambles and branches on that stretch of incline—the hill climbing hard on her right, the river down below her on the left—and she fell hard on her knees once, but she didn't drop Ross, or say the words she wanted to shout at Butch.

She listened to him right behind her, breathing hard, smelling of whiskey and hatred. Her head had stopped bleeding, and that helped, and she pulled herself up and moved on, trying to protect her face with the arm holding the basket.

"There're stairs comin' up. Take 'em down to the river."

Just when she thought she couldn't go any farther, her boots thick with mud, heavy and hard to stay up on, she saw a thinner patch of undergrowth up head. And when she got there, she could see stairs that headed left toward the river, and climbed up on the right too, through thick grass and brush that hid the road completely.

Then she heard the first car they'd met in almost an hour, and saw lights in the darkening dusk stabbing through the line of trees up above by the road.

"In here. Fast." Butch tapped her on the shoulder with the barrel of his revolver, and it startled her so she almost fell, which made Ross start wailing. Butch grabbed her arm and pulled her back into the underbrush, while he hissed at her to shut him up.

"Shh, Ross. It'll be okay. I'll give you a bottle in a minute."

When the car was past, Butch listened for half a minute, then shoved her on toward the stairs and told her again to head toward the river and keep the kid quiet.

The river was very low, and the shallow stairs, overgrown with grass and weeds and shrubs starting up, ended in a strip of sand wide and deep enough to be a kind of beach. It wasn't more than a temporary beach, because when the river was running high all this land below the road would be flooded. With the cliffs and the flooding, this whole strip was nothing now but unused land cluttered with the bones of a few old fishing shacks and the prohibition roadhouse, long abandoned and left untouched by everyday human life.

But there, where the broken stairs met the strip of flat ground, the broad bow of a dilapidated houseboat was pulled up on the sand, the disintegrating wooden stern listing in shallow water.

There were two padded benches abandoned on the sand that must've been in the houseboat to begin with, but now lay covered in mold, the plastic upholstery ripped into strips exposing filthy stuffing.

Jo stood and stared at the cracked wooden siding, and the broken glass in the top of the door, as Butch stepped up on the warped wooden bow—a wide flat square-cornered bow designed like a deck on a house, where one aluminum-framed folding chair leaned against the door.

Butch threw it out of the way and wrenched the door open, the screech of swollen wood cutting across the quiet of the river bank like a knife in Jo's chest, and motioned her up onto the deck with his .38.

She stepped up on the sodden wood, the smell of rot and mold overwhelming, the rain dripping through the overhanging porch as though the roof weren't there.

Butch shoved her inside the cabin and pulled the door closed behind them—and Jo stood and stared at the wreck, at the water covering the rusting floor, deeper ahead of her toward the stern, shallower by the bow.

Black mold grew around the window frames, and lichen stuck to the walls. A metal sink had been half ripped out of its cabinet on the right side close to the door. A built-in table was centered on the left, shooting out from the wall between windows, a wooden chair in front and behind it, the bottoms of their cracked legs standing in dirty water. It dripped in places from the ceiling too, and gathered in beads on the outside walls. Maps curled and hung in strips where they'd once been smoothed between the two windows on the long right-hand wall.

Someone had been there recently. A sheet of plastic covered the table. A bucket sat on it close to the windows to catch a drip from the roof. A loaf of bread and a jar of peanut butter sat in the middle by a jar of instant coffee and an unopened fifth of bourbon. There were two metal cups and a gallon jug of drinking water. And opposite the table, along the right wall, was a raised wooden bench-like bed with a blanket and pillow in a clear plastic bag sitting in the middle.

A cast-iron Franklin stove stood in the back right corner, to the right of the solid rear door, its doors standing open, kindling, newspaper and several small logs waiting, ready to be lit.

Butch had waded over to the table, while Jo looked at the cabin, and he said, "Put the kid in the basket on the table," as he laid the handgun on the plastic with the barrel pointed at Jo.

Jo did, after feeling to be sure the plastic was dry. And then took a bottle out of the diaper bag with a can of formula and a bottle opener.

Butch shoved her down in the wooden chair with its back to the front door, her feet in more than an inch of water, and tied her ankles to the legs of the chair. Then he stood and grabbed her arms and started to tie them behind her.

"Don't. Please. I've gotta hold him and feed him a bottle, and be able to change his diapers. You know. You've got kids, you—"

"Shutup!" He stood and stared at her for half a

minute. Then tied her elbows to the corners of the chair back, leaving her hands free enough that she could hold Ross, who was whimpering already, getting ready to cry.

"He's hungry. I need to give him a bottle. That'll help settle him down."

Butch dropped into the chair on the other side, watching her the whole time, as she sat Ross in her lap and poured formula in a bottle. She laid him down in the crook of her left arm, but he wanted to sit up and lean against her, and she held the bottle in his mouth as best she could, while he held on to it too.

"Why have you done this?"

"Why! I've lost my wife. I've lost my kids. Even my last job. Alan Munro needs to know what it's like to have what you love ripped away!" Butch unscrewed the top on the bottle of bourbon and poured what sounded like a sizeable slug into a metal cup.

# CHAPTER FIFTEEN

Alan left Equine earlier than normal, not much after 5:30. He'd gotten to a spot in a methods report where it made sense to stop work—and he was restless, which wasn't much like him, and he wanted to get out of there and get himself home.

He'd been more tired than usual the last week too, and he'd begun to think that the anxiety and the stress and the interrupted sleep that had driven him for weeks had left him feeling limp and slow once the pressure released.

But it'd been a good day at Equine. He'd inter-viewed a very promising lab director candidate. And the new production manager had made some progress with the viscosity control in the de-wormer paste, making it more likely that they could move to the new Sigma blender sometime soon. Which meant that as Alan drove home he was thinking about what he'd tell Jo about work, and what he should make for dinner. He liked to cook when he had time, and Jo could use a night off.

The rain was horrific by the time he got halfway to

Versailles. He actually had to pull off and wait once on the Lexington Road. But there were hardly any cars on McCowans Ferry, and the windshield wipers were slapping against the glass in a rhythm that made him hum something that sounded to him like an old English ballad, and he was smiling to himself at how badly he hummed as he slowed down the last long hill that took him on toward home.

Then, in the fraction of a second when the wiper cleared the glass, he saw Jo's truck pulled off on an angle on the right side of the road by the pillar at the end of their lane.

He pulled over behind it, and ran to the driver's door, and saw then that the left front bumper had been grazed by another car. The damage didn't look serious. Not enough for Jo to abandon it. And then, when he pulled her door open, he saw the key was in the ignition and her purse lay open on the floor.

She never would've left her purse, *or* her keys, *or* walked home with Ross in the rain. And adrenaline hit Alan like lightning in the blood, firing every nerve, whipping him back into combat, his whole body coiled and tense, as he started the engine, and put it in reverse, and found that it drove just fine.

*There're tire tracks in the mud by the pillar.*

*There's red paint on the fender.*

*Someone ran her off the road, and it's got to be Butch.*

"You bastard!" *If you hurt either one of them you'll wish you'd never been born!*

He pocketed her keys and grabbed her purse and drove his own car up to the house to phone Butch at home.

It wasn't that he expected Butch to be there, or answer even if he were. He had to start somewhere, and eliminate what he could, and make some sort of move fast for the sake of his own sanity.

No one answered, which was no surprise. It made more sense that Butch would call him, and make some threat or demand.

Toss was gone, so he couldn't have seen anything. He'd fed the horses and turned them out, and gone off to play cards with his hunting buddies and wouldn't be back till eleven.

Alan called Spencer, who picked up the phone in his barn. He didn't live all that far from Butch, and he said he'd check out Butch's house, then come on to Alan's.

Alan stood by the phone in the farm office, his fists planted on Jo's desk, staring through the archway into the dining room without seeing a thing.

He limped up the two broad stairs, and on through the dining room, across the front hall, and the living room beyond, then down two steps to their bedroom.

He pulled on a long-sleeved black cotton turtleneck over dark gray jeans, then laced up his old brown work boots with dark rubber soles.

He slid his Swiss army knife into one of his pants pockets, and took a key from a metal box in a high cabinet in the master bath and hurried back to the mudroom, off to the right of the kitchen. He opened the carved pine door Jo had found in a barn sale somewhere that she'd hung to hide the tall metal safe he'd had built in the wall.

He unlocked both its locks, the Yale and the combination, and took two latched wooden boxes off a high shelf and laid them on the kitchen table. He grabbed two holsters and two extra magazines and two full boxes of .45s before he relocked the metal safe and closed the thick pine door.

They were Colt pistols—M1911s—U.S. Army officer issue in World War I and II. He took the magazines out of both boxes and loaded eight cartridges into all four, then slid them, and the ammunition, into zippered pockets in the hooded black raincoat he'd brought in from the mudroom.

He got two flashlights out of a mudroom drawer, and put in new batteries at the kitchen table. Then he threaded his belt through the slits in the holster, and put it on, with his back to the fireplace, making himself close his eyes and take a deep breath.

*Please keep them safe. Help me find them fast. Keep me from taking revenge before I can make myself stop.*


When Spencer ran through the front door, Alan was on the phone in Jo's office, and Spencer said, "Earl?" as he pushed back the hood of his navy blue raincoat, and stood dripping on the sisal rug in dark pants and combat boots, watching Alan check a number he'd written on a pad.

Alan said, "No, not Earl," as he hung up. "*If* we can find out where Butch's taken them, and that's a pretty big *if* right now, I don't want the cops rushing in. You and I'll do better alone, with what we did in Europe."

They stared at each other in silence for a minute.

Then Spencer nodded and opened the closest of the wooden boxes sitting on the old pine desk. He unwrapped the cloth around the Colt pistol, then pulled the slide back and locked it, looking to make sure there was no round in the chamber and no magazine in the grip. He slid a finger across its scored wood, then the dull, dark blued steel barrel, as he said, "Good old John M. Browning. He knew what he was doing when he came up with this. Where's the magazine?"

Alan pulled two out of his coat pocket, along with a box of .45s, and handed them to Spencer before he dialed the phone—and hung up in disgust. "Busy! Again! Where would Butch have taken them? I'm trying to get his wife in Louisville to see if she's got a clue."

Alan dialed again, one foot tapping the floor fast, before he hung up and dialed "0". "Operator, this is an emergency. I'm trying to reach a number in Louisville that's continuously busy, and I have to get through right away! ... No, I can't. It's a matter of life and death!"

He waited, pacing as far as the phone cord let him, till the operator told him to place his call again. He dialed, and waited, and then said, "Frannie, this is Alan Munro. Butch has kidnapped my wife and baby. He's not at his house, and I don't know where to look. Where do you think he'd take them? ... He's from Harrodsburg originally, right? Is there ... Well, where else do you think? ... He wouldn't come to you, would he? ... Okay. Yeah. I understand. Let me give you my number. I'm trying not to call the police, hoping to find them first, but ...

"No! I don't want to hurt him. Not if I can help it.

… So you think he's that unstable? … Yeah, I wondered about Korea. You could see that whenever the topic came up he … Yes, I understand. Do you remember his license plate number? And the model and color of his car? It's red, right? … Thanks. Yeah. Maybe that'll help."

Alan wrote down the number and description as he said, "She doesn't have any idea!" He threw the pen on the desk and raked his hands through his hair, then gripped both sides of his skull. "Maybe I *should* call Earl. He could put out an all-points bulletin, although—"

The phone rang, and Alan grabbed the receiver. "Yes? … Great! … Do you know where it is?" Alan wrote for half a minute, then said, "Thanks. I'll let you know what happens," and dropped the receiver in the cradle. "Frannie. She said Butch had a friend he knew in Korea who was from Harrodsburg, who has an old houseboat docked south of here on the Kentucky River. She said since she left Butch, he's talked about going there for the first time in years, though why she doesn't know. But if he wanted to hide Jo somewhere, that might make sense."

"Does Frannie know where it's docked?"

"She says it's in really bad condition, and if it's where it used to be, it's not far past the bridge on 68, not too far before Shaker Town. She says there's an abandoned bar, or saloon or something, somewhere close by. 'Course we don't know that he's taken them there."

"No. It's nothing but conjecture."

"Right, but we've got nothin' else to go on."

Spencer nodded.

And Alan slipped his 1911 into the holster on his

belt and tossed the other holster to Spence. "If the houseboat's as bad as she says, we oughtta take blankcts, and maybe clothes for Jo and Ross. It's rocky there, right? High cliffs, on both sides of the river?"

"Yeah. Trees too I think. Where there's ground to grow 'em."

"I've got rope in the garage we can take. And we better blacken our faces. There's shoe polish in the junk drawer in the kitchen by the fridge. I'll get the other stuff together."

Spencer said, "What if they're not there? We'll have wasted a whole lottta time."

Alan froze and stared at the fireplace, before he said, "I'm gonna go on gut feeling with this, even with the risk. If they aren't there, we'll call Earl in and see what he can do."


Jo was forcing herself to speak slowly and quietly, as though her heart weren't thundering in her chest, and her blood wasn't beating at her brain—as though she were just her normal self discussing a slightly contro-versial topic with some distant acquaintance. "I think maybe I can understand a little about why it was hard for you when Alan came to Equine. If I'd been you, I would've admired Bob a lot, and really enjoyed working with him. And when Alan arrived it must've looked like he was standing between you and Bob."

"It didn't *look* that way. That's what *happened*! Bob had been real good to me. He took a chance on me when he hired me, and he worked real close with me from then on, till Alan come between us. And he did it real deliberate."

"Bob had so much he had to do, though. Don't you think? He must've needed to delegate some work to Alan. Bob's the only one who can work on the antibiotic development, so when—"

"I liked Bob real well. Best boss I ever had. 'Cept for when …" Butch stopped and stared at the table between him and Jo.

"What?"

"When he shot his mouth off about Korea. That got under my skin." Butch finished the bourbon in his cup, and rubbed his right eye. It was bloodshot and dry looking and he blinked several times before he spoke again. "Bob didn't know a goddamn thing about the war. *Thought* he did. Made me real mad. Figured we shouldda stayed till we won! Shoot! How the hell could we win? Politicians stopped us from goin' north past the Parallel! Red Chinese comin' in by the millions, Russians givin' 'em arms. Wasn't *Bob* watchin' his friends get blown to bits on some goddamn frozen mud hill he didn't give a damn about!"

Jo tried to think of something to say to that, that would keep Butch talking without irritating him even more, and all she could think of was, "Did Bob serve in World War II?"

"Worked with a bunch of scientists fermentin' penicillin. Make him quiet down!" Butch waved his cup toward Ross.

Who was making baby noises, spitting sounds, and "t-t-t" and "b-b-b", while flopping a cloth diaper on his head as he sat on her lap.

Jo said, "I'm sorry. Could he play with the other cup? I don't have toys in the diaper bag." She picked

Ross up and held him around the waist, letting him stand on her thighs, his face turned towards hers.

Butch watched her without saying anything for almost a minute, then pushed the metal cup across the table with the barrel of his .38.

"How old are your daughters?" Jo turned Ross so he was sitting sideways on her lap and handed him the cup she could only just reach with her elbows tied to the back of the chair.

"Bitch don't let me see 'em hardly." He was staring at the table, his mouth vicious, his dark eyebrows pinned against his squinting eyes.

"That's not right. You should be able to—"

"Just shutup!"

She did for a minute, watching Butch pour more bourbon and take a large swallow. His face was flushed, and he was sweating, and he spilled some on the table, and then drew circles in it with a dirty thumb.

"Butch? Are you cold? I am, from getting rained on. Ross is too. You think you could start a fire in the Franklin stove?"

"Why? So Alan can smell the smoke?" He smiled a slow crooked smile, and fished a small bottle from inside his coat.

"What is that?"

"This? Dex." He grinned like a teenage boy who thinks he's gotten away with something daring and forbidden.

"Dexedrine?"

"Keeps me on my toes." He laughed, but it was harsh and grating, and Ross started to cry. Butch picked up the revolver and aimed it at Ross's head. "Shut him up!"

"Shhh, sweetie. You have to be quiet." He sobbed for a minute, but then it slowed and softened, and finally, after a couple of gulps and two big sighs, Ross subsided into silence. Jo had already changed his pants, and she poured more formula in his bottle, trying to keep him quiet and get him to go to sleep. "What kind of gun is that?"

Butch took another gulp, then set the handgun down. "Colt .38 revolver. Police model. Used all over."

"Is the handle wood?"

"Why do you care?"

"Just wondered." Jo held Ross in the crook of her arm tight against her chest, and willed him to fall asleep, while she searched for something neutral to say. "World War II was hard on folks too."

"Yeah? They come back to victory parades!"

"That's true. Yeah. But—"

"Alan bring a few guns back, did he?"

Jo didn't know what to say, and she hesitated long enough for Butch to yell, "Did he!" so loud Ross pulled the bottle out of his mouth and started to whimper.

"If you don't want him to cry again you have to talk quietly."

"You tellin' me what to do, bitch?" He picked up the .38 again and aimed the glossy black barrel straight at Jo's chest.

"No. But I know it's hard for other folks to listen to babies crying, and I'm trying to keep him quiet."

"Did he bring back guns?"

"Some. I don't know what came from the war, but he has a couple of handguns."

"Pistols or revolvers?"

"What's the difference?" She was hoping to keep

him talking. Trying to keep him from drinking more, and getting more aggressive.

"Pistols have magazines that snap into the grip. People who don't know nothin' call 'em clips. Revolvers are like this." He pointed to the cylinder and tapped a fingernail on the end of a shell casing.

"Pistols then. That I've seen."

"Rifles?"

"I think so. Might be a shotgun instead of a rifle."

"He shoot?"

"He's shot raccoons with distemper, and injured deer. Situations like that. He doesn't hunt, or shoot for fun."

Butch watched her, then rubbed both eyes before he sipped from his cup.

"Are you holding us for ransom? Or—"

"I don't have to tell you my plans!"

"I know that. I don't mean to pressure you. I've seen you with your wife and girls, and I don't b'lieve you like hurting people. I think you've had a very hard year."

"Do you? You figure I'm stupid enough to believe you care?"

"Alan didn't kill Carl. Carl killed himself."

"Because of what Alan did to him!"

Jo was suddenly furious. All the weeks of Alan being wrongly accused of murdering Carl—of hearing him blamed for doing what was right too, the whole time he'd been at Equine—it all rose up hot inside her chest and she couldn't keep it in. "He came in and tried to help Bob! He knows a *hell* of a lot more about chemistry, and how to make a product than Carl ever *could* have, and Carl did *nothing* but fight him, because of his own inflated ego—and then he tried to steal what was Alan's! Dragging you into it too! You ought to be mad at Carl, not Alan! He was trying to help you!"

Butch grabbed the .38 again and stood up, weaving some on his feet, staring down at Jo and Ross with fury on his face.


The rain had begun to slacken a little, and as Alan made the sharp left turn on 68, just past the river bridge, Spencer rolled the passenger window down and leaned out across the door, trying to see down toward the river on the left side of the road.

There was some small building collapsing in the undergrowth not too far past the bridge. But there was nothing more but dripping trees and thick dark weeds and shrubs—until Spencer saw a broken-down sign a few yards ahead and said, "Slow down! There's some kind of building. Let me get out and look."

Alan slowed to a stop. And Spencer jumped out and disappeared in the drizzling mist.

Then Spencer was back, opening the passenger door and rolling up the window. "There were tracks into what used to be a drive, and I found Butch's car."

"I'll look for a place to hide this. You keep an eye on his. Right?"

Spencer nodded and headed toward the river.

It was more than a half a mile on, past where the road swept sharply right away from the river, before Alan could pull the car off on the edge of a farmer's field behind a broken-down cabin.

He sprinted back, the coil of rope slung across his shoulders, to where Spencer waited on the edge of the muddy gravel that had once been the drive to the abandoned roadhouse.

Spencer stepped out and stood close to Alan so he could talk quietly and still be heard. "Looks like they went through there. Through the undergrowth here, heading away from the bridge." Spencer was pointing to the tangled undergrowth on the sloping ground below the rocky hill that climbed almost straight up and edged the side of the road.

Alan whispered, "You watch the car. I'll scout ahead."

Spencer nodded after hesitating for a second, as Alan pulled his pistol from the holster, his index finger clamped against the trigger guard.

Alan could see where they'd moved through, in crushed leaves and bent branches, and he moved slowly and silently, listening and looking in every direction, as he followed two sets of footprints—Jo's paddock boots, partially hidden by treaded work boots—in mud and grass and gravel and weeds, till they came to a spot where Jo had fallen—or possibly even been pushed—and had caught herself on one hand.

He gritted his teeth, and his green eyes looked dangerous, in the gray light of a rainy woods, a light mist brushing his face, as he watched and walked through the gathering gloom, listening for any change.

When he could see a lighter patch up ahead, he slowed down, and moved even more cautiously when he saw what looked like broken stone stairs ten feet in front. He waited in the shadows six or eight feet away and listened, but heard nothing but the wind in the trees and the dripping of sodden leaves, and the faint whisper of foggy mist settling on the living and the dead.

He slipped closer and pulled a branch out of the way just enough that he could see what was left of the stairs built into very steep ground that rose on his right to the road.

He slid the branch back and shifted another so he could lean forward and look toward his left, down the stairs to the low-lying river, to whatever flatter ground was there stretching along its edge. He was standing on sloping ground, and he dropped down and crawled toward the stairs, till he could see a stretch of sandy ground mixed with stones edging the river, eighty feet or so away.

There, lined up directly with the stairs, was a derelict houseboat, its bow pulled up on shore, its broken glass door staring straight at the stairs, its stern angled in the water.

Alan lay there and listened, and watched the river lap against the warped wooden sides as rain dripped through the porch roof, and two discarded turquoise banquettes rotted in the mist.

Alan tried to estimate the width of the open space on either side of the crumbling stairs, noticing what grew there, how thickly and how high, and how far the flat land lay from the start of the cliff.

He backed up and stood when he could, and made his way back to Spencer, where he'd hidden himself in a cluster of trees not far from Butch's car.

Alan told Spencer what he'd seen, while he re-strapped his pistol in his holster. "We know what's between here and the bridge. If Butch wants to get to his car, this is the way he'll come. We've gotta move past the stairs up by the road, then get down the cliff where he can't see us from the door. We can scout that side from there, and plan our final approach. Jo fell, or was pushed. She had a hard time getting up."

Spencer nodded, and touched Alan's arm, then started up toward the road, making his way as silently as Alan, till they stood in the undergrowth beyond the stairs at the edge of the narrow road.

Alan tied the rope around the trunk of a large oak, and worked his way backward down the cliff, getting battered and torn by briars and branches, but hidden from below by the trees and shrubs growing on the shallower slope between the cliff and the beach.

Spencer came down behind him, and they crouched and crawled closer to the water, before Alan searched the woods on their right, till he found a fallen limb, maybe eight feet long and four feet wide where its branches spread at the end. He dropped it beside Spencer, then motioned Spencer to stay where he was.

Spencer nodded, and pulled his Colt from the holster underneath his coat.

Alan's pistol was in his right hand again, when he started making his way toward the houseboat with a light rain pelting his face. He crouched in the under-growth on the edge of the beach, and stared along the right side of the boat at the two windows with a three-foot space between them, the glass in the front one cracked and broken, leaving a hole near the bottom.

The deck was four feet wider than the houseboat, so that two-foot widths of deck extended out from the long sides all the way back to the stern. The bow deck was maybe eight feet deep. And there were broken and missing boards up and down the decks. And it was then that Alan had to face the problem he'd been trying to overlook since he'd talked to Butch's wife.

How can you climb up on a boat deck without making the boat dip in the water? The fact that the bow was up on the beach made the bow more stable, but would it be stable enough that the boat wouldn't shift? And could he climb up there without Butch seeing him through one of the right-hand windows? What was the layout inside the cabin? And where were Jo and Ross?

All he could do was crawl toward that corner, and hope that one of the cracks in the siding was large enough to see through.

He slithered as much as he crawled, and made it over to the corner, keeping his head below the deck.

He lay still and listened, and he could hear Butch and Jo, faintly and indistinctly, so at least he knew she was still alive and hadn't been gagged.

And finally, when there was nothing else to do, he raised his eyes above the top of the deck and inched his way slightly to the right, so he could see through a split in the siding into the houseboat's cabin.

He could just see the bottoms of four chair legs, and a boot that belonged to Butch on the far side of the boat, back toward the stern from where he crouched.

He could hear better too, nearer to the side wall, and it sounded to him as though Jo was closer to the bow than Butch, but on the far side too.

Then he heard Butch shove his chair across the floor as though he'd pushed it farther toward the stern. There was a small section of siding missing, a foot or so higher and toward the stern, and Alan held his breath, and slowly, silently, raised his head farther above the deck, a foot or more toward the stern. He could see Jo from the waist down, sitting, facing the stern, on the left side of a rickety table, Ross in her lap, diaper bag on the table, .38 revolver on its side, the barrel aimed straight at Ross next to a bottle of bourbon that was less than a quarter full.

She was talking to Butch, soft and soothing, as though she was trying to sound sympathetic, and Butch sat crumpled against the back of his chair off to Alan's right, his hands hidden in his lap, both of them on the far side of the cabin between him and the windows in that far wall. Jo moved Ross so he was standing on her thighs, her hands circling his middle. But then Butch talked at her, louder and nastier, slurring his words some, and slapping the table, saying, "When I want *your* opinion I'll be lettin' ya know!"

Ross started whimpering, and Butch told her to shut him up.

Alan dropped flat on the cold slimy beach, and backed away from the boat, then picked his way up the sloping woods to Spencer, the mud slick, in the bottom ground, making him slither and slide.

Alan hunkered beside Spence, and whispered close to his ear. "Butch is facing the bow, opposite these windows, behind a built-in table. Jo and Ross are facing the stern, on the bow side of that table. Butch's drunk close to a fifth of bourbon, and he's got a .38 on the table pointed right at them. The front window in the right-hand wall's got a ping pong ball sized hole missing. So if you'll get over there, I'll create a distraction with the branch to get Butch focused there, and get myself to the door to sight in on him fast. You shove the—"

"Colt through the window on the right."

"Yeah. That make sense to you?"

"There's a risk."

"That he'll shoot Jo first before we get him in our sights."

"Yep." Spencer nodded, and waited for Alan's reaction.

"Any other suggestions?"

"Nope. Being drunk'll slow him down."

"That's what I'm hoping."

"It's your wife and son. It's gotta be your call. And it's gotta be quiet. No waves. No splashes."

Alan hesitated, before he said, "Me getting to the door with my handgun on him, it's all about speed. And not rocking the boat."

"Old man like you?" Spencer smiled.

And Alan nodded. Then started down the hill.


Spencer was in place, crouching in the shallows below the front right-hand window. Alan crouched down to the right of the door, by the corner of the deck, and threw the branch into the river on the left side of the houseboat—at the same time he stepped up on the deck, and fixed his handgun on Butch's face through the broken glass.

Butch snatched up his own gun, yelling something incoherent, and grabbed Ross away from Jo, then stood there weaving on the stern side of the table, drunk and drugged and over the edge, shouting "*I'll kill her and the kid if you don't drop the gun!!*"

Jo was fighting her chair, trying to stand up, screaming, "Butch, *please!* Put Ross *down!*"

"SHUT THE HELL UP!"

"*Let me have Ross!*" Jo was begging, her arms

stretched as far as they could go, trying to touch Ross's hand.

"Screw you! I got *NOTHIN'* to lose!" He'd backed up toward the stern, his left arm wrapped around Ross's middle, holding him under his arms so he and Ross still faced Jo.

In that silence, while Ross turned purple, before he started a wild piercing animal wail, Jo said, as quietly as she could, "Butch, please. Alan's staying where he is. Let me take care of Ross. You wouldn't want someone to hurt your girls!"

Butch didn't move. He stood there gripping his revolver, Ross screaming in his other arm, as he stared straight at Alan.

That's when Alan said, "Look over to your left."

"You think I'd fall for that!" But Butch did look. He couldn't stop himself from turning his head just enough to see Spencer, six feet away, with the barrel of his 1911 stuck through the hole in the window.

"*I'm takin' y'all with me*! I got *nothin'* left to live for!"

"Your girls don't deserve a murderer for a dad!" Jo was pleading, her hands reaching out to him.

"SHUTUP!" Butch was weaving from left to right, Ross still in his left arm, legs dangling against Butch's hip.

And then Ross fell—hitting the floor hard, face down in filthy water.

Jo screamed, yanking her chair toward him, while Butch leaned forward, shoving the gun closer to Jo's face as a .45 slug from Spencer's pistol slammed through Butch's right arm, driving that arm up and out, so a .38 round hit the ceiling as the Colt flew out of his hand.

Alan charged through the door and grabbed Ross—who was choking and gasping, blood splattering from his lips, his whole body contorted, and rushed him to Jo —one split second before he grabbed Butch by the shirt and smashed him in the face.

Alan stood over him with his fists clenched, watching as he flailed on the floor, crying and cradling his arm.

# CHAPTER SIXTEEN

Alan didn't say a word to Butch after he'd put a tourniquet on his arm, and tied both arms loosely behind his back with the rope he'd used on Jo. He just pulled Butch out of his chair and shoved him out the door.

It was dark then in the woods and the weeds, by the time they got to the stairs, and the rain had petered out to nothing but what dripped on them from the trees. But it was slippery, and hard going, and they all stumbled and missed their footing on the steepest part of that hill.

Alan and Spencer had to hold Butch to keep him from falling. He was boneless and limp, and they had trouble getting him up the broken stairs in the rock face close to the road. And then they had a half mile or more to walk to Alan's car, where it also took both of them to get him in the backseat. Spencer climbed in beside him, and gave him instructions Jo couldn't hear.

She changed into dry shoes, and added a sweater and a cotton jacket, and dressed Ross in the clothes Alan had brought for him too. His lips had stopped bleeding, finally, though a huge bruised lump had popped out on his forehead, as well as his left elbow.

She found herself holding Ross tightly enough to half-choke him, once she'd gotten into the passenger seat with a blanket wrapped around them both. She made herself loosen her grip and hum something soothing for a minute with her mouth against his cheek.

When Alan started driving (after having cleaned himself up as much as he could with one of the towels he'd brought), the only sound in the car came from Butch. It wasn't any kind of normal crying, but he kept sniffing and swallowing in a strange sort of rhythm, and when Jo looked at him, he seemed to be shaking, slumped against the seat.

Alan started talking to her in a low, very quiet voice, trying to make sure she was doing alright, the same way he had in the houseboat. Then he pulled her over to him and whispered a question she hadn't expected.

"How much do you want Butch punished?"

She thought about that, as Ross half-dozed on her lap, and the headlights lit up the dripping trees and the sharp gray wall of rock on the north side of the river that climbed up on their left. She finally whispered, "I want him in jail for a long time. I'd like him to get some help sometime. *If* he's ever willing to be helped. But I want him kept from doing this again. To us or anyone else. You think Ross could have a concussion? And that falling in that water's going to make him really sick?"

"We'll ask the doctor Earl calls in for Butch to examine Ross too."

"I can't imagine how many germs he swallowed. That water was disgusting. And the gunshots! I never knew they could be that loud. My ears feel weird, and my head's still throbbing."

Alan nodded but didn't say anything. And Jo leaned against him as he drove the deserted roads that led north to Versailles.

When they got to the light at Rose Hill and Main, Alan spoke to Butch for the first time since they'd left the houseboat. "We're taking you to the Sheriff in Versailles, and he'll get a doctor to look at your arm."

Butch said something low and muffled that Jo couldn't understand, and Spencer told him to watch his mouth.

As soon as they walked into the jail, Jo began to feel queasy. Seeing the same dispatcher sitting there at the counter. Smelling the same smells rolling off the walls. Disinfectant, and stale cigars, and what might've been the bathroom over by the cells. It brought back the worry and fear and anger. And she had to walk outside again, and stand there by the corner of the courthouse, and talk to herself for a couple of minutes before she could step back in.

Earl wasn't there so they talked to Pete, the deputy on duty. He arranged for a doctor first, and then took Alan and Jo into Earl's small pea-green office while Spencer stayed on a bench with Butch (whose hands were still tied behind him) across from the guy at the counter.

After they told Pete what had happened, he phoned Earl—who said he was on his way, and told Pete to cuff Butch, apparently right that second, since Pete grabbed his cuffs off his belt and shot out the door.


Spencer wrote out a report for Pete and handed Butch's gun over—Alan's too, the one he'd fired, describing many more times than he wanted to why he'd taken the shot.

Alan and Jo explained what had happened to Earl, who listened hard and asked a string of questions, then nodded and watched them for a minute, leaning back in his desk chair with his hands clasped on top of his head. "We'll lock him up, and get the paperwork goin' right quick. I'll argue against bond, and I'm real sure the court'll go along. 'Course, if the doc says he needs surgery or somethin', we'll have to transport him to St. Joe's in Lexington quick as we can tonight."

Alan and Jo didn't say anything.

And Earl sat up in his chair. "I reckon we can postpone your written reports gettin' done till tomorrow. Looks to me like you folks need to get yourselves on home."

Jo said, "I'd like the doctor to examine Ross."

"Sure. We can get him to do that. I'm sorry for all this. I truly am."

"Thank you." Alan reached across the desk and shook Earl's hand.

"Don't mean I won't have something to say later on 'bout ya not calling me in. Tonight ain't the time. How are you doin', Jo?"

"Okay. I think." Jo shook his hand too, and followed him into the outer office, though as much as she tried to keep it from showing, she still felt rattled in that jail, being that close to Earl.

The bullet had passed through the muscles of Butch's upper arm without hitting bone, so the doctor didn't think he needed surgery. He dug out the cloth fragments, cleaned and bandaged the wounds, and gave him a shot of penicillin.

Earl told Butch he was one lucky son-of-a-gun that that's all that was wrong with him, as he stood there with his hands on his hips, staring down at Butch.

Butch hardly looked at him. He'd thrown up by then, and was shivering on the scarred wooden bench, his right arm in a sling, his left cuffed to the side of the bench, glaring at the bucket and mop the dispatcher'd used to clean up the floor. Spencer was standing six feet away leaning on the wall, wiping the mud off his clothes with a towel, looking at Butch in disgust.

Earl and Pete pulled Butch up by his good arm and guided him through the door to the cells, and he shuffled past Jo and Alan without looking in their direction.

Jo handed Ross to the doctor and explained what had happened, that the water was close to three inches deep, and the metal floor underneath was covered with slime and rust.

Alan used Earl's phone to call Frannie in Louisville and tell her what had happened, and she said she'd drive down to see Butch sometime the next morning. Then she thanked Alan, and burst into tears, before he handed Jo the phone so Frannie could ask Jo if she and Ross were really alright.

Jo was holding Ross, who was wailing again, after getting penicillin and tetanus in both sides of his bottom, and Jo told her he'd be okay, barring some nasty infection.

Alan walked toward the door, limping more than normal. He had been since they'd left the houseboat. And Jo asked how bad his leg was as they walked toward the car. He just said, "It's nothing to worry about," and thanked Spencer again for everything he'd done, and told him he'd give him some clean clothes as soon as they got home.

Alan and Jo got Ross fed and bathed and spent enough time with him to think he was calm enough to put to bed (with Emmy sticking to Jo like glue). When they finally got showered and ate what little they felt like eating, and crawled into their own bed—sore everywhere and bone tired, Jo's nerves still frayed and vibrating, her forehead bandaged, a bag of ice on Alan's leg—Jo said, "When you came through the cabin door you looked like you wanted to kill him."

"I did. In the abstract. I'm glad I didn't have to." Alan looked away from Jo then, their hands holding onto each other, lying quiet on top of his chest. "I know what war can do. Remember the old cliché? 'But for the grace of God, go I?' That one's true. I could've been like Butch."

"No. You'd never do anything like—"

"Oh, yeah. Me, Jo. Given the right circumstances. And now I know what it's like to be locked up, thinking you're facing life in a cell. He needs to be there. He's unstable and dangerous. But I'd like to think that someday he'll build a useful life again. Ouch." Alan had taken off the ice pack, and twisted his knee when he'd moved.

"I do too, in the long run. But I hope he'll be locked up for a good long while to come."

"I know. Me too." He turned toward her and wrapped his arms around her and kissed her on the forehead.

"Do you think he dropped Ross on purpose? Or did he just lose hold of him, as drunk as he was?

"I don't know, Jo. I couldn't tell."

"It makes a big difference how I feel about him."

"Yeah. It does to me too."

*Excerpt from Jo Grant Munro's Journal*
*Tuesday, June 23rd, 1964*

*It's early morning, probably just after five, and I'm in Mom's rocking chair in Ross's room watching him sleep. He seems to be doing okay, but I can't believe what he's been through won't end up in nightmares, or dysentery, or something even worse. Though what that might be I don't know.*

*I dreamt Ross was lying dead on his back on the table in the cabin of the houseboat, and I woke up in a blind panic afraid to go back to sleep. I'll get over it. The dreams'll stop. But I can't write about being kidnapped. Not anytime soon.*

*Saturday, June 27th, 1964*

Spencer backed Tracker down the ramp of his two-horse trailer, then led him into Jo's south barn into the stall next to Sam. They knew each other from having gone cross country with Jo and Spencer and Alan, and they trumpeted to each other, and nosed the boards between their stalls, and stuck their heads over the bottom half of their doors so they could see each other face-to-face—before Tracker circled his stall twice, peed in the straw in the center, then sucked up half the water in his bucket and rubbed his chin on his door.

Spencer had put his dad's gelding, Buster, on the other side of Tracker's stall, after he'd trailered his own mare, Bella, and his mother's gelding, Duff, over to Jo's farm. Duff and Bella and Alan's Maggie had watched the new boys walk through the barn, snorting and whinnying and nodding their heads over their doors—and Jo and Spencer stood and smiled for a minute, before they poured grain in all the feed tubs, and left them to get used to their stalls before they were turned out.

Spencer and Jo walked north toward her house, watching the wind blow in from the south, seeing it stir the trees on their left, on the west edge of the ridge, making the mares and the babies in the paddocks that Toss had just turned out pick their heads up and prick their ears, and sniff the world in the wind.

It was a soft wind in a lazy afternoon cooling into an evening of long shadows and quiet rustlings after a hot humid day of buzzing bugs, and birds feeding babies, while horses flicked at flies and fought drowsiness in their stalls.

The sun was still hot, when it wasn't hidden by the clouds that had just begun to drift in in swirling white mounds, before they got torn into tatters that slid apart toward the north.

Spencer was quieter than sometimes, while Emmy ran around them, sniffing tire tracks on the gravel drive —till she spotted her favorite barn cat in the tall grass along the fencerow on their right where the yearling colts were turned out on the east side of the drive.

It was a game they played almost daily, and Cloe clawed up a distant sycamore, just as Emmy shot off in hot pursuit, barely squeezing between two fence rails, giving a handful of yearlings a reason to turn and run. They all liked the excitement, and Spencer laughed when Jo did, just before a huge horse fly landed on Jo's head—the Flying Fortress of the horse world that can rip chunks out of horsehide. She waved it away, then trapped it on her shoulder and crushed it between her fingers before she told Spencer she was sorry.

"For what?" His blond-brown hair was blowing in his face, and he pushed it back with one hand before he looked at Jo.

"That you've had to sell your farm."

"Thanks. Yeah. I know. But the couple who bought it are in their seventies, and when their granddaughters sell their horses to go to college, they'll move back to Midway. They've given me right of first refusal, so I'm hoping I'll have the business up and running, and can buy it back then."

"You think our tenant house'll make you claustro-phobic?"

"No. I'm working so many hours, all I need is a place to sleep. The important thing is that you're letting me bring the horses here and take care of them myself without having to pay board."

"It's the least we could do with what you've done for us."

"What d'ya think of the name Blue Grass Horse Transport? Dissolving Blue Grass Horse Vans means I've got to come up with a new name. I wanted to keep Blue Grass in it to make reaching old customers easier, but—"

"I think it's fine, as long as folks don't think you pick up horses and deliver them."

"Yeah, that's the danger. If you come up with a better suggestion let me know."

"What are Martha and Richard doing?"

"Well …" Spencer picked up a stick and threw it up ahead for Emmy. "We've had to put Mom and Dad's house *and* the Blue Grass property up for sale to pay the inheritance taxes. They're based on the value of Dad's estate when Blue Grass was worth something."

"Nuts."

"Yeah. But we'll get the insurance money from the fire. It was some kind of a wiring malfunction, so that's been a relief. Anyway, Richard's going to work for a company in Lexington that sells rare stamps and coins. He used to collect both, so I think he'll be suited for it. Martha's gotten a job at the art museum in Macon, Georgia. Her college roommate lives there, and she's converted her family home into two large apartments, and Martha's going to rent one. Her ex-husband pays decent child support, and it's at least a place to start."

"How are they treating you?"

Spencer shrugged as Emmy brought the stick back and slipped it in his hand, so he'd tug on it while he walked. "More or less the way they have since Dad died. They can't get over of the fact that he trusted me to run the business."

"So it's the old 'Daddy loved you better.'"

"He didn't, though. He just thought I'd do a better job."

"Your dad thinking your brother's more competent must be hard too. Especially when it's true."

"I know. Family business. If it wasn't this, it'd be something else."

"Are you going to keep your folks' horses?"

"I don't need four, that's for sure. If I knew somebody who'd ride them and care for them the way I would, then it might be different. It's not like selling a couch."

"No. I went through that when Tommy died and left me Sam and Maggie. 'Course I'd had to put my own horse down, so that made it easier."

They'd passed the trees on the south side of Jo's house, and the long drive that led to it, and they were almost to the tenant house, a hundred yards north, when they heard a car climbing the drive. They turned in time to watch it cross the cattle guard in the front hedge, heading up to Jo's porch.

Spencer said, "Was that Earl?"

"I couldn't see the driver."

They couldn't see much of anything through the evergreen windbreak, and they walked on to the tenant house Spencer had just rented. They stopped on the porch and looked at the chaos inside—furniture shoved against the walls around a sea of cardboard.

Spencer said, "A sharecropper Dad knew as a kid

used to say, 'The worst thing about any job is the dreadin' of it.'"

"Let's just hope he's right."

"I know!"

"What do you want me to do?" Jo was standing with her hands on her hips, gazing from one side to the other of the wide open room that was kitchen and living room and dining room combined.

"I need to put the bedframe together in the bedroom first, but then—"

"How 'bout I put your dishes away and set up the kitchen?"

"Thanks. That'd be great."

"We can shuffle the furniture around once some of the boxes are gone."

"Fine." Spencer stopped in the middle of the room, holding his old pine headboard. "Elizabeth said she'd come over tomorrow and help me too." He looked endearingly self-conscious.

And Jo smiled before she said, "Good," and told herself not to laugh.

"Thank Alan for me too, for what he did this morning. I couldn't have moved the furniture without him."

Spencer had just walked into the bedroom, when Jack parked his pick-up in what there was of a driveway thirty feet from the front door. The back was filled with boxes of books, and Jack asked where he should put them as he slammed the truck door.

"Pro'bly here on the porch for now. The living-room floor's an obstacle course."

"I heard from France." Jack smiled as he pulled out his handkerchief and wiped his face and neck. "She'll get here September 12th. Do you know anybody I could hire to give the house a good cleaning? I clean, but—"

"Charlie Small's sister, Esther Wilkes. She'd do a great job."

"Also," Jack lowered his voice and smiled self-consciously as he opened the tailgate and reached for a box, "when we talked before, you said Camille could stay with you if she wanted. You still willing? I'd like to give her a choice. I've got the extra bedroom too, but—" His voice trailed off and he dropped his eyes, and it almost looked to Jo as though he was ready to blush.

"Sure. No trouble at all."

"And …" He paused dramatically and smiled at Jo. "The people you're doing the restoration for have accepted my proposal for the landscaping."

"Good!"

"This is the first time I've had a chance to execute an overall plan. By the way, did you know Earl's up at your house?"

"No. I wonder what he wants?"

"One other thing." Jack looked at her, holding the box, but still not speaking for what seemed like half a minute. "My father's heart condition's gotten worse. I'm driving up tomorrow."

"I'm sorry, Jack."

"I never should've stayed away from him all those years. It was my mother I didn't …" Jack looked stricken.

And Jo said, "I look back on how frustrated I got with how my mother treated me when she had the brain tumor, and I wish I could do it all over. Your father's so glad to talk to you now, that's all he cares about."

Jack didn't say anything else. He just set the box of books on the porch, and went to get another.


Earl had knocked on Jo and Alan's front door, then opened it and shouted, but hadn't gotten an answer.

He'd seen Jo walking toward the tenant house, but Alan's Dodge was parked by the south side of their house, so he walked around behind it past the arbor, and saw Alan sitting with his back to him by the willow tree on the edge of the pond, sharpening a hedge clipper, with Ross on a blanket beside him.

"Hey. Ya got a minute?"

Alan looked over his shoulder, and said, "Sure. Let me get you a chair."

"I'll get it." Earl was carrying a shoebox in his left hand, but he grabbed a director's chair from the arbor with his right, and set it on the other side of Alan from Ross.

Alan shoved the hedge clippers under his chair, where Ross couldn't get them, while he told himself it was purely Pavlovian, the wariness and flash of distrust whenever he saw Earl. "So what's up? You're actually wearing jeans again."

"Saturday. Took the day off, 'cept for a fund-raiser this mornin'." Earl was squinting at the pond, his broad face furrowed and fixed under the brim of a worn beige cowboy hat, his huge hands planted on his knees, looking as though he felt ill at ease too, or was worried that his small canvas chair wouldn't hold up underneath him. "First off, I gotta say this once. Ya shouldn'ta gone after Butch like you did. It couldda gone wrong real easy for you, *and* for Jo and Ross."

"It happened fast. Finding Jo gone. Spencer getting here within minutes. Hearing from Frannie where Butch might've taken them. I made the decision to move right away because of what Spencer and I did in the war." Alan looked at Earl, as he rubbed his left thigh, his eyes steady and cool.

"I'm just sayin' what's gotta be said." Earl took a pack of gum from his shirt and held it out toward Alan, then folded a stick in his own mouth after Alan shook his head. "Ross is doing real well. Sittin' up like that and all."

"Yeah."

"Anyway, I wanted ya to know the County Attorney's gonna move things along so Butch'll go to trial week after next."

"Thanks for letting me know."

"His wife's been visitin' some, so that's been good. Goin' cold turkey hasn't been easy, just like you'd expect." Earl gazed over at Ross, looking self-conscious again, without saying anything for a minute. "So whatta ya figure he was gonna do to Jo?"

Alan shrugged and shook his head, and handed Ross the rubber ball that had rolled onto the grass. "I don't know. I doubt he would've tried to ransom them. I think he wanted to make me suffer more than anything else. I'd like to think he probably would've brought 'em home, once he'd sobered up. But it was touch and go in the houseboat. I don't know whether he threw Ross down, or dropped him accidentally, but he was ready to shoot Jo then, even if he didn't mean to when the whole thing started."

"Wasn't thinkin' too clear, I know that. How'd he

know to act like the neighbor up the road to get Jo outta the house?"

"From when he worked at Equine, I guess. I probably mentioned that Jo and I knew him, and had him over to dinner sometimes. You want an iced tea, or a coffee?"

"Nope. Just wanted to tell ya where things stand, and give ya back the 1911 Spencer used on Butch. I talked the County Attorney into letting it go once all the documentation got done, with your report, and Jo's and all, corroboratin' Spencer's." Earl took off his glasses and rubbed his eyes, then set them back on his nose. "I'm kinda hopin' this makes it up to you some. For what happened before." He didn't look at Alan when he said it. He gazed out beyond the pond as though there was something worth looking at.

"You did what you thought you had to do."

"I did. But it don't make what you went through go away."

"I can't honestly say that I can look at you and not remember what happened. But I don't blame you, and time'll take care of the awkwardness."

Earl nodded, and stood up, and set his hands on his hips. "I'm real glad Jo and Ross are okay. I'll talk to ya another time."

"How's the election looking?"

"I got no idea. Nothin' I hate more than campaignin', but ya play the hand yer dealt, right?"

"I think it backfired when the other guy tried to make a big deal out of you arresting me. I think folks respected you for admitting the mistake in public."

"You talkin' to the papers helped with that too."

Earl was walking toward the south side of the house

when Alan said, "Thank you for coming to tell me about Butch."

Earl waved without looking back, then disappeared past the arbor.

Spencer went off to have dinner with Elizabeth from the pole barn business, and Jack went home to get cleaned up there, and it was almost eight when Jo and Alan had packed cold chicken and pickled beets, lettuces they'd just picked, a half bottle of good champagne his folks had given them for their anniversary in December, fresh strawberries from Toss's garden, cream she'd just whipped, ice water, and Ross's bottle —and pushed his stroller past the barns, to the old broken-down log and stone cabin on the south end of their land.

There was a big sweetgum sheltering that side of the cabin, just above a deep ravine, and they settled Ross on a blanket underneath it, and sat on the stone steps beside him and laid out their picnic. They'd given Sam and Maggie and Spencer's horses carrots on the way past their paddock, and they could see them grazing and looking pleased with themselves from where they sat in the shade.

They'd brought real plates and silverware, and they were balancing them on their laps, laughing at Ross playing with a stick instead of the toys they'd brought. Emmy was lying there next to the blanket, her eyes clamped on the stick as though she thought it ought to be hers, which made Jo say, "That stick is *not* for you!" while she patted Emmy's shoulder.

"I like the marinade on the chicken." Alan had opened the champagne and was pouring Jo a glass.

"Ginger and soy sauce and garlic, and the juice and rind of an orange. Isn't it great to be alone? Finally. With nothing terrifying going on?"

"Yeah. Look, he's trying not to fall asleep." Alan had waved his fork toward Ross, who'd fallen over on his side and was holding his yellow stuffed rabbit against his face, his big blue eyes closing, then flying opening, then closing slowly again.

Alan speared another bite of chicken, but looked directly at Jo before he put it in his mouth. "So how are you doing? Really."

"I'm okay. If I ever complain about the weather again, kick me right in the shins."

"You sure?"

"That you should kick me?"

"Very funny."

Jo smoothed Ross's hair, and then gazed down the slope of the ravine. "Something happened in the house-boat."

"What?" Alan's fork froze in midair, as he turned and stared at Jo.

"Before you got there. Something that made a difference in how I handled it that I don't know how to explain." Jo stopped then and ate a bite of chicken.

And Alan sat still and watched.

"I knew I was at Butch's mercy. That everything that was happening to me was out of my control. I don't like that feeling at all. Not having any control."

Alan said, "I know," and told himself not to laugh.

"I've always wanted to influence events. To have a definite say in what's about to happen. Maybe it was

Dad dying so young, and worrying about Tommy during the war, neither of which I could change. And you being arrested made me crazy partly because there was nothing I could do to help."

"You helped."

"You know what I mean. So I was sitting there, with Butch getting drunker all the time, waving a revolver in my face, and I knew there was nothing I could do. Ross and I were hanging by a thread being held in the hands of a drunk. And then I thought, 'No, it's in God's hands. All of it. And who else's would I want it to be in?' And once I thought that, I stopped feeling so panicked. And I knew that how it came out would be whatever way it should. And then I was able to slow myself down, and think more clearly about how to talk to Butch, and try to calm him down. It wasn't me thinking that without help, either. And it did begin to calm him down some. And help him see me more as a person, and not just as his enemy's wife."

Alan nodded almost imperceptibly before he said, "I know exactly what that's like."

"France?"

"Yeah. And here. You want more beets and sour cream?"

She shook her head as she watched him, and saw he didn't want to say any more, especially about the war. "You asked me how I'm doing. I could ask you the same thing."

"It can change so fast, Jo. Life, as we so carefully construct it. Just one phone call, or one—"

"You mean the way the phone rings and someone you don't know tells you your brother was crushed on his motorcycle?"

"Sorry. Yes. Exactly. You know that as well as I do. It could be a lump showing up in an armpit. Or a piece of old shrapnel shifting toward your heart. Or one person like Carl Seeger who wants to wreak vengeance. We can't take this for granted. Food enough for a picnic *tonight*. All of us being healthy *right now*. A house to live in that keeps us warm and dry in a place like this that we love."

"I know. I do. Just having you here. When the thought of you in jail for years was almost more than I could stand." She leaned over and kissed him, and dropped a forkful of salad on his knee, before she sat up and listened. "Did you hear something?"

"Yeah."

"Boots on gravel. Emmy!"

Emmy had leapt right over Ross, and was running toward the south barn.

Buddy Jones, tall and bony and blond headed, appeared around the corner of the south barn, moving fast, excitement sticking out all over him. "Hey! Wondered where you two was!"

Jo put a finger across her lips and pointed down at Ross on the blanket, and Buddy nodded and slowed himself down, and when he got to the lawn leading up to the steps, he sat on his heels and grinned at them, while he rubbed Emmy's chin.

"What's up?" Jo smiled and poked him on the knee. "You look like you won the Triple Crown."

"You know who Mack Miller is? Trainer for the guy who owns Cragwood Stables?"

"Engelhard. Sure. Mack and his wife live on Morgan Street."

"Well, I got in touch with him about maybe workin'

for him as an assistant trainer, or somethin'. 'Course, he got an anonymous letter from D'Amato like the rest, but he called Mercer Tate and asked him about me, and Mr. Tate explained about me telling him the illegal stuff D'Amato done two years ago, and Mr. Miller's offered me a job!"

Jo said, "Great! When do you start?"

"Well … that's kinda what I wanted to talk to you folks about. Engelhard's horses get shipped all over. They're here in the fall, but Mack moves 'em to South Carolina after Christmas, and stays there till March. They're back here till June, then Saratoga for the summer."

"Ah." Alan finished the last of his beets before he said, "So that's a lot of moving."

"It is. His family goes with him, even in and outta schools and all, and his wife, she's real good about it, makin' it go as smooth as can be. But they got them a house here they can come back to. Mr. Engelhard puts 'em up in places north and south, but I haven't asked how that'd work for me, only bein' an assistant and all. Once I leave Mr. Tate, I won't have me a house here, and Becky, she's never lived nowhere but Woodford County, so it'd be a real big change."

"You've talked to Mr. Tate? You're ready to leave him?" Jo was cutting her chicken, watching Buddy out the edges of her eyes.

"Yeah. I'd need to give him a couple months' notice, but he's a real kind man, and he wants me to do what I want. You'd lose your babysitter and all, and I don't know, I … It's a real big decision."

"It's a good one to have to make." Jo smiled and patted his knee and handed him a strawberry.

"It is."

"But I guess you need to find out what the house situation would be."

"Yeah."

"You been bellyachin' 'bout wanting to be a trainer since I first set eyes on ya, and now you're askin' advice of other folks? You go home and make up your mind, boy, and don't come back till you do!" Toss was walking up behind Buddy, grinning at him while he lit a smoke.

When Buddy got done looking startled, he stared at Toss and laughed.

"Mack Miller is a *real* good trainer. He's honest as the day is long, and he's got him a real good instinct for what every one of his horses needs. That's all I'll say on the matter, till you decide for yerself."

Buddy stood up, and grinned at Toss. And said, "I'll talk to Becky again, and I'll be lettin' y'all know."

Jo and Alan and Toss watched him go. Then Toss picked up his half-smoked cigarette butt and twisted the tobacco onto the lawn before he looked at Jo. "I'm fixin' to take a couple days off, pro'bly this comin' week. Haven't seen my daddy's cousin Ruby in a good long while."

"She the one in Tennessee?"

"Yep. Franklin. She's gettin' up in years, and her son wrote to tell me he reckons she'd like a visit, and now might be the time. That okay with you? Ya figure you can run the farm without getting' kidnapped, or thrown in jail, or anything else drastic befallin' ya?"

Jo said, "I don't know, Toss. I certainly hope so. All we can do is try."

They all smiled, till a serious sort of silence settled in, and Alan said, "God willing and the—"

"Creek don't rise." Toss grinned and walked over to Ross, who'd turned himself over on his back and was looking up at Toss as he hunkered down beside him. "Hey there, Mr. Ross. Talk to your Uncle Toss." He tickled Ross's stomach, which made him laugh, then he picked him up, and set him on his knee and kissed him on the cheek. "You folks ever have another one, I want him named after me."

"Toss, or your real name? The one you never admit to."

Toss laughed, and started coughing, and it took him a long time to stop.

"Toss—"

"Don't you start in on me, missy. I know what you're gonna say."

"Yeah, well, somebody oughtta say something about it sometime. Smoking didn't do Carl a whole lotta good."

Toss started to bristle, but then he and Jo smiled at each other, and it looked to Alan like it wasn't simple. Like there was sadness in it somewhere, in the ingrained habit of Toss Watkins's family. Of minding your own business and not sticking your nose in, in a lifetime of caring without words getting used.

Jo looked at Alan, as Toss set Ross on his blanket and lit another cigarette, and she shrugged slightly and nodded silently as though she'd read Alan's mind.

# THE WIRE

It's been thirty-three years. And I can look back now on Carl, and the panic I felt because of Butch, and understand why it happened. I've learned by living. Everybody does if they want to. Most times even when they don't.

When somebody's getting talked about in town, I cut off the gossip more deliberately than I used to. And when we find somebody strung up in a straightjacket of their own private suffering, I can sympathize better than I could before, and see more ways to help. I'm not as affected by what other people think, and I'm better at sniffing out bias and carefully glossed-over facts. But trusting in your own understanding's still a perilous path. Solomon's life didn't end well, and he had advantages I don't.

I've seen a lot of choices getting made since 1964 by all kinds of people (including our other two sons, who appeared with their own ways of carving out their lives), and some of those choices are worth writing down.

Alan and I have watched genes and character and upbringing navigate the rocks and rapids in two family businesses that whole time, in ways that can still make me feel for my own pulse, and inflict the details on strangers, when I ought to slip them in a book.

Spencer and Jack and Toss, Bob Harrison and Equine, Charlie Smalls at Claiborne, where he cared for Secretariat when he first went there to stud – I'd like to tell what happened to them all.

I'd like to write about the home places too that get passed on, or sold, or crumble into dust, that teach, or taint, or turn us toward the past in ways that can heal and harm, depending on the ingrown pride in the folks they belong to over time.

The work we do around here with the horses on our land lets us see a little way inside a complicated alien species in a way that's very rare, and there's more I'd like to say about the horses I've raised and lost too soon.

I'd like to write about an unusually gifted equine painter who was injured riding cross country. And what I found in a wall I tore down in an old pioneer house that was home to a very strange horse connected family I've pondered before and since.

But the year it took to write *Behind The Bonehouse* was a gift from God, the way I see it, after more than one doc said I'd be dead two years before. I can't count on another (any more than anyone else), but I'll start the next book anyway. Because contemplating interesting lives in an earlier time keeps me from losing the gift of today in what might happen tomorrow.

We all die alone, we all know that, even with someone we love standing next to us. It's worrying about the pain that'll lead there that wakes me up in the night and makes me ask for the worry to be taken and peace to be put in its place. It has been, always, every time I've asked. And that's changed more than my mood.

Yet I've learned the most from sickness and trouble. They make me grateful for the small and simple. The taste of a peach. Redbuds in the woods. Alan's smile in the bathroom mirror. A two-year-old grandchild holding my hand while we talk about the sky.

The way Alan and I are with each other gets deeper and wider and stronger all the time. And as we've loved our sons, and learned from them, and seen their babies born, as we've done the work we've loved, even when it's exhausting, we've seen the gifts and grace more clearly than we could before.

There're so many stories I hope I can tell. And maybe that's part of why I'm still here. But with what I've seen in our lives and others', whether or not I write the next book, it'll happen the way it should.


Jo Grant Munro

December 25th 1997
Rolling Ridge Farm
McGowan's Ferry Road
Versailles, Kentucky

# ACKNOWLEDGEMENTS

Frank Mellon is a chemical engineer and innovation-process consultant who's worked with my husband over the years, and become a very good friend in the process. He helped me to conceptualize the formulation and scale-up processes in *Behind The Bonehouse*, as well as what making a paste at Equine would've entailed in the early '60s.

Dr. Rick Martin was the vet who cared for my favorite horse, Max, through the loss of his eye (which is part of the plot in *Watches of The Night*). Rick's gotten used to my peculiar questions, and when I asked, "What kind of equine pharmaceutical would've been an interesting way of killing someone in the early '60s?", he came up with several options, but leaned toward the organophosphates, Dylox in particular. I did too. Which led to more questions, which he answered patiently, before and after he found me a Merck Veterinary Manual from 1961 on e-bay that's filled with detailed information on vet medicine at that time.

Jeff Nelson, our long time family attorney, very kindly helped me with the employment contract non-compete issues and the options Bob would've had in dealing with Carl, as well as various procedures related to Alan's arrest.

Jim Rouse is a well-known Woodford County attorney (whose farm I've commandeered and given to Jo and Alan) who helped me with Woodford County history and legal procedures as well. He also arranged for me to interview Loren "Squirrel" Carl, a former Woodford County Sheriff.

Squirrel, who's now a U.S. Marshal (and yes, I couldn't keep myself from asking about the nickname), described how the investigation of the crime scene would've been conducted, as well as what the court proceedings would've been like in Woodford County at that time. He also told me that the pay phones in Versailles were privately owned in 1964, and that that's where records of calls would have been found, which smoothed a wrinkle in the storyline.

Betsy Pratt Kelly (who once owned the house I describe as Jo and Alan's, which is actually on McCracken Pike and is now a part of the Irish stud farm where American Pharoah is standing at stud) knows so much of the history and social context of Versailles and Woodford County that there aren't too many questions she can't answer. She's also introduced me to all kinds of people who've told me things I've needed to know, and given me ideas for characters as well. When I told her I wanted Esther Wilkes to live in an African American community somewhere in the country, she took me to Frog Town (where there were no signs of a town, much less frogs, and the origin of the name has been lost in time). I saw a house Esther could live in and drew a quick sketch before we drove around a curve – where we saw an old gentleman working in his garden. Betsy thought he looked vaguely familiar, and she stopped the car and got out. As soon as they started talking, they discovered that they'd known each other when she was a child, for Betsy had lived on a farm nearby where his parents and older relations had helped from time to time. It was good to watch them reminisce about folks remembered but long gone and what their families are like today.

Betsy's husband, Bob Kelly (who's lived and worked all over the world, first in the Air Force, later in academia), did research on aspects of Keeneland I hadn't thought to investigate when I was there. In the course of various visits, he also helped me develop a better sense of what it was like to be raised in Woodford County and watch it change since the '40s.

# HISTORICAL NOTES

Mack (MacKenzie) Miller was a real life Thoroughbred trainer of admirable character and substantial accomplishment. See the Acknowledgements and Historical Notes in *Breeding Ground* for more information about him and the time I spent with him and his wife, who have both passed away since. I found the book *MacKenzie Miller: The Gentleman Trainer from Morgan Street* by Jonelle Fisher to be well worth reading.

Jack Freeman's experience with the OSS and the French Resistance in the Loire Valley during WWII grew out of a wide range of reading on both underground groups. The Resistance leader in Tours was not set-up by a traitor in his organization, but others in France were. The depictions of the factions within the Resistance are accurate, and the tensions between them did compromise the functioning of the underground, and complicated politics all across France after the war.

For those interested in reading more about the OSS and the French Resistance see the Historical Notes at the end of *Breeding Ground*.

# ABOUT THE AUTHOR

Edgar Alan Poe Award Finalist Sally Wright's most recent novel, *Breeding Ground*, is the first in her new Jo Grant mystery series, which has to do with the horse industry in Lexington, Kentucky. *Behind The Bonehouse* is the second in the series.

Sally has studied rare books, falconry, early explorers, painting restoration, WWII Tech-Teams, the Venona Code, and much more, to write her university-archivist-ex-WWII-Ranger books about Ben Reese, who's based on a real person.

Sally and her husband have two children, three young grandchildren, and a highly entertaining boxer dog, and live in the country in northwestern Ohio.

36113902R00217

Made in the USA
San Bernardino, CA
13 July 2016